PRAISE FOR

SOULGAZER

"Rich in myth and wonder, *Soulgazer* is a tale rife with longing, extraordinary tenderness, and delicious tension. A glorious escape for the heart and imagination."

—Roshani Chokshi, *New York Times* bestselling author of
The Last Tale of the Flower Bride

"A stunning world of lush magic and tantalizing romance. Every word stuck with me long after I finished!"

—LJ Andrews, *USA Today* bestselling author of
the Broken Kingdoms series

"A high-stakes romantic adventure steeped in magic. I loved it!"

—Kristen Ciccarelli, *New York Times* bestselling author of
Heartless Hunter

"Strikingly beautiful and as romantic as the sea itself, this gorgeous fantasy debut has both the lure of a song and the power of a tide."

—Brittney Arena, author of *A Dance of Lies*

SOULGAZER

MAGGIE RAPIER

ACE
NEW YORK

ACE
Published by Berkley
An imprint of Penguin Random House LLC
1745 Broadway, New York, NY 10019
penguinrandomhouse.com

Book design by Kristin del Rosario
Map by David Lindroth Inc.
Interior art: Triskele © Anne Mathiasz / Shutterstock

Library of Congress Cataloging-in-Publication Data

Names: Rapier, Maggie, author.
Title: Soulgazer / Maggie Rapier.
Description: First edition. | New York: Ace, 2025.
Identifiers: LCCN 2024036389 (print) | LCCN 2024036390 (ebook) |
ISBN 9780593819272 (trade paperback) | ISBN 9780593819289 (ebook)
Subjects: LCGFT: Fantasy fiction. | Novels.
Classification: LCC PS3618.A72585 S68 2025 (print) |
LCC PS3618.A72585 (ebook) | DDC 813/.6—dc23/eng/20240923
LC record available at https://lccn.loc.gov/2024036389
LC ebook record available at https://lccn.loc.gov/2024036390

First Edition: July 2025

Printed in the United States of America
1st Printing

The authorized representative in the EU for product safety and compliance is
Penguin Random House Ireland, Morrison Chambers, 32 Nassau Street,
Dublin D02 YH68, Ireland, https://eu-contact.penguin.ie.

For Corinne,
whose soul-piercing gaze recalled the wild I nearly lost.
Soft doesn't mean weak. Silence is not golden.
Stay vibrant. Stay loud.
Stay you.

THE CRESCENT

Isle of Frozen Hearth

Dermot's Castle

Isle of Reborn Stalk

Spring of Leighas

Isle of Ashen Flame

Dromlach Cliffs

Saoirse's Cottage

Aisling's Cove

Scath-Diol

The Teeth

THE KNOWING SEA

Isle of Painted Claw

Isle of Unbound Earth

Isle of Bridled Stag

Mount Iolair

PRONUNCIATION GUIDE

PEOPLE

Aisling ASH-ling
Clodagh CLO-dah
Eabha AY-vah (like Eva)
Faolan FAY-lan
Gráinne GRAW-nya
Odhrán Oh-RAHN
Róisín ROH-sheen
Saoirse SUR-shuh
Sionn Shawn
Tadgh TIE-g

PLACES

Iolair Eye-oh-LAIR
Leigheas LAY-huss
Scath-Díol Scath-DEE-uhl

OBJECTS/THINGS

aisling de na sióga ASH-ling duh nah SHOH-gah

bean sídhe bahn shee (banshee)

bodhrán BOW-rawn

caipín baís CAH-peen BOH-sh

carnyx CAR-nix

Damhsa Babhdóir DOW-sah BAV-door

Daonnaí DAY-uh-nee

dhia DEE-yuh

grianchloch gree-yahn-claw (guttural chh, like "loch")

murúch muhr-ROCH (guttural chh, like "loch")

oilliphéist OH-lih-fihsht

rí REE

ríona REE-ohna

seanchaí SHAH-nah-chhee (guttural chh, like "loch")

tuar ceatha TOOR CAH-thah

SOULGAZER

SOULGAZER

ONE

I am the lone magpie in a sea of silver-winged swans. Lithe, artless girls who flick their bone-white skirts to the beat of a bodhrán, heedless of the waves lapping at their ankles. As they revel in their costumes, lit like jewels by the fading sun, I shrink deeper into my feathers and pray the light does not seek me out.

There are dark-eyed, starving things waiting onshore.

Sweat beads across my palms, dots my spine, until the gown clings to my skin, as a man stalks the edge of the water, head bent low like he's scenting blood. A bear's pelt cloaks his shoulders, fur lashed to his wrists with strips of tanned hide. Behind him, a woman arches her back so that braids of kelp stretch taut across her stomach, thousands of shells clattering into a single song. They watch us enter the waves without flinching—two beasts among hundreds, waiting to devour us whole.

A touch dramatic, my brothers would say.

I fight the urge to search for their faces, blink until the beasts become human.

Blink until the sting fades to a distant throb.

Aidan and Conal are not here.

I've waited years to attend the Damhsa Babhdóir, our one

tradition to outlive the gods. Six clans gather at the birth of every summer, abandoning their old bloodlust for a chance to strike bargains of marriage instead. For three days we live under a truce, dancing among feasts and finery to form fragile bonds that our noble families can pick apart like crows seeking the choicest bits of carrion. It is a challenge to our bloodlines, a feat meant to be undertaken alone.

But my brothers always swore they'd find a way to guide me. Conal would wait onshore to collect me after the first ritual was done—Aidan smothering his laughter as I trembled among the waves. Beneath the eyes of our sovereigns, they told me I would invite the sun to set upon my youth and would emerge from the water fully grown, ready to wed at last. Or, more likely, resembling a half-drowned rat.

I've never felt their absence more keenly than I do now. It is a snarled knot in my stomach, tangled tighter every time I pull at the threads.

Neither of my brothers will ever see me wed.

A girl wearing an otter's pelt brushes against my skirts. I twist my hands into the limp fabric of my dress and shy away before her skin can touch mine.

It took three months to create this gown. Black and white linen straining against my needle until a thousand wee pleats formed into feathers. I pricked my thumb on nettle, crushing woad to stain the bottom layers that same unearthly shade of blue witnessed every time a magpie takes flight. If I were to spread my arms, wings would fall from the delicate bronze cuffs at my wrists and elbows, ready to catch the wind.

Such a foolish notion, wanting the sea or the open sky. A pitiful grasp at hope.

Cursed things belong in cages, after all.

"Children of the Crescent!"

The voice is the snap of a twig in winter's flame, cutting through the wind without effort. It sails across sea-foam and sand to where we stand among the waves, drawing our attention to the eldest queen—a weathered dagger sheathed in silk. "Descendants of the Daonnaí, those six who sculpted our world anew. Who comes to claim their birthright?"

"I!" Hundreds of voices lift at once. Mine is the barest hum.

"And who among you would dare to slaughter a god?"

No one utters a sound.

Wind tears at Ríona Etain's braid, silver strands splitting her wrinkled face like lightning as she rakes her gaze over our forms. Finds them wanting. "Our ancestors were cunning. Strong. Beautiful. Wise. As reckless gods rotted on their gilded thrones, it was *they* who plotted the destruction of the divine. Together, the Daonnaí drove the gods down from their mountains and dragged them shrieking out of their golden coves. Together, they brought time to its knees."

These are not the stories I grew up with. My mother speaks of the gods with reverence—beseeching them night and day to forgive our ancestors' actions. To rid me of the curse they left behind.

But the Slaughtered Ones never respond.

"Bound by a strange darkness, the sun a solitary ring of gold, our ancestors held the gods at their mercy until one after another, they slit their throats. And what did the Daonnaí discover as the gods bled into our starving lands?"

The answer pricks my neck like the stroke of a blade.

"Magic."

I resist the urge to step back, slipping my fingertips over the pulse rushing at my throat instead. Down the golden chain nestled against it, leading to an amulet and its promise of relief—sickening and sweet. Three slender spirals mark the surface in a chalky white, connected by their middles and all rotating left. I hesitate, my finger poised just above a sharp point directly at the center.

Better to be numb than dangerous. To forget rather than mourn.

I press down in a single firm touch as another person jostles my side until the point breaks skin, flooding my veins with ice.

"Ten years it took to hunt the last of the gods down. Another five for their descendants, three for the bastards and blessed. With each fresh slaughter, our islands drank deep until the divine blood called forth magic the likes of which we'd never seen—power they never permitted us to touch."

Ríona Etain raises one gnarled hand into the air, as though breaking the barrier between this realm and the next. It beckons us forward until the waves are only a whisper at our feet.

"What once we had to beg for, we could now *take*."

A final drum echoes across the water just as I reach its edge, and Ríona Etain smiles—a slash of red that distorts half her face.

I grip my amulet tighter, swallowing hard.

"And so, descendants of the Daonnaí. I ask you again. Who comes to claim their birthright?"

"I!"

Through a haze of salt spray and smoke, the queen lifts a bronze carnyx to the sky. Said to be sculpted by Odhrán, god of her isle, the stag-shaped trumpet produces a sound like I've never heard—half keening, half cry. It weaves between our bodies like a clever spider's web, coaxing us closer until waves become ripples, then nothing but foam and dry pebbles underfoot.

A final note splits the air, like a breakage of time itself.

And then the Damhsa Babhdóir begins.

Silver coins sewn like scales glitter on the back of one lad as he hooks the waist of a crane, sending her crown of sweet-gale blooms flying. It's caught by a girl masked in raven feathers, inky black silk cut across her bare shoulder blades where true wings would be. She twists into the arms of a fawn with white-speckled shoulders, anointing her with the flowers as I jerk clear of their path.

I do *not* belong to this menagerie. I never had the chance to.

Heat lashes my skin as I stumble farther onto shore, away from the writhing bodies and wild laughter. They've all done this before, somehow—I'm certain of it. Dancing round the solstice fires, gathering at harvest with the rest of their clans. Three girls wind around one another like a braid, while beyond them, men clatter together like boulders with the strength of their embrace.

My throat runs dry to see how easily they all touch, loose limbs outlined in a hazy golden glow.

"Och, would you look where you're going, lass?"

A weathered hand snatches my skirts just as I stumble back from a fire's edge, one of a dozen scattered across the beach.

"I'm so sorry! I—"

But the woman's already lost interest. She stands among a patchwork of elegant figures with lined faces and silver crowns woven of their own braids. Each of them, from the tallest man to the shortest woman, bears the hands of Clodagh tattooed across their collarbone: the markings of the seanchaí.

I nearly cry with relief.

Seanchaí are storytellers, trained from childhood to guard our histories and keep our laws. Above family ties, friendship, payment, or blood, it is their sworn duty to witness our world and reflect what we've become.

They might also be my only chance of surviving tonight.

I shuffle closer and try not to think about how my brothers would tease me if they saw this feeble attempt to get by—but Aidan and Conal never had to undertake a Damhsa alone. Da prepared them to face suitors drunk on power and possibility, willing to do *anything* to wed a true child of the Daonnaí. His pride cloaked their shoulders; mine still ache with the force of his grip.

"Listen to that lot," the first seanchaí says, her spine notched and jagged beneath the line of her dress. "Carrying on as though it's something to be proud of, breaking the natural order of things. No mention of what came after—or what the slaughter cost."

"Aye, because *that's* what's on everyone's mind tonight. The consequences of death."

I curl my toes into the ground as they cackle, digging my nails into my thighs.

Death will be a kindness if you make a fool of me, Saoirse.

My father's final blessing, after he unlocked my cell door—careful never to touch my skin. Even after seven years of exile, with the amulet secured at my throat, he won't risk the magic. Not when any small intimacy could allow it in.

Maybe that's why he's never been soft.

You will join the others until I find you, and for star's sake, don't look anyone in the eye. They believe you simple, sent away to heal your fractured mind. You'll earn your place with silence, and, gods willing, we'll put an end to this before the night is done.

I didn't dare ask what he meant by those words, or how I could please him by offering nothing. But if I could talk to the seanchaí . . . my shoulders ease at the mere thought.

I'll just ask for a name. Someone who might want my title or Father's resources—who'd be content to forget me as soon as we wed. Someone who could balance the scales of what I've cost.

Someone I could survive.

Perhaps then I'd earn Da's ambivalence in the place of his outright contempt.

I reach the circle's edge. "Blessed seanchaí?" My voice falters, catching on the wind. "I beg you to h—"

"All the magic in this world is meaningless, so long as we cannot pass on to the next." The oldest seanchaí's veins stretch in purple streaks from one knuckle to the next as he sweeps his hand through the air, narrowly missing my head. I flinch back. "For two hundred years, the dead have choked our lands—thousands upon thousands of souls left to rot. And for what? For those six eejits to preen each other's feathers and polish their pretty crowns?"

"Be fair," another seanchaí says, her hair more copper than silver like the rest. She looks not at the first speaker but beyond, where a cluster of men gather around a single point. Their voices tumble over one another, competing with the music and the elderly storytellers both.

The younger seanchaí raises her voice, a scowl lining her lips. "Ríona Kiara's half-decent at least. I heard she's called for another quest, only *this* time her cousin is joining."

A scoff. "What, the pup who calls himself a wolf?"

"Aye." The copper-haired seanchaí's words take on an edge. "They say he's never once failed to find what he seeks. And if rumors are true, he's looking for a girl here who can lead him to the lost isle. A girl with—"

"Ocean eyes!"

I whirl away from the seanchaí as though someone's caught hold of my wrist, tugged along by the solitary, fierce thread of that voice. It emerges from the thicket of bodies clustered around the fire nearby, the lines of it blurring the more people join, until suddenly, one figure breaks free from the rest—a man.

No.

A *wolf.*

He stands half a head taller than me, bare above the waist and painted with streaks of mahogany, umber, and ash. Wayward curls sweep his shoulders, as ruddy brown as an evergreen's bark stripped at the height of spring. When he raises his arms, the air grows thick around him—tinged violet with the essence of twilight and smoke.

And he's wearing a tail.

None of those gathered see the absurdity, their eyes transfixed by the legend walking the earth. But I cannot look away from that ridiculous length of fur-lined cloth, sewn by a shoddy hand into the back of his trousers so it sways with every quicksilver step.

"She'll be something special, this girl. Excellent with her stitching, or a damned good fighter. Blue-eyed, green? Hell, sometimes the sea is pure silver as it was three winters past!"

A roar of laughter breaks out over a story of the Wolf's exploits I've yet to hear—the sort that used to set my heart to flying.

It sours my stomach instead. Aidan hasn't shared a tale with me in seven years.

I start to turn toward the seanchaí again, but I cannot stop watching that pitiful tail. The Wolf of the Wild is a creature belonging to my brothers' stories and my own dreams—ones where sirens can be seduced and shipwrecks survived by cunning and skill. He's a pirate. A myth.

And yet somehow, impossibly . . . just a man.

"The point being, lads, she's *here*. I feel it in my gut." The Wolf drops his fist, and I swear I feel an echoing tap against my ribs. "And with my cousin's blessing, I'll take her to sea, where that damned island can't play coy any longer."

I stumble back a step. Another. When did I draw so close?

Gooseflesh erupts across my arms as the Wolf twists slightly, until firelight blazes across his profile. Beautiful lips tugged back into a dangerous smile. I retreat as close into the shadows as I can—but I'm not fast enough to avoid them, the legends I once collected like plump berries off a vine.

"Together, we'll find the Isle of Lost Souls!"

I close my eyes. Breathe in the crowd's violent swell of hope. Breathe out the beautiful lie.

It does not exist.

Still, my body remembers praying for the island, lungs burning with the need to push forth a song. I would plead daily for the god-forged utopia to return, begging until my knees bled for the chance to touch its healing waters, said to cure soul wounds, break curses, and even release the dead.

But if the Wolf of the Wild is only a man wearing a poorly sewn costume, then the Isle of Lost Souls is nothing but an empty promise.

I sweep a thumb over the amulet's rough surface, tracing the bone-white swirls carved within. A shiver racks my spine when the raised center again pierces my skin, and for a moment there is something still and sharp in the air between us—the Wolf of the Wild and me. Roped lines of muscle go rigid in his shoulders. Wind catches my feathers, unfurling my wings from where they lie.

His heel shifts upon the sand, and I feel the grit of it beneath my fingertips.

Eyes hunting the darkness, landing everywhere but me.

I am weightless.

Heavy.

"Saoirse."

The Wolf's gaze snaps to mine just as a mountain steps between us, forged into the body of a man.

TWO

The man stops a breath away from me, boots twice the size of my own bare feet. He wears no costume, auburn hair braided back from pale skin and eyes that are a sharp kind of beautiful. The sort that could be soft as cornflowers but prefer thistle spikes.

"Your name is Saoirse, yes?" His voice is a rockslide tumbling down my back. "Rí Dermot's only daughter, descendant of the fifth Daonnaí. You've come here unclaimed?"

It's only then that I see the young seanchaí at his side.

Cheeks burning, I drop my gaze to the gleaming chestnut leather of his boots. "Aye."

"Then I've come to collect a dance." His hand fills the air between us, curving like a scythe toward the darkening sky. It's rough, thickly calloused, but the embroidery on the edge of his sleeve is pure silver. "Unless you've something else in mind?"

Nothing comes to mind. No clever turn of phrase or even a simpering smile. It's all I can do to slip my fingers along that starlight embroidery, avoiding the skin below.

The man nods to the seanchaí in a dismissal, and I do my best to keep pace as he walks off—but sensation rolls through my body like thunder, the drums an iron hammer against my heart. It matches the frantic press of bodies around us, their hopes and desires tugging at my consciousness in a way that makes it difficult to breathe. What would it be like to touch them? Strip myself bare and allow them all to slip inside, until nothing of me is left?

I tuck the fabric feathers tighter. It's too close. Too chaotic. Nothing like that moment when time ceased to exist because the Wolf stole it all away.

I glance past my shoulder, breath caught in my throat.

But the Wolf is already gone.

"A drink first?" The auburn-haired stranger shifts his grip as he walks toward a row of flattened logs lined with barrels of mead, whiskey, and wine, his thumb now resting on the bronze cuff at my wrist. "I cannot abide the clamor without it."

I cannot manage a single word in response. A few linen feathers and the cool curve of metal is all that separates our skin. One more shift and we'll be touching.

I pray the amulet's numbing power holds.

A heady scent of liquor drenches the air as we approach. Coins flash one after another, tossed into copper bowls while wooden cups and carved horns exchange hands just above. I chance a look at the stranger's face and find a firm jaw set below a furrowed brow—stern, but like it was carved that way from creation.

"You're pale as grianchloch, woman."

Instinct draws me back, but the man does not allow me to pull free. Light flickers over the red-gold dusting of his beard as he tilts his head, examining me with a hawk's gaze. "Are you ill? Faint?"

"No, I—" A knot forms on my tongue. His grip tightens, fingers sliding over my sleeve until the rough pad of one fingertip brushes against my tender blue veins. I grit my teeth and wait to feel . . .

Nothing.

I feel nothing. There are no emotions or impulses, no visions of impending death. Relief uproots the panic blooming in my chest so abruptly, I nearly collapse.

The amulet works.

"I'm cold. That's all."

The stranger's frown eases, fingers relaxing until they fall against his thigh. "Wine will warm your bones." He drops a coin into the half-filled bowl, nodding to a woman with a violet-stained apron on the left. "And in any case, I'm not much for dancing. It was only ever a means to an end."

The woman hands over a drinking horn, which he presses into my palm—amber bleeding into onyx at the curved tip. I drink the deep purple wine without prompting, and it's a relief when the black cherry and earth unlock my tongue. "Thank you."

"She speaks," he says, "but can she manage more than two words at a time?"

My forehead bunches, but . . . there's a new twist to his lips. Almost like a smile. "I prefer to listen."

"A trait I heartily wish more people would adopt." The man touches his horn to mine and steers us toward not the dark, empty night but a gently crackling fire. We sink onto a log, and another cord releases along my spine, shoulders dropping so that I can breathe again.

Until he tilts his head, studying me closer in the light. "Are you certain you're well? Your eyes are . . . strange. I thought they were blue."

"They are." I jerk my head down so that my fringe falls into place, obscuring my eyes from view. "It's the fire playing tricks. They're blue."

And green, gray, brown—changing hands from one day to the next, or tumbling all together in a mad swirl. The last time my curse broke free of its cage, I made myself sick watching the colors churn.

I drink, my heart lashing itself against my throat. "They're just blue."

"Is that why you're not lined up with the others, hoping the Wolf will claim they're the rare color of the sea?"

More knots gather between my ribs as I follow his derisive gaze to another fire, farther down the beach. Women gather like clouds ringing a mountaintop, and I see him again—the Wolf perched on a damp log at their center. He cups their faces and tilts them this way and that, making a show of inspecting each one.

I fight down the horrible urge to laugh. "What would be the point?"

"Curiosity. Romantic notions of an idiot who never grew out of playing with his toy boats."

I think of the tail and barely restrain a smile. "He's just a story."

"And the isle?"

My throat burns with the acrid taste of that fantasy, turned to ash on my tongue.

I drink until I taste nothing but wine. "The Isle of Lost Souls fell with the gods."

He grunts, eyes raking over me. "Practical."

"Aye. I'm nothing special."

"You're not?"

His tone is dry. Flat.

Regret swallows me whole as I scramble to say something—anything—until he makes a sound like the dry clatter of rocks. Laughter. He's laughing at me. Heat crawls over my limbs, an effect of the wine or perhaps the hopeless mess I'm making of my father's task.

"I'm sorry, I have to—"

"You're not experienced with courtship, are you?"

The words stop me mid-rise, or perhaps it's just the tap of his finger along my wrist. I flinch as he traces the delicate skin, tipping my palm up into his own. Creases and calluses mark each joint.

"No. I'm not."

"And you're certainly not as fragile as you're painted. I expected a waif lost to the wind."

An uneasy laugh startles past my lips. Is that an insult? A compliment? Is he supposed to be touching me—and am I meant to let him?

Panic seizes my tongue as I glance to the side, where other couples twine together like serpents. Father said nothing of this—*Mam* said nothing of this. "I haven't broken yet."

"Yet."

His touch slides higher up my arm. I jerk my face back to his own.

"You seem practical enough. Sturdy. Smart. But this gown . . ." Something quickens in my belly. Severs me from my body until all I can do is watch as he traces the whisper-soft edge of my sleeve. It took twenty-six hours of sewing to get the folds right. "It's a fanciful thing, isn't it."

His eyes capture mine as he tears it with the slightest twist of his fingers.

"Are you a fanciful girl?"

I drop the cup. Wine splatters across my hem, flecked like blood along the white as the black darkens to pitch. The stranger watches with an expression carved from stone—until his eyes flick past my shoulder just as another voice cages me from behind.

"Answer the king, Saoirse."

My father steps into the light. "Rí Maccus has never been known for his patience."

Maccus? I blink, and another name floats to the surface, whispered long ago by my brother with equal parts fear and awe.

The Stone King.

Ruler of the Isle of Unbound Earth. Maccus's land once belonged to the god of stonemasons, blacksmiths, and miners, abundant in minerals and every sort of gem. Yet by his father's reign, it was little more than a chain of barren mountains, unleashing disease and waste the deeper they dug. Many have died attempting to bear children there, including his first wife, and with her their newborn son.

But it is not this truth that unmoors me.

It's that this man, Maccus, sought me out. He spoke my name, drew me into the light—not out of curiosity or kindness, but because he wanted to inspect a broodmare he'd already claimed for purchase.

Shame carves a cruel path down my spine.

"I . . ."

I have nothing to say.

Rí Maccus's thumb holds the weight of the earth against my shoulder, crushing the frail ember of hope I'd dared to rekindle. "I apologize for finding her before you could introduce us, Dermot. I wanted to see what's left of the girl's mind."

Da's keen eyes fall on me. "And your verdict, my king?"

"She is intact." A muscle twitches in Rí Maccus's jaw. He does not let me go. "It's strange that you kept her away for so long. Seven years, was it not?"

"Aye."

Maccus taps once against my collarbone—then hooks his thumb beneath my jaw, forcing my face to the light. With that firm touch, a dark emotion at last trickles in. Slick and snakelike, coiling past the amulet's numbing shield straight into my heart: contempt. I shudder from the unfamiliar weight of it inside me, stomach threatening to purge it along with the wine.

"Strange, too, that she should arrive the same night as Kiara's cousin. Did you hear the tale the Wolf is spreading? About a girl with ocean eyes."

Da goes still. Then he adjusts the signet ring on his smallest finger. Crinkles his eyes, lip twitching up like he's in on the joke. My pulse had started to falter; now it flies twice as fast.

It's worse than a rage, watching my father shed one skin for the next.

"Is this the same 'Wolf' who claimed to seduce a selkie last year, right after he skinned that giant squid? Or am I getting the two stories confused—he has ever so many of them. Such a wit." Da tilts his head. Smiles. "But I'm surprised at *you*, Maccus. You've never been susceptible to his particular charms."

Maccus drops his hand. It takes everything in me not to scream—with relief at the release of his emotion and with horror at what's to come. But who would listen to me if I did? Not a damned person here would dare interrupt a talk between two kings.

I swallow it down and wrap my arms around my waist as Maccus becomes a mountain once again, shoulders blocking the firelight until I am nothing but his shadow. "I am asking if there is anything to be concerned about, Dermot."

Da's humor melts away. "Nothing that won't be resolved tonight."

"Good." Rí Maccus turns to me, and I can't help but shrink. For a split second, something crosses his features—something like regret. It's gone by the time I return my gaze to the ground. "Best to leave any romantic notions now, because they won't buy you kindness in my home. It's a brutal land, crafted without mercy. Bear a healthy child, lass, and you will be rewarded. Is your role understood?"

"A-aye."

"It's done, then. Dermot?" Rí Maccus turns to my father, and it takes all my strength not to crumple to the ground. "We'll settle the affair with the seanchaí—your daughter's hand for the masonry and labor to fortify the southern caverns of your island. I'll send the first share once the marriage is consummated, the next when she's carrying my child, the last when it's born healthy and whole. Agreed?"

"Agreed."

My future is sealed by the slapping of two palms coated in spittle.

Da's chin tilts up as Rí Maccus walks away, shadows clinging like a cape. Beside him, I see Mam for the first time since Da unlocked my cabin door this morning to let me out, standing just as she's taught me my whole life—posture straight, eyes downcast, hands folded serenely in front of her. She looks like she could break with a stiff wind, her collarbone forming sharp peaks below her throat.

She won't look at me.

I reach out before I quite know what I'm doing, the tips of my fingers barely skimming her sleeve. "Mam, please don't let him—"

A hand clamps around my arm and I stop a second too late. Da's grip is iron and ice, drawing me up short as pain echoes up my shoulder and out of my lips in a hiss. It is nothing compared to the fury his touch unspools inside me. His voice comes low at my ear, any hint of charm gone with the Stone King.

"You dare to ask for mercy? I *told* you to find me as soon as the dancing had begun."

"N-no. Yes. Da, please—"

His eyes are bottomless and cold, like the cursed well behind my old cottage that sings after it storms. My throat runs dry, fracturing my voice into nothing as his hand digs into my bone.

"You lost the right to call me that the day you took my son."

THREE

I didn't mean for Conal to die.

The three of us were racing across the beach, rare sunlight drinking up our winter-pale skin. Conal was the first to leap into the water, clothes flying off behind him. Aidan was next, teasing me for my slowness—never mind that at fifteen, my legs had widened whereas his grew long. I was last, rushing to unravel the laces of my new gown because at any moment, they could lose interest or Da could steal Conal away for lessons and Aidan for training.

The amulet broke as I pulled the gown free.

I was never supposed to be without it. The last time I'd tried, Mam told me I brought on her miscarriage—but Conal always said she was weak in those days, passing hours with the healer before I ever touched her belly. And Aidan swore he used to hold me often as a wee one, bearing no consequence.

I believed them. I *wanted* to believe them.

So when that amulet split upon the rocks, I did not hesitate to rush into the water and seize my brothers' hands.

Only when the vision landed like a blow to my gut did I realize what I'd done.

Power drove me to my knees, vomit climbing up my throat as

the sea and sky swapped places. I heard someone scream, deep in my mind. Saw the body floating on the waves, my mother wailing as she clutched their dark curls to her chest. And even after the curse released me, gasping as my still-living brothers let go of my hands to dive, I *knew* that if we all went into the water, only two of us would come out alive.

I knew, and yet I could do nothing because Mam had been telling the truth.

It was *I* who brought death to our door.

Da releases me and I bow my head, free hand coiled tight within my wine-sodden skirts. Where he gripped my arm, four feverish lines mark the flesh.

"Clean yourself up, then come meet us at the pavilion."

"How will I find—"

"Have you grown simple? Follow the flags." A sharp gesture turns me toward a row of wooden stakes driven into the earth, each bearing a sigil for the island it represents. Together, they form a crescent from one end of the beach to the next, broken only by a platform built several lengths higher than the earth. It is there I spot the crowns.

My brothers used to tell me what it was like, when the Ring of Stars collected together. Half a dozen kings and queens, each wearing a diadem fashioned from the elements of their home isle. Crafted of molten stardust, twirling coral vines, or ever-frozen icicles shaped from Mount Iolair's highest peak, the crowns are a wonder only the Daonnaí's descendants are permitted to enjoy.

"We'll take your betrothal to the Ring of Stars for approval and announce it before the first fire's gone to ash." Da's voice bends in the middle, and it takes me a moment to realize it's because he's smiling. "If all goes well, Saoirse, you'll be wed in two days' time."

It takes only three seconds of strained silence to realize he wants me to thank him. But my tongue has gone thick, useless in my mouth. I'm powerless to do anything but stare at those turning constellations on the pavilion, failing to imagine a crown of stone upon my head.

Da shifts, then straightens his collar into a sharp point, beckoning once to my mother, who falls neatly into line. "Don't be long."

I touch the amulet where it lies below my collarbone as my parents walk away, tracing those three pale spirals to the sharp point at their center. Within seconds I am bleeding again, but blessedly numb. A small price to pay for escaping madness or death.

Nearly two decades have passed since the day I was cursed and Da presented me with the first amulet. Carved into sunstones, then dipped into our late goddess Eabha's holy well, the amulets were designed by his apothecary to protect me—a safeguard against the magic's effect. Each would last a full moon's cycle, requiring only a drop or two of blood to work.

But I could always tell when their protection wore thin.

The servants' discontent would stick to my bones, their restless energy and unspent desires crowding my mind as they combed my hair. Mam's heartbreaks would become my own with a touch, as would Aidan's mischief and Conal's worries. And that is to say nothing of the grief of the dead.

But with these amulets, I've survived a soulstone curse. Somehow—impossibly—*I'm* still alive.

It's only cost me everything.

I stagger from one fire to the next, head swirling with the potent scent of wine. I should go to the water—wash until all I smell is the briny sea. Instead, I drift closer to the tree line, where I lose sight of my father and the other rulers altogether. There, an amber moon has replaced the sun. It kisses the treetops bordering the beach, where food passes freely from hand to hand: steaming, golden boxty and crumbling rhubarb tarts. Everyone is smiling, the younger set twirling round one another like birds in a mating dance while the elders embrace and laugh, old friends reunited each summer.

My throat swells with a sob that I cannot allow to surface.

I lied to the Stone King. I *am* a fanciful girl.

A ridiculous, stupid, hopelessly fanciful girl, because after seven years without a vision, I dared to think perhaps it was finally done. The amulets had worked properly at last—or more likely the curse was sated on my brother's blood and would leave me to what little peace I had left. I thought when Da fetched me for the Damhsa, I could find someone to tolerate me. Be safe, and numb, and learn to bite my cheeks until the smile felt true.

But maybe this is the gods' justice.

Why should I live free when Conal is bound forever by death?

"Oi, sparrow! You're trying to cheat, aren't you?"

I don't realize the words are meant for me until a length of cloth covers my eyes, hiding all but the smallest pinpricks of firelight. "What are you—"

"She's not a fecking sparrow." A girl snorts, shoving the boy's hands aside to pry at the material until my vision clears. It's a mask. "You ever seen a sparrow sporting feathers like that? She's a blue tit, I'm telling you."

"Come off it! She's a cheat, that's all—no one's supposed to know what they're getting 'til the night's through!"

I stumble back from their argument, fingers spread wide to keep the mask in place. It's a tradition I forgot, a mask worn on the first night of dancing to confuse faeries seeking their own brides. Da took my mask when we arrived, saying he didn't want to lose me in the mass of people. But as the music strikes up again, I realize I'm no longer safe on the edges of the crowd.

I'm right in their midst.

Drums and fiddles blaze through the air, weaving a spell that pulls near every person into a frenzy. They beat the earth with steps I've never seen, exchanging cries and howls as though they're truly animals come to life. It's a scene ferocious enough to wake the . . .

A silver light flashes at the edge of the woods.

Sweat gathers cold at the base of my spine.

"She's a blue tit!"

"Sparrow!"

They are watching us. I can feel them. Not the dancers, not the rí or ríona.

The dead.

Curious, broken things left to decay on this earth just as their bodies once did. Some spirits dwell among those they once loved, unable to touch or speak—watching as the lives they built crumble to nothing. Others *wish* for nothing, trapped in endless repetition of their own violent deaths without the means even to scream. And the rest simply . . . linger.

An incessant, gaping wound.

My hands drop to the amulet as a silver light takes shape, flowing over the curves of a body that no longer exists. The ghost wraps herself around a tree at the forest's edge, silver-pale skin tinged blue beneath the branches. She looks hollow. Hungry.

I shudder as her longing sinks like a rotting tooth into my flesh.

"You don't feel it," I whisper, pressing the amulet down until its edges dig into my skin, as two other spirits flank her. A fierce ache brushes against the amulet's numbing power, blurring my grasp on what's real. It's always been this way. The dead have no need to touch me as the living do—their memories and emotions, their very souls, bleed into the edge of mine with their presence. Even the strongest, newly wrought amulets are not enough to dull the raw, raging bite of a lost soul.

Prayers form and falter as I wait for the lonely ache to be quelled—or for anyone else to be half so affected, but the others hardly notice. Only those dancing nearest to the trees falter, glancing at the spirits and then firmly away. Whatever they feel, it's easy enough to look away.

I *want* to look away.

My fingers press harder as I try, forcing my gaze to the ground.

I feel nothing. I want nothing. I am nothing.

It doesn't work. To my left, a woman rubs catlike against a man before her, both their arms sliding against mine. Her indifference and spite take root in my gut. Before me, the couple arguing drunkenly over my costume bump into my chest—releasing irritation and lust in their wake.

I drop the amulet, reeling back from the weight of all these souls crushing mine.

"Blue tit!"

They need to go—no, *I* need to get away. There are too many of them. I can't bear it—can't *breathe*.

"Sparrow, you bastard!"

It's all coming undone. Everything I've tried to contain, splitting at the seams.

I am seconds away from curling over myself as tight as I can go when a hand suddenly catches mine. Calloused fingers press into my palm, lifting my arm high and away until my sleeve unfurls like a sail, dozens of blue-green linen feathers rippling between us.

"Clever thing. You're a magpie, aren't you?"

His voice is a rough caress of salt-stained silk, drawing tight over my bare flesh. Chills bite down my spine as sweet, empty promises coil deep in my belly, lifting the delicate hairs along my nape. I breathe, and the frantic crash of my heart becomes the steady hum of waves pouring in, and out.

In. Out.

Let it out.

"You caught my eye earlier, but I half think you might've stolen my heart as well." His finger slides along my jaw, coaxing my face to the side with an aching, terrifying familiarity. "Be a dear and give it back?"

It is a lover's touch. And a stranger's. I shouldn't look, but, stars spare me, I can't help myself. My eyes snap open, and I see—

Wild.

The man before me is made of wild—nearly feral with it. His face is made of defined angles softened only by a beard, uneven sprays of freckles ending at the corner of his mouth. It twists with laughter, his eyes singing the same pattern amid deep currents of blue. Twin daggers rest in leather sheaths strapped to either hip, topped with intricate, carved bronze wolves. And there is the tail, peeking round the edge of his thigh.

It's *him*. The Wolf.

I feel the truth ripple in a hum across my skin.

"Well?" The man taps my bottom lip with his thumb; I nearly take it between my teeth. It's wrong—*so* wrong—to keep still for fear his touch will fall away. Every instinct tells me to lean in, nuzzle and lick. Beg for scraps of affection after seven years without a single ounce.

I have never felt such a ferocious want—not one that belongs solely to me.

My gaze falls to his smirking mouth, and it widens at once.

"If it was a kiss from the Wandering Wolf you were trying to steal, love . . ."

A kiss. Is that what I want?

The answer is a devouring roar, consuming every scrap of fear hosted within my blood. *He* is the only thing that makes sense in this storm of sensation, blotting out the rest of the world with the sheer force of his presence. Something foreign—something primal— urges me onto my toes past any sense of reason or the instinct to shy away. And though a splinter of ice attempts to pierce through the drunken waves of desire, an echo of the amulet's mark, it's a weak effort. Easy to ignore.

I've craved touch for far too long.

The Wolf's hands drop to my waist as mine flutter in the air between us, unsure of where to land—until he raises a single brow. His bemusement spikes through the sticky heat of my mind.

"Darling, I'm afraid that's not how you—"

I bury my hands in the pirate's hair and crush my mouth to his. A mistake.

Oh *gods*, I've made a mistake.

His lips are a firm, unfamiliar plane beneath mine, and I haven't the least idea how to explore it. A puff of hot air rushes past my cheek. His eyes are bright with amusement, warped by how close we stand.

Embarrassment devours me.

"I'm sorry." I start to drop back, his laughter chasing across my lips. "I'm so sorry. I—"

"Where exactly do you think you're going?" Before I can draw fully away, the Wolf catches my earlobe between his fingers, folding the edge lightly over his nail. "If you're going to do a thing, you'd best do it proper."

Fire licks across my entire body. I feel eyes on us by the dozens—see it in the way his chest puffs out, arms flexed to keep me close. Irritation flickers inside me, only to vanish when his fingertip finds the hollow below my ear, stroking once.

"Come back here, Trouble."

Cupping my face, the Wolf guides my lips back to his—parting them as though I am a ripe plum, sweet for the tasting. He traces their seam with the tip of his tongue. My hands knot in his hair.

That is when it happens.

It's sudden—relentless—the beating of our hearts against my skin. My soul drowns in the noise until salt explodes across my tongue, and I realize too late that after seven years of silence, it's finally broken free.

The curse. My vile magic.

The Wolf's hold falters as I buckle forward, choking on the waves of it because I *know* him, this stranger. I see a hundred different versions of his face, feel the weight of his hand upon my chest—I know that I'm going to tear through his world like an arrow through flesh, and he will bear those scars for the rest of his days. I will steal his rest, and he will rob me of mine.

We are going to break each other.

I collapse under the vision's abrupt retreat, caught by this stranger's arms.

Not a stranger. Not for long.

I don't realize I'm crying until the mask bunches beneath my cheeks. The Wolf reaches for it, and I stay his hand—trembling and pale, whatever urgency from before gone with the rest of the magic.

"Ah. Shite."

"It's fine." I can barely breathe, my eyes locked on his. The deep blue iris is nearly swallowed by black. "Just—"

His jaw goes slack, and it's only then I realize my second mistake.

Because while I've been fighting an entire ocean inside myself, he's watched the battle wage in the colors of my eyes. Blue to green, gray to brown, churning like the sea captured in a vicious storm—the mark of the magic. My soulstone curse.

But as I study his face, it's not surprise that lingers. It's . . .

"It's *you*."

The word has barely left his lips when a high wail splits the music once more, catching the ear of every reveler gathered around us. He twists to see the eldest queen blowing on her carnyx once again—and I rip my arm from his grip.

I hear the Wolf's shout as I burrow between bodies to the slender promise of safety.

"People of the Crescent!" My father's voice lands like a sharp blade in a thicket of thorns against my skull. I want to melt into the earth—escape this madness. "It is my great privilege and honor as rí of the Isle of Reborn Stalk to announce the first union of this Damhsa Babhdóir."

Dizzy with nausea, I break through the last of the crowd only to turn and see Da standing on a dais in his crown of silver-crafted mushrooms capped in glowing quartz, the Stone King just beside him. My skin crawls, muscles jerking beneath like a dozen spiders have chosen them for their nest.

"Rí Maccus, king of the Isle of Unbound Earth, will take my only daughter, Saoirse, to wed on the final sunset of the season."

A laugh climbs my throat. Maybe a cry.

I stumble farther into the dark.

"May the stars, skies, and Slaughtered Ones bless this night."

FOUR

"Bandia Eabha, spill your moon over my soul. Dia Odhrán, raze my impurities with your sun."

The air inside my cabin is thick. Stale. Built into the belly of my father's ship, it offers only the smallest window and holds onto a damp, earthen smell marked by rings along the ground where barrels of mushrooms used to stand.

I drop to my knees in the center of one.

"Bandia Clodagh, bind this sickness with your dawn."

Charms form a familiar tangle around my wrists as I whisper to the six fallen gods, holding the amulet tight between my hands. The magic does not fade. I press harder, until the amulet's freshly carved swirls bite into my palm, the small spike at their center drawing blood—but still it's not enough. There is no reassuring rush of ice through my veins. No quiet or calm.

Only a raw, violent sense of yearning that echoes across a thousand living souls on that shore—as though they are infection and I an open wound.

I stifle a whimper with my teeth.

"Please help me."

It's been months since I prayed to the gods in earnest—who

could scream endlessly into an apathetic void? For twenty-two years, no matter what I've sacrificed, or promised, or pled, *no* one has ever answered. And how could they, when they're all dead?

But the amulets *work*. They have since Da's apothecary first carved their surface with an inverted triskele: the reverse pattern of a soulstone. Three waves curl over themselves, drinking my blood to swallow the magic back—but it's only ever taken a drop.

I squeeze my fist until pain forces me to let go, blood lacing across my palm in a dozen rivulets. The amulet is a slippery, vibrant red.

It isn't working. The magic will *not* be tamed.

"Bandia Róisín, hear me—*release* me. Save me from the soulstone's curse!"

I swear I can hear the coy goddess laugh.

There is a price for those who tamper with the gods' greatest gift, after all. Did I truly think I could avoid it? Spiraled shells of moon and sky that form on the tongues of those who've died, the soulstones were made to protect our fragile human spirits from corruption even as our bodies decayed on earth. It was said that long ago, at the quarter year's turn, emissaries from every island would gather the stones of their dead into gleaming baskets, releasing them into the waters of the Isle of Lost Souls. Only there could they be purified, freeing the spirits to the realm beyond.

Now the soulstones crack in their growing piles, a reminder of our greatest mistake.

We are a people who cannot mourn, for the dead cannot pass on—trapped in crumbling stones that curse any who dare touch them with the fate of madness or death. I was a child of three when I crossed paths with one, washed up along the beach. Mam says it was an accident. Da tells me I knew not to go near.

But no one stopped me until I'd already invited the magic in.

I drop the charms. Rake my fingers through my hair as tears carve molten paths down my cheeks.

Mam promised me we would find it someday, the Isle of Lost Souls. She swore the island's blessed waters could wash away the rot inside me, painting me as pure as the world was before we all entered into it. Every year, another wayfarer would set out with the kings' and queens' blessings, and every year, they would return, claiming the Isle of Lost Souls no longer exists. Over time, Mam's conviction faded into halfhearted hopes, then increasingly frantic prayers, and finally silence. Defeat.

Still, I wanted to find that land more than anything—would pay *any* price for my redemption.

But the searches continued to fail. The curse only grew stronger. And then my brother died.

I push the amulet into my palm until blood trickles down my wrist.

"Just take it. Take it, *please*—or take me so I cannot feel it any longer. *Plea—*"

Heavy boots pound across the planks overhead, and I nearly swallow my tongue as they stop outside the open door.

"Saoirse."

The lines of Da's face are deep. Severe. I remember a time when they would appear only at the corners of his eyes when my brothers were caught in mischief and he had to fight a smile at their nerve. When his hands were gentle things that ruffled their hair and occasionally passed through my childish curls as well.

They form fists at his sides now. My throat runs dry.

"You didn't come after the announcement. You made a fool of Rí Maccus. A fool of *me*."

"I-I know. But, Da—" My words come to nothing when my mother enters behind him. She's shrunk herself to a waif, blue-green eyes grown too wide in a face as delicate as bird bone. Still, her hand flies to her stomach as it almost always does when she sees me. Like she feels the ghost of me, there in her empty womb.

"Dermot. Her eyes." Mam reaches a shaking hand toward my cheek. Stops only a breath away. "It's happening again?"

My vision blurs as I nod, peeling my hands apart so the amulet drops to my chest. I wipe at the smears of blood with my skirt. "Aye—but I swear I didn't take it off this time. You saw me put it on, didn't you?"

Da scowls as he hooks the chain away from my skin, until the amulet dangles between us. I force a breath before his closeness steals the rest. "I wore it all night, and I keep praying, but it still won't—"

He breaks the chain with one hard tug.

I claw at my throat as the amulet drops, but for the first time in seven years, all I touch is bare skin.

"Enough of this." He straightens, and I struggle to my feet as well—until it hits me. I *don't* have my protection. And the tides are pressing in, and *gods*, it's too much to feel. Even without touching me, Mam's panic weaves through mine alongside Da's resolve and fury, and a dozen other sensations that force me low until my forehead scrapes the ground.

I want it to swallow me whole.

"Dermot, what are you doing?! Saoirse *needs* to wear it. You said yourself it was blessed by the druid on Eabha's cliff, dipped into her well! We could offend the goddess if she doesn't—"

"I said enough!" I look up in time to see Mam cower as Da paces forward, his boot ripping a hole in the rug. But he doesn't strike her. He's never had to. "Wise up, Leannon. It wasn't the gods' doing—it never has been. This *thing*"—he shakes the amulet—"was only ever meant to smother her magic until I could find a permanent solution. And I have."

Mam's hurt collides with my own confusion, threatening the boundaries of my mind. I dig my fingers into the rug with one hand and wrap the other around my throat until I find something that makes sense—something angry and scared and *loud*.

The frantic pulse of my own heart screaming at me to run.

Dimly, I hear Mam say, "What are you talking about? The gods spared her the night she touched the soulstone. She was marked for death, but they allowed her to live. You *told* me that's how you discovered the amulets. You said—"

Da's laugh ripples through the cell they kept me in. "I lied."

I squeeze until my heartbeat becomes a tether, snapping the world back to rights.

Da stalks to the doorway, amulet fisted in one hand as he barks an order to the guard outside. Mam stands in one corner with her arms tucked like clipped wings, praying under her breath. Each of us is an island, encircled by musty barrel rings worn into the ground.

Except here on my knees, there is a sickly hue to the color I hadn't noticed before.

I scrape my smallest finger along the ring's edge and stare at the milky blue-white stain left behind. The same unsettling white embedded in each swirl of the amulet Da holds in his fist—the one mimicked in the mushrooms sculpted of crystal and metal dotting his crown.

The color of the caipín baís.

"You . . . you used the death caps?"

His body goes stiff, but even with his face in profile, I see the twitch of his lip. The one my brother pointed out to me once, like a forest going silent when the owl is near. "What else do you think would be strong enough to stop you?"

My hands fall uselessly to the ground.

The gods never helped me. It was only ever the mushrooms.

I want to laugh.

Weep.

Rage.

Vivid as moonlight, growing deep in the caverns he's selling me to protect, the death caps are all we have left of the goddess's magic on our island—the last creation to spring forth once our ancestors spilled her blood on the ground. For centuries we've used the caipín baís to heal and forget, ease pain and quicken death. But there are also rumors. Whispered reports I wasn't meant to hear, of workers in those caverns who spend their days harvesting mushrooms and forget their children, their homes. Their own names.

It wasn't until Da found an apothecary when I was three that he discovered new, powerful ways to use them.

Ones that filled our dwindling coffers and made him a wealthy king.

My stomach revolts, and I clutch a handful of those ridiculous feathers I spent so many hours creating—stopping only to bruise my knees over and over again, praying to gods Da promised would listen if I offered enough of myself. It was *Da* who built half a dozen altars to the Slaughtered Ones by the time I was six—and Mam who guided my knife across the throat of my first pet in sacrifice. As the earth turned black and putrid beneath those altars, Da swore my offerings guaranteed the gods' protection. He said they were what truly made the amulets work.

Anger rips through my shock, sending me off-balance until I fist both hands against the ground.

Not a single day of my childhood passed that I did not touch my lips to those bloodstained stones.

"This whole time . . . you made me think this was something I could control. That I wasn't praying hard enough to change it, or—or that I somehow asked for this curse, but—"

"What part of this can't you understand? *You* are the curse, Saoirse."

My father's voice—this splintered, misshapen version of it—sinks into my gut like a knife. I search his face for the man who once held my chubby hand to steady my fledgling steps across a flagstone hall.

There is only loathing in his eyes now.

"I should have cast you into the sea the moment you opened those eyes and I recognized you for what you were. A death bringer, full of the ocean's madness and want."

Stitches pop where my fingers tighten in the folds of my dress as, slowly, Da crouches until his face is level with my own. "I thought you were smart enough to wear the amulets. Thought they might be enough to last. But like my mother, you are weak. And I have no place in my home for useless creatures."

The room blurs around me. I search for my mother. She's looking away.

My whole life, she's only ever looked away.

"I'm—sorry. I'm sorry. I'll try again. *Please* let me."

Da shakes his head. "I spared the babe who clutched my finger in her cradle. And look what that mercy has cost."

I hate the way my chest heaves with each breath now. Hate the keening sounds of my sobs echoed by Mam's across the room, even as I stifle them with a sleeve. But I hate the storm of magic more—sensations peeling me open from the inside.

I reach for Da's hand in one last, weak attempt at childhood belief. The amulet dangles from his fingertips. "I-I'm sorry, Da. Please let me wear it. I c-can make it work."

He jerks his hand back before I can take the amulet, disgust mapped across his features. "Sionn, it's time."

The shadows bend as my father's apothecary steps through the door.

FIVE

My body rebels at the sight of Sionn's gaunt frame, eyes gleaming too bright for the low candlelight. He has aged in a way that comes from substance, not time: hair so pale it's nearly white, skin draped like wax over his prominent bones. I have only ever seen him lingering in the shadows—passing corked bottles of elixir in exchange for coin. Aidan used to hurry me along if we ever passed him in the halls.

The apothecary is Da's greatest secret, guarded as ferociously as he ever hid me.

"Hello, Saoirse." My name feels wrong on his lips, like a pearl perched on a viper's tongue.

I wince, but as he steps forward, Mam shifts into his path, her shoulders stretched as sharp as wings. "No."

"Leannon," Da says, his voice low—but she stays.

For the first time, my mother stays.

"She's done nothing wrong, Dermot. It's the soulstone. That's all." Her knuckles are white where she rubs them, fingers locked over one another as though she's guarding her bravery inside. "I know you're concerned, but can't we wait a bit longer?"

"Leannon—"

Mam takes a half step forward, and the rigid line of his back softens. Her hope flutters between us, coaxing air back into my lungs. "The Wolf is launching a quest for the Isle of Lost Souls. I know you dislike him, but with his reputation—there's a good chance he'll actually find it."

"And if he doesn't?"

There is a bitter edge to Da's voice as he flicks one hand in a silent order. I scramble back, an echo of my mother's retreat as Sionn shuts the door. "You're asking me to gamble the fate of our entire island on a fairy tale when *she* has already cost me my heir."

The reminder of Conal's death is all it takes. Mam's hope dies like a starling in the shadow of a hawk.

I cower, alone, against the wall.

The apothecary empties his leather pack on my small bed, then lights three more candles around the room. They stink of animal fat, crudely made compared to the beeswax tapers I created in my cottage by the sea. My hands ache to shape them again. I want to be there—so badly that for a moment, I can taste the salt.

Until I realize it's only tears caught between my trembling lips.

Sionn lays out a series of beaten metal instruments forged of sharp lines, and another handful fashioned of bone. But something else steals my focus when it comes, paralyzing my body. My lungs.

It's a small vial of lurid white ink.

Da tosses the amulet on the bed with a shake of his head. "Undo her dress, Leannon. Just the back."

Mam doesn't hesitate this time. I try to swallow—to speak—as she plucks the laces of my dress until it eases down my shoulders. But no words come. I wrap my arms across my front to hold it there, eyes stinging, when Mam stops. Hesitating before she spreads her hand flat over the notches of my spine.

Her lament is a poison cord, woven through each of my tendons to create a doll she could master and love. I understand now why Mam has never touched my skin willingly—why she used to flinch if I reached for her hand, then smile and brush me away.

I am the embodiment of my mother's regrets. For all her prayers, beliefs, lectures, and lessons, she hates me for touching that soulstone.

And she hates herself for hating me.

Mam takes back the hand she meant as a comfort, and I fold into myself as small as I can go—a lone, pitiful creature trapped in the barrel ring. Another tear slides down my jaw as she wipes her palm against her skirt.

"What will you do, Dermot?"

"Mark her with the same pattern we used for the amulets," Father says, watching Sionn remove a needle from his pack, as slender as an eggshell and tapered to a point. "A triskele, with the spirals turning west. She needs a permanent bind on the magic."

"And the poison?"

Sionn uncorks the vial and dips the bone needle into the ink.

My heart thrashes like a rabbit caught in a snare when he steps behind me.

"We've tempered the ink. Tested it many times—the last three people functioned well enough after." Da stands beside her as I feel the apothecary's cold hand spread where Mam's was only seconds ago. "It's time to take the risk. Maccus has agreed to a betrothal, and we cannot send her along like *this*. The curse must be contained, one way or another."

I want to throw the apothecary's hand off. Shriek at them to stop.

But isn't this what I wanted? Protection from the madness, safety from visions and the call of the dead?

The needlepoint pushes against my skin. I gasp for breath that will not come, arms straining against the urge to push the apothecary away and run—except I killed my brother with this curse. Summoned death with a vision. Is this fate truly any different from banishment to the cottage for the last seven years? Or worse than rotting in a dungeon, buried in the earth?

If *this* is the only way to atone for Conal's death—to be the daughter they wanted, worthy of the mercy Father bestowed . . .

The needle breaks skin, sending liquid fire into my veins that swiftly calcifies, as brittle as ice.

I am numb. I am burning inside. I am—*nothing*.

I scream.

They have to hold my arms—hold *me* in place like they haven't held me since I was small. Gods, was I ever small?

I scream as Father's hands lock my shoulders into place, and Mam grabs my face between her hands, trying to soothe me—no, to stifle the ugly sounds pouring from my mouth.

This is wrong. This is cleaving me in two.

"Stop—*please* stop—stars, I *can't*—"

"Keep her still! One wrong mark and she'll never move again."

Their hold becomes iron, and I moan as something snaps inside me with the next scrape of the needle.

The first spiral is done.

I can't feel a part of myself—can't even remember what to call it. It is the hollow ache of a missing limb.

The apothecary starts on another, and I feel myself breaking away. My insides spasm, and sweat breaks out across my skin.

"I can't . . ."

"Be still!"

It's between one stroke of lightning-hot pain and the next that I vomit.

They all jerk back, leaving me to collapse into my own sick—heaving until those retches give way to sobs that tear through my entire body. Air nips at the raw skin on my bare back, trickles across my chest. I wrap one unsteady arm around my front, dragging the ruined dress back into place as shame burns alongside the acid on my tongue. "I can't—I can't do it. Please don't make me do it."

Mam is senseless. Da is too busy wiping vomit off his boots to look my way. And the apothecary . . .

He frowns at his needle. The mess I've made of the floor. Like I'm a roast pig he was eager to carve, only to find it snatched away by hounds before he could truly start. "Her shaking will disrupt the pattern too much if we continue now."

I'd laugh at his disappointment if my horror wasn't choking everything else out.

"It would paralyze her, like the others."

"Make my daughter worthless, you mean." My father's eyes harden to slate. "I've had enough of that from her."

The apothecary grunts as I stare at my twitching fingers, too terrified for relief to settle in. "It is strange, though. I recall Gráinne reacting just like—"

Da grabs the apothecary's arm and shoves him toward the bed. "You shut your *fecking* mouth about that wretch and get out. We'll finish this tomorrow."

Sionn scowls but lowers his head in a wary bow. "As you wish, my king."

Da doesn't speak until the apothecary is gone, taking the caipín baís ink and his instruments with him. I fix my gaze on the floor of this stinking, stagnant cell, clutching at my stomach as if that might keep the insides from being slashed to ribbons. But Da takes my hand away, only to curl it around something cold and heavy.

For once, I feel not a flicker of emotion from his touch.

"You will clean yourself up and accept Rí Maccus's offer to-morrow. And for once in your life, Saoirse, you will prove you were worth keeping."

I stare at the betrothal torc hooked over my palm, crafted of iron set with gray agate from the Isle of Unbound Earth. It slides down my arm as Da slams the door shut behind him.

Are you a fanciful girl?

I look at the torn linen feathers, the hem soaked in my own sick, and release another weak sob.

No, I'm not fanciful. I'm just a fool.

Tears choke me until a touch to my shoulder jolts me half out of my skin. When I look up, it's into the stricken face of my mother, her lip bleeding where she bit it through.

"Mam?" I am on my feet before I can register the weakness in my own body, catching her arm with both hands. She falls heavily on the trunk at the end of the bed, and I am quick to remove my touch. I don't know what is welcome here. Her regret lingers in the space between my ribs. But before I can step back, Mam seizes my skirt.

"H-he doesn't mean it."

A pucker forms between my brows. "I don't understand."

Mam shakes her head, rocking slowly from one side to the other. "When you were born, Dermot was the first to hold you in his arms. He wept that day, Saoirse—*wept*. Just as he did with both your brothers."

I close my eyes. Try to swallow. "Mam, please don't—"

"And the night you turned three? When he found you holding the soulstone?"

I catch her hand, only because she's clawing at her own throat, leaving angry scarlet lines behind. "Aye, I remember. He said . . .

he said I slipped away from my nanny. Someone must have drowned at sea, and the soulstone washed up—"

"It's not true." Mam turns her hand over until her nails drive into my wrist, her eyes suddenly fixed on my own. "The soulstone was put there on purpose, Saoirse. The curse is your grandmother's fault."

The pain ebbs. My shock takes over.

"My grandmother?"

"*Gráinne.*"

The name shivers across my aching muscles, stirring memories that don't feel as though they belong to me. A fading sensation of skin like crinkled silk passing over mine. Da claimed she took ill when we were small and was sent away for her health before she died. Neither Aidan nor Conal remembered her well, but . . . she used to hold me, didn't she? Aside from my brothers, she was the only one unafraid. And there was a song. One that lit up her eyes.

Eyes the color of . . .

Pain spreads at my back, clouding my mind. The memory is gone as quickly as it came.

"I don't remember her. Da always said she died when I was wee."

Mam shakes her head, silver-threaded hair tumbling against her cheeks. "She was *there* that night, Saoirse. Mad—she had been mad for years, and kept under guard. That's what your father refused to tell you. He was only trying to protect you. But Gráinne once held a soulstone too."

My jaw goes slack. "What?"

"Gráinne gave the guards the slip. It was the night of your birth celebrations—everyone had been drinking. She sneaked past your nanny and then took you out to the shore." Tears flood my mother's eyes, painting the colors thin where they'd been stroked by summer before. "She believed that if she bled you into the sea, it would break her own curse. She—stop shaking your head, it's true! By the time Dermot and the nanny found her, she already had your head underwater and a knife to your throat."

The torc clatters to the ground as I wrench my arms away. "What are you—"

"Your father saved your life. He wrestled you from Gráinne's arms, and while he was trying to make sure you could breathe, she attacked the nanny onshore. The girl was dead by the time Dermot reached her, her soulstone sitting on the sand. A-and as Dermot went for your grandmother, you . . ."

I stare at my fingers like they might unearth some new truth. "I picked it up."

The knowledge hangs between us, noxious and empty. Changing nothing.

"It was all Gráinne's fault," Mam says, rocking herself slowly back and forth. Her own prayer charms tinkle together at her wrist. "That's why Dermot sent her away after—and why he must have made the amulets. It was to protect you. Wasn't it?"

Oh.

I close my eyes, sinking unsteadily to the ground. "Mam . . ."

"Your father just wants to protect us. And the gods have been so quiet—of course he used the caipín bais. It's hard to understand, but they're made with the goddess's blood, after all. He still believes. The magic is still their blessing."

My hands are clammy as I bury my face against them, tucking my knees tight—hissing when my freshly scarred back touches the wall.

"He's always known best which path to take, Saoirse. He saved the island from ruin—he's kept you alive." The desperation in her voice is palpable. "It's a miracle. A cure. You won't be dangerous, or feel the pain any longer."

I won't feel *anything* any longer. I will be nothing.

Is that what they both want?

I curl inward as tight as I can, until her rambling becomes prayers and then songs to the gods who died long before they could hear them.

SIX

When I was a girl, I thought that veils were enchanted things—woven of birch, fox fur, and snow to make the world winter-quiet. I imagined the relief of sitting among dozens of people with their countenances softened, their voices reduced to a hush.

The reality is a jarring web of shadow and light that clings to my lips every time I take a breath.

I bow my head low, combing my fingers through the mound of rich golden petals perched precariously in my lap. It threatens to collapse every time a breeze slips beneath our awning. Made of driftwood and finely spun cloth, the awning is one of several sheltering the royal families as our matriarchs and patriarchs gather into their Ring of Stars. It is they who will decide which marriages to bless or reject, what trade laws to pass or punishments to deliver.

It was their verdict that wrapped this iron torc around my throat.

"To the first match of the season!"

I tilt my head until the heavy lace shifts, creating a small window between one design and the next.

Da holds court among the others, standing as servants pour

mead into their gleaming bronze cups—a toast for himself and the humorless Stone King sitting beside him.

It is not the usual order of things. I see it in the cool glances exchanged between Ríona Etain and her granddaughter, Aisling, both of them draped in pale gowns peppered with violets and wild clary stamped into the silk. They have the same wide, dark eyes and bronze skin, though Aisling's is tinted with the poppy blush of youth. She flicks her dark braid over one shoulder and threads a flower through the end. As heir, her place is to observe, not engage.

I gather more marsh marigolds, a frown pulling at my lips.

None of the Ring appear quite the same as they did when I was a child. As host of the Damhsa Babhdóir, Rí Tadhg of Frozen Hearth ought to be congenial and smiling. Instead he scowls at the cup in his yellowed hand, fingertips as twisted and fragile as half-burned twigs. Rumors have it that winters grow harsher with each passing year, cracking open the island to release a flesh waste into the very springs once renowned to heal. Only three remain pure, where once there were hundreds.

Two of the other regents have died since I last saw a gathering, replaced by their children: Ríona Kiara of Ashen Flame, and Rí Callen of Painted Claw. Kiara sits on the other side of Aisling, an imposing blur of red and gold I cannot quite see, but Callen—called Calla until they were six—crosses one sharp leg over the other directly across from me. Their stare pierces through their curtain of white-blond hair and my veil, both.

I drop my gaze, fire licking my wound in response.

They were my friend, once. Before it became too dangerous to be friends with anyone.

Father fills the last goblet to the brim. "Rí Maccus is a just man who rules with an iron will and steady hand."

I glance at those hands—thick, and free of jewels or gentleness. But he was gentle at times last night. Wasn't he? Will his hands go soft when he finds me an empty doll, made without will or curiosity or wonder? Or will those fingers trace the violet-tinged paths left by his heavy engagement torc around my neck?

Will I even care, once the tattoo is complete?

I pick up a fresh stem and tear out the fragile threads of its golden heart.

Will *I* be anything at all?

"And in this age of depletion, when the magic seems to be running scarce, I must believe such unions offer hope for the descendants of the Daonnaí. Surrounded by the constant reminder of death, we can only hope that in birth our legacy will continue, and our Crescent will prosper."

Father finishes to scattered applause. I pull the last petal free from the marsh marigold until it is naked and plain. Then I cast it onto a pile with the rest.

"Congratulations, Rí Dermot. Rí Maccus." The voice is low. Almost feline—nestled in the speaker's throat like a purr. "I'm sure the bride is thrilled to champion your cause. Or at least I'll have to assume, considering you've hidden her beneath a tablecloth."

Rí Callen's smile is a razor's edge, cutting Da's pride into bristles. For half a second, I want to smile too.

Until Da casts me a look, and the impulse fades away.

"During the week of her own wedding, your aunt was plagued by spirits. The ghosts of her parents, grandparents, siblings lost to winter, and nephews to the sword." Da sinks into his seat. "And without a veil, she had no means to hide as the gathering drew the dead near. One week of their presence—the constant reminder of all she'd lost—and she threw herself into the sea. That is why you wear her crown now. Is it not?"

Callen taps their finger against the bronze cup—hollow clicks that raise chills along my arms. "Yes."

"You'll forgive me, then, for taking precautions with my only daughter. I have already lost a son."

They all go silent at last.

Clever thing. You're the magpie, aren't you?

The words come unbidden—and unwelcome, trickling through my body in a pitiful echo of last night's rush. It was quiet then too. Like the whole world had been swallowed up by time the moment I first saw the Wolf.

Pain scrapes across my skin at the memory of his touch, shuddering through my body until it draws back to a needle-fine point. I grimace and shift until my dress stops brushing against the incomplete spirals cut into my back. But it does nothing to relieve the emptiness inside me.

I reach for another yellow flower.

"We all mourn for you, Dermot. There is not a one among us who hasn't experienced a loss. Yet I cannot help but wonder how marriage and birth are meant to conquer an unending tide of death."

A patch of clover made of lace obscures the speaker from view, but I know her voice well. Ríona Kiara is not a queen to be dismissed. When she was barely more than a child, she inherited her crown and an island on the brink of destruction, consumed by wildfires and poachers after their precious horses. Bred on grasslands fed by the goddess Maira's blood, the steeds are unmatched in endurance, battle will, and strength—their hooves able to yield a month's worth of the same when boiled beneath a full moon. Yet as the Ring of Stars united and warfare died out, so did the need for such talents and beasts.

There was more than one occasion she came to speak at my

father's court when I was small, asking for aid or an alliance against the thefts.

He always seemed to relish saying no.

But when she speaks now, they all sit straighter. Even my father does not dare interrupt.

"We are living with a festering wound. How many generations must pass until our islands are completely overcome by the dead? Until the seas cannot be sailed for spirits clogging the waters, and every last resource dried up as we all go mad?"

My handful of petals tears in two, leaving a jagged edge along the marsh marigold's center. Dark veins rip through the cheery yellow, and I can't help it.

I look up.

Ríona Kiara is staring right at me. Unlike my father, she does not need to stand to command attention. She is like her cousin in that way.

Like my brother Conal.

"The lands must heal. The dead *must* move on. Until that changes, there is no hope for true legacy." Ríona Kiara lifts her chin. "Not unless we steal it out of fate's hands."

I drop the flower. Stare at its mangled remains.

She's talking about the Isle of Lost Souls. About her cousin, and the quest.

It's a myth—a *lie*—but one I could believe is true by the mere power of her words.

But Da was right; it's not worth risking more death for the sake of a fairy tale. Is it? I'm the only person I've ever known to survive touching a soulstone—and that is only due to his ingenuity with the caipín baís and his apothecary's ink.

Da is the only reason I am alive.

So I will wed Rí Maccus, and pinch my mouth until it bleeds, lock my magic—*myself*—away, and never again fall prey to so much sensation that it lands me in the arms of a Wolf.

Even if kissing him was like touching the sky after a lifetime leashed to the ground.

. . . *I will steal his rest, and he will rob me of mine . . .*

I shut my eyes tight. Release the petals in an ugly clump onto my lap, then bury my stained fingertips in the skirts below.

Better to have fled the wild last night than feel its loss.

Better never to have wandered at all.

They're all arguing now, the glittering Ring of Stars. Callen doesn't see me anymore, glaring at Tadhg while ancient Etain taps her collarbone to calm her blood. Kiara and Aisling join hands behind the chairs, Kiara's head high as Da sneers from across the awning, his fist white-knuckled at his side.

And Maccus laughs. Like this is a game he's already won.

We are going to break each other.

I don't realize I've stood until I'm surrounded by a million flecks of sunlight. The basket lies on its side by my feet, petals clinging to my veil and skirts, dragging like fingertips across my cheeks.

All eyes beneath the awning fall to me, and my face burns as I kneel in a fruitless effort to gather up the mess.

"I'm sorry—I wasn't thinking."

But I was. Because I can't do this.

I can't be *nothing*.

Ríona Kiara would not lay her stake with the Wolf unless she believed he could do it. She would not campaign to the other kings and queens unless she truly thought he would find the Isle of Lost Souls—and why not? *He* is the reason Kiara holds so much power now. He's found everything he's ever sought—creatures we thought extinct, plants only rumored to exist, clever currents between every island, and a friend in every port. The Wolf could charm even a goddess back to life, if the songs ring true.

He looked into my eyes last night as though he recognized them. As if he's been waiting for me all along.

And I am already broken. What is there left to fear?

"Saoirse!" Da's voice stops my hands short, petals falling between my fingers like rain. "A servant will take care of that. You should rest before the festivities tonight."

I swallow as something forms in my mind—something dangerous. The path leading away from these pavilions splits just at the edge of the woods. One runs toward the beaches and docks, where my father's guards await, ready to escort me to the cabin on his ship. The other leads into the woods.

It would be easy, wouldn't it, to hide in the milling crowds drifting past vendors and food stalls at the split?

Easy to find the man whose name lingers on everyone's lips.

I stand, brushing my skirts free. "Aye, my king. Thank you." I bow as Da dismisses me with a wave.

But Rí Maccus's cold gaze stays at my back until the crunch of shells shifts to moss-covered earth beneath my boots as I reach the shadow of the trees.

People cluster around vendors like bees sampling the same flower, turning over earth-toned tunics and leather belts, beaten-metal torcs and stone-studded cuffs to inspect their craft. A handful of lads clusters around a firepit, swapping coins for sticks of roasted meat. One of them has his back to me, arms woven around a swan from last night. His dark, wavy hair is tied in a knot behind his head.

I stumble over a tree root in my attempt to see his eyes past the veil—and immediately regret it when the couple startles to their feet, glaring. "Watch yourself!"

"Sorry." This man's eyes are brown. The Wolf's are blue.

I wrap my arms tight around my middle, trying to ignore their muffled laughter as I walk on. But the faces passing by are tricky to make out through the veil. One is too round, the other's smile too sincere. Their voices blend together like birdsong until all I hear is an indistinct melody.

I step off the path into a thicket of beech trees, hazy blue smoke drifting in between, and laugh.

I truly am a fool.

The Wolf wore a mask last night. His smile was arrogant, lips painfully soft, but firelight and magic obscure my memories of the rest. Did I truly think it would be easy to find him? I'm used to looking at the world through windows, not standing in its midst.

A nearby seller removes an ochre cloak hanging from the line tied to his cart, creating a wee gap to the other side. I wander closer, tightening my hold on myself as the overwhelming urge to flee settles in.

It was stupid to come here. For all I know, the entire legend of the Wolf is built on lies. And the island's been gone for centuries, since before the gods' demise. Why should I think he could possibly—

A second cloak comes down, and in the space left behind I see *him*.

Leaning back against his own beech tree, holding a leather flask in one hand. The Wolf of the Wild is taller than I remember, or perhaps it's just that now he's wearing boots. Elaborate rings dot each finger as sunlight teases liberal streaks of red out of his dark brown hair. Half the curls are tied back, revealing a series of gold rings at the shell of his ear. He smiles like he understands *exactly* his place in this world, just like Aidan said.

Gods. *Gods.*

I bite my lip. Take one slow step forward to duck around the remaining cloaks.

And find half a dozen people surrounding him on the other side.

SEVEN

This is a mistake.

I turn to flee—but my boot strikes a twig with a crack so loud, it draws all six pairs of eyes directly to me. I cover my veiled face without hesitation, begging the ground to open below.

"Right. We'll start the betting at a ten-piece that her friends put her up to this. Stars above, but the lasses are getting an early start today!"

The words startle me nearly enough to look up, just so I can put a face to the deep, honeyed voice. Before I can, another person chimes in—lighter this time, her words trembling like she's holding back a belly laugh.

"Shall I cut a lock of hair for the girl, Captain? It'll do you some good, missing a chunk in the front there."

Chuckles ripple among the others and I attempt to swallow, but my throat is as dry as sand. "I-I'm sorry, I just . . . L-last night—"

Full-blown laughter drowns out my words, chased by a deep groan and the strike of a hand against a shoulder. "Winds o' fury! Faolan, lad, tell me you didn't seduce an innocent last night—and this one a bride! We can't take any more enraged grooms threatening to set fire to our sails. Or fathers, or brothers, or—"

"Oi! Lay off the poor thing, would you? You all know damned well innocent's never been my type."

It's *his* voice. I'm sure of it.

Silk and salt.

Tentatively, I lower my hands enough to see a tall woman with a rounded belly standing closest to me, coppery hair cut just above her broad, heavily freckled shoulders. A man stands one head above her, his deep brown skin and dark eyes gleaming like mahogany polished in the sun.

Are they the ones who made the bets?

The Wolf leans forward, and sunlight glares off the beaten-silver pendant hanging from his neck: three wolves chasing one another in a tight circle across its surface, clasping one another by the tail. "Darlin', it's sweet of you to find me, but you'll want to get back to your betrothed now. In my experience, they don't take kindly to women who run with the wolves."

"That's not—" I try, but the others cut in, most of them hidden by the stupid veil.

"It's bad luck to send a bride off without a kiss!"

"Aye, Captain, can you imagine the stories she'd spread if you cursed the poor soul?"

I flinch, and the Wolf cocks his head. Steps toward me as I scramble back. "Is that what you're after, love?"

"No! I . . ." Sweat coats my palms, and I glance at the others— then once more at the Wolf. He wears a shirt of finely woven linen with stars embroidered along the collar, and a coat dyed such a deep green it would take weeks of foraging to get the color just right. A leather glove wraps over his left hand, tied at the wrist. He smiles beneath my inspection, but it holds the promise of a bite.

I swallow. "I need to speak with you. Alone."

The Wolf stands close now. Too close.

"Is that so?"

I startle when he slides a finger between the betrothal torc and my bare neck. A ripple of laughter runs through his friends, and my stomach draws tight, anticipating the curse's response to his touch.

But no magic flares between us.

I tilt my head until I can meet his eyes again—a deep, decadent blue that reminds me of the ancient crypt beneath my home, veined with sapphire and vibrating with spirit song.

They narrow with recognition. My throat closes in.

"Aye, well . . . far be it from me to deny a bride's final request. Nessa?" The Wolf slips a hand into his pocket and tosses a silver coin in the air. "Take the crew for another round of drinks."

The redhead—Nessa—catches it with an easy grin and nudges the deep-voiced man beside her. "Right. We'll just find you round the Maypole later, shall we, Captain?" She tosses me a wink, then slips off into the trees, the others trailing behind her.

"You're wearing the Stone King's collar."

I pull back from the Wolf so sharply, the torc strikes the line of my bone. "I-it's not." I frown and touch the cold, sharp stones set in iron, then the sensitive skin beneath. "It's a mark of betrothal."

"All it lacks is a chain."

The words don't startle me half as much as the sincerity in his tone, the distaste in his expression. It causes the torc to weigh thrice as heavy, cold metal curves digging in. "Rí Maccus meant it as an honor."

"Really?" The Wolf snorts. "I wonder how much honor he'd show if he knew you kissed me last night."

I glance around us to see if anyone has overheard, but there's no one. The vendor has walled us off with his line of cloaks, and some part of me wonders if the Wolf's crew isn't responsible for that. "That wasn't—I didn't mean to—it won't happen again."

"A damned shame, that."

"What?"

He drapes himself against the tree like it's a throne, a slight smirk banishing the dark from his eyes. "It wasn't terrible. Clearly you're new to it, but with a bit of practice . . ."

"It won't happen again, Wolf."

His mouth snaps shut, the rest of his expression masked by lace, and I can't stand it any longer. I lift the veil back and find him smiling—smirking really, as though he's barely managed to contain a laugh.

"Wolf?"

My face burns. "What else would I call you?"

He searches my eyes like he could drink them up, until his mirth eases into something softer. Curious, but wary. "Faolan."

I fold my hands to hide their trembling. Taste the name on my tongue. "Faolan, then. Are you truly everything they say?"

"Depends on who 'they' are."

I frown. "Can you find things?"

"I found *you*, didn't I?"

Heat crawls up my neck, drifting into my cheeks. "That's not—it doesn't count. You weren't looking for me."

"Och, but I was. The only trouble is, I wasn't expecting you to be the daughter of a king."

I pull back. "How did you . . ."

"Don't worry, love. That and the betrothal to old Stoneheart only complicates our plans a wee bit. Wouldn't you like to know what they are?"

He's grinning now, and it's so . . . unnerving to be played with,

I bite my lip in a refusal to respond. It only takes a moment of quiet for him to sigh.

"All right. Some of the stories about the Wolf are exaggerated, aye. The giant squid was only a tiny fellow, I've never slept with Ríona Aisling—you've my cousin to thank for that—and my ship's not crafted of actual starlight, though that's my favorite bit of the legend. But yes, I'm *that* Faolan." He looks me over and my toes curl hard in my boots. "And you're Saoirse. The girl with ocean eyes."

He grazes the fragile skin beneath them with a fingertip, and my body doesn't know how to respond. To being touched—being seen. Pain flares across the freshly carved swirls in my back as magic whispers in my mind, then quiets.

And all the while, he watches. Like he knows exactly the effect his touch had on me last night and is waiting for my eyes to shift colors again.

I push his hand off, stepping far enough away that he can't reach me. "Don't say it like that."

"Like what? A story?" Faolan smirks, twisting a ring around his fourth finger. "Because that's exactly what you'll be. The only one who can guide us to the Isle of Lost Souls." His gaze cuts to mine, sharp this time. Bemused. "I've searched half the world looking for you, lass."

Oh.

I lay a hand over my ribs until I'm sure they'll expand.

I forgot what it's like, to be wanted. To matter to someone, even just a little. And the way Faolan watches me with unflinching focus, I could almost believe he can see into my very soul—the hopelessly fragile wreck of it. Because try as I might for apathy, or dismissal, or even rage at all my father's lies . . . some part of me still believes in it.

That the Isle of Lost Souls could be found.

Just not by me.

"I think you've wasted your time."

Faolan cocks his head, as if he can scent my wavering doubt. "I highly doubt that."

"Why?" I shake my head. "I'm not—"

Special. Worth it?

I am nothing.

"Safe."

His laugh is a rasp, one that lifts the hairs along my nape. "If safety was such a great concern of mine, do you really think I'd be out on the sea?" Faolan tucks a smile into his cheek as he adjusts the leather glove until it wraps his knuckles like a second skin. "They don't tell stories about safe lives, Saoirse. Pious fishermen, humble innkeepers, or good daughters who wed whichever bastard they're told to."

My face pales as Faolan ties the glove off with his teeth. "Even if that bastard is a king. But I promise you, Trouble, they'll tell stories about *us*."

I tear my gaze away to the trees, the patchwork sky through their canopy, the line of cloaks rippling in the wind. Anywhere but the impossibility of him.

Stars. Every breath hurts now, ice threatening to consume my lungs as it leeches from the inked swirls between my shoulders each time a new feeling arises.

I always suspected fate to be cruel, but it is unspeakably so to have met Faolan only now—*now*, when I'm to be married tomorrow. Now, when I will lose my magic and myself completely tonight.

Now, when my brother is already dead.

"Come with me, Saoirse."

I blink away tears and find Faolan standing before me. The

pendant flashes silver as he breathes, then lies flat against his chest when he reaches for me, hand hovering just over my cheek. He gives me the choice to meet it this time, and every bone in my body bends toward his touch. I've never felt so exposed—never wanted to be seen so badly.

"Let me make a legend of you."

I breathe in, and his smallest finger drops to trace the movement. Breathe out as his nail scrapes my jaw.

There is no going back from this. My entire being knows it, locking against my will, hands curled close to my heart as embers shift beneath the tattoo. Yet it is that pain that prompts my lips to part, pushing the words at last beyond them.

"What if . . . I'm not a legend? What if I'm a cautionary tale?"

Faolan's triumphant smile flickers. "Sorry?"

I take another step—closer this time. Until I swear I could hear his heartbeat if I concentrated hard enough. "The reason my eyes shift colors. The . . . ocean trapped inside them. It doesn't mean anything good; it's just . . ."

A crack in the earth hiding a collapsed cavern below? The first stroke of green in a sky already swirling with storms. It's a warning bell—a witness to a coming death. A calling card to it as well.

I should have cast you into the sea the moment you opened those eyes.

My stomach lurches, and I press both hands over its shaky center. "I'm sorry, I can't—"

"*I* can't find this island without you, Saoirse." Faolan's voice snatches me back from the swirl of memory as his hand drops to my chin, but his touch is featherlight. "Believe me, I've tried. So tell me what it means."

I wrap a fist around the amulet Father returned this morning. "I-I don't know."

"Bullshite." The word is a breath—a whisper—against my lips. "You wouldn't have risked coming out here to find me if that were true, would you?"

"No. But—"

For once in your life, Saoirse, you will prove you were worth keeping.

I stumble back, and Faolan's hands drop between us. My whole body rebels in response. I don't want to be without his touch, but before I can reach out, he clasps his hands behind his neck and sighs. "Just a few words, love. Help me understand."

As if that wouldn't be a betrayal of everything my father's ever done to keep me safe.

The scent of whiskey cut by sea air is stifling, and my skin crawls with magic that *cannot* find purchase.

I want to rip it off. I want to scream.

I am *not* nothing yet.

"Saoirse—"

"Because I'm cursed!" The words fly out like they've never known a cage. His mouth falls open, eyes gone blank. I'm shaking, but there is no stuffing the words back inside. So I release a few more.

"I touched a soulstone. I held one in my hand as a child, and somehow, I survived."

EIGHT

It began innocently enough. I'd know when my brothers were
playing a prank, or when that night's fish would spoil our stom-
achs for a week.

But the gods did not spare me as a blessing.

When I was five, I touched Mam's swollen belly and asked if
the new baby could take my selkie doll down to the crypt, for fear
it might get lonely away from us all. She lost the babe a week later.
By the time I was eight, crowds drowned me in their emotion—a
shrill note of song no one else seemed to hear. By twelve and with
it my first blood, I could hardly bear to be touched. By thirteen, I
avoided the woods, where spirits would flock to me as flies to rotting meat, wanting salvation I could not give.

And at fifteen, when I chose to break my own careful rules . . .

"How is that possible?"

I search Faolan's face for revulsion or disbelief—fear.

There is only wonder.

He takes a step closer, catching my hands while I root myself
to the ground. "How in shade's realm did you survive touching a
soulstone without being marked?"

"I . . . Father said it faded after a few days. Most people die before the marks can." Faolan makes a thorough sweep of every crevice, callus, and scar with his thumbs. When he lingers on the chalk-white cuts left from the amulet last night, a sharp breath rushes past my teeth, and I jerk my hands free before he can fully map the pattern.

That is one secret he is not permitted to have.

"I'll tell you what I can," I say slowly, repeating his promise from before. "But only after you tell me why you need me to find the Isle of Lost Souls."

Faolan's brows flick together, lips quirking to one side. "Cheat."

"I am not—it's a truth for a truth."

"Smuggled out of my hand only because I still want to know what's hiding in yours." He taps his nose, and a little of the tension melts from my shoulders. "Cleverly done. You're thinking like a pirate."

The word sends a shiver down my legs. "Well?"

Faolan rubs at his scruff, then tugs at the gold ring dangling from his ear. This time, he does not meet my eyes. "It . . . starts with a song. A piece of one, anyway."

My incredulous stare must speak for itself. But he doesn't laugh. Why doesn't he laugh?

"A song. You're doing all of this because of a song?"

"I've taken greater chances on less." He lifts one shoulder, slipping a hand into his pocket to retrieve the flask. I barely restrain myself from knocking it away.

"This isn't a chance, though. This is—"

He tips the flask back, and I watch his throat shift around every swallow.

This is *everything*.

"You don't know what it's like." My voice trembles, as he slowly lowers the flask again.

"What, love?"

"*This.*" I flatten a hand over my heart. "Being cursed. I can hardly touch another person without inviting a piece of them inside. Souls call to me constantly, both the living and dead. I don't know when the visions will come or go—I can't *force* them to stop. And the only reason I've not died or gone mad is—"

The amulets. My father.

Right?

But another face appears in my memory, crinkled skin and . . . gray eyes? Green? A song lost to memory, like Faolan's pitiful scraps.

Daughter of . . . gaze sworn . . .

My temple throbs with the effort of remembering. "I probably am going mad, just like Gráinne," I whisper.

Faolan lurches forward, flask dropping to the ground. "What did you say?"

"I said I'm going mad, same as Gráinne. My grandmother." The word tastes wrong, coating my mouth in dust. It doesn't belong to me. Not in the way it should. "Mam said she touched a soulstone too—that Gráinne is the reason I'm cursed."

There's something in Faolan's eyes, growing dark and wild as they hunt my own. "And you believe them?"

"I—of course. Why . . ." Humor quirks his brow. My hands curl in response. "Did you know her?"

"I met her once."

I stagger back. "How?"

His lips pull into a sideways smile. "Where do you think I heard the song? 'Daughter of the knowing sea, gaze sworn long ago to me . . .'?"

My body goes slack.

"Unfortunately," Faolan goes on, scooping the flask from the ground, "I didn't know she was your grandmother until just now.

Would've saved me months of sailing round the Crescent if I'd known where to look—but this just proves my point further." He straightens, and whatever shadows lingered in his expression are gone. "You, my wee clever magpie, are meant to find this island. In fact, I daresay you're the only one who can."

The absurd urge to laugh rattles through my shock. I rake my hands through my hair, dislodging the veil entirely so that it slides into a silken heap on the ground—a spider's web of lace and lies.

I cannot quell the childish impulse to kick it away. "This is not a game to me, Faolan—this is my freedom."

"So take it."

"What?"

Faolan taps the iron torc hanging round my throat. "You want freedom—from marriage to the Stone King, and from your old man."

From the magic.

From myself.

My heart constricts as Faolan opens his hand between us, emerald and opal rings casting prisms across his palm. "Join me, Saoirse. Help me find the Isle of Lost Souls, and I swear that freedom will be yours."

The wind stops. Birdsong stifles.

There is a faint ringing in my ears as I contemplate Faolan's hand.

It would be easy—*so* easy—to believe him. I've heard stories of the Wolf of the Wild since I was twelve and he a lad of sixteen, first carving a place for himself on the violent sea. During my banishment to the cottage, when I would wake in the nights alone and raw with grief, it was the Wolf I imagined coming to my door, ready to whisk me off on one of his wild adventures.

I tear my hand away, cradling it close to my chest, where it brushes the heavy torc resting on my collarbone. "Rí Maccus would be furious. He'd never forgive the slight."

"Aye." Faolan sounds far too pleased about it. "Your da too— but it won't matter once we've found the isle of the lost, now will it?"

My laugh is too bitter for the sunshine streaming around us, the clover at our feet. "*If.*"

"You doubt me?"

I doubt myself. "I don't even know you."

His eyes have no right to look so wounded. He stuffs his hand into his pocket, kicking his boot back against the tree and sending a shudder through the leaves. "So what's the alternative? Stay here, become a Stone Bride, die young, and be forgotten?"

I wince with every word, ice slaking down my spine to coat the panic until it's slippery—present but impossible to grasp or wield. And that is what terrifies me most. Being trapped in my body, feeling all the horror of it, yet completely unable to react or break free.

"There is no guarantee we'll find it." The words sound small, even to me. "What happens if we don't?"

"Then I drop you off in a lovely, small cove to hide, and make things up to Kiara."

I stare at the pendant hanging around Faolan's neck. His family's sigil. One he's altered to suit him because the original belonging to Ríona Kiara has a trio of horses, not wolves.

Kiara. His queen.

Stars above.

"I'm supposed to be married tomorrow. They—gods, they'll all think you stole me. Or that Kiara orchestrated it . . . Faolan, we'd set off a war if I went." I can barely speak the words. "Between my father and Rí Maccus, or both of them against your cousin's people!"

"So let them think it."

I laugh, because the words are perhaps the most outlandish ones he's uttered so far.

And yet.

The laughter dies on my lips as I stare into his eyes. Look over his frame—all those symbols of power marking him as the Wolf of the Wild. If I abandon my betrothal and they catch us, Faolan's protection would be meaningless. Unmarried, I am subject to the laws of my home, and though I'm of age, my father is still the king. A single word from him could end me, and no one in the land would dispute it.

But if I could change that one small fact—no longer be the *daughter* of someone, but instead . . .

"Who saw me kiss you last night?"

Faolan's lips twitch, breaking into a wide smirk even as he turns one of the rings round and round his finger. Restless. "Most of the Damhsa, I have to imagine. My cousin. The crew. There are few lasses daring enough to try it these days—especially the innocent ones."

"And I was the only one dressed as a magpie." I weave my hands over my stomach and press down until I am steady. "What if I ran away with you? Not because I was kidnapped, and not to defy my father or Rí Maccus's hand, but because . . . I wanted to marry someone else."

Faolan goes still, gaze locked on mine. "Aye?"

"But it won't work if they don't believe it. And I'm not risking my father's fury or the Stone King's war without a guarantee of your protection—the sort that takes more than words."

His eyes narrow into a suspicious shade of midnight. My throat threatens to collapse, but I force a steady breath into my lungs. Lock my hands together and push the words out.

"If you want me to come with you, Faolan, you'll have to wed me first."

His laughter bursts free like the snapping of waves against a cliffside. I compel my spine not to bend, keeping my chin level even as I tuck my shaking hands into the folds of my skirt to hide them. When I don't join in, his laugh dies between one gust and the next.

"You were serious? No—no, I'm never going to marry anyone."

"Well, if you want me on your ship—"

"I don't *want* you on my ship; I *need* you there."

"And I need some guarantee that I'll survive it."

Faolan flings his hands into the air. "You're never guaranteed anything on the waters; that's what makes it so damn exciting! Any moment you step foot on those planks is a moment you could meet death."

"I *know* I'll meet death if I leave with you now."

"Well, that's a bit dramatic, isn't it?" Faolan's smile returns halfheartedly, like he's waiting for the joke, but I only stare until it disappears altogether. When it does, he grimaces and rubs at his neck. "All right. All right, look—Saoirse. How about a chest of gold? A home of your own? Servants, lovers, a new feckin' name. You come with me and you'll have all of that—more if you'd like. We'll be heroes when we return, completely untouchable!"

"*If* we find it."

He scowls, and I shrug. "Like you said, you're a story." The words are harsh, but the pain lancing across my tattoo is harsher. "I don't know which parts are true."

Faolan bites back a groan, raking a hand through his dark curls. "Lass. If you're looking for a lover or some gentle, kind man to keep that tender heart of yours, I'm sorry but I—"

I shove hard at his chest, anger bubbling up my throat and

burning behind my eyes. "I'm not asking for that! Shades damn you, I'm just trying to survive."

"Aye, but you still want your freedom and I want *mine*." His words are emphatic, his voice tight. "I cannot marry, Saoirse."

"And I can't go without that protection." My lungs ache as I force as deep a breath as I can manage. Then I lower my hands, watching him for one long moment as I try and fail to reconcile what I am about to do. If this doesn't work . . . "So I guess you'll have to find the island on your own."

Shards of wood and fresh spring blooms grind beneath my boots as I turn, leaving the shock on his face behind. I'm nearly sick as I take one step. Another.

Surely he'll stop me? I can't have told him all that for nothing.

I don't dare look back as I walk. I don't breathe.

I'm at the line of cloaks again when his hand curls around my upper arm, drawing me up short. "A handfasting."

My mind roars like the wildest winter wind. He's furious—I see it in the firm line of his brow and the flatness of his mouth. But there's respect as well, and his touch is gentle even as it falls away.

"What?"

"A handfasting. That's all I can give. It's binding, but we can both walk at the end of this journey if we want."

I am speechless. Numb. Ants crawl across my skin as a hive hums behind my ears, the ocean churning gently in my mind. And though metallic fear coats my tongue, for once it doesn't overwhelm me. I know what I'm going to say before it comes out—know all over again that I'll likely regret this someday.

But at least this destruction will be my choice, and mine alone.

"Aye." I watch him for one second longer before I spit into my palm and offer my hand like Da did yesterday. Faolan echoes the gesture and shakes my hand firmly enough to jar my shoulder.

"Well. You've got your wish—a leash on the Wolf of the Wild. Shall I deflower you now or later?"

I tear my hand away from his so violently that I fall back into a cloud of ferns, their vibrant green fronds cool against the raging heat of my face.

"I don't think you understood, I-it's not *that* kind of marriage."

His laughter is wild as he grips my arm, hauling me out of the leaves. "Stars above, your face! You'll have to grow a thicker skin than all tha' if you're going to survive on my ship, lass." He looks me over, cocks his head to the side, and before I can stop him he's caught either side of the betrothal torc and pulled it free from my neck. "No use for this anymore."

I rub at the raw skin left behind, biting my lip when my fingers find an especially tender place. "Thank you."

"Besides, if I'm going to be bound up in marriage, might as well piss off two kings in the process."

He's ducked before I can fully process the magnitude of what we're about to do, plucking my veil from the ground. "Come to my ship after the fifth sacrifice. Everyone should be well and truly drunk by then. If we time it right, we'll be tethered and sailing off on our merry adventure long before anyone realizes we've gone."

This cannot be reality. I am not this girl.

"Which ship is yours?"

Faolan's smile is wicked as he slips a wolf's-head ring off his pinky and slides it onto the longest finger of my left hand.

"The one made of starlight."

NINE

A column of smoke disrupts the pristine, silver-streaked sky, casting a haze upon the moon. On the southern beaches, they'll be burning effigies of the gods—Róisín first for the island of artists, storytellers, and twilight bargains. I imagine the smooth wood of her skin peeling back as flames lick higher, marsh marigolds mingled with blood and ashes at her feet.

My fingers twitch in response, casting skeletal shadows over the heavy wool blanket below. It's too thick in the sticky summer heat of the cabin, but I couldn't refuse my mother's offer to cover me.

I couldn't refuse anything at all.

Somewhere in the stifling room, I hear a sound like tearing fabric echo again and again. Five long seconds pass before I realize it is just my breath—short and sharp. Shaking on every exhale.

My fingers twitch again.

"Tie her down." The apothecary never looked my way, attention fixed on his vial of precious ink. "I'll attempt the second circle, and if it succeeds—"

"You will complete it tonight." Da's voice held none of the apothecary's apathy. "And never assume to order me again."

I cowered when he came for me, fighting every instinct to run as

I begged for more answers—more time. Until Da ripped them from my hands.

Slowly, painstakingly, I curl my hand into a fist and twist it knuckle side up. Four sleek bruises stripe my arm above the wrist.

"Not the ropes, Dermot. They'll leave marks on her skin. I'll hold her."

And she had.

I glance down to see my pulse throbbing relentlessly at my wrist as though it, too, wants to escape. Out the window, a second stream of smoke ignites. I manage to dig my fist into the mattress and roll onto my side—gasping with the monumental effort. Sweat trickles down the small of my back and across the pads of my feet as tears slip down my chin.

This is the first time I've felt them in hours.

"Why has she gone quiet?" Mam's voice was a splinter in the silence. My throat was burning—everything was burning—but I couldn't scream. My body was the earth, and the earth was crumbling. An entire island lost to the sea.

Jerking. Shaking— Why couldn't I stop shaking?

Phantom tremors dance across my bones. I've never been more terrified of myself than I was in the eternity after my father's apothecary completed the second swirl of the triskele, separating my body from my mind.

I thrashed on the ground without reason, a plea lodged tight between my teeth. They rattled together and my mother sobbed, holding fast to me—why had she never held me like this before?

Until it stopped.

And I couldn't feel Mam's hands on my shoulders. Or the pain at my back.

I couldn't feel anything at all.

My legs prickle as a thousand spiders seem to writhe across my calves. I kick until they flee, sending the dense wool covers to the ground.

Outside the window, a third thread of smoke joins the other two.

I grit my teeth and heave against the mattress until, with a sickening lurch, my body topples to the ground. There, my limbs twist and jerk as I crumple between chalk-stained barrel rings, pressing my forehead to the filthy ground. I breathe slow and deep, rocking back and forth until every limb is mine again—aching, but *mine.*

"*Why has she stopped moving? What the feck have you done?!*"

Boots landed heavy on the floorboards, inches from my nose. A bone dropped, the needle splitting in two as ink sprayed across Da's robes.

The apothecary sighed. "I warned you she'd react poorly. We should have begun the moment we collected her from that shack— small pieces, over time. Is that not what I advised?"

"*Your advice is worthless if you do not fix her* now!"

Four sacrifices bend in columns of smoke to the sky, and I lock my eyes on the window. Ease onto my knees—bite down a cry when my strength falters, sending me back to the floor. My mouth tastes vile with the apothecary's elixir.

If I can just make it to the water.

On a weak sob, I start to crawl.

Was I finally nothing? Were they happy now?

Da continued to argue as Mam sponged my brow. I couldn't turn my head away from the irritating drips of water, or keep it from lolling as she dragged me onto the bed. The air was stifling when she tucked me in, singing prayers over my head. When the apothecary tipped a bottle into my mouth, I swallowed the best I could.

My mother had taught me nothing if not to endure.

To obey.

I nearly tip the basin over, grasping for the clay jug tucked inside. Water streams down either side of my mouth as I drink, saturating my dirt-smudged gown. It's not enough. I need more water. Air.

Wild.

The Wolf's face flashes across my mind, and I drop the jug. Its handle splits as it hits the ground, the body lying cracked and worthless beside it. There is something in the mess I've made—a thing I've forgotten. But the pool of water is stunning, capturing all the moon's blessed light.

"Tomorrow, then. We will complete the tattoo at first light. And gods be damned, Saoirse will wed Rí Maccus before the sun sets."

I trace a finger through the liquid, silver threads rippling out from the point. In another moment, it will be gone—absorbed into dusty knots of yarn, forgotten beneath someone's heel.

Is that what I truly want?

My gaze flits to the window, where a fifth beacon of smoke has just barely begun.

The fifth sacrifice.

Faolan.

"No."

Something inside me snaps into place at his name, the memory of his touch, like a limb returned to its socket.

And I am raw with sensation.

Fear sends the world spinning until I drop to my knees, my body wrapped over itself in a child's idea of protection: if I can make myself small enough, maybe the threat will go away. The amulet lies on a chair beside the bed, useless as the curse rams into my tattoo like a swollen river against a dam. But the magic will *not* be contained. Swirls of pasty ink will only turn it inward, flooding my soul—breaking my mind.

I cannot live with war raging constantly inside me.

The charms are in my hand in seconds, pulled from their constant home tucked beneath my bodice. I don't even know if I believe in them anymore, but I press my lips to them all the same, fingers weaving between the tiny metal slates until I've prayed three times to each of the holy gods.

"Bandia Eabha, spill your moon over my soul. Dhia Odhrán, raze my impurities with your sun."

For years of my life, the six charms and all their stories were a comfort. A hope of salvation. I truly thought if I prayed enough, behaved, and sacrificed, whichever god had seen fit to curse me for touching the soulstone would end it, and I'd be all right.

But it was a lie. It's always been a lie.

I whisper the prayers frantically now, desperate to hear something. *Anything.* Over and over I repeat their names in a plea, a rage, a sob, until my fingers tangle so tightly in their cords, my skin mottles like an overripe plum. It's a macabre tapestry—a lamb bound for slaughter.

I stop, my tongue poised against the roof of my mouth, lips shaping the next god's name. Róisín's broken antler presses to my palm like it wishes to pierce the skin—a tiny fleck of metal among half a dozen that have demanded blood for nineteen years of my life and not *once* given a damn thing back.

Because only a fool seeks mercy from a god slaughtered by mortal hands.

The antler breaks my flesh, and a bead of blood trickles down my wrist.

I was that fool. But no longer.

My fingers go white as I pull my wrists apart, slowly at first and then with singular focus, gritting my jaw at the sting of my flesh until one by one, the leather cords snap free. Charms rain into my lap with a furious cry—not the gateway to the gods I once believed in, but a pile of tiny, harmless scraps of metal.

Nothing more.

I'm not sure if it's a laugh or a sob that escapes me as I stand on shaking legs, wiping my wrist against my skirt. Faolan said to come after the fifth sacrifice. It's not too late. With unsteady fingers, I tug the satchel free from beneath my bed and drag it to the door. The wolf's-head ring is nestled deep inside.

Never again will I beg the air for salvation from this curse. If the Isle of Lost Souls will wash it free, then to its waters I shall go. But first . . .

The ship is quiet as I slip down the hall, my own door unlocked since I'd been unable to move when they left me behind. My bare feet find well-crafted rugs and smooth panels of oak as I count each door. My father's cabin, that of his advisers, Mam's lady's maid.

I stop at the very last one.

The apothecary's door is latched, but this ship was built for luxury, not protection. It's a struggle to lift it on its leather hinge, wiggling the handle like Aidan taught me long ago until the latch slips free. My hands drop, exhaustion sending dark splotches across my vision as the door swings open.

Pools of melted wax litter the ground, dripping off flat surfaces secured to the walls where instruments and bottles lie strapped in by slender leather cords. Clay tablets covered in elaborate drawings are nailed beside them, and a smell clings to every surface, sweetly spiced as rotting flesh.

I gag, fumbling to retreat, when I spot it. The bag he brought to my room.

My skirts drag across discarded papers as I kneel to lift the top. There are the other bone needles, the bloodstained cloth he used to wipe my skin. A bottle of noxious orange paste sits beside one that looks like sulfur, another filled with glistening liquid black.

And there, at the center, is a tiny glass vial swirling with milky ink.

I weigh it in my hand. Wonder what it cost my father to make. They spoke of tests—others they tried the inverted triskele on who lost use of their limbs, their minds. Did Da know what he was doing? Did he care about the cost?

Do I?

My fingers close around the bottle, tendons rolling against the glass.

I'll take this with me. A promise—a vow. If we cannot find the Isle of Lost Souls and the curse cannot be cleansed, then I'll lock it away myself. Finish the tattoo and be free of the magic one way or another. Whatever life is left to me after, I'll take it.

I don't need to be a story, but I won't be nothing either.

TEN

Faolan's ship is a finely carved extension of himself, cutting out of the water like it was born of a crashing wave. Perhaps the stories hold a thread of truth, and starlight did go into its making. After all, I've never seen sails glow quite like that. Even bound to their masts, they seem to catch every moonbeam from the sky.

My heart drops by a measure as, one by one, they unfurl.

"No."

I break free of the trees to career down the eastern beach, my gaze locked onto the sky. Faolan said to come after the fifth sacrifice, when everyone was drunk but the ceremony not quite done. He promised his ship would be waiting for me. Yet by the time I'd floundered onto the docks, sweat-soaked and shaking, all six columns of smoke had tapered into one sooty, violet mass rolling into itself like a pot of boiling nettles.

The mass is gone now, replaced by a smattering of melancholy gray wisps.

It's too late. He's leaving me behind.

I make it as far as the water's edge before sinking to my knees, shoulder aching under the weight of the single bag I managed to smuggle out. Cold sweat gathers across my upper lip and the grooves of my palms. I wrap them on either side of my neck, pressing until the nausea subsides and clarity takes its place.

Harsh and unforgiving.

He was never going to take me, was he? Who was I to think I belonged in a story next to someone like *him*. Faolan probably had a good laugh about it with his crew—taking bets like they did this morning on whether I'd cry.

Rough, green-tinged boulders dot the beach, smelling of seaweed and the coming tide. Past them, a wooden she-wolf stands guard at the bow of Faolan's ship, her smooth head thrown back as it drifts toward the open sea.

Moonlight glances off the water, painting my skin translucent so the veins stand out twice as strong. I can't stand their faint blue quiver. As I twist my arms close, silver light glints off a finely wrought scrap of metal: the wolf's head set with eyes of sapphire.

I stare at the ring. Turn it slowly around my finger.

Faolan wouldn't have left it behind—not unless he meant to have it back. He likes games, tricks, wordplay. And I'll bet he hated allowing me the upper hand during our negotiation.

So much so that he'd want to even the scales before facing his crew again.

Waves crash on the sand, spraying my face and lapping at my boots as they creep higher with the tide. I cast his ship one more hard look, judging the distance between it and my place onshore. Then I tug at the laces of my boots, pulling them and my stockings free.

If this is a test, I'm not about to fail. Not when every second I linger, a guard could catch me—drag me back to my father, his apothecary, and the Stone King's altar.

I'd rather be the fool in Faolan's story than nothing at all.

I wrap my cloak around the boots and stockings, then tuck the

bundle as far into my bag as it will go. My hands shake in antici-
pation of the cold water, or perhaps because whatever strength I
used to get this far has left only dregs behind. But I still manage to
unbuckle the leather-roped belt from my waist, winding it around
the bag until I'm sure my belongings won't be swallowed by
the sea.

I edge into it then, in small measures, clenching my teeth
when it hits my thighs. Though summer shone brightly this morning, the ocean hasn't forgotten winter's kiss. Soon, I am fighting to
keep my head above water through sheer will alone, cutting the
waves with awkward sweeps of my arms as I kick furiously below.

Damn the Wolf and his tricks.

The water shifts, circling my legs like a shark, and it's been so
long since I swam that I've forgotten what it means. It's not until
the current pulls hard at my calves and sweeps my feet forward
that I see the hungry wave cresting just over my head.

Salt floods my mouth and nose as I'm tumbled head over feet
again and again, the leather strap of my bag cutting into my throat
until another shift tears it free from my arm. When my head
breaks the surface, I retch as darkness spins around me, then
slowly rights itself. It takes effort to remain afloat—to separate the
stars from the sea. I breathe.

And then release a stream of curses at the sky. "Pox-riddled,
wolf-obsessed—bastard!"

"Well, that's a wee bit harsh, isn't it?"

My full-throated scream lasts only a second before I slip beneath the waves, drawing in water once more. A hand knots in the
back of my dress like the scruff on a wayward pup, hauling me
through the air. I barely register the wooden edge of the currach
when Faolan drops me onto one end of the little boat. My toes
catch between the ribbed slats of wood at its base.

I'm still coughing as I stare at him, scrambling for purchase against the curved hull. "W-what are you doing?"

"Rescuing you. I told you to come find my ship, not dive head-first into the waters, eejit."

The currach rocks violently as I lurch to my knees, gripping the boat's sides along with my sanity. "You *said* to come find your ship. But it was already out on the water—I thought you meant it as some stupid test!"

Faolan blinks and then releases a howl of laughter, his head dropping back with the sound.

I clench my teeth hard to keep them from chattering and glower at my sodden skirts, attempting to drag them closer to cover my legs. I've barely cleared a space when my equally waterlogged sack drops to the curved panels between my feet, hardly making a sound.

"Ah, winds o' fury, you're serious." Faolan wipes actual tears from his eyes. "You'll be a right bit of chaos, won't you, Trouble? I've been waiting all this time by the rocks. Half thought you'd changed your mind, but it turns out you're just bloody late."

He turns a lazy grin on me, and I flinch, looking away. "I was kept."

"By drowning?"

The thick fringe of hair cut across my forehead drips salt water into my eyes. I push it back with a swipe of my hand, not caring for once that it exposes them. They're what he's after, anyway.

"By my father." It's only then I notice the water isn't making a sound as it laps the sides of the boat. "I . . . didn't hear you approach."

"Right, and you wouldn't have. Too fixed on that test, weren't you?"

A flush scorches my skin at Faolan's smug reply. I glare at the curved wood beneath my feet, where seaweed clings to the bottom edge of my skirt.

He shifts. Clears his throat.

"You've heard of the tuar ceatha from the Isle of Painted Claw, haven't you?"

"Aye." The crane's iridescent feathers were said to render a wearer silent when woven through their hair, but Faolan's is untouched by feathers or other adornment. Curiosity steals my embarrassment. "Are you saying this boat is lined in them?"

"No." Faolan brightens, giving a hard tug on the oars. "But one of my crew figured out that if you take the sap of the trees they like to roost in, you can mix it into a lacquer—along with a few other things, mind—and coat the bottom of a vessel, oars, ropes. As long as it's a decently cloudy night, or they're not looking directly for our ship, we can slip by silent as we please."

I frown at once. "Why do you need a silent ship?"

Faolan's smile tightens at the corners. "Why not? Anyway, there's no ship quite like mine. D'you know her name?"

I shake my head and shift a touch closer to inspect the oar as it rises.

Faolan leans in, blocking my view. "Neither do I."

An incredulous huff escapes my lips, and his grin returns full force. "What? It's true. Every time I've faced her down and asked, she goes feckin' coy on me. It's a damn shame because a ship is only as notorious as its name. I worry, sometimes, that she'll be forgotten."

All I know is that every blast of wind off the sea burrows its way deeper beneath my damp dress, and I can't quite sort who I'm angriest with: myself for taking to the water, or Faolan for playing such games this morning that I thought it might be a test at all.

"I don't." I don't see how it matters much either as I study his face. "You haven't changed your mind, then? About the marriage?"

His eyes lock on mine in the semidark, fingers drumming the oars before he hauls them back in a weaving pattern. "No, I gave my word. And if I believe in anything in this life, it's that." He grins. "Besides, who wouldn't want a wife willing to swim fully clothed during high tide just to reach his arms?" A hand drops to his chest. "Really, I'm touched."

I glare at those same arms, flexed with every pull on the oars. "You could have stopped me."

"And missed seeing that lovely, determined wee scrunch to your nose? I think not."

"Now you're just being clever."

"Better clever than cruel." The ship looms overhead, and I try to sit up straighter, hugging my arms tighter at my middle. He follows my gaze to the barnacles clinging overhead and clears his throat. "My cousin's on board to perform the marriage rites. That's why we had to wait for the fifth sacrifice to be done—not that it mattered much in the end."

I stare at the railing, so far above my head, it's hard to distinguish against the evening sky. My parents' ship was secured to the docks, wooden steps or ramps allowing us to ascend with ease. There are no such structures here on open waters. "And how are we supposed to reach 'on board'?"

A soft laugh chases Faolan before he pulls up beside the ship and lifts his hand to his lips, letting out a piercing whistle. A heartbeat passes, and a rope ladder tumbles over the railing, striking the side of the ship before us.

I can barely make it to my feet, already dreading the graceless climb ahead. I can only imagine the humiliation that will come when I reach the top, sweaty and red-faced, *if* I even make it to my own wedding.

Gods.

My fingers have barely curled over the bottom rung when Faolan hauls me back.

"What are you— Faolan! Stop that, are you— *Stars o' fire*, you can't just throw me over your shoulder and—"

My voice grows progressively higher as I push at Faolan's arm and back, trying to right myself, but it's no use. The waves glint mockingly below my face as he tightens his arm across the backs of my thighs, shoulders trembling on another bout of laughter, and begins his climb.

ELEVEN

My fingers knot fiercely in the back of Faolan's shirt as he flings one leg over the railing, jostling me sharply. For just a moment, I see only stars and ink spread across the night as his hands find my hips, guiding my body free from its perch. Then the still air shatters on a burst of hoots and whistles as my entire face goes hot.

"On your feet—there's a good girl," Faolan murmurs once my bare toes meet the deck, but a smirk belies his gentleness. He's bloody proud of the spectacle he's created. I'd step back from his chest—or shove him away, possibly—if I could trust I wouldn't collapse after that climb. But when I open my mouth to tell him as much, a clear, low voice cuts through the din.

"Faolan, lad, what in the shade's realm do you think you're doing?"

Before I can move, Faolan twists me round, fitting my back snug against his chest so that I'm still reeling when the most beautiful woman I've ever laid eyes upon steps forward.

Ríona Kiara is as memorable as her cousin. I've seen her before, of course, but not since I was a girl and never as close as this. Her hair is cut short, nearly shaved bare along the sides, save for a dark red tousle of curls the wind clearly adores. Muscles flow in perfect tandem beneath the taut lines of her shirt. When she tilts her head, her green eyes bear a haughty mixture of curiosity and skepticism.

"*This* is your girl with ocean eyes?"

I want to fling myself back over the railing.

Eyes burrow their way into me from every direction as the tattoo pulses beneath my dress, fresh cuts scraping damp fabric until all I want to do is tear it off, toss myself to the ground, and scream *I am not this girl*.

Faolan releases me, and for a moment I consider following through, until a heavy weight settles over my shoulders in place of his hands. A weight smelling of salt and whiskey, stitched with fine threads into deep green fabric dyed a shade more earth than emerald. His coat.

I'm wearing the Wolf of the Wild's coat.

Stepping half in front of my body, Faolan winks at me and slips his hand around mine.

"She's the one, Kiara. I'd stake my life on it."

His conviction is staggering. Suffocating.

I grip the coat as the queen of Ashen Flame takes my full measure, brow cocked and eyes narrow. Faolan strokes my smallest finger with the edge of his own.

"Very well, then." Kiara kicks one foot over the other, dropping back against the railing with a sigh. "It's yours to lose."

"We both know I'm no good at that." Faolan grins, and I feel the lights dim when he lets go of my hand. Kiara cocks her head to the side, noting the gesture, then whistles once as I rub it against my wet skirts. A man wearing a brooch of her house's sigil steps from the shadows, a small wooden chest in hand.

"And you're sure you want to go through with this part as well?"

Kiara flicks the chest open with a light touch, withdrawing a strip of fabric from inside. "You already got the girl on your ship."

"A deal's a deal. You of all people know that."

"Then approach, little wolf." Kiara's lip curls like she's tasted something foul. "Daughter of Dermot."

It is the way she says my father's name that finally steadies my legs from the coltish wobble they'd borne since our climb.

Faolan's hand falls to my lower back, guiding me across the deck on bare feet until we're standing before Ríona Kiara. He trails his hand down my arm to hook at the wrist, catching my fingers firmly in his. I am powerless to do anything but stare at the unfamiliar calluses stamped across his palm, the tiny scars littering his knuckles.

I don't know these hands. I don't know *him*.

Stars, what am I doing?

Kiara steps closer, a full head taller than me, and reaches for the long, bedraggled ribbon still dangling from my hair. Much of the color has bled free from the silk, leaving it a pale shade of pink. Next, she takes the flexible cord woven with three strands of leather from Faolan's hair, so it falls thick with curls just past his shoulders.

It's only then, cords wrapped round her finger, that Kiara stops. Looks him in the eye.

"This is your last chance to change your mind, Faolan. It's a lot of trouble to cause over . . ."

A flush claws up my neck as Faolan snorts, rolling his shoulders back. "Get on with it, would you? We've a long voyage ahead."

Kiara levels a gaze at him, then reaches into her pocket, extracting a vibrant length of costly silk I recognize from her phoenix gown last night. As she weaves the three items into a single cord, my stomach ties into similar knots—ones I'm not sure will ever be undone.

Still, I tell myself this isn't permanent. It's only until we find the Isle of Lost Souls. This is *my* choice.

Isn't it?

"Give me your hand."

"What?"

Kiara extends her hand, and foolishly I lay mine upon it. A glint of metal is my only warning before she slices into the meaty flesh just below my thumb.

Gasping, I jerk instinctively back, but she catches my wrist and layers my hand over Faolan's until our wounds align. Blood carves rivulets across our skin to drip onto the deck, their paths broken only by the silk and leather bindings.

"I call upon the stars as witness, the wind and raging sea," Kiara says, her voice deepening by a measure from the teasing it held before. She guides the cords slowly through one another so that when we pull our hands apart, a knot will appear. "Guide these two souls together in a bond not easily undone."

Her words are unfamiliar to my ears, and I realize only now that I've never witnessed a handfasting. But I used to wonder over them as a child. The poetic language made it seem sacred—but if that's true, who safeguards it now the gods are dead?

"As their blood flows as one, so their bodies soon will follow. May their path be struck always together, neither forcing the other nor leaving them behind. May good fortune follow their journeys, and their enemies cease all pursuit. May they hold fast to their vows as they exchange them above the tides, below the moon."

Silence follows and I look at Faolan, whose jaw is tight, though his smile remains fixed for the audience lingering in the shadows.

But it falters when he glances at our bound hands and the flecks of blood now blooming like flowers upon the silk.

Magic swells where our lifeblood mingles. Fades beneath the tattoo's blanket of ice.

Guilt floods me straight after. "Faolan, I—"

"Listen close, Saoirse, daughter of Rí Dermot and Leannon. You'll only be hearing this once."

Faolan catches my eyes with a look heavy enough to drown.

"I pledge myself to you for as long as we both desire. Should a dagger strike toward your heart, let it be my body that meets it first. Should another cast slander or cruelty your way, let it be my words that are a balm to your spirit, my fists that enact your revenge."

He steps closer, gaze dropping to my lips, and it's only then I realize they've parted. Like they remember that brief, stunning press of his own.

"Should your body cry out of loneliness, let it be mine that offers relief sweet as honeycomb."

A whistle does break out then, low murmurs chasing across the deck. But my gaze is fixed on his. They are just words—beautiful, aching words that pour from his lips with the ease of water from the sky. Soft and meaningless.

Sweet as honeycomb.

My throat runs dry.

"All this I vow to you, Saoirse. I ask only that you honor my freedom to explore the seas now, and for the rest of our days."

The emotions swelling inside me rupture at once, leaving me reeling. How could he offer all these promises and demand the opposite? Isn't bondage to me in marriage a loss of his freedom? Won't it be the loss of mine?

Or is it all a show, put on for the sake of his cousin and crew?

Faolan's fingers tighten on mine, and I swallow. The words

don't flow easily when they come—a fumbled version of my mother's chiding over the years on what a wife should be. "I vow to you Faolan, son of . . ."

His eyes flicker as a string of longing curls from his hands to mine. "Barden and Iona."

"Barden and Iona." I lean closer until pain jolts across the tattoo, severing our connection. The rest of my words tumble out on a series of gasps. "My honor and—respect as I follow the path you lay. I p-promise to guard your name from slander and your body from sickness, warm only your bed, keep your faith, a-and honor your freedom. All of this I vow, for as long as we both should choose."

There is no talk or laughter now as Kiara and Faolan cast me strange looks, Kiara's faintly disgusted. Finally, the queen shakes her head and tucks the ends of our bindings into the loops so they form a seemingly endless chain of cloth between us.

I'm tempted to lean back and test if it will hold.

"Let it be known, let it be struck. Should you choose to separate at the end of this time, I myself will sever the bond between you and cast the ends into the sea. Should you remain, keep this as a reminder of the vows you swore today." She smirks and takes a step back. "Or consider casting new ones."

A scattering of shouts and claps echoes around us, the crew finally let off their leash. I glance across the deck but can't make out their faces where they hover outside the cast of lantern light.

"Give us a kiss, Faolan, go on!"

"Aye, lad—'tis bad luck your whole life if you refuse to seal your vows with a kiss."

Their words blend into a hum just behind my ears, vibrating in the roots of my teeth, and panic blooms fast in my chest as I recognize the pull of magic in my gut. The pain of suppression from my back. I start to step away from Faolan, but before I can get far, he catches me round the waist with his free arm.

"As a pirate, you'll learn that superstitions are best dealt with swiftly." He's grinning, the swagger firmly back in place. When he sees my face, though, something slips. My lips press into a hard line against the shifting inside me, fingers wrapped tight in his shirt. Faolan glances once more over his shoulder, then turns me slightly away until I'm hidden by his shoulders, and kisses my cheek—just at the corner of my lips—to a fresh chorus of cheers.

I'm still reeling when Kiara speaks again, voice just low enough for the two of us. "We'll speak down below. But get your wife something dry to wear first, aye?"

With that, she disappears into the shadows across the deck, leaving me barefoot and bound to a husband I barely know.

TWELVE

Faolan leads me into a jewelry box of a room. Colorful clothes lay strewn across the floor while a quilt patterned with the night sky drapes over the end of a bed shoved against the ship wall. Trinkets line every surface—glittering creations from the island of artists, striped hides and brilliantly colored feathers of beasts I've never seen. A single window catches the lamplight, throwing shadows across the central desk with its many instruments and the strange experiments they've wrought. More bizarre still are the two full tapestries nailed to the flat wooden wall separating Faolan's room from the hallway beyond.

My saturated bag slips from my shoulder with a heavy thunk.

I'd thought myself clever, dressing as a magpie the first night of the Damhsa. Clearly, I've just married one.

Faolan falls back against the doorframe, and the movement nearly jerks my arm free from my shoulder. I stumble against the wall and grimace, working a finger beneath the braided cords that bind us to rub at the raw skin below.

"Forgot about those. Hold still, would you?" Faolan's smile is sheepish as he pulls a dagger free from his boot, but a warning rings in the back of my mind just as he lowers the blade.

"Wait!" I catch his wrist and push it far from the cords before turning my attention to the knots. It takes long, quiet seconds, the steady weight of his gaze unnerving me, but finally the long cords loosen enough for us to remove our hands.

"Sentimental, are you?" He flexes his fingers, his eyes never leaving mine.

"We need the proof. Kiara can keep this to show our handfasting was real—that you haven't kidnapped me." It's an easy thing to coax the long cords back into a triple knot, until it's small. "*This* is how we prevent a war."

"Oh. Right."

An awkward sort of quiet stretches between us, interrupted only by the plips of water falling from my skirts. I turn the knot over in my fingers a few times, glance at my bag and then at him, because I don't know *how* to ask a man to leave his own bloody room so that I can change in privacy. My only consolation is that now we're out of view of anyone else, he seems just as much at odds with what to do with *me*.

Mercifully, a knock comes on the door behind us and Faolan whips around with more than a little relief on his face. "Go on, then. Kiara and I will be in the quarters to the left. Ah—I'll take that." He plucks the knot from my fingers with the same caution one would use when carrying a snake, and then pulls the door shut behind him.

I drop to my knees without delay, fumbling with the buckle that's kept my possessions from spilling out of the bag so far. A groan rolls up the back of my throat when I see that every single garment inside is soaked through. Voices register beneath the door, footsteps sounding back and forth in the cabin beside, and there's no time to second-guess. I rifle through the trunk nearest Faolan's bed.

Two pairs of eyes greet me when I walk through the door, barefoot and wearing borrowed trousers along with a soft brown knit jumper on top. Kiara walks past me to shut the door, and I scurry to Faolan's side.

At least he's given a vow not to harm me. Kiara's expression promises bloodshed.

"You're the one he's been searching for. The girl with ocean eyes, who will find the island, restore the purest waters, all while using some mystic, special gift. *You?*"

Her voice drips venom straight into my most vulnerable parts. She's only asking the same questions I had of Faolan—the ones that kept sleep at bay through the night. My mouth gapes like a fish, wide and useless, and I don't realize how small I've made myself until Faolan's hand flattens beneath my shoulder blades, pushing my back straight.

"Aye, she does. I've seen it myself and—"

Kiara's laugh is as sharp as glass. "Don't give me a handful of dung and call it gold, you gobshite. If I had a coin for every time you've 'seen' something yourself, we wouldn't be in this situation."

To my surprise, Faolan's smile remains easy. "I've sailed the Crescent for over ten years under your reign. Have I ever once failed you?"

Kiara goes quiet, but it's no mark of submission or compliance. Instead her frown dulls into something much cooler. More calculating. My muscles tense as I push against Faolan's hand until it slips to the small of my back, then the crook of my waist. I've seen that look on my father's face enough to know it's worse than the fury.

"Can you prove it?"

"What?" The word is somehow mine, strangled though it is.

"You have magic that my cousin *supposedly* witnessed—and

I'll admit, I've never seen eyes like yours. So go on." She waves a hand. "Convince me."

I have no control over the curse's magic. It's always worse when I touch someone's skin, but now I have the tattoo, there's no telling how it might react or whether I'll feel anything beyond flashes. It hadn't seemed like such an issue this morning, with Faolan spinning silver thread from his tongue, but Kiara does not seem to be a queen who suffers fools—and I am most definitely one of those.

"It doesn't work like tha'," Faolan says before I can make another feeble attempt at speech.

"How does it work, then?"

"It— Her eyes shift round and . . ." I glance at Faolan and for the first time see pink in his cheeks above the scruff, a boyish look about his face as he shuffles from one foot to the other. I can practically see his mind racing through options as his fingers tighten unwittingly on my elbow, where they've settled once more. "Look, why are you always trying to explain the unexplainable, eh? Embrace the wonder of the unknown for once."

Kiara levels him with a look. "Deal's off."

"No!" Faolan releases me to step forward. Any hint of his charm and humor are gone. "You said I'd get a year from when I first brought up the island, and I still have six weeks left. The deal's done."

"That was before I knew you'd be taking on a pathetic runaway princess as your bargaining chip—magical abilities." She sneers. "Come off it."

"I've given you *everything* you ever asked for, Kiara." Faolan stops a hairsbreadth from her, voice dropping to a snarl. Kiara does not flinch. "Since I was sixteen years old, I have chased down every creature, every problem, every *myth* you've tasked me. How is this one different?"

"Because it was only ever your life we put at risk. Not our people's." Kiara glares past his shoulder to me. "It was a fair trade for what I spared when I gave you that ship in the first place. You still owe me—"

"I've paid you back for my life tenfold—I have! And you promised me last summer that the Isle of Lost Souls was the last job. *Ten years*, Kiara. I'll owe nothing more after I find it for you. Are you telling me I can't count your word to be reliable, *my queen?*"

Faolan lands his mark. The cabin air goes still as a midwinter night until I swear I can hear the soft metal song of a blade drawn, the edge of it slicing down my spine.

I double over, gasping, when a hand seizes mine.

There is a flash of red hair.

Blood?

Something inside me vibrates, pushing against the tattoo and amulet both. A howl rends the air—then a pop like a lyre string split in half.

An arrow . . . in her hand?

The vision leaves me as quickly as it came, broken into a dozen fractured pieces that refuse to form a single image again. Fear sparks nausea, and I wind my arms tight across my ribs as my head throbs with suppressed magic. It is unpredictable—terrifying.

Faolan releases my hand only to brush the sweaty, dark strands of hair from my eyes.

"Let her see," Faolan says, his voice muffled as though spoken through water. But obedience is the one thing that comes easy to me, after a lifetime in my father's home.

I lift my chin. Immediately, Kiara startles back a step, her frown etched into deep lines. I can see her trying to sort out the change, reckon if it's in her mind or not, but my tongue is thick and my throat dry.

I've no explanations left.

"Faolan . . ." She turns on the young captain. "If this turns out to be one of your tricks—a ruse or a game—if you've wasted an entire year of my time on this or try to run on your bargain, don't forget there is nowhere you can sail that I won't find you. And I swear I'll make you suffer for it."

Her eyes cut back to me, the same glassy green of soft spring leaves when the sun flickers through. I nearly swallow my tongue, knowing there's a wasp hidden beneath each one. "Same goes for the lass. Now you're married, whatever consequences you face will be hers as well." Her lips flicker into a grimace. "Remember, she'll happily follow the path you lay for her."

I cringe at the nasty twist she's placed upon my vows, hearing them properly for the first time.

Hearing *everything* properly.

"Consequences?" My voice is too soft to be heard as Faolan murmurs something that yields a reluctant smile from Kiara. I steel myself as blood pools beneath my cheeks. "What do you mean—"

Faolan squeezes Kiara's shoulder and then marches to the door, flinging it wide. "Well, we'd best be off now if we want the stories to do this justice. And you've got to let the groom know his bride's run off—won't that be fun?"

Kiara weighs the knotted cords in her hand. "It almost makes all this rubbish worth it."

"I'll send my reports." Faolan taps the doorway once, and she rolls her eyes, slipping a knife from her belt. With one easy flick of her wrist, she slices a lock of hair free from the back of her head and presses it into Faolan's hand.

"I'll inform *Tavin* to send them, given he's the only bloody person who actually can. See that he gets this, would you? Eejit."

The word is affectionate, as is the tousle to Faolan's hair as she walks out.

There is a trick here I am too exhausted to understand—one Faolan clearly does, seeing how he nudges his cousin along like a sheepdog nipping at a ewe's feet. There's a final flash of green eyes, and then Faolan stands alone in the doorway with his fingers drumming against the frame like rainfall. His jaw divots as he clenches it, grinding slowly from one side to the other.

I can see it now, the way his mind spins stories. He's writing one this very moment—something fantastical and quick. A net to catch me and wrap me up tight before I even know I'm falling. It's only now I realize how badly I'd wanted to be caught before.

Freedom. That had been his promise, hadn't it?

Faolan's breath hitches, but I speak before he has the chance. "What consequences is Ríona Kiara talking about?"

He avoids my eyes for the first time since we met. "She's dramatic, that's all."

"No . . . No, you said she'd given you permission to find the island but you never told me—you never said this was just for her benefit." My voice tightens. "You never said this was to pay your debt to her."

"*Our* debt, darling."

My head snaps up and I take a step back, my thighs meeting the edge of his desk. "What?"

Faolan turns abruptly, and his smile is anything but charming—full of irony and a taste of bitterness. "It's our debt now, lass. You ensured tha' when you blackmailed me into marrying you."

My fingers curl hard over the edge of the desk, keeping me upright. "You owe your cousin for your life?"

"Aye." Faolan tugs the collar of his shirt free. "When I was fourteen, I ran away from court to join Keegan's crew from Unbound

Earth—only turns out he was a shite captain and a raging drunk. We were caught on a smuggling job two years later and dragged before the Ring of Stars to be trialed. Hanged."

He glances my way, linen gathering at his wrists as he shrugs off the shirt.

"Except for me. As luck would have it, Kiara had just inherited her crown and I'd learned a fair bit on the sea. She pardoned me at the execution, then gave me a ship a few weeks later—and plenty of orders besides."

There's more to the story. I know there is, but it hardly matters now.

"Faolan, you never said yesterday that we were searching for the island under Kiara's command. Or that I would owe her—" What? My *life*? I shake my head. "We don't know anything about my magic, or the Isle of Lost Souls for that matter. All you have is a bloody song. We can't just—"

"We can, and we will, because—well, we don't have much of a choice, now, do we?" Faolan pushes off the doorframe and walks toward me, lips hitching at the corners. "Besides, can you honestly say you'd have come with me if you knew?"

"I . . ." My head is heavy and spinning at once. Have I really done this? Run away from my parents, married a pirate—promised to use the magic that once killed my brother?!

Faolan's hand lands on my arm and I stare at it, because I can't help wondering now if it's meant as a comfort, or a manipulation. "You took a risk for a free life, Saoirse. I've done the same. I won't apologize for it."

"Even if you've damned me alongside yourself?" I hate the weakness in my voice. He slides his hand beneath my arm, nudging me through the door into his bedroom.

"You're the one who vowed to follow my path. It's sort of your own fault, aye?"

"That's different."

"Is it? I'd love to hear you elaborate on how."

I dig my heels into the ruby-colored rug laid beneath his bed as we pass it by, unable to look away from the rumpled pile of quilts and sheets. There isn't another place to sleep in this room. "There is one vow I have no intention of keeping, Faolan. Have you forgotten?"

His hand drops from my arm, wrapping lightly around a bedpost. "No. I'm only surprised you actually meant it."

"I meant it." I study his fingers, elegant and long. The patch of skin exposed at the collar of his shirt. Remember the feel of his lips against mine, brief though that touch was.

Remember the Wolf has a woman waiting at every port.

"I heard the stories at the Damhsa."

"Then you know I've yet to leave a lover without hearing them scream my name first." He cocks his head, canines flashing as he smiles. "That doesn't intrigue you, even the slightest bit?"

"I—" My face burns. "I know that having your child would only complicate things."

"Oh, love," Faolan says, leaning closer—careful not to touch me now. "There are plenty of ways to make your body sing that *don't* involve getting you with child."

The room is too small, his body too near.

I smell of Faolan and the sea—not myself at all.

It's too much.

"No." I barely manage that single word, but force another behind it. "Please."

Faolan jerks back. "Stars, lass, I only meant—there's no need to . . ." Whatever he sees on my face, it erases the self-assured smile from his own. "Marriage in name only. You have my word."

My shoulders drop, but I remain wary until he reaches the door and turns, tilting his head to consider me. "At least, until you're curious enough to ask for more."

I latch the door behind him, then crumple into the center of that lonely bed, burying myself in unfamiliar scents and fabric until the world ceases to exist.

THIRTEEN

I awaken to the wind lapping a sweet trail across my wrist. It pours in through the open window, dappling the warped glass with sea spray as the ship crests one wave and glides neatly into the next.

My first sign this is only a dream.

I turn my face into the pillows and groan when they smell of whiskey rather than lye. A hint of it clung to Faolan the first time I met him, lingering long after I'd raced from the beach back to Father's ship. But the window of my room could not open.

And Faolan's wolf ring still glints just below my knuckle.

I raise my head and a breeze trickles beneath my collar, running along the fresh, tender scars. Tremors erupt across my body, gathered in furious pools at my temples and the hollows behind my knees. As I shift onto them, the bed creaks, ropes tied below the mattress putting up a fight until I go still. Wide-eyed and ghostly pale.

Or at least, my reflection looks it in the polished bronze surface nailed to the opposite wall. I trace the blueish-purple smudges along my throat where Maccus's torc dug in. Glimpse four similar lines on my arm when Faolan's sleeve drifts past my elbow. The fringe Da always insisted I cut to shield my eyes is plastered to one side, the rest of my hair falling in dark, heavy tangles to the generous curve of my waist.

None of that matters, though. Not as much as the tattoo burning between my shoulder blades.

I bite down on my lip and ease the laces farther apart. Faolan is larger than me—it takes only a few tugs until his shirt is loose enough to dip past my shoulders, exposing the top of my back, where two-thirds of the tattoo is complete.

Below the stark white marks, my skin is angry, painted bright pink as though I lay in scalding water for too long. Unlike the woad tattoos common among our people, these markings are unnatural, almost glowing in their brightness. My stomach rolls as I reach to trace the curve of one spiral.

"Good morning, wife!"

I nearly tumble out of the bed. The door muffles Faolan's voice, but barely, as he nudges it open with a boot. I scramble to pull the shirt back into place. "You looked so peaceful this morning, I hated to disturb you. But then I thought, even a mystical lass with ocean eyes must want to eat at some point."

He grins from the half-open doorway, and I try not to look like my heart's just leapt clear across the room. "You weren't here this morning."

Faolan cocks a brow. "Wasn't I?"

My gaze drifts to the bed. The divot in a pillow beside mine, and the nest of blankets where someone must have kicked them off through the night. "I—I didn't notice you come back last night."

"Well, you were dead to the world, weren't you?" Faolan smirks. "If you hadn't started snoring, I'd have checked your pulse."

Heat splashes across my collarbone, surging up my neck. "I don't snore."

"Aye, you do. But it's a precious wee sound, like thunder off the horizon." He chuckles as I glare, touching my nose, like that will give me any more truth. "Music to a pirate's ears."

"You could have slept somewhere else." It's my last defense—one he laughs off instantly as the door swings shut behind him.

"And risk my crew thinking I've lost my touch?" Faolan lays a wooden tray on the bed beside me, and I pull back as though it contains venomous serpents. But it's only . . .

"What is that?"

"Breakfast." He nods to it, hands on his hips, a wicked gleam in his eye. "Some of the finest you'll have, I'm afraid. We eat our best when we've been docked on land for a time, but the farther we get on the sea, the more shite the food. Shall I give you a tour of your meal, Princess?"

"No." My nose wrinkles at the moniker as I study the clay pot of strawberries and the slab of nutty brown oat bread drizzled in honey, with a round of sausage just beside it. It's the flower that captures most of my attention, though. A bright yellow marsh marigold, dropped in dead center so no one could miss it.

This tray is not a kindness. Or if it is, it doubles as a prop.

"How much does your crew know?" I glance up in time to see his brilliant smile falter.

He drops onto the bed before it can truly shrink. "They know where we're headed. That you've some ability to guide us there, and that you and I are wed." Faolan nudges the tray closer to me. "Eat."

I pick a berry, the familiar sweetness turning tart on my tongue. "But they don't know it's only temporary."

Faolan snorts. "You're the one who set that particular trap, love. Everyone saw the magpie kiss the wolf that night, and you said it yourself that Dermot and Maccus needed to think you'd run away on your own." He studies me. "My crew is one of the best—loyal to the end—but I've never exactly been one to curb gossip. If I'm honest, I've even encouraged it, time to time, so it's for the best they think this is real."

I force a bite of the bread next. "And if we can't convince them?"

"Oh, *I* can convince them just fine. It's you we have to worry about. D'you realize you hide nothing on that lovely face of yours?"

The bread hits the tray with a clatter. "I grew up in court. I know how to behave."

"It's not behaving yourself that's the problem, Saoirse. You should be wild. Mad with love." Faolan picks up the bread and offers it to my lips. I shove his hand away as he laughs. "Acting like the luckiest girl in the world, to have tamed the Wolf of the Wild at last!"

Impossibly, laughter lurches in my chest as well. I'm so unused to it, I press my hand there until the sensation eases, but still a smile tugs at my cheeks. "You're . . . ridiculous."

"Aye, from time to time. D'you mind?" Faolan drops the bread and eases back onto his elbow, head far too near my thigh for comfort. His hair is dampened at the ends, curling over his firm jaw and trailing down his throat. It becomes a touch harder to swallow.

"No. It's just surprising."

"Speaking of surprises." Faolan slides a hand into his pocket, and I take another strawberry between my teeth. "Silver or gold?"

I frown at the sight of his fist. "What?"

Faolan nudges it against my knee, his smile somewhere between lazy and mischievous. "I've a piece of jewelry in my hand, and I want you to tell me what it is. Silver or gold?"

"You can't be serious."

"As the plague. Now, stop stalling and give it a go."

I can only stare at his fingers and the pale line marking one where his wolf ring had been. The one currently nestled around my fourth finger. "Why?"

"We've got to start somewhere, coaxing the magic out. I figure this is as good a way as any."

The night before seeps back, and any hint of a smile drains from my face. He's not teasing this time. Faolan doesn't know about the tattoo, or the magic beyond what I've told him, but clearly he thinks there's a way to draw it out. That I *must* draw it out. And my freedom—my entire life—hinges on the ability to awaken it. Starting with a guess as to whether Faolan is holding a piece of silver or gold in his hand.

My voice catches when I speak. "Silver."

His smile drops, lips contorting as he turns his fist over and reveals the gold earring in his palm. My chest sinks. "I'm sorr—"

"Oi, is everyone decent?"

It's my only warning before the door flies open, and the tall, broad woman from the market steps in. Her hair is a vibrant shade of red in the morning sun, matched only by the spray of freckles across her nose and down her collarbone. When she smiles, the expression lights her whole face. "Well, isn't this a lovely sight?"

I am on fire. The blankets are trapped below Faolan's body, and I'm wearing nothing but his shirt. Words fold over themselves across my tongue as I tug the hem lower, only just now realizing Faolan's lain beside me for several minutes, and I hadn't even noticed.

A lie. I'd noticed.

I just hadn't cared to do anything about it.

Faolan clears his throat and eases to the side enough for me to tug a blanket fully over my figure. "Nessa, your timing is impeccable as always."

"Happy to serve, Captain." Nessa leans against the wall, looking me over with shameless curiosity. "The crew and I were just wondering if you plan to introduce our newest member, or if you'll be keeping her all to yourself. Considering we've been searching for her most of the year and all."

"And you couldn't wait another hour?" Faolan groans, but the sound holds no real disdain. "Right. Give us five minutes, would you?"

"You can only last that long? Captain, I'm shocked."

"Away with you, demon!" Faolan laughs as he tosses a pillow at the closing door, and I clutch the blankets with a white-knuckled grip, jaw slack and eyes wide.

"You let your crew talk to you like that?"

"Why in shade's realm wouldn't I?" Faolan rolls onto his back, running a hand across his face. "People shouldn't curb themselves of harmless impulses. Besides, if I tried to control all their tongues, we'd never get anything done."

I think of my father's silent guards, the oil-slick speeches at court and whispers in the dark. I also remember Faolan at the Damhsa that first night, and the way half his audience had stars in their eyes for whatever tale he'd spun.

"I see."

"Grand so." Faolan pushes off the bed, energy ebbing and flowing from him faster than the wind shifting over the sea. "Never mind the silver and gold trick. We'll have another go later. And again after that—as many times as it takes to spark something. And if that doesn't work, I've a whole chest down below full of bones, cards, and druid fodder."

Faolan turns to me, hooking the gold earring through his left ear, where it snatches the morning sun. I close my mouth with a snap, panic trickling into my chest.

"And if none of it works?"

"Something will. Don't forget, I've seen those eyes of yours churning." He pauses. Tilts his head. "Why did you run that night, after you kissed me? I meant to ask you before."

"It was nothing." The words come too fast. I fill my mouth with bread before any more can slip out.

Faolan frowns but reaches for a pair of knives on his desk, belting them around his waist with practiced ease. "Nothing had you at a full sprint away from me at the Damhsa, did it?"

I almost choke as I swallow. "You surprised me."

"Aye, well . . . at least we know something works." Faolan winks, plucks the flower free of the tray, and tucks it into my hair. I go perfectly still.

"Now, get dressed. It's time you met the crew before they all find some pitiful excuse to barge in."

FOURTEEN

I'm still attempting to secure the two braids I wove behind my head with a ribbon when Faolan drags me onto the deck, whistling a bird's trill that draws every eye right to us. My fingers slip, and dark hair falls into my eyes again until he circles behind me, gathering the pieces to tie them himself.

"Oi! Tavin, Nessa, Brona—come meet my wife, would you?"

My breath catches as three figures peel away from ropes and wooden things I've no name for, having been on a ship exactly once in my life before. And Da barely let me out of my cabin before we reached the Damhsa.

The first of the crew to approach is a tall man with wiry limbs, tawny skin, and a strong profile. His hair is the color of onyx, long and straight aside from a knot formed just at the top to keep it from tangling in his short beard. His dark eyes slant up in a fashion common along the eastern waters of the Isle of Frozen Hearth, and they warm considerably with his smile.

Faolan claps a hand on his shoulder. "This is Tavin, the finest quartermaster and seanchaí you'll ever meet in your life. You get into a squabble with anyone on deck, he's the one you want to settle things."

"You think this mouse would get herself into a fight, Captain?" The pale, freckled woman from before stops beside Tavin with a smirk. "Nessa. First mate and master of weaponry."

"Nice to meet you."

Faolan lets his arm fall behind me. "You'd be surprised, Ness. She's got some teeth, my Saoirse."

I jerk away from the hand he settles at my back. I've never been anyone's before, not truly.

Do I . . . belong to him now?

No—not with all his talk of collars and freedom. It's just a game. He said as much in the cabin below, didn't he?

A new figure steps into the circle, smaller than the others and delicate in a way I always longed to be. Her hair is so dark, it's a match for the shadows cast below the sails, woven into three thick braids that swirl together in a knot at the base of her skull. She's of an age with me, and wearing the first dress I've seen since boarding the ship, though it's a nut-brown, practical thing without the courtly embellishments of my own home.

"Brona," Faolan says, and something about the gentleness of his tone draws my gaze up to her face and the pair of beautiful deep brown eyes staring back at me. "Our navigator. She hails from the Dromlach Cliffs, along the eastern coast of the Isle of Reborn Stalk."

My eyes widen. She comes from my homeland—the most brutal, derelict part of it. The cliffs' magic is as deadly and unpredictable as the people who inhabit it, boasting blades of untraceable ice and snowcaps that can burn someone with cold from the inside out if slipped into their drink.

Brona holds some of that same ice in her veins and the rigid line of her spine as she turns on Faolan. "Not much of a navigator when the only thing you can tell me is 'get us the hell away from her parents.'"

"Well, you've done a bloody fantastic job with it so far." Faolan's smile is unflinching as he folds his hands behind his head and arches his back. "And then there's the bosun, Lorcan. You saw him by the market stall, aye?"

The man is larger than anyone else on deck, his skin a rich shade of umber, arms and back thickly roped with muscle. I know how bright his smile will be before it appears, teeth gleaming like pearls as he comes over with a small loaf of bread in hand.

"Aye. But I don't know what that word means. Bosun?"

The navigator—Brona—gapes at me, but a laugh deeper than any of the others I've heard pours from the bosun's mouth as he comes to a stop just behind her.

"Maintenance, mostly. It's my job to keep this old pile of wood floating like she ought to, fix any damage we pick up along the way." His voice is as rich as his laugh, pouring from his mouth in a melodic lilt that matches that of those born on the Isle of Painted Claw—a small land full of artists, singers, poets, storytellers. I'm studying his arms for any of the beautiful tattoos the island is famous for when he takes my hand and presses his lips to the back. "My name is Lorcan. It's a pleasure to meet you, Wolf Tamer."

I pull away, searching his face and then Faolan's, noting the way his lips twitch. "How many monikers have you given me, Faolan?" I ask, fingers curling into my palm until Lorcan's forced to let go. "Ocean Eyes, Wolf Tamer—"

"Daughter of Dermot." Brona's voice holds such a bite, I wince and look at the toes of my boots. "Does that name suit you better?"

It takes effort to draw my gaze back up. "Saoirse. I'm just Saoirse."

"Very well." Lorcan tosses me the bread and wraps a broad arm around Brona's shoulders, dragging her alongside him. I'm half-surprised when she tolerates it. "There's our striker, Oona. She's in charge of keeping us fed, hunting down fish and whatever else happens to be lurking about." Lorcan points across the ship to where a girl with short, strong legs and hair as light as sunbeams winds a bandage around her calf. "Fixing the mess I made of her leg. I'll be the first to admit that I'm a clever talent when it comes to shaping wood—"

"But absolute shite with a needle," Nessa says where she lounges against the railing, watching me along with the rest. "A piece of advice? Avoid anything that'll poke you full of holes or take a limb. Lorcan can fix a ship all right, but I'd not trust him near your flesh."

"You don't have a surgeon?" I ask as Lorcan's laughter drops into a cough and Nessa's lips twitch higher.

"Not since the squid. But you should ask your husband about that one."

Faolan cocks his head at the word but doesn't flinch as I do. It's the smallest jerk of my hand, weight shifting from one foot to the other—easy to miss unless someone is watching.

And Brona *is* watching, her eyes hard as flint.

"I'd like to hear a different story," she says, stepping free of Lorcan's arm. "The one where you tell us what possessed you to steal the Stone King's bride, or why we've been sailing all over the feckin' Crescent for months, and—"

"And making plenty of coin along the way, hitting every port on time, and pleasing our lovely queen who sanctioned our marriage just last night. Did she not?" Faolan's smile is tight, but there's no trick to it. No threat in the way he touches Brona's shoulder, as light as a bird's perch before taking off again. "Saoirse is my wife now, that's all there is to it. And Kiara's handling Maccus."

"But what about Dermot?" Brona asks, and I ease forward onto my toes. There's something in the way she says my father's name. As though it's familiar, and foul.

"Too much of a coward to put up a fight." Faolan cuts his eyes to Lorcan, who takes a half step closer to Brona's side. Her stance eases the moment their arms brush. "Besides, he'll be too busy saving face until the Damhsa is through to give us a chase—imagine your only daughter taking off with a pirate. The cheek."

Some of the others laugh, but dread knots every muscle I possess. I hadn't really imagined it—not until this moment. There wasn't time. Mam will probably tear into her own flesh again with worry, Da's rage honing into a fine, cold blade in the dark. I do not know yet what Maccus is capable of, but I felt his eyes on my back like needles slipping beneath my skin as I walked from the pavilion yesterday morning.

Faolan claps his hands as I grip the ship's railing. "Right. Now we've found the girl with ocean eyes, our first stop is the Teeth. We'll decide the next heading after that. Lorcan, Tavin?" He waves to the quartermaster. "A word."

Faolan leaves my side, and all my breath escapes in one smooth rush.

"Damn his smooth tongue." Brona skirts past me to a barrel with a hide laid over the top, weighed down by a lantern and other objects. "The Teeth, Ness? Honestly?"

Nessa nudges my elbow once in passing, a faded version of the easy smile back on her face. "You'll know the reason, won't you, Wolf Tamer? All that business about your eyes." She tries half-heartedly to inspect them, but I duck my head so the short, dark pieces of my hair obscure them from view. Nessa clears her throat. "Perhaps you have a special skill with the sails, or currents? An ability to map patterns by the stars?"

"I'm the only one who reads the stars here," Brona snaps, tracing patterns across the hide with a fingertip. She's painted it into a chart full of dots large and small, some in patterns and some scattered seemingly at random.

I can't make sense of them.

All I can see is my father's back after he pushed that betrothal torc into my hands.

"Not the stars. I—"

My tongue falters, then lies prone behind my teeth. What could I possibly say? I'm cursed? Marked by a soulstone? Believe in the gods, and the Isle of Lost Souls, because my only other choice is to hate them and accept I will be nothing in this life?

Brona flips the chart over with a scoff. "Look at her, Nessa. She's useless."

"Ease up a bit, would you?" Nessa rubs at the back of her neck, smile all but gone. "I'm sure there's a good reason she's here. Besides, Faolan only collects useless things if they're works of . . . Anyway." She turns to me. "You'll have knowledge. Secrets about the politics and trade—or something to do with your da's island?"

My throat's too tight to speak, so I shake my head.

Brona scoffs. "Doubt she even knows where those pretty clothes came from. Certainly not her father's dirty hands. In fact, I doubt she knows how to do anything useful. Scrub, weave nets, take bloody orders—feckin' hell, I'm talking to Faolan. There's got to be a mistake."

"Brona!" Nessa reaches for her, but she's already off in a storm.

We stand in the quiet, the small loaf of bread heavy in my hand. I haven't earned it, but when I try to set it near the hide, Nessa waves me off. "Nah, we're not going to starve you even if you're usele—" She coughs. "We'll find something for you, lass."

"Perhaps something to do with sewing?" Lorcan appears at her side once more, a far softer expression on his face than any of the others I've seen so far. "Faolan says you made your own costume that first night. Magpie, wasn't it?"

"Aye." I smooth the damp fabric of my current gown, a faint

streak of salt limning the wrinkled edges. "I've a fair hand with a needle. If you showed me what stitch to use, I could mend the sails?"

Nessa's smile goes sheepish. "As much as I'd love to hand that task off, sails are a bit of a stretch for a new recruit to take on, seeing as they're just about the only thing standing between our survival and sinking if the structure goes wrong."

"Oh."

"But you could mend our clothes for a start? Earn a bit of trust."

I note the tightness around her eyes. The way Lorcan chews on one cheek. Both are trying to be friendly, neither quite succeeding, yet I can't blame them for their wariness. Who am I but a mythical stranger—some odd creature with even odder eyes their captain went to a world of trouble to capture on board? And that's to say nothing of Rí Dermot's and Maccus's wrath.

Brona's suspicion is not unwarranted. They should all be terrified of me.

I smile in the same stiff way reflected on both their faces, and fold my hands into a tidy knot behind me.

"I'd be happy to."

FIFTEEN

The light of the dying sun streams through my linen skirts and wool dresses, casting shades of mustard, sage, and heather onto the walls of Faolan's room. They drape over the backs of chairs and hang from a slender rope I tied to the door handle, the other side attached to a wooden bedpost. A pale line of shifts marks the hooks on one wall, fluttering with each brush of air from the open window.

If I closed my eyes, I could be in my cottage once more. Banished by the sea.

Harmless.

Footsteps shatter my delusion, and I turn just in time to see Faolan burst through the door with a chest in hand, sending all four of my gowns to the floor. Beside them lie three separate baskets of rumpled clothing covered in tears, threadbare patches, or stains. His brows shoot up, highlighting a little white scar at the corner of one, but he doesn't apologize. "Making yourself at home, are you?"

I don't bother to respond. Instead, I gather the gowns up one by one in my arms, my mind racing over the snippets of information I learned from Nessa and Lorcan as they guided me along the ship to collect everyone's torn clothing. There are a dozen names for every wheel, beam, and mast, and hundreds more words to explain what to do with them. Ropes for pulling, hoisting, tying down, catching an eastern breeze or pushing the westward wind away. Nets require a complicated weave, fish their own particular stroke of the blade to separate bone from workable flesh.

And I am inept at all but the mending.

Every task they tried to set me, I failed in some way. My nervous fingers slipped on the knife, in spite of years working with blades at the cottage to cook my own supper. I didn't dare touch the ropes for fear of collapsing a sail when it needed to rise, or venture near Brona and her maps again. Only the surgeon's cupboard held any promise when we stopped to collect needle and thread— a jumbled disaster of old bandages and glass jars turned so dark, it took hours to determine every herb or mixture they contained.

But it wasn't wasted time. I asked questions of Nessa as she helped me work—questions about Faolan and Kiara, the crew's adventures around the Crescent, and whether they'd ever journeyed through the Teeth. Lorcan was the one to answer that, stopping by with lunch in hand. He told me they are a jagged patch of uninhabitable land that spends half the year submerged in the sea and the other half rotting more with every low tide. Settled just off the coast of his homeland, the Isle of Painted Claw, they're a devil of a time to get through, with very little reward.

As it turns out, neither of them could answer what's possessed Faolan to go.

I run a finger over the delicate row of forget-me-nots embroidered along the bodice of my sage-green dress, then shake it free of wrinkles and add it to the others.

Useless *and* fanciful.

Faolan clears his throat. "Nessa tells me you're going to take on the crew's mending. And that you spent half the day sorting through the surgeon's stores?"

"Aye." I reach for a shift next, but Faolan gets to it first, knitting his fingers in the near-translucent fabric. My heart jumps as I fail to take it back.

"It's a pitiful job to seek out. Bags of herbs with no sense to them, cramped wee doorway—and the lantern kept in there needs replacing. It stinks."

I fight the urge to smell my hair as he looks my way. "It's work that needs to be done. You don't have a surgeon, and I know my way around herbs, so I thought—"

"You already have a task, love." Faolan taps one of the stars embroidered along the shift's edges, then tosses it to me. My hands go cold as I glance at the chest, the skin between my shoulder blades taut where the tattoo cuts in.

"I can't just bring it on. I-I don't know how."

"Which is why I brought this." Faolan kneels before the chest and shoves the top free, the hinges groaning in protest. "My advice? Start with the bones. I've had them cast by druids or soothsayers at least a dozen times by now, and they always have something interesting to say." He holds out a small, misshapen sack that clatters with every jerk of his hand.

I don't move. I can't.

A pain gathers at the base of my skull.

"Faolan, they won't . . . Your crew won't understand—"

"Leave them to me." He dismisses me with a wave, and I fist my hands in the shift.

"If you'll just let me have the job—mending the crew's clothes or cleaning out the hull. I could even scrub the deck."

That catches his attention. Faolan stands to face me, and I duck my head, clutching the shift against my front.

"Saoirse?"

I fold the piece over itself again, and then a third time, until the fabric strains against my hands. And when he takes it from me, I stare at the ground between us.

"Trouble." He taps my chin once, and like an idiot, I lift my gaze to his. It is painfully bemused. "I spent nine months looking for those eyes of yours. Not for a new deckhand. If you'd really like to be of use to me and the crew, you'll find a way to make them work."

"I . . ." I cut my eyes to the chest full of divination tools, stomach seizing. "I don't know what I'm supposed to do. Or how to keep everyone safe when I do it. It might go wrong—"

So wrong. Conal's face flashes across my mind.

I grimace as I draw my arms hard round my waist. "I-I just need more time to sort it out."

Faolan's smile flattens, and then he releases a heavy laugh. A hard one. I shrink back. "Well, unfortunately, time's the one thing we're a wee bit short on." He takes my hand from its hiding place, opens the sack, and pours its contents into the center. Knobby pieces of bone piled atop one another, jabbing sharply into my palm. "You're a legend now, Ocean Eyes. Best start acting like it."

The door clicks shut behind him. I stare at the ugly things in my hand, wrapping my fingers tighter until they're a milky yellow blur within. And then I fling them as hard as I can against the opposite wall, releasing the sob I've held back for days when they shatter.

I was right. This was a mistake.

My magic is vicious and careless, and inviting it back inside is like courting death. If any of his crew catches wind, they'll hold the same view as my father. This magic is unnatural—not worth the risk.

And Faolan wants me to wake it as quickly as possible?

Another sob breaks free, and then another as I stumble to my knees and bury my mouth hard against my sleeve to stifle the noise. I cry for the stupid girl I'd been last week, sewing a magpie's wings and hoping to find someone who might like her enough to take her home. For the grieving child who drowned her oldest brother with a vision of dark water and swirling skies.

For the woman who tried to rewrite her fate with a marriage pact and a moonlit swim, but ended up cursing herself all over again in the process.

It's not until the door creaks shut that I realize someone's opened it in the first place. Brona stands petrified beside it, her jaw locked and eyes unreadable as they rake over the pathetic mess I've made. Breaths rip out of me in sharp little gasps even as I attempt to smother them.

"A-accident" is all I can manage after the silence becomes too thick, and then I roll onto my knees and reach for the nearest pieces of bone. I've only managed to gather two when she crouches beside me with a sigh and plucks a shard from my hand.

"Bullshite. Faolan piss you off, then?"

"N-no—"

"He's a pushy, irritating son of a bitch on his best days, and an irredeemable pain in the arse on his worst."

I can't help but gape as she methodically collects pieces of bone and drops them into the sack. "And you still call him captain?"

She cuts her eyes to me, a brow quirked. "Better than husband."

My own laugh surprises me, shaky though it is with the tears still gathered in my throat. I bite my lip after, and sweep a small pile into one hand as she holds the sack and leans back on her heels.

"So why'd you choose him and not the Stone King?"

The question draws me up short. "What?"

Brona rolls her eyes and turns my hands with hers, tipping the bones into the sack. "We're all wondering about it. Nessa said you evaded her questions, and Faolan won't admit a damn thing. So I'm asking you. Why would a princess be so damn eager to trade a whole island for life on a ship?"

"I . . ." Ice and flame trickle across my skin, leached from the tattoo. "I wanted to find the Isle of Lost Souls. I always have."

"So you fancy yourself a hero, then?"

I can't help but laugh, rubbing at the spot on my throat where the torc dug in. "No—not exactly." Her lips quirk down, and my stomach lurches. I force words past the wall of nerves. "There are so many dead on the Isle of Reborn Stalk. Aren't there? Spirits walk the waters and land, whisper in the night. They're so . . . restless, and because of my—" I wave a hand toward my eyes. Swallow. Uncertain of what's safe to tell her, or if there's a lie Faolan's already spun. "I see their emptiness more than most. Feel their longing and pain. I've always wanted it to stop."

Even if that's only one of the reasons—the *smallest* of reasons— to seek the Isle of Lost Souls, I hope that it's enough. But when I glimpse Brona's face, it's clear I was wrong.

Whatever kinship had just settled between us snaps. Her brows drop and her lips turn down as she slowly releases my hand, crossing her arms. "You just want it to stop. All those bothersome ghosts wandering the earth. How inconvenient for you."

No. It wasn't enough. I scramble for something else— something clever like Faolan might say—*anything* but the truth of my soulstone curse or Conal's death. She speaks before I can manage another tangled word.

"Where do you think all those spirits come from on your precious island? Or are you too selfish to care?" Her lip curls back in disgust. "Do you have any idea what your father's done?"

"I don't—"

She drops the sack of bones. "So we're sailing to the Teeth—the one scrap of land notorious for sinking the most ships in the feckin' Crescent—and pissed off not one but two kings in the process, for a girl who doesn't even know what that decision cost?" Brona knots her braid around her fist. "Can you at least tell me *how* you plan on guiding us to the Isle of Lost Souls? I'd like to know what makes you so bloody special it's worth risking all our necks."

My silence damns me.

Brona's laugh is harsh, landing like a slap. "Forget it. Just like Rí Dermot, aren't you? Careless with any life but your own."

Da's name jars me back to life. "And how would you know?"

The question is not a defense of my father—far from it—but before I can blink, Brona's jerked my sleeve up to reveal a pale arm marked by the four long, dark bruises. Mam left them there, but only on his orders. "I know what kind of man your father is. Don't think for a second I didn't see these soon as you walked on board."

I nearly lose my lunch in my attempt to pull my arm free, but she's already let go. I fumble the sleeve, tugging it down as Brona walks to the door, her braid falling loose to flick between her shoulder blades. I want to ask what she knows about him—why she *hates* him. To understand what I'm supposed to feel for him when everything I thought I knew has changed in a matter of days.

She reaches the doorway before I can get another word out.

"Storm'll hit in three hours. Brace yourself."

SIXTEEN

I'm told to stay below, though the wood groans like a starving creature. In the darkness of the cabin, clinging hard to the blankets, I watch as a patch of moonlight flits across the floor and back again with each heavy rock of the ship. It's worse than that last night on my father's ship—at least then I could track the passing hours by the steady creep of its silver light. Here, I can do nothing.

Useless.

The moonlight suddenly shoots past the floor and straight to the wall—my only warning before I tumble from the bed in a tangle of legs and blankets as the ship tilts sharply on its side.

"Gods!" I roll until something hard catches me around the middle, knocking my wind free.

Smooth wood leads up to hard corners. Faolan's desk. He's bolted it to the floor—which has now become the wall—and I cling to its edges as I kick the blankets free, trinkets clattering past my feet.

The door. I need to get to the door.

Twisting, I reach for the handle as my muscles burn with the effort to hold on. It takes barely a tug on the latch for the door to fly open with a crack against the wall. Then it's all I can do not to fall straight through into the hallway.

Stars, we're going to sink!

Another groan shakes the wood beneath me, and as if we are a toy in some god's fingers, the ship slopes slowly in the opposite direction. I pull myself through the doorway and then lie flat against the wall as the entire thing leans back, until I'm near horizontal again.

My stomach churns. I force myself to breathe as my hair lifts from my neck, dangling toward the ceiling.

And then it rights itself, slamming me into the ground.

I will *not* drown like a rat.

The moment the ship steadies, I scramble toward the staircase leading above and slam my shoulder into the hatch, exchanging stillness for the roar of wind and a face full of stinging water. Sodden ropes lie in heaps around the deck, the crew ducking between their lines to manipulate the sails and rigging, each of them impossibly agile.

My legs tremble so much that I can barely stand.

But I'm alive. Free, and—

A wave larger than anything I've seen crashes onto the deck, knocking me to the ground as the ship tilts nearly on its side once more. For a moment, the movement attracts Nessa's eyes and they widen as if she's shocked I haven't kept upright along with the rest of the crew. Then the water drags me by my ankles toward the edge.

My scream is joined by one sharp whistle, and I'm just about to slam into the railing when an arm locks around my waist, tugging me through the air one last time to collide with a sturdy wall of flesh.

"You don't like to stay put, do you, Trouble?" I can hardly breathe as I stare into Faolan's eyes and hear the lunatic laugh as if it's not all completely terrifying. Lightning splits the sky above our heads and he glances up, then nods once and hooks his other arm beneath my trembling legs.

Words that barely make sense pour from my lips as I cling to his shirt. "Don't put me back below. Please—I don't want to die like that."

His brows quirk together as he walks us across the deck, then sets me down at the helm, where Tavin holds the wheel. Faolan taps him on the shoulder, and the moment Tavin steps aside, Faolan catches the wheel with one hand and locks his arm around my waist with the other, keeping my back pressed flush against his chest.

He's mad. All of them are mad. I shut my eyes tight as instinct takes over, reaching for the charms to pray, but all I find is a bare throat.

Right. The gods are dead. And my life is in the hands of a daredevil.

As if I've called his name, Faolan shifts behind me until his lips brush the shell of my ear. "Saoirse."

I shake my head, and his chest jerks with a laugh.

"Lass?"

"No."

"Open your eyes."

"No." I want to keep them closed and pretend I've made good decisions in joining his crew—in binding my life to his. Faolan's fingers curl lightly over my ribs, then dance across them like a spider. I gasp, pitching forward into the wheel as my eyes fly open.

"Faolan—"

My rage stifles before it can truly begin as I witness the monstrosity of a storm at sea.

It is something my bones know to fear. Clouds boil in the heavens like the cauldron of blackberries I used to dye a new skein of wool just one year ago. Rain falls in torn sheets, blown about by the volatile wind that splits every few seconds with jagged bolts of lightning.

It's wickedly, wildly beautiful.

"How are we not dead?" I have to turn my head to be heard, and nearly jump out of my skin when it puts my face a breath away from Faolan's. "The ship should've capsized hours ago, against all this. There's no way . . ."

He smirks, one brow arched, and the answer strikes me hard.

Magic. Of course.

"We'd be a load of fools to travel to the Teeth without a few tricks up our sleeves." Faolan tightens his arm around my waist. "Every summer, a heap of kelp washes up on the shores of the Isle of Ashen Flame—black leaves pebbled all over with ugly yellow warts. They're a sight, aye, but once you pound them into a paste, there's not a damned thing that can break through. We plaster the hull with it, and it makes for an easy repair when you're in a rush to keep the old girl from sinking. Then there's the clusters of Dhia Eamon's quartz from your old betrothed's island; we store some at each point of the ship to keep us balanced along the waves, no matter where the water takes us."

Faolan regards his crew with the same pride my father always held when watching my brothers train with their blades. "And o' course, we all wear a strip of goat's hide from the Dromlach Cliffs tied round a shadow crane's feathers tucked in our boots. You'd have to work damn hard to take a fall with those on your person."

My brows snap together as a hazy memory attempts to unroot itself. "The Dromlach Cliffs? No, that can't be right. My old nanny told me stories about those goats, and how as a girl she'd watch them hop across the cliffs without once losing their footing. She always swore they had wings. I begged to see them too, someday, but she told me . . ."

What was it? I squint against the rain, studying his face.

"She told me the cliffside they inhabit is so steep, my great-grandfather outlawed any attempts to catch them. There were too many lives wasted."

Faolan's fingers abruptly stop their drumming against my waist, lying flat instead. "You really believe that?"

"Why wouldn't I?"

His laugh jolts against my back, sending heat over my neck. "I suppose you would, living a life tucked away in a palace."

The words sting more than I think he means them to, rubbing salt into the wounds Brona left behind. The castle was never mine, nor the cottage Da banished me to. I held no control over the nursemaids or nannies, the conversations I overheard or what I was directly taught. And at the cottage, I had no one but myself. How was I meant to learn otherwise?

He must feel my rigid limbs; his laughter cuts short, then shifts into a sigh. "The Ring of Stars forbade attempts to catch them because their agility led us humble wayfarers to be far too good at our jobs. We were getting wealthy, buying up land, settling down—no incentive to keep at the adventuring when you could retire in a few years to a good life, eh? They couldn't have that. It's the same with about fifty other objects of interest or resources left by the gods. Wayfaring is a dangerous business, and none of them want to risk their own hides for the magic their world runs on, but they don't want us getting our piece of it either."

A fresh wave of thunder drowns whatever pitiful response had formed on my tongue. I close my eyes to let it seep beneath my skin, where his words slot neatly into the gaps and questions that've grown every year since I was small.

It makes sense. The wealth wayfarers gained by their plunder is exactly the sort of threat my father would have foreseen—a threat he'd have found a way to diminish with his clever words and false concern for their well-being. And though Faolan embellishes when he speaks, I'm learning he's not a liar for lying's sake any more than he's a hero. I don't have any reason to disbelieve him, as strange as it is to speak of the Ring of Stars as a lofty, conniving group of lawmakers and rulers rather than the just, kind leaders I've been raised to see.

Faolan squeezes my waist once, drawing me closer to him. "Believe what you want, Saoirse, but—"

"I believe you."

I'm not sure who's more surprised by the words. He stiffens against my back, his breath suspended in his lungs. "That so?"

My nod jars his chin, and I bite down on my lip when I feel his arm hitch lower over my hips, steadying us both against the next swell—but they're getting slower, the waves calming without much ceremony. Splashes of deepest indigo appear through the gray as the sky gives a final complaint, then stills.

Nessa looks to Faolan, crimson strands of hair plastered to her face like scars. He nods, and she flashes a smile before relaying orders to the rest of the bedraggled crew to clean up the deck and get some rest below. Faolan's fingers lift away from my ribs one after another until the whole weight of his arm is gone, draped over the wheel's spike to my left.

I could duck free of his arms if I want to—return to the cabin alone.

I trace my fingers along the wheel and lean carefully back into his chest instead.

"Is that why they call you a pirate?"

Faolan snorts, reaching for one of the fine daggers sheathed at his side. Its hilt is the body of a wolf, carved of pure bronze that flickers to life every time he draws it through the air. "*Technically,* I'm a wayfarer."

"What about the Wolf?"

Faolan pauses, a muscle feathering in his jaw. "My mother gave me that name."

He ducks down before I can see more of his face, slipping the blade beneath a strip of hide tucked into his boot and cutting it free. A moment later, dagger between his teeth, he ties the same piece around my ankle.

"Winning these daggers in a game only solidified it. I was a lone wolf when I started, until Kiara sent Tavin to mind me. He was as miserable to be stuck with me as I was with him. But shortly after we started is when Nessa joined the crew, then Lorcan, and finally Brona. At some point . . . we became a pack." He knots the leather cord, fingers teasing across my ankle. "I had more to look after—which meant more wee trips *off* the official record to keep us afloat. Protection comes at a price."

"I thought that was your cousin's job."

His muscles tense, arms brushing my shoulders as he eases the wheel to the right. "Kiara is my queen."

I twist just enough to see his frown. "I know."

"Then you know it's her name that gave me the ship in the first place. Opened up every port. Spared my life. So whatever tasks she comes up with, they're not the sort I can accept or deny." He huffs a laugh. "For now. But she's not half so bad as the rest of the kings and queens—and worse than the other handful that are decent. Honestly, the whole lot of them have gone to rot."

"When did it happen, though?" The words sound naive, even to me. "Our ancestors slaughtered the gods to ensure equality and justice. Wasn't that the whole point of forming the Ring of—"

Faolan buries his groan in the curve of my throat.

"*Stars.*" I jerk against the wheel, wholly unprepared for the heat of his mouth. Or the weight of the air separating our bodies. It settles against my skin like the memory of a touch—except no one has ever touched the places it's gathering now. And he must know what he's doing, because Faolan has gone still. Lips parted, just below my jaw.

Where he must feel every savage beat of my heart.

"Are you afraid of me, lass?"

"Y—" The word dies on my tongue. Is this fear? Sensation pricks across my skin as though it were a lyre, aching to be played. I can't catch a proper breath. My fingers clench hard on the wheel spokes—but the urge to run is nowhere to be found. "No."

His smile against my neck casts a shiver down my spine. "Good."

A sharp whistle interrupts us from the starboard, where Brona stands. A pulse seems to sweep the deck, drawing the crew to awareness and Faolan to his full height as dawn teases the horizon.

I lean forward until my fingers wrap over the wheel spokes just beneath Faolan's. The ship slows beneath our feet, dragged by wind or anchors or perhaps the sails and their ever-shifting rhythm on this ship.

All but one are furled now, and in only seconds I understand why. Massive formations of black-and-white marbled rock tower on either side of the ship, leading to a narrow passage. They are rough and misshapen, full of pocked holes, and they emerge one after another from the angry sea.

The Teeth.

SEVENTEEN

The sky is threaded with rose and gold as the sun climbs over the Teeth's rotting maw. Shadows flicker back and forth across the deck with each new monolith we pass—the ancient jawbone of a voracious sea monster, if Faolan's story is to be believed.

"The goddess Róisín was no warrior. Her fingers branched like tree limbs, nimble and many-jointed, her feet sculpted of pure glass. But when the oilliphéist came, she went out to greet him among the waves." Faolan's hands curl over mine on the wheel, steering his true love safely through. "Her voice coaxed new stars into existence and commanded others to fall—the only weapon she needed against a creature so fearsome as that.

"One word, and the first star fell directly into the oilliphéist's eye. A stream of them, and the sea serpent was left writhing on the ocean floor. She was clever, but not quite wise. Fair Róisín turned her back before the job was done, thinking the beast parted from this world."

A chill brushes my face as the next shadow passes over.

"It cursed her with its dying breath. The channel Róisín's people sailed, the currents and the tides. Any who dared disturb its bones would risk death—by storm or sea, the oilliphéist would have its due."

I don't miss the tattered remnants of a shipwreck caught between every other tooth and the next, nor the way tension knots Brona's shoulders as she studies the map in her hands. But it's not until I see the first spirit lingering beneath the water's surface that my heart sinks a little, banishing any heat lingering from Faolan's story.

The farther into the Teeth we sail, the more the dead will come.

"What are we doing here?" I whisper, shying closer into his arms. "Be honest."

He sighs. "There's something here to help us find the Isle of Lost Souls." Faolan eases the spokes along with a touch until the ship vibrates beneath our feet. "But it's best to discuss that part belowdecks."

Ten other questions flit across my mind as Faolan whistles a whirling little rhythm. His first mate—Nessa—glances up from a conversation with two of the others, and I startle at the sight of her smirk. When she walks over, my jaw goes slack.

"You whistle for your crew like . . . dogs?"

Nessa must hear, because she cackles as she takes hold of a thick rope, swinging around to face the wheel.

"Believe me, Wolf Tamer, if it was anything like that, we'd have chucked the captain overboard a long time ago. No, we all keep our own signals. Saves us having to shout."

"We'll be needing to find one for you next." Faolan tugs a lock of my half-dried hair, and I have to blink hard. Not because it hurt, but because it's been so long since anyone teased me like that. If he notices, he doesn't say anything. "Ness, we're going below to change and talk over the next steps. Tavin's busy, so can you get us through to the bay all right?"

"Aye," Nessa says, already nudging us out of the way, but my heart has forgotten how to pace itself.

We're going below to change. Together.

My feet are moving, Faolan's hand spread on my shoulder. I'm aware of the wet fabric chafing between my thighs with each step now, the way my shirt must cling. But the full weight of Faolan's words doesn't sink in until he's left me in the doorway to yank his shirt overhead, casting it to the side.

"W-what are you doing?"

Faolan pauses with a finger hooked through the knot at his waist keeping his trousers up. His eyes spark like wildfire just before he grins with full abandon. "Does a nominal marriage mean I'm not allowed to change in my own bloody cabin now? Or are you afraid you won't be able to resist me?"

My blush would hint at the latter, so I roll my eyes instead and start to turn my back. Only to stop. If I change, he might see the tattoo. I can't allow that to happen, not after the incident with the bones.

Pivoting slowly, I tuck myself closer to the window where a tapestry hangs—a gift from one of those lovely girls at the Damhsa enamored with his stories. If I had to wager, nearly half the items in this room must be gifts, marked with the colors, materials, or techniques scattered across all six islands. My favorite is a basket of colorful wool and thin bronze needles that would be better replaced with wood.

It's a ridiculous hoard. And a lovely one, even strewn across the cabin as it is now after the storm.

Half-facing the wall, I peel my shirt free from the clammy skin beneath, careful to shake my hair after so it hides the mark. The trousers prove more difficult. Still, I can't help the prickles of awareness that skate down my back like fingertips.

Like the feel of his lips at my throat.

I won't look back. It would only make him smug.

"You had something to tell me?"

"Aye." There's a smile in his voice. "But I'm afraid I can't hear you very well, facing that wall."

Bastard.

I tug a dry shift over my head, breathing easier once the soft linen falls into place. It's far too thin for the morning light streaming in, but my fingers are too stiff to pull on anything more. I turn, arms crossed over my chest, jaw locked in case he starts to laugh.

But he's not looking at me. Of course he's not.

Instead, Faolan studies another tapestry on the opposite side of the room—smaller, and better made. It depicts the Crescent as though from the eye of an eagle hovering high above, the smallest of the six islands nearly kissing on the right as the others grow gradually larger curved to the left. It's a sight I'm somewhat familiar with.

The expanse of his bare body is not.

"I—thought you were getting dressed."

He glances over one shoulder roped in muscle and smiles. "I got distracted. Don't just stand there like a lecher—toss me some trousers, would you?"

I gape at him as indignation and . . . something else wars within my blood. Terrifying and beautiful, captivating as the storm.

My voice is hoarse when I speak. "You agreed to a marriage in name only, remember?"

He cocks a brow, and my hands go rigid where they curl over the softness of my waist. But it's not fear that arches my back when his steps draw near, or panic that tilts my chin high. Faolan won't hurt me—not for speaking my mind. If I've learned anything on the ship, it's that.

In fact, that is the only thing I'm certain of at this moment.

Faolan tilts his head to one side. "Is that your way of telling me to fetch my own bloody trousers, Trouble?"

I swallow, and he tracks the movement with his gaze. "Aye."

He grins. "Good girl."

I stumble back as he roots for a fresh set from the mess of cloth and trinkets clustered round the legs of his desk. He steps into a pair without much ceremony, and it's all I can do not to collapse onto the bed.

There's no trick. No threat. His smile is bemused but not the least cruel.

"Faolan—"

"What do you know about your grandmother?"

My hand falls to the bedpost as he ties the trousers in place. "Why do you ask?"

"Because Gráinne is the reason we're here."

Warmth leaches from me as fast as it came. I search Faolan's eyes for humor, only to find them serious for once—no spark of mischief igniting the midnight blue.

I should have cast you into the sea the moment you opened those eyes and I recognized you for what you were.

My nails bite into the wood. "You said you only met her once. That she is the one who sang about the Isle of Lost Souls—about me?"

He nods. "Aye, but I didn't know *who* she was exactly at the time. Otherwise I'd have sailed straight for your father's land to steal you away, wouldn't I?"

The wood slips beneath my sweating palm. "Would you have?"

Faolan's smile goes crooked. "Darling, I had a whole plan to kidnap you two nights ago if you hadn't shown up onshore. Give me a wee bit of credit."

A laugh perches on the tip of my tongue. The memory of Mam's confession chases it away. "My father said Gráinne was mad. That she—" Tried to drown me. "She's the reason I'm cursed."

"And we both know what a reliable narrator he is." Faolan drops into the chair beside me, woolen socks in his hand. "Gráinne wasn't a royal, or a descendant of the Daonnaí. Did you know that?"

I don't know much of anything, it seems.

"Your father's done a fair job covering up anything to do with her, but the oldest of the seanchaí still remember. I sought them out at the Damhsa, and they told me that before Gráinne met your grandda, she was a regular soothsayer who read bones at every gathering. She was never made queen—his family wouldn't allow the marriage—but she was known to be levelheaded and wise until her husband passed on."

The tattoo on my back stings as Faolan leans forward, fixing his gaze on mine.

"They say it was only *after* he died that her mind split."

I grip the mattress. "You think she touched his soulstone?"

"I'd stake money on it." Faolan tugs on one of his socks. "Dermot all but scoured his mother from the public eye after that. Ran the story she'd gone mad with grief, then tucked her neatly away where no one could see."

Like me.

My stomach hollows as Faolan stretches the knit so casually over his ankle, like he hasn't just painted the story of my own life.

"H-how did you meet her, then? If Father banished her."

"She escaped. Our islands aren't that far from each other—she could've handed a bit of jewelry off and taken passage on a wayfarer's ship along the coast to reach our docks. Or a fisherman might've pitied her? Hell, maybe she's like her granddaughter and fancied she could swim."

My brows snap together. "I *can* swim, I was only—" Weak from the tattoo.

A tattoo the apothecary said they'd tried on my grandmother first.

I shake my head. "And where did you find her?"

Faolan loops an arm around the bedpost, one of his knees brushing mine. "At the docks. The poor creature was rambling to thin air about the Isle of Lost Souls, and no one else would go near her. But I was curious, so I took her into the pub and bought her a meal while she spun her tales." Faolan taps his fingers along the wood, watching me from the corner of his eye. "I never could resist a story."

I tear my gaze away. "So she told you about the island, and then—what. You left her there?"

"No. At least not in the way you're thinking." A thin band of pale skin nestles beside carved bands of gold, where the wolf's-head ring used to be. "I was only a wean at the time, thirteen at most? She gave me this ugly old ring of hers, then sent me off to show my parents, and . . . I obeyed."

A smile flits over his mouth, but it's all wrong, bitterness catching at the corners. "I should've left the stupid thing behind, but I didn't. And then . . ." Faolan rubs at that bare strip of skin. "Anyway. I never saw her again."

My heart sinks. "That must have been at least a decade ago."

"Thirteen years or thereabouts, but—and this is important." Faolan taps me once underneath the chin, his smile drawing the light once more. "You've married a very smart man. I had a hunch, so before we left the Damhsa, I got Dermot's head seanchaí alone with a bottle of whiskey and found out where

Dermot had his mother sent. Or rather, where the ship holding her went down."

Blue light flickers across his face, and I glance out the window to see more souls clinging to the pitted rocks outside. Spirits half-formed, tossed in the waters above a wreckage we sail past.

Understanding settles in a tired lurch to my gut. "You think she died here."

He nods. "Aye. And seeing as you're cut from the same cloth, I figure finding her bones or soulstone is worth a shot. If the magic is stronger when you touch someone's skin, what will it be like to hold their very essence?"

The thought of holding my grandmother's bones leaves a sour taste on my tongue, but as though he senses it, Faolan slides a hand down my arm. "I could be wrong. And just in case, she's not the only reason we came. Rumor also has it there's a breed of fish here that can allow a man half a day below the water without needing air."

I shake my head. Stand to reach a dress folded neatly on top of a trunk. Do anything not to think about the grandmother who, whether mad or misunderstood, had shared the burden of magic with me. "No, that's the freckled whales. They've been gone a whole generation, haven't they?"

"Aye, the bastards from Ashen Flame hunted the poor creatures to the point they've either left the Crescent for good or they've passed on to the same realm as the gods. No, I'm talking about a fish bred two generations past by the Isle of Painted Claw for their beauty. Sailors in those parts claim that if you cut out their gills and lacquer 'em in the same kelp we use for the ship, a person could *breathe* below the waves nearly half a day—sunrise to sunset. If they're lucky."

I tip my head back. Release a long, slow breath. "And we're

doing all of this because of the song? The one you can hardly re-member."

He must hear the doubt in my voice, because his hands abruptly fall to my hips and squeeze, sending me squirming back toward the bed. "Oi, ye cheeky wench—aye, it's because of a song. Most of my adventures are. You've just got to work your way through the pretty lyrics and find the truth beneath."

I can't help but snort even as I struggle to pull the dress over my head, heart unsteady in my chest. "Fine, but if the fish yield such power, how is it they're so unheard of?"

"Well . . . they're shy little beasties. Quick as lightning. And they've got teeth."

"Right." I try and fail to lace the side of my dress together. My fingers are still numb with cold. "And how long will we be here?"

I'm on my third try when his hand pushes mine aside, drawing the fabric together with a few easy tugs. Neither of us says a word until he's done, his fingers wrapped in the laces for just a moment more before he smiles and steps back, tossing me a fresh pair of socks from my bag.

"As long as it takes."

I can do nothing more than watch as he adjusts the damp leather glove tied around his left hand and slips out the door.

EIGHTEEN

A s long as it takes" turns into two full weeks of trial and error.
Mostly error.

The crew attempts to track the fishes' patterns, weave stronger nets, lay baited lines, but the fish slip or bite through their traps every time. And all the while, morning and night and every moment in between, Faolan tries his damnedest to coax my magic free.

I grind my teeth at the thought of his last attempt, locking me up in his study for half the day with the chest full of divination aids: more casting bones, prayer medallions, and ritual objects I've seen the druids use. When he tried to come in later with a bucket of entrails to interpret from whatever nonmagical fish they'd caught for supper, I flung it at his feet. He's left me alone about it since.

"I can just feel it! Today's the day—just you wait. It'll happen."

"How's tha' different from the last five?"

Faolan's voice drifts across the water, and I fight the urge to roll my eyes. Instead, I watch my fingers cut tiny divots into the water as the currach glides between two of the Teeth. It's a spot free of shipwrecks, the spirits blessedly absent for now.

"Your husband's pretty sure of himself."

I glance up and Nessa is grinning at me, her sunburned bottom lip split in the middle. "Is he ever not?"

Faolan's currach turns a corner, followed by a second holding Tavin, the striker Oona, and her brother, Bowden. Their names come easily to mind now, though our conversation's been middling at best. A fumbled handful of words when I handed their clothes back, neatly patched and free of stains. Tavin's been pleasant at least, noting our progress for Kiara, though I still haven't figured out how he communicates our path from this far across the waves using only her hair. I haven't been brave enough to ask.

"No." Nessa laughs and steers us around one of the formations, both our noses wrinkling when we get too close and the smell of rot becomes unbearable.

"Why are we taking this path again?"

"Faolan had a feeling. Weren't you listening?"

I laugh once and shake my head. It's easier to ignore my husband than absorb his charms—especially when I have to lie beside him each night, waking to every restless dip and jerk his body makes against the bed. It's worse than the sea's fitful nature, the way my husband battles his own sleep. No matter how many quilts I fold between us, or the precise lay of my limbs, I wake to a twisted storm of sheets and limbs threaded loosely with mine.

A shiver wracks my chest as I remember the strange, feverish flash of yearning that shot through me this morning—one that jolted me from sleep, sweaty and damp in places I try to ignore. It's not the first time I've woken to a feeling or half-formed memory I could not claim.

In sleep, Faolan's skin drags constantly over mine.

So I tolerate his ambushes and guessing games for the sake of the magic, if only so he won't start asking why my eyes remain still, or why I avoid his gaze each morning. And for all the sheer amount of space Faolan takes up on this ship, I can survive it so long as he doesn't touch me under daylight.

And he hasn't, apart from that brush of his lips after the storm. Faolan's kept his promise.

Even if some small, traitorous part of me wishes he wouldn't.

Nessa sighs, guiding the small boat after the others. "He reckons there's got to be a reef or something tucked away in a shallow nearby where the fish spend most of their time."

I pull my hand from the water. "Even if they did, it's unlikely they'd let us close enough to—"

A whistle flies around the bend in a low-high pattern I understand now to mean we'd better get there sharpish. Nessa grins, adjusting her feet against the lower boards to pull hard on the wooden oars. "Winds o' fury, the lad had better be onto something. I'm getting pretty damn tired of the setbacks."

The sight that greets us around the corner brings me to my knees, fingers gripping the sides of the currach tight as my jaw hangs free.

Shadows zip back and forth across a wide shallow leading to a particularly jagged formation, creatures cutting through clouds of gold beneath the water's surface. Sharp trills echo back and forth in time with the shadows' movements, and a second later, a sleek fin emerges between waves just before a flurry of the fish take to the air.

Dolphins. An entire pod is here hunting the things, and Faolan looks like some mad idea is spinning round his mind as he watches them move. More shadows fall across our tiny boats one after another, as well as prisms of color and light, announcing the arrival of the tuar ceatha—enormous cranes with sleek black necks, white faces, and iridescent feathers—that come from the Isle of Painted Claw.

Chaos descends in a flurry of splashing tails and feathers as dolphins feast from below, rounding the fish into tight circles, and the cranes dive down to catch their own fill.

"Tavin, get your net ready!"

"Wha'?"

A dolphin jostles the side of our currach. By the time it steadies, Faolan's leapt into the water with one arm raised against the birds, the other slashing through the waves to try to catch . . .

"Stars above, is he serious?"

"Apparently!" Nessa shakes her head and then heaves against the oars to bring us closer to the mayhem, their screeches, shouts, and swears blending into a single hum that takes root in my jaw.

Rakes across my skin like scales.

"Oh. Oh, no."

Ice crackles across my back, draining me of humor as I lift my hand slowly and stare at the red-violet streaks of blood left behind. A dying fish flaps feebly where my fingers just rested, a jagged gash splitting its golden tail.

I cling to the side of the boat. Stare hard into the water, though every part of me screams to look away, because if I don't see whatever is coming to me, then no one will die.

Faolan won't die.

Right?

The thought is ridiculous, almost childish in nature, because in truth, I've no idea what this magic is capable of. Whatever we've attempted—bones, cards, stones—nothing has worked to awaken its power or summon a vision forth. Nothing but lying skin-to-skin for hours every night, when my guard is low and my mind vulnerable. Yet if I feel things from the mere brush of skin, how much more powerful a gateway is the heart's own blood?

I blink, and the colors blur. Blink again, and see feathers coated in blood. Hear bone shatter against flat rock. Scaled bodies lying still beneath an open sky, slender bones plucked from flesh. It's vivid and terrifying, and—

Another blink, and I'm surrounded by the Teeth once more as the painted cranes swoop harmlessly overhead.

Cranes suddenly streaked in scarlet.

Head pounding, I turn my face to the sky and take in the strange flat top of the nearest Tooth. It is as pockmarked as the rest of them, with a black, mottled base peeking up from the waves. And at the top . . .

At the top, wings beat against the sky in a rage, cranes dipping over the edge to drop objects that I swear glimmer like gold.

Stars above.

We don't need to try our nets or useless arrows—the answer is in the skies.

"Faolan!" I twist around to see Nessa's left our currach, wading through the shallows to join her captain. The dolphins aren't happy with her invasion. They slap their tails against the water, sending salty sprays into Faolan's and Nessa's eyes. I crawl to the edge of the boat and cup my hand over my mouth. "FAOLAN!"

"I'm sort of busy here, lass! Nessa, just try and—oi, you barmy little maggot, stop splashing me, damn you."

"Faolan, look up! I felt—" *Magic.* "I felt the—"

"Not now, Saoirse!"

I bristle at the name. Not Ocean Eyes, Wolf Tamer, wife, or any of the other things he's called me for weeks. Only Saoirse, said with the same edge of dismissal that nearly everyone else in my life has ever used.

My teeth grind together as I watch another crane pluck a fish from the water and take it high into the sky. If Faolan would bloody look up and see my eyes shift, he would know. He'd *listen*. But I'm

not going to shout about the magic in front of all these people—
not when it's finally told me something useful instead of terrifying.

"If you're not going to listen—"

Oona joins them in the water with a warrior's shriek, weapons
at the ready to spear through as many fish as she can, and the arguments that descend drown out any remaining attempts to get
Faolan's attention.

"Of all the feckin' times." I bite off the string of curses and
shove myself over the edge of the currach opposite all the rest. The
water is warm here, lapping at my rib cage as I wade toward the
pitiful excuse for land. Whether it truly is a decaying beast's tooth
or only a legend, the strip of dark, spongy ground is hardly wide
enough to stand on. I step closer to the pitted surface, where deep
crevices split the wall large enough to fit a foot or hand.

It's only as I put my fingers into the first one that doubt slips in.

I have to tilt my head back until my neck strains, just to catch
a glimpse of the flattened top. I'm hardly more agile now than I
was two weeks ago, and I've never climbed anything higher than
a tree. But the magic's call is only getting stronger. With trembling
hands, I pull down on the ledge above my eyes, fit my boots into
another, and climb.

"What in shade's breath are you doing?"

I drop hard to the ground, jerking around to see Brona standing at the edge of the Tooth, brows fixed in a straight line. She's
wearing the same scowl she's had for days, but something about
it—about the magic humming in my veins and irritation over
Faolan's dismissal—has me scowling back.

"Why do you care to know?"

Brona huffs. "If you fall and break your royal neck, who do you
think will pay for it?"

"Myself, seeing as I'll be dead." The words are bitter, scraping away whatever nerves I had left. I turn back to the monolith. "I'm just careless, remember?"

"No, you're not."

My hand slips from a crack, falling hard against my side. "What?"

"I've been watching you." Brona crosses her arms, turning her glare onto the sky. "And you're so damn timid. Irritatingly quiet, avoiding the rest of us when you can—and I'd think you hate us all if it weren't for the forlorn looks you cast our way after you've sat yourself in a corner while the rest of us eat."

My laugh is shaky when it comes. "But not careless?"

"No." She kicks a rock into the water and finally meets my eyes. "Thanks for mending my shirts."

I say nothing. Not until the magic tenses in my belly again, urging me forward. Up.

"Would you look up?"

"Sorry?"

"Look *up*." I jerk my chin toward the sky, and Brona snorts. But I know she's humored me when her breath hitches a moment later.

"The tuar ceatha. They're killing the fish by dropping them— why didn't you tell Faolan?"

A whoop carries across the water, followed by a splash. "I tried."

I expect Brona to bite again, tell me I didn't try enough. Instead, Brona's stony expression softens by parts until, for the first time, she watches me with curiosity rather than open suspicion. "Aye. Well, sometimes Faolan gets on to one subject or another and only wants to hear his own voice."

My laugh surprises even me, sending a sharp ache through my chest and a flicker of confusion through her eyes. We stand for just a moment, the distant splashes and shouts hanging between us, before she lifts her chin. "Right. Lorcan told me the other day that he thinks I might've been a wee bit harsh with you at the start."

I can't help another laugh. "A bit?"

Brona kicks a shell into the water. "I won't apologize for it, so don't ask me to. Just . . . answer my question and I'll help you climb up. Why are you really here, Saoirse?"

My smile drops. What can I possibly say?

There was a starlit night and a bonfire, the painful collar of an unwanted betrothal. A feral man dressed as a wolf who touched me like I'm not something other and whispered how special I was. The promise that my magic could heal for once, find and restore life rather than take it away.

I swallow. There is only a small piece of the whole I can give her, and I know instinctively it won't be enough. But if I'm to survive this, I'll need allies. Friends.

It'll have to be a start.

"My whole life, I've believed a lie about myself—about the world and my place in it. I believed my father's version of things."

Brona's grimace nearly stops me, but she forces it back. Watches me with intent in her dark eyes.

"Faolan showed me otherwise. And now I—I want to know the truth about myself. I *have* to know it. But the only way to uncover it is by finding the Isle of Lost Souls, and I couldn't do that married to Rí Maccus or—"

Banished on my father's lands. Not even Faolan knows that part.

I rake my fingers back through my hair, until the Tooth is all I see. "It was my choice to come. If anything happens from here, Ríona Kiara's made that known. I've never wanted anyone else to face the consequences of my actions."

My foot slides easily into the lowest crevice, but another joins at its side.

Brona nudges me until I make room, then scales the section in three easy lurches of her small frame. "Follow my pattern. And for gods' sake, don't fall."

NINETEEN

K eep up, Saoirse."

I lift my forehead from where it's dropped against the wall, sweat pouring down my temples and spine. There isn't a single part of me that doesn't tremble as we ascend the crumbling, pock-marked surface. If it weren't for the footholds, I'd have no chance at all.

"Saoirse!"

Brona's sharp tone has me reaching for the next divot, and the next. For once in my life, I can't look down. If I do, I'll fall.

But as we near the top, where it plateaus, something shifts around us. The wind, which had only nudged my back before, rips through my hair, coaxing me higher. I see the edge, and a thrill burns its way from my stomach up to my heart, then out to every limb.

Brona slips over the top, turning to catch my hand after. She pulls me up, and then we're lying beneath nothing but sky, both of us breathless and shaking with the awe of such a discovery as—

The smell hits us at the same time, making our gasps turn to groans as we push onto our knees.

We're kneeling on a surface just as wide as, if not wider than, the main deck of Faolan's ship. Cranes cover every inch, their noises easily overshadowing our heaving breaths and the ruckus from below. Mates dance alongside one another as younglings trail after their parents, ruffling their fresh feathers. Nestled in a row of small, pebbled nests far along the edge, a dozen gray weans squawk and tip their heads back with beaks too big for them to carry, waiting for a feast.

Carnage surrounds us all.

Wherever there aren't birds, there are streaks of blood, scales, and piles of near-rotted fish. The smell turns my stomach worse than the magic did, and that's before I see a crane fly overhead with a fish writhing in its beak until it opens. The fish slams into the Tooth with a horrible thwack, killing it instantly as blood spatters the ground.

"Right. Better get on with it." Brona pulls a knife from her boot and passes me another, brow raised. There's a faint smirk on her lips and a dare in her eyes. I'm reminded of how Aidan used to challenge me. "Unless you'd rather collect shells and feathers? I can't imagine the daughter of a king has ever scaled a fish."

Shrugging off my unease, I force a smile and take the knife from her. "Never a magical one." I crouch before the fresh kill and bite down hard on my tongue as I work my knife into the vulnerable stripe of its belly. "Have you ever heard of 'An Bradán Feasa'?"

A half hour later, we've filled an entire sack to the tune of my story—one about an ordinary salmon who lived in a well and ate nine hazelnuts that granted him the knowledge of the world. I sift through the piles of fleshy gills and tie off a pouch of fishes' eyes and another of scales, recounting another tale my nanny gave me, and a third all my own. Anything to distract from the gruesome work. I nearly throw up twice by the time it's done, but when we straighten with our arms streaked in blood, I can't help a smile.

"Not bad," Brona says, swiping at a loose curl before she ties a long strip of leather tight over her sack. "Better than the others have fared, I'll bet."

I glance over the edge we climbed and spot Faolan at once where he lies back in one of the currachs, all the others back in their own boats. There's only the smallest splash of gold in his hull, none in the rest. A reluctant smile edges onto my lips as I weigh the sack in one hand. "Do you think he'll be annoyed?"

"I hope so, the eejit."

My smile widens as Brona joins me, snorting at the sight below. She kicks a rock off the edge then, and waggles her blood-streaked fingers while we wait for the splash. It comes three beats later. "There's our way down."

"What, falling?" I laugh until I realize her grin is not a show of amusement. She's dead serious. "No."

"You barely made it up at all." Brona nudges another rock over. I feel its splash like a ripple in my blood. "I'm not trying to be rude, but do you really think you stand a chance of climbing down when you have all *that* to contend with as well?"

My grip on the sack tightens. "I'm not going to jump."

"Please, Highness, enlighten me about all the other choices at your disposal, then."

"Brona, please don't call me . . ."

Time stops as my vision narrows to one central point in the near distance. A flag—badly damaged, colors fading, barely more than threads at this point. But the familiar trio of silver-threaded mushrooms still manages to catch the light where it peeks above the still waters between one Tooth and the next.

"I'll make it easy for you."

"No—Brona, wait!"

Her hands meet my shoulders with a strength I had no idea she possessed. For a moment, we hang suspended over the ledge. Then

I'm falling through air and space, and I don't even scream for the surprise of it all. Water slaps my side when I land, swallowing me whole. A splash sounds to my left a heartbeat later, knocking me into the wood of the boat, and then my head breaks the surface just beside Brona's.

"Feck!" The word slips from my mouth, and we blink stupidly at each other before she breaks into a laugh—a genuine one. The first I've heard from her.

"That's the best you can do, Wolf Tamer?" Brona asks, and for some reason, a laugh tears free from me as well.

"Give me a minute, and I'll do better."

"Aye, I'll bet—" Brona starts before Lorcan catches her by the waist and hauls her into his currach. She immediately shoves his arm away, cheeks flushing in spite of her glare, but I'm still laughing as someone helps me into the other boat.

It's only when I'm settled down in one end that I notice Faolan seated on the other side.

His lips are always tilted up at the corners, but there's something new to their set now. His chest is puffed out, shirt gone, one arm wrapped and bloody propped along the side of the wee boat as though he hopes I'll ask about it. And there between his feet are two fish, mangled as though he had to wrestle one of the dolphins to get them.

Faolan stares at me, and it's so clear he's waiting for praise, I can't help it.

I burst into laughter—harder than before.

Every time I glimpse his face, the fit gets worse. I'm doubled over myself, cackling, gripping the boat as his expression goes from taken aback to confused and then to a childlike pout.

"Oi—do you know what I had to go through, getting these? You could at least act a wee bit impressed."

My breaths are a wheeze, fingers curled hard over my side where an ache has begun, and it's all I can do to look at Brona, who's watching me with the smile back on her lips. She snorts and tosses the sack of gills directly into Faolan's lap.

"You were saying, Captain?"

My unruly laughter tapers down to a few soft chuckles as Faolan unties the bag and stares at its contents, looking from Brona to me and back again. "Right. Well . . . feckin' good job you've done here, Brona."

"Don't look at me. It was your wife's idea."

I expect my body to crumple at the sudden attention, the weight of all their eyes. Instead, I shift slightly back and wind my arms loosely over my knees, watching them all over the tops.

Faolan watches me right back, dark brows knit in a line. "How'd you figure it out?"

I glance at the others, conscious of their listening ears. "I . . . felt like we ought to look up, once the tuar ceatha arrived. And then I saw the cranes carrying fish to their nesting grounds on top, so I . . . What?"

Faolan's lips have spread into a wolfish grin that lights his whole face. It punches me clean of breath.

"You *felt*?"

"Aye. But— Don't touch my stomach!" I squirm back from the finger he's teased against my soft middle, and he laughs, shaking his head.

"Sorry, but where'd you feel it? There, in your gut?"

I shake my head and, before he gets any more ideas, lock my arms protectively over my waist. "No, it was just—I just—"

I'm beginning to doubt it was even magic now. My power has always led to pain before, hasn't it?

"If anyone else had tried looking up, they'd have seen it as well. Anyway, that's not the important bit."

"It seems pretty damn important to me," Faolan says, lifting a gruesome set of gills from the sack. He drops them when I touch his wrist, eyes snapping to mine.

"I saw my family's crest on a flag right before we jumped. It's crafted in the old style, before my father changed the pattern. Just past that ridge." I glance past his shoulder, then study Faolan's expression as it shifts from excitement to awe to something else. Something I've wanted to see my whole life.

Pride. Lining every part of his face.

"You found her."

I nod, my throat thick as Faolan releases a half-broken laugh, then catches my cheeks between his palms. I hardly have time to breathe before he's kissed the tip of my nose.

It's a nothing spot. Should be a nothing kiss.

But for all the ease with which he handles the others, forever jostling and clapping them on the back, I've never seen him kiss anyone else. Not once.

Heat tears through my chest, raging across my cheeks and drawing my eyes wide as he pulls away, beaming like he hasn't just taken my heart into his hands. "Clever thing. We'll know for sure by tomorrow."

"Know what, Captain?" Lorcan's voice startles me enough that I rock the boat when I pull back.

"Whether or not Saoirse's grandmother is buried in a spot just over there." Faolan gestures toward a jagged mast, where the flag moves feebly with the wind. I steady myself with a hard grip on the wood on either side of my hips as the crew exchanges looks, their smiles gradually fading. My joy evaporates alongside them.

I'm not ready for their questions. For this moment to end.

Brona is the first to break the silence, water still dripping from her curls. "And why do we need to know that information?"

"Because we're going to dive the wreck at sunset." Faolan nudges the ragged fish away with his foot and reaches for the oars. "Saoirse's grandmother is the one who knew where to find the Isle of Lost Souls."

"*Knew?*" Nessa's smile goes stiff. "Captain, what are you playing at?"

Faolan drags his gloved hand along the oar's handle, damp leather creaking against wood. My chest tightens, waiting for him to spill the truth.

"Her family kept the story, and legends don't die. You'll see. Get the lacquer ready."

He pulls us away from the others before they can ask for more, oars cutting through clear water streaked here and there with gore. I wait until we're out of earshot, then nudge his leg with mine.

"What will we tell them?"

"About what?"

He's not looking at me anymore, his expression vague, brows tugged low.

I dig my feet against the hull. "About my grandmother. We can't tell them we're looking for her soulstone or bones."

"And why not?"

"Because—" Because then they'd know what a strange creature I am. Just how dangerous it was to allow me on board. "Because it's too much of a risk. Finding her body could yield nothing—or I could touch her soulstone and truly go mad."

"You're not going to go mad."

"You can't know that."

"Saoirse." He steals my hand, the one bearing his ring, and squeezes tight. "I know it."

My lips part at the rush of sureness I feel. Faolan believes in me. Not in the way I've believed in the gods—begrudging and fearful—but with a pure, raw intent from the very core of his being. I cannot fathom how to respond.

He flashes a smile, and it sears straight into my heart.

"Think of the reward, never the risk."

TWENTY

"Y ou're positive the gills will work properly?"

"Tavin, we've tested them three times now." Faolan winds a long woven cord around my neck, threaded through a set of gills lacquered a vibrant, angry red. It's nearly the same shade as his skin, flushed from the sun's force today.

My stomach draws tight as Tavin examines another set of gills. "Aye, but we could've tested them longer. Waited until tomorrow. The sun's barely cured these."

"The fact we were able to breathe *with* them instead of just holding it all in like the other methods was proof enough for me. Besides, we only need a few minutes, don't we?" Faolan's fingers slip over my throat, adjusting the gills before he knots the cord to keep them in place. "All right, Trouble?"

I try to swallow, then flatten my hands to my stomach instead. "Aye."

Tavin glances toward the railing, a pale blue light flitting across his face. It would almost be beautiful if it wasn't a reminder that dozens of souls likely linger in the depths we're about to swim. "Ríona Kiara wouldn't like it."

"Kiara isn't here. Besides, it's a new moon tonight. If we're going to risk diving waters infested with all those soulstones, now's the time to do it. Spirits go docile in the pure dark. Less likely to affect us."

I battle the urge to touch my tattoo where the skin feels raw, itching, and exposed. Though the crew has been quieter in the spirits' presence, reflective and a touch morose, I've dreamed of my brother and a half dozen deaths I've never seen. The longer we sail the Teeth, the more it feels like walking with a festering wound. "Can I have the sponge?"

It's Brona who passes it to me, gritting her jaw while I dip it into a bucket of water. "You don't have to do this."

Over her shoulder, Faolan's eyes lock onto mine—burning with that same belief I felt before. Seawater trickles down my throat as I press the sponge there, cooling a blush as it fights to rise along my skin. "It's all right."

"No, it's not. He's only pressing you because you haven't learned to say no like the rest of us. Just tell him to piss off and wait until morning, and then we can—"

"I want to, Brona."

Her mouth snaps shut, and any further response dies on my tongue as breathing air becomes painful, the gills knitting with my flesh.

Across from us, Lorcan grimaces as he paints his own gills with the sponge. The largest of the crew, he'll come along in case a board or doorway's fallen to block access to the ship itself. "Feck, that'll take some getting used to."

"So don't get used to it." Brona's tone is short, but a deep crevice lines her forehead as she looks from Lorcan to me, then to the water. "Faolan, this is stupid. It'll be pure dark soon."

"We've hours of light ahead," Faolan says with a quick wave of his hand, sweat dotting his temples and plastering his shirt to his chest. He tears his gaze from mine. "Oona?"

"Here!" The small striker appears, hair caught back in a tight braid and wearing a pair of worn trousers and a single strip of cloth over her breasts. I duck my head immediately, staring at the loose shirt I've already prayed twice over won't turn translucent with the swim. It's not just the tattoo I'm keen to hide. "What exactly are we looking for again?" she asks.

Too many eyes turn on me at once, and I wince as my back meets the railing, every breath raking through my lungs like talons. "I-I'm not sure. Faolan thinks my grandmother might have left a . . ."

I falter, and Brona directs her hard stare at him. "Left a *what*, Captain?"

"You'll see soon enough. That's the adventure of it." Faolan rubs at the bandages on his arm and grins, his eyes a touch too bright as though they've captured the setting sun. "Ready?"

Could someone ever truly be ready to search the sea for their elusive, mad grandmother's bones?

Just her bones. Let her spirit not linger with them.

"Aye."

Lorcan helps me onto the railing, neck stretched so his own gills don't rub against one another. "If something goes wrong down there, Captain, we'll all three be haunting you."

"In shifts," Oona says, grinning from my other side, "so we don't waste the whole of our afterlives chasing round your sorry arse."

Faolan's rough laughter is the last thing I hear before we drop into the sea.

Silence swallows the world in seconds.

I fight the urge to gasp as waves tumble across my skin, sapping every ounce of heat from my body. Silt and small bubbles rush past my vision, interspersed with eerie blue-lilac lights, and I kick hard until a hand wraps my jaw, forcing my mouth open. Water floods my throat and lungs, pools in my belly, then rushes out—working through the gills. They flare at my neck in a thousand pricks of sensation, fluttering with every breath.

I want to rip my own throat out. *Gods.*

Lorcan taps my arm, and I nod in thanks, forcing my focus onto the shipwreck lying just below us.

Most of the wood has rotted away, the deck caving in under a decade's worth of barnacles. The mast juts out above the water, bearing that same outdated flag I'd noticed up on the Tooth, but its twin slithers snakelike from a rusted ring by the captain's door. And that's to say nothing of the wild surrounding it.

I've swum in the ocean since I was small, chasing after my brothers among the waves. But our waters at home are vengeful, the currents changing without prediction. We were told never to cross the first drop, where the water reached our hips. Anything of interest to see lay beyond that forbidden point.

Here, flat, speckled rays with needle-thin tails sail over our heads as a cloud of bright fish takes one shape after another. Kelp steals the final rays of sunlight, glowing bottle green save for the spots of blue, gold, and scarlet—creatures I have no name for living among the silken strands. Even the spirits seem surprisingly at peace here, drifting in and out of focus along the base of the ship.

My grandmother is not among them.

Lorcan jerks his thumb in Oona's direction, and I turn to see she's already halfway past the green field, swimming like she was born of the sea. For all I know, she may have been. It wouldn't surprise me if Faolan's crew included a child of the murúcha.

I follow just beside Lorcan, avoiding his powerful kicks until we reach what's left of the deck, and heat ripples like lightning across my back.

My lungs clench, arms flailing through the water.

A song hums in my ears.

A call . . . a warning?

The magic.

Lorcan swims past, and I grab at his shirt. "Not in there." The words are garbled, round like the bubbles that escape my lips, but they're enough. He casts me a strange look, then holds up a hand for me to wait and swims after Oona, who's already halfway through an opening inside the ship.

Daughter of the . . . knowing sea . . .

I catch hold of the railing until it crumbles beneath my fingers and squeeze my eyes tight against the words. Force one unnatural breath after another through the gills, because that song is not out in the water.

It's inside *me*. Drifting through my mind.

But I can't listen—can't give in. Not here.

Every muscle strains as I fight the curse, pain tearing across every spiral of the tattoo and sinking deeper into flesh and bone. Whatever fight I have, it's not enough.

Unnatural cold floods my veins. Colder than the ocean's kiss or winter's bite. Colder than the Stone King's gaze. It coils around my body from my wrists to my ankles and pulls me down, down, down—

And that's when I see her.

Gráinne.

My grandmother.

Her face is familiar and foreign—a hazy dream of a dream still-born inside my head. She wraps blue-tinted fingers around my ankles as her lips part wide in the silent shriek of death. Yet her eyes are what arrest me: fathomless. Empty.

I'm still searching for a person in them when that whisper of sensation turns to iron at my ankles, pulling me down.

My scream is lost in a stream of bubbles, ears ringing as she drags me into the kelp. It doesn't make sense—ghosts can't *touch* mortals—but she jerks me through the emerald clusters until my elbows scrape against broken shells and coral littering the seafloor.

"Please stop—*please!*" I scrape the sand for anything to hold on to—to strike against her ghost. But just as my fingers close on something long and thin, her grip falls away and the world goes dark and quiet again.

Even the faint song is gone.

Panic creeps higher up my throat, threatening to break free, when a weak ray of light pierces through the silt, illuminating the shape of a skull inches from my face.

I jerk my hand away, and a splintered portion of bone comes with it. When I tip my head back, I can no longer see the ship. The sky is a distant blur, barely lighter than the waters surrounding me. She must have dragged me down a ledge.

My frantic breathing slows as I stare at the bone in my hand, then squint harder, waiting for the debris to calm and the pathetic light to trickle through until I see it. An entire skeleton, brittle with age, nearly grown over by coral so thick, it's as though my grandmother wears a peony gown in her death.

I trace the curve of her skull with a fingertip and shudder when it cleaves in two. The halves drift apart in lazy spirals above the seafloor, revealing—

Her soulstone.

Nestled in a bed of coral framed by the curve of her jaw, it ripples with light and color—pink, silver, lapis, lilac. My fingers form a cage around it before I've made the conscious decision to move. A bluish light glimmers in the water as my grandmother's spirit returns, hovering over her remains—no longer terrifying but longing.

Desperate.

I grind my teeth together.

I can do this. I was *made* to do this.

My back throbs in protest, but I take as deep a breath as I can tolerate and then close my hand, nails dragging through sand until the soulstone rests directly against my palm.

A palm that's puckered and scaled with age. Yellowed nails curve too tight together, veins bulging beneath my wrist. When I force the bent fingers open, it is not a stone in the center, but a ring unlike any I've ever seen.

"Daughter of the knowing sea, gaze sworn long ago to me." The voice is ragged and high—unnerving.

Not mine.

And yet, somehow, it is my body that rocks back and forth, my heart that beats weakly in a rattling, caved-in chest. No longer surrounded by water, but warm, stagnant air smelling of mead and ripe bodies. Sunlight drifts through the mottled glass of a window, past heads bent over pints of ale.

"Captive soul . . . c-captive soul . . ." The rest of the strange words evade me, slipping through my mind like strands of tattered silk. "Captive. I am a captive—the captive, not queen. This is all a dream. This is all a dream."

The ring cuts into my lifeline the tighter I hold it, until blood seeps over the curve and my mind fragments again, a hundred times over. Such pretty pieces they form.

But my little Soulgazer will collect them for me. She will find it. Someday.

"Captive soul, your blood shall free . . ."

I part my fingers and let go, watching as the ring paints a line of blood across the wooden table and lands in the open palm of a sharp-eyed lad with a wolfish grin.

Lost.

It is lost—I am lost.

"The Isle of the Lost."

A blink, and I am my own again.

Saoirse.

But the weight of what I've seen—of what I just *lived*—sinks into my stomach like a fist as I double over and gag on the water that's meant to be my air. It's too thick, and the pain coming from my tattoo's attempt to blot the vision makes me sick. Gráinne's soul-stone grows still in my palm, but I can *feel* her, like her spirit's touching mine.

It's too close—too intimate.

I kick off from the seafloor and swim away as hard as I can. Away from the bones and broken spirit, away from the strongest magic I've ever experienced, away from the darkness until I am swallowed whole by it and can no longer remember which direction to go because the ocean is fathomless and night has fallen and I am *just* one woman.

I feel nothing.

I want nothing.

I am nothing.

My next breath strangles me, and I don't think. I dig my fingers into my throat and claw the gills free—flooding my lungs instantly with water.

TWENTY-ONE

I wake to the splatter of salt ripping from my throat as a firm hand lands between my shoulder blades.

"Easy, easy, now. There's a good lass—dammit, Faolan, we should've waited."

The hand pushes me onto my side once I've stopped retching. I blink hard at the pair of deep brown eyes hovering over my own. It's Lorcan, dripping wet and shaking. Brona stands at his side, half-drenched herself and holding two sets of gills in her fist.

"It's not my fault she went ripping them off halfway through."

"You're lucky he saw the kelp move!" Brona thrusts the gills at Faolan's chest. "If these were properly cured, they wouldn't have sloughed off at a scratch like that."

"Aye, well—" Heavy boots cross the deck, and with another blink, Faolan replaces Brona in front of me. His cheeks hold angry streaks of color, eyes wild and face drawn. He reaches for my face, then stops himself. Curls his hand into a fist. "She's alive. That's something."

"No thanks to you. What the feck has gotten into you, Faolan?! Ever since you decided we needed to find the Isle—"

"Saoirse could have said no. I've given that choice to everyone here—and have I ever broken that vow?" Faolan lurches back on his heels. He does not meet my eyes. "The Isle of Lost Souls is a greater gamble than we've faced before. Than anyone alive has faced. It comes at a higher risk, yes, but a higher reward as well. Aren't you all hungry for it?"

Lorcan's jaw is tight as he kneels by my side, lifting me away from the pool of water I just expelled. He sets me on a blanket tucked beside Oona, who sports a scrape down the side of one arm. Blood trickles down my own throat where I scratched myself, welts and pebbled marks dotted along my limbs.

It's all I can do to stay upright, head swimming with the loss of consciousness and all their words. If I didn't know better, I'd think . . .

Nessa peels my hands from my face, inspecting it with a frown. "Look at the state of you."

"Proper roughed up, isn't she?" Lorcan asks, holding out a skin of freshwater. I try to take it, but my hand trembles too much.

"Still better off than my first dive." Brona appears with a sigh, grabbing the leather skin and holding it to my mouth until I drink. Beyond her, Faolan stands alone, mouth parted as he watches his crew surround me. "I told you that you weren't ready. What were you thinking, taking off into a kelp forest alone?"

I drink until my throat feels less raw. "I was turned around. Couldn't tell which way to swim."

"You would've drowned if not for *that*," Lorcan says, casting an uneasy look over his shoulder to where a scrap of cloth lies open several paces away from anyone else. The soulstone rests at its center, glimmering like a fallen star. "It was caught in your shirt. You're damned lucky it didn't touch your skin or mine—where did you even find it?"

I shy back until my whole weight lands on my elbows, jostling Oona in the process. "I-it's my grandmother's."

Lorcan frowns, the expression so unfamiliar on his face. "How do you—"

"The family crest on her necklace. It was beside her bones." The lie comes too easily. I'm learning fast. "She . . ."

She was cursed. Her spirit trapped in the water, just as I feared. My mouth falls open to tell them how she dragged me into the depths, or the way I felt her mind split down the middle a dozen times over—leaving her reeling, and painful, and *alone*.

So terribly alone.

The world tilts again, and my head threatens to burst as another memory from the vision surfaces. One of a smiling lad with teeth too sharp and eyes too cunning.

A lad who's grown into the man crouching at my feet.

I stare at Faolan where he leans back against the railing, emotions weaving a complicated web at the center of my chest. His face is unrecognizable—flushed and hard-edged, without any of the usual charm. He is the man who kissed my nose earlier because he was proud I'd used the magic at last—the one whose conviction reached my bones when he touched me.

The same one who sounded utterly nonchalant when I was coughing up the sea just moments ago.

She's alive. That's something.

Tears slake my raw throat and settle in a sharp sting behind my eyes.

I'm a fool. A fanciful fool.

"She died here." The words tumble past my lips, rough and far too small. "I thought she might have left me something."

Nessa tucks my blanket tighter, and Brona stares at the soulstone by my side.

I could tell them the truth. That my grandmother was mad when she directed Faolan toward the Isle of Lost Souls because she'd held my grandfather's soulstone when he died. That this entire journey was sparked by a song neither of us remembers. I could tell them about the visions—how Gráinne's soulstone swept me into the past and returned me here, dazed but alive.

I could tell them about the magic.

But then I'd also have to tell them why I kept it a secret in the first place. About Conal, the baby before him, and the tattoo that restrains my power, keeping us all safe but possibly keeping us from the Isle of Lost Souls as well. And then there's the song.

Daughter of the knowing sea . . .

Frustration shivers down my spine. I don't know what I'm meant to feel now, after holding my grandmother's soul in my hand. I don't know what the song means—or how in shade's realm *my* eyes are meant to guide us to the isle when I don't understand how it all works. I don't know what to think of Faolan's attention or dismissal, or the crew's sudden kindness and concern.

But I do know where I can find answers. And at least one of them should lie within my husband's nest.

"Faolan?" My voice is sharp when it comes. "I need to see your hands."

He stiffens. "Why?"

I sit up, pushing the heavy strands of black hair from my eyes as Brona and the others shift away. "I almost drowned. Do I need a better reason?"

His laugh is a hollow version of its usual sound. "No, I don't suppose you do."

Flexing his hand once, Faolan walks forward into the dying

light, shirt clinging to his torso as if he is the one who swam with a ghost. His eyes dart across my skin as he nears me, taking note of every scrape and cut. When he reaches the blanket, he drops into a crouch and offers his hands: one gloved and one bare.

Nine lovely rings rest above his knuckles, beaten of gold or studded with gems shaped beautifully by a master's skill.

None of them are made of bone.

"Where is my grandmother's ring?"

Faolan releases an unsteady breath. "What?"

"Her ring." I search his empty expression, looking for recognition or the hint of a lie. "Golden-white, carved of bone. I think it had a blue jewel in the center?"

He stares, openmouthed, and my own insides draw uncomfortably tight.

"You said she gave it to you. Faolan, I *saw* her—"

"I know!" Faolan's voice is the crack of a whip, and I react to it the same: legs shot to my chest, face turned away. Instantly, he recoils, lips parting as he shoves a hand through his hair. "Feck. I'm sorry." He reaches that same hand toward me, then stops when I press back against the railing. "I'm so sorry, Saoirse."

I shake my head, neck rolling across the wooden bars. "Explain, please."

Faolan looks as though he wishes time were a creature he could charm into turning back. But he doesn't reach for me again.

"I did have her ring. Wore it for years until someone stole it during a bet."

I blink. Try to comprehend. "Someone stole your ring."

"Aye." Faolan wipes the sweat from his forehead with his sleeve. "Remember when I told you how I won these in a card game?" His hand drops to one of the wolf-hilt daggers strapped to his waist. "That ring ended up in the same betting pool."

"But you *won* the game."

He shoots me a half-apologetic smile that twists into a grimace. "Doesn't mean much, playing a crowd like that. The pile grew so bloody big that night, heaped with coin, jewels, and the like, it took days to realize the ring had gone missing at all. And I'd always hated the damn thing, so . . ."

My arms tremble as I fail to push to my feet. "You can't be serious. You're a pirate—no, not just a pirate, the *Wolf.* How did someone manage to steal your ring?!"

Nessa glances at Lorcan and Brona, then clears her throat and hauls the striker up from my side. "Right. Clear out, you lot. Mam and Da are fighting."

Her words are lighthearted, and on any other day the others would laugh. But as Faolan slumps against the railing beside me, all his usual bluster gone, I'm left shaking with a fury I'm too exhausted to hide. The others scatter fast.

"Who has it?"

"One of three especially clever wayfarers—code for pirate, if the company's polite." Faolan kicks at the railing once, squinting at the waves. A muscle spasms at his neck. "There wasn't a damn thing magical about it, you know. I carted that ring around for years, asking the master jewelers on Unbound Earth and Painted Claw to break down its elements and test it for ability. That ring's nothing special."

I bury my face in my hands, bitterly wanting to laugh. "That ring is what's meant to guide us to the island, Faolan. *That's* the piece you've been looking for all this time."

"Well, shite."

My laugh escapes at last, obliterating a path through my skull. "Shite."

"Never thought I'd hear you curse without blushing."

Pain removes the last of my veils. "You usually leave with a perfect, clever word before you can hear anything I say."

He falls quiet. I drop my head back against the railing, eyes trained on the oiled wood mast disappearing into a darkening sky above. "How long before Kiara expects us to find the isle?"

Faolan snorts, the sound hollow. "A month now, give or take a few days." He hesitates, then slides down to sit beside me, careful that our bodies don't brush. For once, I regret it. I'd have liked to hit him earlier, when he blamed me for removing the gills.

As if he can read my mind, though, Faolan twists a ruby-crusted ring around his third finger and releases a shaking sigh. "I really am sorry, Saoirse. You almost drowned, and it was a stupid wager—you learned nothing more than we could've figured out on our own."

I flinch. "Do you think so?"

"Well, sure, you . . ." His gaze rests on my throat, the flesh tender and undoubtedly pink. "You're not serious."

My laugh is quieter now, tapering off as I hug my legs to my chest and look across the deck. The others have gathered beneath a lamp, tension easing with every curl of steam from their bowls. For the first time . . . I want to join them. And I think maybe they'd like me to as well.

"You're becoming a wolf, you know."

I twist round to see Faolan staring at me, eyes glinting like beetle wings in the dark. "What does that mean?"

"It means you'll have a harder time pretending to be a lamb." His teeth flash on a smile. "Though how you ever had anyone convinced of that is beyond me."

"I've never pretended to be a lamb."

"No?" He chuckles. "With all your docile manners and sweet

words. Perhaps I ought to start calling you Mutton Chop as well as Wolf Tamer—"

"Don't you dare!" I catch his hand when he reaches for my eye, laughing in spite of myself as I trap it flat against my cheek. It's like fire against my chilled skin, his pulse running a quick rhythm to match my own. Faolan meets my gaze unflinching, just as he's done from that very first night—looking too close, seeing too much.

My smile fades.

I don't know what I want from this yet. My husband who's not a husband, this body that yearns in a way I still can't understand. Irritation and hurt mingle with hope and desire, and I'm lost in the throes of it all every time Faolan speaks. Saying *just* the right things, which are all so horribly wrong.

He parts his lips, unable to stand the silence for long, and I lean forward on instinct.

Stop myself only a breath away.

Frown.

"What's wrong with your arm?"

"It's nothing."

"Faolan—*gods*." I tug his arm farther into the lamplight, revealing the bite wound that should've stopped bleeding hours ago. Twelve tiny punctures gape in a crescent, golden threads seeping at the edges of every bright red mark.

"I know. It's not ideal, but it'll be fine."

"You can't know that." I try to hold on, but he pulls free of my grip. "You're not a surgeon!"

"Neither are you."

"We need to wash it out. Bandage it, but I should probably—"

"I told you, it's fine. I've dealt with far worse." Faolan shoves to his feet, and I don't miss the way he lurches for the railing above my head. But whatever strength he has, I've only a fraction left. "Let me get us some food and rest, and I'll be just grand. Stop your worrying, Trouble."

He staggers toward the crew and stops. Grins.

"Though it's sweet of you to start now."

TWENTY-TWO

"... wide in the ... broad ... ocean eyes."

Faolan's breath tickles my ear and I try to bat the sensation away, but my arms are pinned to my chest beneath the weight of his hold. I shift, and his sweat-slicked skin slides against mine—bare chest pressed to my back, arms round my torso where my shirt's drawn up, one leg tossed over mine.

My eyes fly open and I glance down at the hand spread out over my ribs just below my breasts, confusion warring with the heat he puts off—gods, is his flesh made of fire?

"Faolan?" I wriggle one arm free and shove his hand off my stomach, twisting in the process. This doesn't make sense. He always falls asleep on his stomach and spends the night tossing while I keep to myself on the opposite side. Not once has he tried to touch me like this on purpose. "What—"

His fingers slide over my lips and I taste salt as he pats my face clumsily, nuzzling my shoulder. "Shh. I'm tryin' to get it right."

He carries on humming for a second and I'm too shocked to do much more than lie beside him, staring hard at the window and the faint light showing through from the sliver of moon, because his finger is tracing my bottom lip in tiny sweeps that I feel through my entire body. Yet the emotions slipping beneath my skin, re-pelled by the caipín baís tattoo, are as wild and impossible to com-prehend as my husband. I'm about to roll off the bed to escape the confusion—or perhaps roll closer—when he lets out a "Ha!" and turns me onto my back himself.

His eyes glitter like sapphires beneath the weight of damp curls, and when he strokes my cheek with the backs of his fingers, some-thing in me falls away.

Faolan's gaze falls to my lips. Stays there. And just when I'm sure he's going to kiss me—when I think I might want him to—he lets out a low chuckle and starts to sing.

"I once met a girl with ocean eyes. She was quite wee, yet broad in the thighs. One kiss from her lips, and surely I'd die. Oh the mighty sweet Saoirse, my bride."

One kiss and he'd die? Sweet?

Broad?

"Faolan, I—" Something glints across his arm. I choke back a scream as I shove him away and scramble out of bed, reaching for the silver box of Bruidin flame. With shaking fingers, I pull one of the dried leaves from Faolan's isle free and crack it in half, spark-ing a flame. I light a lantern in seconds, returning to the bedside to catch his arm and pull it over for a proper look.

The wound on his forearm didn't close. It's worse. So much worse, swollen to twice its usual size and colored an angry red laced with gold the same as the fishes' scales.

"Stars help me—Faolan! Oh gods, you're burning up." I see it now. It's so fecking obvious I want to scream. The flush to his face when they pulled me onto the deck, the strange temper and fever glittering in his eyes. The nonsense song and all those touches. He's not in his right mind—of course he's not.

And neither am I.

Shoving my hair back, I snatch Faolan's green coat from a chair and slip it over my shift. He watches me with a stupid smile on his face, crimson flags raised high in his cheeks.

"Where in shade's realm are you going, love? We were just getting started."

"You're sick, eejit!" The word breaks as I speak it.

And I'd thought he wanted to . . . had I really . . .

My vision blurs as I fling open the door. "Stay there, all right? I-I'll just fetch Lorcan. And the surgeon's chest—thank the gods I didn't listen to you."

"You never do. But that's one of the things I like about you."

I stare at him for two endless moments, then race through the door.

Lorcan's brow furrows so tight as he examines Faolan's arm that I'm convinced the wrinkles will remain forever. "You didn't want to make this easy, did you, Captain?"

"Where's the—fun in that?" Faolan's sitting up now with the wind ruffling his hair, chest rising and falling in rapid bursts. There are no more absurd songs, but there's hardly anything else from him either. The white heather we brewed from the Isle of Frozen Hearth managed to calm his fever enough to return his mind, yet did nothing for his arm. Even willow bark is barely touching the pain.

"Why don't you keep a surgeon?" My voice shakes as I pound calendula and elm bark with a mortar and pestle, the pieces so shriveled I'm not sure they'll be of any use. "For this many people— as *dangerous* as your lives all are—you should have one."

I glance up to see Lorcan biting down on the tip of his tongue, avoiding my gaze. I turn on Faolan.

"Why don't you have one? Or at least a half-decent stock of supplies?"

He appears sheepish for once, no more energy for the show. "We were supposed to visit the northern healers of Frozen Hearth after our last, ah, run-in with trouble. But it's a few days' hike inland, up their mountain pass, so I gave the orders to carry on."

Lorcan twists Faolan's arm lightly in his grip. Scarlet lines radiate from every puncture in the flesh.

"Why?" I ask, the word barely audible. I don't want to hear the answer.

Faolan grimaces when the movement pulls at his broken skin, but he tries for a smile nonetheless.

"I was eager to meet my wife, of course."

Tears flood my eyes as Lorcan grunts, pressing a cloth to the seeping wound. "You just had to dive headfirst into the thick of it, didn't you?" he mutters.

"No other way, was there?" Faolan's laugh rattles when it comes. "Well, until Saoirse found it. Bloody smart, she is." His eyes seek me out, and my jaw clenches tight.

I cannot remember the feel of his kiss. I can't think about his arm around me when I woke.

I can't dwell on what happens if his fever doesn't break.

Lorcan blows a breath between his lips, then drops the infected arm and shakes his head. "I could just cut it off?"

My body seizes at the suggestion just as Faolan snaps back into himself. "Absolutely feckin' not."

"Well, I can't see another way around the gold spreading. Look at it, Captain. It's already near the bend."

Faolan scoffs. "Bollocks on that, it's— Saoirse?"

I'm not a healer. I'd never been to Frozen Hearth before the Damhsa, or trained in medicinal arts. But when I was a girl, Mam would let me go to the kitchens and work the gardens there. An older woman with poor vision taught me how to recognize plants by smell and feel, as well as sight. I never got to say goodbye before I was banished, but I continued my practices in the cottage by the sea.

"You should have a surgeon, Faolan," I say, my voice a low, faraway sound. It carries behind me as I shove a cabinet open and retrieve the bag of fish scales tossed inside. "A real one. This is stupid and—avoidable, and—I don't understand how someone can keep *tapestries* and fifty different coats on their ship but can't employ a single bloody healer?"

Anger is still a forbidden emotion. My fingers shake as I return to the mortar, tipping a handful of scales inside. One firm strike of the pestle, and they resemble the glittering powder streaked on some women's cheeks that first night we met.

"Is that all, love?"

"No." I grind the things further with a roll of my wrist. Ignore the stinging in my eyes.

Lorcan hesitates, then peers over my shoulder. "That's a bit of a risk, using the same thing that—"

"I know." I lock eyes with Faolan and watch something strange pass over his face, there and gone again in an instant. It's a look that's bound to keep me up at night. "Just . . . let me try. Please."

The scales are hardly more than a paste now, but I keep going, just to keep my nerve from breaking. "Do you know how we treat the bites of the adders that fill our caverns on my home isle?" Curls cling to my forehead in sweaty strands. "We grind their fangs into a poultice, to draw out the venom."

Faolan winces, and I wish for the first time in my life that my father were here. Or at least, the mushrooms he's so carefully cultivated. One bite of the cap, and Faolan's pain would vanish.

I glance at Lorcan, then test the texture of my paste with a slow roll of the pestle. The only comfort I have is that not a damn person besides myself has any better ideas. "Is the kelp ready along with the bandages?"

"Just about." Lorcan pulls a strip free from the bucket of salt water drawn an hour ago, and bends it to test the flexibility. "It'll be ready once the paste has set."

"Thank you." I shake my hair out of my eyes and slowly get to my feet, only to sink onto the bed beside Faolan's trembling form. The fever is seeping back into his mind—I can see him slipping away.

"Hold still," I whisper, and scoop the thick gold-blue mixture into my palm, spreading it over his wound. I use every last ounce I can scrape free. Once it's done and the kelp's secured all the way round his arm, we sit in silence and wait.

Wait for nothing, because for once in our entire time together, Faolan is silent and still. A corpse in a colorful tomb.

I jump when Tavin enters, a golden nautilus cradled in one hand. He asks something as he holds it out, but my tongue is too thick to relay Faolan's injuries, hands clumsy and caked in half-dried paste. Lorcan takes the shell, words rolling across his tongue like thunder—I can't concentrate. My gaze dulls, splitting between Tavin as he pours violet-tinged sand into the shell, and Faolan, whose chest rises and falls in shallow waves.

"She shouldn't be here for this."

"You try telling her that, mate."

Tavin locks his jaw as he unfastens a small leather pouch, extracting a single gleaming red hair. It clings to the nautilus's edge as he holds up a final offering: a shard of ice from the Isle of Frozen Hearth, held just below the lantern's flame. One drop inside the shell, and purple steam erupts.

Lorcan drops a hand to my shoulder as I flinch, watching Tavin breathe in the smoke until his lips turn lilac and his eyes roll back. "W-what is he doing?"

"Reporting to Kiara." Lorcan squeezes once. "But you don't have to listen. We could go on deck and—"

"He's going to survive this." My gaze leaps, frantic, from Lorcan's kind eyes to Tavin's closed ones. "Faolan is the Wolf. He can't . . . he *won't* . . ."

Die.

The pity that blooms on Lorcan's brow sets my stomach turning—or maybe it's the smell of that plum-colored smoke. The way our seanchaí measures Faolan's injuries against his vitality on a scale that seems rigged. Outside the window, sunlight teases the horizon toward dawn, but I feel like the world should be darker. Dimmer as Faolan straddles the line between this life and the next.

My body stiffens as Tavin relinquishes his message to the wind: a streak of lavender, and then nothing. Gone. He blinks twice, then turns my way.

"Saoirse—"

"Please leave. Both of you."

I see the fear in their eyes. Their concern. But whether it's for me or Faolan, it doesn't quite matter. If he dies, my father will come for me—or Maccus, or both. Kiara won't protect us. So there's only one solution: Faolan has to live.

I return to the bedside and rake a hand back through the pirate's sweaty curls, biting my lip at the burn of his flesh. But burning is good. Burning means he's *alive*.

As Tavin and Lorcan leave the room, I bend over and press my lips to Faolan's temple. Taste whiskey and salt as I make one more promise, just between us.

"I won't let you die."

TWENTY-THREE

Two sleepless nights pass beneath a pitch-black sky as Faolan's fever and the toxic gold threads recede—but it's painfully slow. An agonizing ritual of packing the wound, grinding more scales, adding boiled water to the dregs of an old bottled elixir, and praying it will revive the mixture enough to work.

I peel back the latest bandage, my poultice cracked along the edges where infection has seeped between the paste and kelp. Twelve open punctures remain.

"Dammit, Faolan."

I massage the pink, puckered skin between my thumbs until each hole weeps a drop of milky fluid mixed with gold. Sweat trickles down my shoulder blades as I repeat the process, over and over, until all they release is blood. And the whole time, I wait for a vision to strike—practically beg for one beneath my breath to prove that he's alive and healing. That he'll return to me soon.

No magic arises. I turn to the mortar and pestle once again.

"You still haven't slept?"

Brona hovers in the doorway, shoulder propped against the wooden frame. Heavy afternoon sunlight streams down the hall behind her, illuminating her skin so she resembles the bronze statue of a small, particularly vengeful god. I must look corpselike by comparison.

"There hasn't been time."

"Right, because Faolan demanded you chain yourself to his bedside should he ever get injured. I forgot that bit of your wedding vows."

"I'm sure he'd argue it was promised between the lines."

She laughs, and I smear a fresh batch of paste over the wounds, my fingers stained yellow with the stuff. It clings to my skin alongside the kelp, reluctant to release me. Reminding me of my grandmother's grip.

A shiver wracks my limbs as I tie a fresh bandage off and lower Faolan's arm to the bed. He doesn't stir, save for the slow rattle of his chest rising with every breath. It's bare and flushed, sprinkled with reddish hair and scars, roped by muscle. I'm certain he'd tease me for looking if he ever woke up.

Please wake up.

"There's a decent breeze tonight." Brona curls her lip as I wipe off my hands. "It would do you some good to breathe air that's not tainted. Eat something—hell, maybe even have a drink."

"It wouldn't be right to leave him like this."

"Because fretting at his bedside is going to keep Faolan's sorry arse alive?"

I drop the cloth—gasping as fear folds me in two.

"Feck. I told them not to send me." Brona curses, swiping it from the ground. "Faolan's not going to die. He's too bloody stubborn for it. And anyway, that's not why Lorcan sent me. He just thought . . ."

"Thought what?" My voice tilts off-kilter, eyes locked on Faolan's chest. Brona releases a hard breath.

"He thought that maybe I could talk sense into you, because

I'm the only one willing to say it. Saoirse, there's no prize for being a martyr."

I whirl on her, my mess of a braid falling to pieces when I do. "A *martyr*?"

She lifts one shoulder, but her eyes aren't dismissive. If I had to guess, the look in them is something like concern. "You don't owe him penance. Faolan was an eejit for jumping into the water, and the fact he got hurt isn't your fault. In fact, it serves him right for being so careless with that dive. But you don't have to feel so guilty—"

"I don't feel guilty, Brona, I'm just—terrified he won't wake up!"

The words catch us both off guard. Her jaw slackens as I sew mine tightly shut, and all the while Faolan lies on the bed in a horrible, unending stillness. Again, I wish for the magic's terrifying, reassuring tug.

"I thought you didn't like him much."

A laugh burbles up from my chest. "I don't. He annoys me like no one I've ever known."

"Then why—"

"Why did I marry him?" *Don't say it.* The warning clangs in my head like a funeral bell, but exhaustion and fear pull at me like the tide. "I used to dream of the Wolf of the Wild. Back when I was small enough to crave stories about a boy barely four years older than me. My favorite was the tale with the murúch, even though everyone says it's impossible for a person to be half fish."

She drops onto the edge of the bed. "You were one of those girls, were you?"

"Aye." I can't bring myself to try to deny it. Not when tears pool at the corners of my eyes. "I dreamed of Faolan like I dreamed of growing wings. He was flight and freedom—the sort of person I could never be. And all my life, I wanted nothing more than to become one of *you*."

Brona's silent as I swipe at my cheeks, regretting every unfettered word that slips out.

"But I wasn't stupid enough to think it would ever happen. Not until the Damhsa, when I learned about your search for the Isle of Lost Souls and—*gods*, Brona, I'm not a martyr. Not even close. I—" The tattoo stings as my emotions swell, blanketing the magic with ice. "I . . ."

I can't tell her. She *can't* know yet—none of them can.

Not until Faolan wakes up.

Loathing pours through my veins in a rush, and my entire face crumples as it turns on me as well. I start to bury it in my hands until Brona captures my wrists, jerking me to my feet without warning.

"You're an idiot for marrying your hero." For a split second, I think Brona will embrace me. Might even want her to? Instead, she grabs the cloth and swipes it at my fingers, the edge of my jaw where some of the paste found a home. "And I wish you weren't a fecking royal, because if Faolan dies, we'll all pay for him taking you on."

"I'm sorry." They're the only honest words I can give. "I'm so sorry."

Brona stops her sharp movements long enough to meet my gaze full-on, one thick brow arched high. "Would you choose different, if you could?"

Everything in me wants to nod and swear I'd have chosen to be selfless, heroic, and kind. That I should have locked myself away along with the magic and spared everyone the risk of taking me on.

But I can't. And Brona knows it.

"Then save your apologies, and come on deck." She gives me a light shove toward the door, and I steal one more glance at

Faolan's face, as placid as the sea at dawn. "Besides, if anything will inspire the bastard to wake up, it's that. He hates missing out."

The deck is pure chaos as Lorcan, Tavin, and Nessa toss dice and coins in a circle while others of the crew work a cork from a small barrel, peppering the air with a scent of whiskey and aged wood. A roar of laughter emerges from the game, Nessa slipping a coin from her pocket to toss among the rest.

I stop at the entry, transfixed by the sight. "How can they all be so calm? Faolan is *dying*."

Brona sighs and taps my arm until I move again. "They're not. This is just how we deal with it. Look."

I do, and it's only then I see the shadows beneath their eyes, the lines in Tavin's brow. Nessa laughs again, but it's too bright, false-bottomed and ready to cave in at any second. "Oh."

Brona nods and whistles as we get closer, sharp and high. Every one of their eyes falls on us.

"Oi!" She scowls. "What are you playing at? Drinking and gambling on the job—you lot are a disgrace."

Lorcan looks at her like she's just spoken the sweetest poetry he's ever heard, but Nessa only snorts.

"If we cared about decency, we'd be working on a different ship. Shall I deal you in?"

"Not yet. Lorcan? I need you."

He clambers to his feet at once, towering over us all—catching hold of the nearest rope when he does as the warmest smile spreads on his face. "Anything. Is it to do with the captain?"

Brona shakes her head, jostling my arm with her elbow. "His wife."

I fight the urge to shrink back, tugging Faolan's coat closer instead. I've worn it since his fever started, and haven't had a good enough reason to take it off. "Brona, what are you doing?"

She smirks at last, full lips twitching as she walks forward to hook a hand in Lorcan's collar and tug his face down to hers. My stomach flutters as I see his eyes drop to her mouth—and I tell myself to look away. But Brona only plucks his laces loose enough to drift apart, revealing the woad tattoo of a wolf below his left collarbone.

I gape at the marking as Brona releases her grip and then turns around to lift her own shirt so I can see a different wolf curved along her right shoulder blade. Tavin tucks his cards neatly into a line, coughing once. "Should we be—"

Nessa's grin is pure cheek as she flicks his sleek black hair to one side, unveiling a wolf at the back of his neck.

"Odd moment to initiate the captain's wife, isn't it?" Nessa rolls onto her side where she sits and tugs her trousers down to show a fourth wolf curled playfully over her round hip. "But I guess it's about time."

"What are you . . ." It's a stupid question. The wrong one. I shake my head, skin prickling all over. "Did Faolan make you get those?"

All four of them laugh, Nessa's a full-bodied cackle as she reaches over to snatch one of the wooden cups poured out by Oona at the barrel. "Aye, and then he demanded we match our wardrobe to his every day, and wear pink ribbons in our hair—gods, can you even imagine him trying?"

"Yes. Easily." Brona tucks her shirt back into place, then turns on me. I'm learning her expressions better with each passing day. Her brow is often furrowed, lips naturally pursed in suspicion or a scowl. But there's light in her eyes—a depth that's rare and inviting, if guarded most of the time.

They regard me openly now. "You said you wanted to be a wolf. Did you mean it?"

My breath falters. Heart thrumming hard in my chest.

"Yes."

Brona smiles. "Then, Lorcan?" He hasn't moved since she touched him, thumb tracing a ridge in the rope just above her head. She taps his knuckles once, and my stomach flips at the way his smile warms. "Get your needles and woad."

"Aye, Captain," he murmurs, winking before pushing off across the deck, steps straight in spite of the empty bottle at the center of their game circle.

Brona passes it by to snatch up another cup from Oona with a thanks and bring it over to me. "You'll be wanting some of this."

My hand fumbles the carved bit of wood, liquid amber splashing across my skirt. "It—thins the blood."

"Aye, but it helps with the pain."

Laughing, she takes up her own drink as I stare into mine, muscles locked at the memory of my other tattoo. The apothecary's cold hands. Pain searing my flesh to the point of seizure. I didn't want that mark on my back—didn't ask them to cut into my flesh. Even weeks later, it still burns if I'm not careful how I lie down at night.

My neck prickles, and I glance up to find Tavin's eyes on me.

He is quieter than the rest. Less prone to humor, far more patient and particular with his words. He hasn't sought me out like Lorcan or Nessa, and we've had no quarrel like I did with Brona before. Yet I've noticed that when Tavin speaks, the others listen. "You don't have to do it, Saoirse."

I tighten my grip on the wooden cup. "And if I want to?"

Tavin hesitates, glancing across the deck where Lorcan prepares a carved wooden box of bone needles, Brona seated beside him to crush the woad into paste. Something like pain crosses his face. Yearning too. "There's no going back. Once a wolf, always a wolf."

I stare into his eyes. Think of Faolan's words, the night before his fever raged.

You're becoming a wolf, you know.

The whiskey burns on its way down.

"I don't want to go back."

TWENTY-FOUR

Morning light streams through the patchwork of soft yellow wool threaded between my hands, warming the web to a shade near honeycomb. The skein of yarn tumbles slowly between my legs as a strand passes from one bronze needle to the other in endless patterns, dancing over the wolf now laid over my veins.

She is a pretty thing, crafted of delicate blue patterns and intricate paths that flow from one part of her body to the next. If I bend my wrist, her nose scrunches like she's caught a scent. A tilt of my arm, and she's all long, languid lines—yet there is power in her stillness. I can't help smiling at the sight.

Until twelve loops of yarn escape my needles, and I have to chase them all down. The craft is a pitiful distraction, but a necessary one.

When I returned to the cabin last night, half-drunk on my initiation to the wolves, it was to find Faolan rolled onto his side, his fever broken at last. But try as we might, no one could wake him. I wore a path into the rug for three hours after the others left and resorted to knitting on a trunk in the corner just after dark.

My needles clatter together as a stitch again slips its place, sending the scarf sprawling over my apparently broad thighs—a cruel reminder all over again of that stupid ditty he sang. I glare at the gaping holes where other stitches have dropped, then try to hunt this one back out from the mire.

Faolan had better live long enough for me to find out what he meant by it.

One kiss from her lips . . .

"My. Don't you look the wee domestic."

I nearly drop my needles altogether, a cry lodged in my throat. Faolan is watching me with a faint flush and his old half smile, propped against the pillows where he'd lain supine before. His beard is unkempt, his hair sticking up at odd angles where I brushed a comb through it last night. But he's talking.

Alive.

"Don't tell me you're making yourself another pair of socks, as if the twenty in your luggage weren't enough." A tremor wracks his arms as he pushes himself further upright. I want to help—to weep—but it's like he's punched me clean of breath with one look.

"Or is it something naughtier? A fake beard to run away with— though yellow's an odd choice." Faolan squints at me. Tilts his head. "You could pass for a man with a proper hat and coat, though, I'd wager. Except you'd have to bind your . . . Are you all right, lass?"

My mouth drops open as all that panic coiled tight inside me unfurls into a wave of rage. I snap my arm up, sending the scarf and needles flying at his head. A hot thrill rushes through me when he yelps as it hits his eye.

"I was making a scarf for *you*, you arse! Autumn is coming, the nights will get cool, and—you have no idea what it's been like!" I shove myself free from the trunk, making for the door, but Faolan catches my wrist as I pass by the bed.

"Wait. I didn't mean—"

I push his grip free and am nearly to the door when his voice stops me in my tracks.

"I've smuggled myself in a dress before. Stuffed the bodice, shaved my jaw, passed as a woman. Twice, actually. And then I kept the skirt because it's bloody fun to wear."

The image his words paint is so clear, I find myself twisting to see his face—see if this is the truth or another fabrication. But his eyes are serious as he watches me, cheeks hollow in the early dawn.

"What does that have to do with—?"

"Because I wasn't insulting you when I said you could pass as a man. It's a damn clever idea, and dead useful. Believe me." Faolan looks me over, then stares down at the scarf for a long moment before he clears his throat. "How long was I . . ."

"Three days this morning." My back meets the door and I hold myself hard as all that fury shifts inside me like late-winter wind. An ache starts in the back of my throat. I can't play with him now, or hear another stupid comment about this scarf—not when I've spent hours staring at his chest to make sure it moved. "I didn't know if you'd wake."

"You?"

I wince. "We. The crew."

A pause. "I see."

The bedclothes rustle, the ropes beneath creaking, and I look up only to gasp when I see he's trying to draw his legs over the side to stand. I lurch forward, pushing him back into place. "Stop that! You're too weak."

"Aye," he grunts, panting beneath my palms. "But if the crew's out there wringing their hands, I figure it's best to put them out of their misery."

My braid hits his collarbone as I shake my head. "I'll go tell them. You just—"

"Especially since the crew's worked itself to the bone, keeping me alive—bathing me, as well." Faolan sniffs the air once and I stop, one knee pressed into the mattress. His mouth twitches, betraying a smile. "Oats and sea aster. Isn't that a soap you favor?"

I shove myself back from the bed. "You think you're so clever—"

"I don't. Not where you're concerned, anyway." Faolan takes up the discarded wool from where I left it, nuzzling it once against his cheek. His smirk has already shifted to something softer, a strange look in his eyes as they track me through the room. "Were you really scared for me, Trouble?"

Tears blur my vision as I sag against the door, telling myself to reach for the handle. Leave before he can affect me more. "Don't."

"Saoirse—"

"Don't tease me now. Please, I can't—"

My voice breaks, and his gaze dips briefly over my body. Snags on the new tattoo at my wrist. Faolan takes a breath and holds it for three long seconds before beckoning to me with one hand. The scarf lies limp in the other. "I'm not teasing, lass. And I'm not dying—at least not anymore. Come over and see for yourself."

Agony blooms as I take in the sight of the Wolf holding my pitiful scarf. I shake my head.

His eyes narrow, lips quirking up. "Saoirse. Come here."

"Stop that."

My command lacks bite.

Faolan's smile returns, ripe and infuriating across his face. "Stop what?" He leans against the pillows, draping the scarf over his chest. "I thought you vowed to obey, wife."

It's that word that draws me back across the room, flushed and furious as I reach for the scarf.

"Stop pretending like this is anything more than it is! I think—" *Breathe.* "I think you use that same growling tone to charm every woman from every island. And I think you're still delirious from fever, and—I just can't do it, all right? For three days, I believed you were going to die, and— Let go of it, would you?"

I tug on the scarf, but his grip tightens. Before I can blink, he holds it high over his head in such a childish move that my panic all but vanishes, a candle blown out. "No. You said it's mine."

"I did not, I— Give it back, all right? This is so— Faolan!" I reach for it, but when he shifts away at the last second, my attempt turns into a mad swipe.

"It's soft, and I like it. It'll be a reminder of my wife's affection to wear for all my days and—oi!"

I reach too far and tumble headfirst onto the bed.

"Feck. I'm sorry." I try to pull back, but Faolan's arm locks around my waist like it did during the storm. When he sits up this time, he takes me with him. My legs curl on either side of his thighs, hands tangled in needles and wool where he dangles it above our heads. His eyes lock on mine, and I swear I'm drowning in blue.

I'm not sure who lets go of the scarf first, but it drops to the bed with a soft clatter.

My hands spread across his chest as he cups my cheek, skin interrupted by leather where it wraps round his palm. It's the one part of him that's consistent—a barrier between himself and the world, one I couldn't bring myself to remove when I bathed him. I part my lips to say his name—say anything that will make sense of the sudden stillness between us—when his gaze drops to them.

My mouth goes dry.

It's not fear. I know that now.

But I should be afraid, seeing the way his eyes darken the longer he looks. Feeling the pulse of longing—of heat—slip past the tattoo's guard on my back. I should want to shrink my body into itself rather than unfold, drenched in a warmth that feels like pure sunlight.

One kiss from her lips, and surely I'd die.

Just one kiss. Perhaps the only real one I'll ever get.

His nose brushes mine, and my breath all but stops. I almost want it to. Would it be so bad to die in this moment and stay here, where I am finally wanted?

But no, it was just a brush—he's not going to kiss me. He's going to pull back and say something awful, and I'll cry, and—

He nuzzles again, fingers sliding from my cheek to my jaw, and I understand in a dizzying rush that it's not a rejection.

It's a request.

Longing unfurls in my chest, as acute and urgent as the first night we met. One single, shaky nod is all that I can manage before Faolan gathers me close and presses his lips to mine.

It is achingly soft, Faolan's kiss, seeping warmth into my bones as though I were drinking honey. He must sense this new sweetness, because his tongue slips free to trace over my bottom lip. I melt against him.

It's not so soft now. His thumb strokes the frantic pulse at my throat, and I part my lips on instinct, tasting him just as he does me. His fingers slide into my hair, and when a whimper passes from my lips to his, those hands become fists.

I am made of pure sensation. Nails that skate across his shoulders, lips that part and press more willingly every second. A body that jerks hard against his when he bites down on my bottom lip. It's overwhelming. Delicious. Even my wildest dreams could not paint such a picture as *this*.

"Faolan, I—"

His hips roll in a singular wave with mine, and I cry out as a sweet, sharp ache settles directly between my thighs. But when my grip falls to his arms, he jerks back on a soft swear.

It's as though someone's doused me with cold water. "Oh gods. You're still hurt. I'm sorry, I—"

"Saoirse, look at me."

I do. Faolan's skin is stained red, eyes glittering like the fever's returned full force. But his fingertips are just warm where they slide down my throat—not burning or clammy. They sweep a delicate circle just over my pulse, and I can't control the way my body arches in response. My sigh as his mouth replaces that touch. It's as though every ounce of worry of the last three days has been compiled into tinder, ready to burn with the barest spark.

"If you think," he murmurs against my collarbone, "I'd rather be convalescing than sitting right *here*." His other hand falls to the small of my back, dragging my hips roughly against his own. "You've lost your damn mind."

I laugh even as my head spins and body shakes in a way that's foreign to me. I clutch his shoulders, burying my face there.

"You're still injured."

"Aye, my arm's fecked. But there's nothing wrong with my mouth." Faolan nuzzles the tender curve below my jaw. Tugs loose the top laces of my gown. "Or my hands."

His smallest finger dips below my shift in such a tender exploration, a lump forms in my throat. Can I truly have this? Am I allowed to want this much?

No. He's not mine, and I'm not his—not really. But when his tongue dips in the hollow of my throat, it's easy to forget. I rock without prompting, hating myself a little for giving in to the fantasy and fevered dreams. Desperate to understand how they might end. "We're not—really married."

Faolan stops, one hand half-buried beneath my shift, the other wrapped around my thigh.

"Saoirse?"

Touch is a thing life has starved me of. I tremble against the urge to lean into it—*try* to remember that he's just a story. A ravenous man's imaginary feast.

One taste could never be enough.

"Saoirse."

I drop my forehead to the Wolf's and breathe in deep, hands fisted in his shirt. "It's only pretend."

"That's all life is." Faolan's hand flexes once at my thigh, his leather glove the only barrier between us. My leg stiffens, toes curled in the sheet. I feel his smile against my skin. "I could show you. If you'll let me." The fabric of my shift gathers in tight little furrows as he slides that fingertip along the heavy curve of my breast. Stopping at center's edge.

"Please—" I start, but I don't know how to finish. Don't know how to ask for *this*.

As if he knows it, Faolan draws back just enough to see my face. Waits until I can meet his heavy gaze. "I meant what I said that first night. No child, no risks. I won't ask for more than you're willing to give—and if you want me to stop right now, I will and we'll speak no more of it."

Faolan's touch slides up my spine and into my hair, combing through the knots he left there. He strokes until it lies smooth again, my throat closing tight because it's been years since someone offered me affection that didn't demand a price. "But . . . you're curious. And I'm starting to catch on that you might not even know what for."

His lips press to my forehead. I hope he doesn't hear my breath catch. "Let me show you pleasure, love."

"I . . ."

The hand on my thigh slides higher. Thumb rolling over dimpled flesh.

Desire explodes within me—mine or his, it doesn't fecking matter. *That* is real, and it's what I hold on to as the last of my resolve crumbles to dust.

"Yes—"

Faolan groans as his mouth moves again, nudging the fabric of my shift aside just as his hand slips fully between my legs.

His sharp intake of breath is a near-perfect match to mine. And perhaps I should feel ashamed at the slick caress of his fingers, or the way they coax my entire body to rock and moan like the ship facing a storm. But I don't. I can't anymore. Instead I hold on to Faolan's shoulders—and when that is not enough, I seek his lips again and knot my fingers in his hair.

I don't know if he's pleased with my reactions, or if I should be quieter—prettier and sweeter, more controlled. His hands sculpt my body into something new, and that understanding of it strikes a bittersweet note in our heady song. It's never been a thing I could trust before. Never felt so pure as it does now.

When my body seizes, jerking with a sweet sort of violence, I balk.

"Don't fight it, love. Let go."

Faolan croons my name as I bite down on his own, pleasure tearing through me like thunder splitting a cliffside with bursts of silver light. That same summer fire that used to break from the sky dances through my blood until I'm gasping and spent, my forehead dropped against his.

It's only *after* the world stops tilting that I hear him say thank you.

"Thank you?" I'm still blinking the stars from my vision as he fixes the laces of my gown, skirts already smoothed back into place. "For what?"

"For everything. The scarf, the gills, the hint about the ring. Worrying whether I'll make it, nursing me back to health." His eyes darken, but this time, no butterflies flood my stomach.

It sours instead.

"That's what this was. A thank-you."

Not because he wanted me. Because he felt he owed me.

I slide free from his lap before he can stop me, gaze on the ground, my cheeks full of fire. I don't dare meet his eyes again. I wouldn't survive whatever is written there. "I'll send someone with dinner. And Lorcan, to check on your wound."

Gods, I never even looked beneath the bandage when he woke.

"Saoirse?"

I've slipped out the door before he's finished saying my name.

TWENTY-FIVE

The news of Faolan's recovery sweeps the deck like a gust of fresh air. Tavin immediately slips below to check on him as Nessa claps me on the back and shoves a plate of food into my hands with a wink. Mercifully, she doesn't mention my rumpled dress or swollen lips. In less than an hour, the atmosphere's what it was before he was injured—all of them eating and swapping tales from home as the sky lightens above.

I can't understand why it's the stories that weigh heaviest in my stomach.

"You think your da was harsh? Mine had us up at the arsecrack of dawn, doing forms before sunrise. The man was obsessed."

"Not so bad as mine. He made us swim the loch behind our house every bloody morning—even in winter. Had to break through chunks of ice just to get inside. Can you imagine?"

"I can, considering the size of your bits."

Laughter ripples around me, but all I can do is stare at the fish bones on my plate and prod them into new patterns with a finger. Tavin sits across the deck, a fresh pile of coins cast between himself, Nessa, and Oona as they gamble with slats of carved bone. Lorcan rests against the railing nearest me, one foot kicked back to balance as he weaves intricate braids into Brona's hair. Faolan would typically perch on the center barrel, a part of every conversation and yet always an island of his own.

I stare at the empty spot. Thumb the wolf ring where it glints beneath my knuckle.

"See, that's where you lot all got it wrong," Lorcan says, tipping a wink to me over Brona's head as he threads one slender braid through another. "Having a father at all. You *should* have tried growing up in a brothel—I'm telling you, it's the only way!"

Brona snorts as he bends a slim cap of metal around the pattern, locking it in place. "Right, we'll just slip back in time and warn our younger selves, shall we?"

"Aye," Lorcan says, fingertip lingering on the line of her jaw. I force a smile and tear my gaze away. "Only it's best to warn them they'll not get anything past the girls there. Mams, aunts, and nosy birds as far as the eye can see. Once, when I was small—"

"Were you ever small?" Nessa asks, kicking one leg over the other as she lounges back against Tavin's side.

Lorcan groans. "When I was small*er* . . ."

I don't understand stories like theirs, where cheek is answered with a laugh instead of a strike. Tales where the parents tousle the daughter's curls in a mock fight, guide the son's bow arm higher until the target is just in line, grin with delight as their little hero charges into life without hesitation. Lorcan, Tavin, Nessa—there is a warmth to all their voices.

Like they've never questioned if they were loved.

I used to think being quiet and small was enough to earn my parents' affection. That so long as I followed their rules, prayed to their gods, eventually they might love me. I thought it was my own fault Da looked through me any time I spoke—or worse, the times when he didn't look at all.

A fresh wave of laughter breaks through until Lorcan throws his head back with a huge smile. "And don't get me started on my mother!"

Mother. The word calls forth frantic swipes of a dry hand to my clothes until they hung looser, adjusting my hair so it covered my eyes. She was so hollow, even when I was young. Once, when I was a wee laughing creature performing some bizarre dance to Aidan's practice on the lute, she shook her head at me and said I'd stolen half her joy the moment I left her womb.

Guilt still pulses through me at the memory.

But I was only a child. Wasn't I?

So were Conal and Aidan.

An unfamiliar emotion bleeds into the usual pain—ugly, and unfair to feel alongside all my grief. Yet the name arises far too easily from the shadowed corners of my mind: resentment.

I resent my brothers. And my parents, for favoring them over me. I resent my father's "protection" and my mother's submission, and every *single* reminder of how unloved I was. How little they trusted me, and how much I owed them for keeping me alive.

My jaw aches until I release it, setting the bowl of fishbones to the side. It does nothing to stop the pounding in my head, left from Faolan's touch and the tattoo's attempts to block whatever it was he felt.

Thank you.

Another resentment.

Nessa's cackle is sharp enough to draw my full focus, her face flushed a deep red thanks to the celebratory drinks passed around once I'd announced Faolan was awake. "Right—here's the best damn advice I ever got. My mother, holiest o' creatures that she was, said the only man worth keeping is the one willing to go on his knees and worship you proper! Words to live by."

Worship? The entire crew erupts into howls, and I snap my mouth shut, knowing whatever I was about to ask would only incite more. The men swap knowing looks and even Brona's eyes glint as she smiles.

Irritation swallows whatever confusion and frustration are left.

They're all so familiar with this world I've barely explored, their bodies safe havens for their own hands and others to explore. It's a world I've spent a lifetime denying myself, only to experience the smallest taste of it a few scant hours ago. My legs still tremble when I think about it.

I *try* not to think about it.

"Oi, what's this about mothers?" As if summoned by the mere memory, Faolan leans against the doorway that leads belowdecks. He's paler than I've ever seen him, but grinning just the same. "'Cause I've a fair number of stories from me own. A healer she was, born to the guardians of the Spring of Leigheas. If she were still alive, she'd do a right sight better job tending to my poor arm than a certain glorified carpenter."

Lorcan sits up at once on the railing, letting Brona's dark braids slip through his fingers where he'd been gathering them to tie in a high knot. "It was your wife who fixed up your arm, you scut."

I nearly melt myself into the shadows, certain what we did is written all over my face.

But Faolan's eyes find me without delay. He blinks, bewildered, then grins. "O' course it was. You know what else wives are bloody good for? Keeping a man warm—would you just look at this wee beauty?"

To my horror, Faolan pulls the unfinished scarf from his pocket as if he'd waited for exactly the right moment and wraps it around his neck. It's too short by at least an arm's length, and the ends hang in long, uneven strands.

Brona's dry voice cuts the silence. "You look ridiculous, Faolan. It's all coming undone there at the ends."

"Shut your damn mouth about my wife's work—it's feckin' gorgeous." Faolan lifts the end of it, studies the way the stitches are already coming undone, and then catches every strand, knotting one after the other until it's bound together again.

Stars.

A stubborn pang of affection sweeps through me, nesting in my heart where it has no right to lie. His eyes meet mine again, and I swear I'm about to—

A bell clangs from the crow's nest above, and like the sudden shift of wind before a storm, every smile drops. The lookout waves a scrap of red fabric, and all the hazy warmth that had settled in my heart drains away at once.

Red means bloodshed.

"Brona, where are we?" Faolan's voice is crisp, lacking any hint of its usual charm as he searches the horizon for what they've spotted, but the air is thick with fog. His fingers run an incessant rhythm along the railing.

"Just past the Isle of Unbound Earth."

"Shite." I'm not sure who's said it, myself or Faolan, but when our eyes lock I know we're thinking the same thing. Rí Maccus is not a man of mercy, and Kiara must have failed to soothe his wounded pride. I reach on instinct for my amulet and charms and find nothing but my own bare skin.

Brona looks between us sharply, her lip curled back. "You said Kiara would take care of it! We've never had a problem sailing through their waters before, and you were out like a light. Summer storms are coming, and we'd have been crushed by the Teeth if we'd stayed—I had to make a call."

Faolan's jaw is tight, but he nods. "Understood. Tavin!"

The quartermaster is halfway across the deck when a drum starts up across the choppy waves, vibrating through the air into our very bones. The slide of metal chases the sound, and I glance over my shoulder to see that nearly every member of the crew has drawn a weapon, their eyes fixed on the fog past the bow. They're preparing for a battle.

I am already sick with guilt.

The drums pound through the boards of the ship and rattle my teeth, growing closer together into a near-continuous bellow all around us. Rolling, one note on top of the other, like thunder-clouds cut by lightning.

Until it stops.

For the span of a single breath, I can pretend I haven't risked the life of every single person onboard.

Then the fog births a ship, as sleek and silver as the end of a blade.

The crew leap into frenzied action as Tavin barks orders and Faolan curses a blue streak, jumping down from the upper deck to head back for his cabin. Nessa beats him to it. She has his sword in hand and is strapping it firmly around his waist as Faolan tests his injured arm, bending it back and forth and wincing with each movement.

"You can't fight, can you?"

I nearly leap out of my skin at Brona's words, air rushing into my lungs in a way that makes me wonder if I've ever truly breathed at all. "No."

"Right." Brona glances over her shoulder at the fast-approaching ship, then ducks down to pull a dagger free from its sheath at her ankle. "Take this and hold the handle tight so you don't drop it."

She presses it into my hand until my fingers curl over the leather-wrapped handle. It's heavier than expected, but I suppose that's the point—heavy enough to sink through flesh and bone. My stomach turns.

Brona snaps her fingers in front of my nose. "Go for the groin, gut, below the arms, or throat. All that fails? Shove your fingers in their eyes and pray they don't return the favor."

The images painted across my mind will haunt me forever, but already I'm nodding along, my feet taking me backward until a gloved hand drops to my shoulder, too familiar to startle me now.

"To my cabin, Saoirse." Faolan strokes my cheek with the back of his finger. My breath hitches and does not release. "Latch the door, bar it with a chest if you must—and for feck's sake don't re-arrange things again." The smile in Faolan's voice is jarring against the flurry around us, but as I face him the sight grounds me to the deck.

"I-I'm sorry. I didn't mean for this to happen."

"Hush. Maccus has had it in for me for years. This was just bad timing." Faolan tips his head to the side, and then with a cheeky smile, he unwinds the scarf and wraps it around my neck, tying it lightly in front. "Keep this safe for me, would you? I'd hate to get blood all over it."

I stare at him, one hand weighted down by the dagger, the other tangled up in soft wool. It's as though my entire world tilts before he catches the back of my neck and kisses my brow.

"Go on." With a final sweep of his hand down my back, he's gone.

I waste no more time in getting below.

TWENTY-SIX

I hardly recognize the woman reflected in the oval of polished bronze. Her hair is dark and tangled, save for the long fringe that barely conceals a face pale with fear. She's wearing a dress, but her body holds it different beneath—filling the fabric in paths shaped by someone else's hands. A dagger rests in one of her own.

I blink, and her eyes change color. Haunted and deep, shifting between shades of blue, green, gray, brown. My skin pulls taut with the tattoo's restraint, stretched beneath threads of cold so intense they burn. The curse, which was already drawn from its hiding place by Faolan's touches before, sings across my skin in response to the atmosphere above.

The magic, like me, wants to be set free.

Feet pound the boards above my head, and I tear my gaze from the mirror. Watch the cracks overhead for the sign of dripping blood. How soon until the dying starts? Until I hear the screams of those I've traveled with for weeks? My breath trembles as it pours free, fogging the flat of the blade in my hand. I nearly fling it across the room.

Stars above—I'm not a fighter.

Don't fight it, love. Let go.

The words resonate through me so suddenly, I fumble the dagger and have to scramble back as it sinks into the ground.

Humming. The air is humming. I'd thought it was the tension of the fight, but as metal sings through the wood above my head, I *know* it's an otherworldly sound. Vibrating at my temples. Sliding unnaturally across my jaw.

Pain radiates from the caipín baís tattoo as I snatch my dagger from the ground.

"What do you want?!"

No response comes. And I'm sick of it.

"I didn't ask for this power!" My voice rises, holding more bite than I've ever allowed before as I whirl around—stupid and pointless, like the god who cursed me might be looming behind Faolan's bed. A sob fights with a scream in my throat as my skull tightens. Gods, I've never hated myself more.

"I've never wanted it. I can't use it for anything good. So why—"

The pain brings me to my knees. Blurring my vision, plucking the breath from my very lungs. A cry is not enough to release the pressure behind my eyes—though I dig the heel of my hand against them. Something flashes across my eyelids. Bright. Horrific. I don't want to see.

"Please—please make it stop!"

Let. Go.

A garbled cry echoes overhead followed by a heavy thud, and I curl into myself as tight as I can.

"Please!"

It was foolish to think I possess even the slightest control over my magic. It crackles beneath my skin until my heart races, and it's all I can do not to claw at my clothes and throw myself out the window. My body wants to run—to fling itself against the wind and escape everything above and below. I bind the impulse the best I can, so focused on fighting myself that I don't notice the pounding of wood has shifted from the ceiling to the door.

Not until the latch splinters and the door crashes open, my magic breaking free with it.

"Feck."

I'm on my feet and darting around Faolan's desk before the man can grab me, but his hand still brushes my skin. Visions of scarlet and black flesh race across my eyes. He stops at the end of the desk—as broad as Lorcan but blond, half his face streaked liberally with silver dust. As I trip on Faolan's discarded scarf, he grins.

"There you are."

We move at the same time. I'm fast, but his reach is long. He catches my arm just as I clear the corner of Faolan's desk, dragging me over the wooden top until I'm sprawled on the ground before him. My shirt catches on the corner, tearing down the back.

"Please—" He has me by the hair and I scream, writhing against his hold before instincts kick in and I curl into myself as before. A stupid decision. If I close my eyes, hold on to myself, the evil will retreat into the shadows, won't it?

He hoists me up like a sack of grain.

This is how I die. Not drowning by a storm or at my father's hands, not looking for a lost isle, but laid before the king I spurned trying to take charge of my own life. My fingers tighten around the dagger and—

The dagger.

I wrench my wrist free and swipe, splitting his arm open from wrist to elbow. Blood sprays the ground seconds before I meet it as he drops me. My shoulder and hip hit the wood first and I gasp, fingers flying apart, sending the dagger skittering across the ground.

"No!" I roll onto my knees and am halfway to my feet, searching for the glint of the blade, when he catches my ankle, throwing me onto my back. Stars swim across my vision, but I kick until something crunches. Scramble on hands and knees toward the door.

Get to the deck. To Faolan.

I've not crawled two paces when the man jerks me onto my feet and strikes me across the face. Twice.

The shock throws me back against the desk, where I latch on to the edge, choking on air. His own breaths are ragged at my back, so close my skin crawls to get away.

"Try anything else, little princess, and I'll return you to Maccus in pieces."

Leather bites into my wrists as he attempts to bind them, yet as he presses me into the desk, I catch the glint of metal at last. Not the dagger, but a wee silver box engraved with whorls of smoke and seven-pointed leaves.

Bruidin flame.

I lurch forward, breaking his grip just long enough to flick the lid free and take every leaf in hand. One hard twist has me facing him, and though my wrist screams in protest against the bindings, it's nothing to what I'm about to feel. My jaw clenches tight as I shove my hand over the man's eyes and curl it into a fist, breaking all ten leaves at once.

Flames erupt from my palm.

I wrench my hand back, but it does nothing to dull the pain—nor the sound of his screams. Fragments of fire cling to his face in a macabre display, transforming his skin into a blistered map of scarlet. I gape, horrified, as he gouges his cheeks with tattered nails, trying to rake the burning leaves free.

I stumble out the door, scooping up the forgotten dagger as I go.

The ship tilts sharply as I reach the hallway, slamming me into the opposite wall in a pitiful tangle of limbs. I don't recognize the animal sound that escapes my lips when my burned hand strikes wood, nor the clumsy series of thwacks coming from the stairway opposite me.

Not until a body rolls over the final step and crumples at the base, useless and broken. Somehow, I don't scream. Instead, I walk back as quietly as I can manage in the semidarkness, my gaze locked on the steps. My back meets a curved wall that holds for a breath, then gives behind me.

"Feck!" The swear escapes before I can bite my tongue, and I writhe against ropes of fabric, desperate to get free, when someone hauls me up by the arm.

"Winds o' fury, lass, you—oi!" Faolan catches my wrist just in time to stop the dagger from sinking into flesh, and my eyes stretch as wide as they'll go.

It's *Faolan*. He's speckled with blood and gods know what else, shirt torn down one arm—but he's smiling, and the sight is so foreign and familiar at once that I drop the dagger to the side and collapse.

He folds me into his chest like I'm a rag doll. The last of my strength ebbs away as an ugly sob rips from my throat. "I'm s-s-sorry—" I try to pull back, horrified by my lack of control, but his hand forms a cradle to guide my head to his shoulder.

"Calm yourself, Trouble. You're safe now. The danger's past."

I gasp against his throat, tasting a pulse beating as frantically as my own. "You're not dead. I thought I saw—"

Faolan buries his lips against my hair, crooning the one phrase that could break me.

"Legends don't die."

I cry like I haven't in years, pressing my mouth hard to his shirt to stifle the harsh sounds as he pulls me closer. Some distant part of my mind screams at me that there is still an enemy inside, someone who could plant his sword in my back even as Faolan's hand spreads over the exposed skin. But Nessa races past, her steps coming to an abrupt halt as she makes a choking noise.

"Eabha's mercy. Faolan, you'll want to see this."

The gentle weight lifts from my head, and I squeeze my eyes shut. His warmth is the only thing distracting me from the pain in my hand—the terror of what's next to come. But at Faolan's sharp curses, I force myself to look.

Nessa and Lorcan hold the blond assailant by either arm. His skin hangs off his cheeks in tatters, the flesh beneath turned purple-black in places. Whatever is left of his eyes is no longer covered by lids. They've been burned away.

I burned them away.

My knees crumple beneath me, dark spots crowding into my vision. Faolan has to catch my arm to keep me from falling, turning my face away from the sight. "Easy, love. You . . ."

His grip falters. Fingertips sweep across my bare shoulders where my shirt tore down the back.

Where two spirals of the reverse triskele curl in stark white lines beneath my skin.

"What— Feck, your *hand*."

His touch shifts from my elbow to my wrist, lifting my useless left palm. I fix my gaze on his face as a harsh chide passes between his lips. "You couldn't have just stabbed the bastard?!"

His eyes have never been so dark. Not even when we kissed— gods, was that only a few hours ago? But despite the joke, not a hint of laughter remains. I don't recognize this face. It's brutal, cold, unforgiving, and for a split second I wonder if his fury is directed at me. I couldn't blame him if it was.

I should have asked for fighting lessons ages ago or the second I boarded his ship, knowing the dangers ahead.

I should have told him about the caipín baís tattoo, instead of leaving myself blocked. Worthless.

I should have—

"Get him on deck with the rest. I want him alive."

The words barely sound human. Nessa and Lorcan don't hesitate to drag the blond upstairs, but Faolan already has an arm round my waist. "You're coming with me."

TWENTY-SEVEN

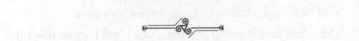

We've barely made it through the doorway of his bedroom when my stammering begins. "Faolan, I am s-so sorry. I t-tried to stop him on my own, I swear, but—"

The words collapse on my tongue as Faolan sweeps a thumb beneath the tender mark left on my cheek by the attack. "Saoirse. I never want to hear such a thing from your lips again. All right?" His gaze travels down my body to my ruined hand, teeth grinding together. "You don't have a damned thing to be sorry about. Just— sit here a minute. Actually, no, sit *there*."

He steers me to a tall trunk spilling over with cloaks from every isle and then returns to the bed. It takes one great heave to lift the mattress onto his shoulder, and then Faolan unhooks two of the ropes beneath to reveal a panel of wood notched in the center. With his teeth, he turns the smallest ring around on his pinky and fits its textured face into the hole. A single twist, and a compartment cracks open.

"Here we are." Faolan lifts free one of the smallest bottles I've ever seen, made of what appears to be frost-cloaked glass. Wrapped partially in leather to keep it from damage and capped with cork, it seems plain enough until he passes it from one hand to the other, and the liquid inside swirls from milky white to a brilliant blue-green. My heart stops.

"No. How did you . . . ? The spring's been dried up for a century."

"It's been in the family about that long." Faolan drops the mattress back into place and returns to my side, light emanating from the glass with every step. "My mother was one of the guardians of Leigheas. Or was supposed to be, anyway."

Once, the Spring of Leigheas on the Isle of Frozen Hearth was welcome to anyone who could manage the climb, was able to cure near every ill so long as it was taken before death. Families with sick children or wives fearing the worst from labor would send relatives to fetch a vial of the gods' blessing and bring it home. Failing that, they could hire someone like Faolan to do it for them.

But as one queen died and her greedy son took over, it became near impossible to obtain. Taxes on the waters tripled in the span of a year, and guards were posted along the perimeter. Within another growing season, even those few who lived upon the mountain itself dared not approach.

Yet the stonemasons of Maccus's isle did. Suspicious of the Serpent King's growing coffers and army, they crept up the mountain one night to destroy the spring and divert its waters into ruin. It halted the king's plans for expansion and wealth and obliterated the world's most potent balm—the final and most vicious crime of war before the six kings and queens formed their Ring of Stars.

"Your ma was from Frozen Hearth, then? She was a healer?"

"Wanted to be a seanchaí, but, aye, she was—and my gran, and her da before her." Faolan glances up, and a touch of warmth returns to his eyes. "But before you ask, I'm shite at healing. Really just bollocks at it. I can wrap a wound and manage this, but otherwise you're best trusting your own needle."

"And yet you don't keep a surgeon?"

As quickly as his smile appears, it falls when he looks at my hand. "I thought . . . maybe the healing instincts would kick in when it really counted."

A wave of pain pushes through me at the reminder, clawing up my arm. "Faolan. You were dying two days ago—or it looked like it, anyway. If I hadn't . . . if I hadn't known what to mix together, you'd be gone." I shake my head, then wince at the way it spins. "Why didn't you tell anyone to fetch this for yourself?"

"Well, I didn't say I was bad at healing *myself*. I'm alive now, aren't I?"

I frown, but when I try to protest further, Faolan drops to his knees in front of me. The sight does something to my head—or perhaps it's the shock, because absurd as it is, all I can think of is Nessa's story at dinner. "Are you going to . . . worship me now?"

Faolan fumbles the cork. "Sorry?"

The pain loosens my tongue, turning my skin hot, then cold. "Earlier. Nessa said her mother told her the only men worth having are those who worship a woman on their knees. Only . . . I still don't know what she meant."

Faolan stares at me for a full five seconds, and then his forehead drops to my knee as a heavy laugh wheezes from his chest. "You could try the patience of a feckin' saint, Saoirse—skies o' fire." Something like relief chases across his face when he lifts his head, and then his eyes flash dark. Without warning, he leans forward and presses a kiss to the soft inside of my thigh.

It doesn't matter that my skirt forms a barrier between us. Heat blooms like a water lily in morning from the spot he's kissed, unfolding inside me until the pain dulls to the back of my mind and all I can imagine is those lips traveling until they find skin.

"At a better time," he says, nuzzling that same spot with his cheek, scruff scraping through the fabric. "When I know you mean it. Ask me that again, would you?"

"A-aye."

Faolan captures my gaze one more time, then tears the cork free with his teeth, cradling my hand in his own.

My skin is black and burgundy, with wide-open blisters creeping along the lines of my palm to the network of veins at my wrist. Bone shows through on the end of my smallest finger. Strangely, I hardly feel it. It's the other injuries that hurt—my head, the mark on my cheek, the parts that struck the desk and wall. Yet the horror of the sight lurches in my gut all the same.

Faolan must feel it, too, because his smile drops. The hand holding mine grows slick with sweat. A vision starts in spurts from where our skin touches—fades to nothing thanks to the pounding in my head.

I start to slump over, and he swears, rocking forward to scoop me up with his uninjured arm. In a flash, Faolan presses my back to his chest, guiding my head into the crook of his neck while pain eats away at my sense.

"I'm sorr—"

"*Hush.*" Something warm and soft presses to the top of my ear. His lips? Faolan's words brush against that same spot, and my eyes flutter shut. "I already told you, Wolf Tamer, you don't have anything to apologize for."

A weak laugh escapes me. "You don't know what I've done."

He snorts, but the hand cradling mine shakes. "Remember who you're talking to, love. Regret's just a part of living. Now, brace yourself."

I open my mouth to ask what he means when Faolan blows on

the burned flesh of my palm, then mutters something that sounds suspiciously like a prayer. A scant second later, he tips half the vial into my palm.

"Faolan, why don't I feel—*feck!*"

Worse curses die on my tongue as I flinch, then buck, but Faolan's grip on my wrist is like an iron manacle and I've no choice but to sit and suffer through. Blisters become islands as the glowing water slides across my flesh, until they rupture and that strange blue-green light covers my palm. The colors shift as red eats away at the black, and a thousand tiny needles shove their way into my flesh.

"Steady—your skin's just knitting itself back together. Look."

I don't look. I *can't* look. All I can do is arch halfway off his body as the needles turn into blades, then flames. A scream wrenches from my lungs as my neck strains until I drop my head back.

And then it's over, as quickly as a storm blowing past.

"*Stars above.*"

Vaguely I'm aware of Faolan's lips at my throat, his breath as ragged as mine. The grip on my wrist slackens, then falls to one rounded thigh. Again, he kisses my ear, and then chases it with a command.

"Look, darling."

I do, only to see the magic water's lost its glow, slipping between my fingers as ordinary as anything. But my hand is not. In fact, the closer I look, this hand is not one I recognize at all. Every scar I bore—the jagged one along my pinky Aidan put there when trying to teach me how to fish, the calluses from my garden, the ragged ends of my nails I constantly chew to the pink. All of it is wiped clean, leaving soft, perfect skin.

I'm still staring when Faolan exhales, heavy and low, then

corks the bottle firmly. He pats my thigh twice in a sign to get up, and I do on legs as weak as a newborn fawn's.

Then it's just us. Alone, in the cabin, rumpled and breathless as we were only a few hours ago. The knot at Faolan's throat bounces when he swallows, and I barely keep from reaching out to see how it feels beneath my newly healed skin.

A knock sounds at the door. "Captain? You're needed on deck for questioning."

Faolan weighs the bottle in his hand, eyes never leaving mine as he calls out, "Aye, we're coming."

We. As though it never crossed his mind that I wouldn't be included. A shiver races up my spine. Slowly, Faolan steps past me to the bed, where he lifts the mattress and tucks the bottle back into its hiding space. I don't move until he's nearly reached the door.

"Faolan—"

"Best keep that secret between us, aye? My mother . . ." He clears his throat. "It was the only thing she gave me. Wouldn't want to waste it."

My head jerks in a nod. He grins.

"There's a good girl."

By the time we reach the deck, the husband who cradled me below has vanished. In his place is a man who looks every inch the Wolf of the Wild I've heard about for years.

"What have you got out of him so far?" His voice doesn't waver, but neither does his smile. That's what makes him so dangerous, I realize now—the charm and easy grins, the flirtation and stories. They all hide a cunning mind and a deadly bite.

"Nothing we don't already know. Maccus sent him and the rest after her." Tavin nods at me, and I falter a step—then almost slip in a pool of blood. Faolan's quick to catch me by the waist, but even once I'm steady, he doesn't let go.

"And why is that?" His eyes lock on the blond man, and I can see now that while one eye is untethered and useless, the other is as gray and cruel as before.

"What do you think happens when you steal someone else's property, mate?" The words are awkward as they tumble through blistered lips, and I have to look away lest I lose whatever is left of my stomach.

"We're properly wed. The entire crew bore witness—and my cousin—so whatever claim the Stone King thinks he has on her is done." Faolan's fingers tighten below my ribs. "Or does Ríona Kiara's mark of amnesty mean nothing anymore?"

A strangled laugh escapes the blond. "Means less than you think, these days."

The crew shifts around us, wood groaning beneath their boots as Faolan cocks his head to the side, jaw twitching once. "It means enough. But very well. We'll leave the queen's protection out of it." He finally releases my waist to step close to the man. Close enough that I wonder if he'll be smelling burned flesh for days to come.

"That woman is not property, nor did I steal her." Seizing the blond's shirt, Faolan drops his face a scant inch away and points back to me. "She is my *wife*. She rests under *my* protection. And you can tell tha' son of a bitch Maccus if he wants a war with me, he'd damn well better prepare his funeral pyre."

My ears ring with his words. I try to swallow. Fail.

It's not real. I know that.

But Nessa steps to my right, bloody sword in hand, and Lorcan braces a strong hand between my shoulder blades. Like I'm someone worth protecting. A treasure of their captain—no. The woad wolf at my wrist proves I'm one of the crew.

Just when I think Faolan is about to step back, he shoves his shoulder into the man's chest and, with a grunt, tosses my assailant neatly overboard. It's only then that I see the silver-painted ship drifting on the water beyond, half its sails engulfed in flame. Bodies bob along the waves in between.

"Even if tha' bastard doesn't survive the swim, Maccus will understand the message clear enough." Faolan catches my hand on his way to the bow and I fall numbly into place. "Tavin, prepare to sail."

My feet grow heavier with each step as disbelief replaces the awe until my insides swim with it. I wrap my free arm over my middle and watch the ground. Once we're out of earshot, I can't help saying the words aloud.

"This marriage isn't even real, Faolan."

I hate the words nearly as much as I hate myself for reminding him. His affection is intoxicating.

To my surprise, he rounds on me, walking until I'm forced to retreat. My back hits the nearest railing and his hands meet the wood on either side, trapping me between them.

"Let's get one thing square between us, Trouble." Faolan tips my chin up with a finger until I see nothing but his eyes. "We exchanged vows. There were witnesses. We're bloody handfasted, and not a damned person can contest that." He leans closer. "We are *wed*."

I don't blink. Faolan watches me for a long minute—long enough that I start to wonder if he means what he says, or if it's another game to him. I'm leaning toward the latter when his gaze drops to my lips. "Until we find the island, anyway." He brushes his thumb across my lower lip before turning sharply around.

"Brona! We've a full hull to trade and a ring to find. Set course for Aisling's Cove. We should be able to reach it by nightfall. I'll send word to Kiara there to clear up the mess about Maccus's fleet, then we'll set off to the Scath-Díol first thing the morning after, aye?"

"Aye, Captain."

Faolan turns before I can ask. "The Shadow Exchange. It's a black market—the very same I gambled at when I won my daggers and lost your grandmother's ring. Whichever of the three traders took it, we're likely to find them there."

"All right."

He studies my face. Reaches out a hand, then lets it drop warily to his side. "Get some rest."

I do not move until the bodies and smoke are well out of sight.

TWENTY-EIGHT

Aisling's Cove is lit by an eternal sun.

As our boats glide through the tall grasses surrounding a narrow canal at dusk, I shudder beneath its unnatural kiss. Crafted of sand glass mixed with Bruidin flame and blood, the fires within are meant to last an eternity. A gift from Ríona Kiara to her lover, or so Faolan says.

In truth, its heat is stifling after weeks spent on the open sea— the air thick, drenched in flowers.

"Shade's realm, look at the state of you."

I glance up to find Nessa holding Brona's chin aloft, her neck gleaming several angry shades of purple.

Brona rolls her eyes and pushes Nessa's hand away. "What of yourself? Was it the axe that nearly took your arm off, or a sword?"

"Axe." Nessa grunts as she examines the ugly split at the seam of her shoulder, still weeping blood. "It's just a flesh wound."

Brona snorts. "For now. Watch yourself—you'll be singing a different tune the second Quinn or Colm show their faces at the palace. Carrying on until they stitch you up."

Nessa grits her teeth as the currach scrapes rock, close to shore.

"Can you blame me? Between her breasts and his thighs, I'll forget I ever faced down death today."

Brona raises an imagined bottle in the air, and Nessa clicks her tongue as she taps Brona's knuckles with her own. "Sláinte."

They're laughing, but I can't blink hard enough to rid my mind of that man's mangled face. Can't stop opening and closing the hand Faolan healed, my thumb pressing the place a scar once marked. All I can do is haul the oars over and over again—a task they've finally allowed me, considering the state of Nessa's arm.

"The Wolf Tamer's a sight for once as well. You all right there, Saoirse?"

I jump, rocking the boat and causing Nessa to hiss in pain. "Sorry. Yes, I'm . . . fine. Alive."

"The best thing you can be after an attack like that," Nessa says, her voice wavering as she wraps a hand over her wound, glaring just ahead to where Lorcan, Tavin, and Faolan climb out to pull their currach ashore. "Och, but that's going to hurt like a bitch."

"Brace yourself," Brona says, gripping the side of the boat with one hand and Nessa's elbow with the other. I follow her lead, my grip clumsy—body shaken and sore after the scramble belowdecks. But it's not more than three seconds before Lorcan's lifting Nessa out as the boat runs aground.

I've just made it to my feet when Faolan appears, wrapping his hands around my waist.

"Easy," he murmurs, lifting me clear of the water with his good arm. But his touch doesn't linger this time, eyes cataloging every injury on myself and the crew as he helps them to shore. He smiles when they tease him for acting the mother hen, but it's fleeting— gone by the time they've started down a well-hewn path.

"Tav?"

The quartermaster lingers beside Nessa at a break in the tall grass, cocking his head to one side. Half his face is coated in blood from a gash just above his eye, but like the others, he doesn't seem horrified. "Aye?"

Faolan tosses him a leather pouch. "Drinks on me. Send one of Aisling's girls out for some healer's supplies—it was bloody stupid to risk sailing this long without them. We'll do a proper run next time we're near Frozen Hearth. And pass on the messages we discussed to Kiara."

Tavin cuts his eyes to me, brows meeting in the middle. "You're not coming, Captain?"

Faolan doesn't look at me. "No. There's some other business I need to attend."

"Is that what we're calling it now?" Nessa asks from Tavin's other side, her smile growing lush. "You know, Faolan, if you need us to pick you up some powdered antler—"

"I don't."

"Aye, but if you *did*, I'm fair certain Lorcan could build you an excellent crib. In fact—"

"Nessa." Faolan's smile is strained. "Please."

Tavin nudges her side, and Nessa yelps as his elbow brushes her injury. "All right, all right—stars above, that smarts." They trail after the others into a heavy copse of trees, slender branches bowing under the weight of midsummer fruits. A marble wall lies just beyond, though it's impossible to tell if it's part of the same slab that towers above our heads, shot through with veins of rose, or a structure built by the queen herself.

"You should go with them."

Faolan's back is a knotted map of muscle beneath his shirt, shifting with each tug of the rope as he ties off the boats one after another. Any playfulness he'd maintained for the crew is gone.

I twist the wolf ring once on my finger. "Why?"

"Because you've never seen it."

"There's a lot I've never seen."

"Aye, but Aisling's palace? It's a bloody marvel." His tone is light, but I know his voice well enough after weeks on the ship. He's forcing a smile to warm the notes. "They carved it straight into the southern mountain here. Feels like you're walking into a pearl. And of course Bridled Stag's known for its pleasure houses—"

"Faolan."

His back goes rigid beneath the weight of my hand.

I very nearly snatch it back. And perhaps I should—the crew's closeness is something they've fought for, touch and intimacy a thing each of them has earned. But Faolan's breath shudders against my palm as it pours out, and I dare to take a step closer. One more.

Until my arms slide around his waist, hands tucked neatly across his ribs as I drop my face between his shoulder blades and sigh. "Thank you."

His laugh jolts my forehead, the sound hard and humorless. "For what? I nearly got you killed."

"I chose to come, remember?"

"Only after I gave you no other—"

"I *chose* this, Faolan. Don't take that from me." I release my hold, trying to see his face, but Faolan grips my wrists. Draws them tighter around his waist. I swallow and stare at the patch of blood staining his shirt to my left. "I knew what I was risking."

He turns abruptly to catch my face between his hands, eyes flickering over the bruises at my cheek. Lower, to the burned remnants of my sleeve clinging to pale, perfect fingers that were black this morning. Faolan eases them into his own leather-wrapped hand. "No, you didn't."

"Well, I know now."

A laugh startles out of him. "You're a stubborn arse when you want to be, love. Anyone ever tell you tha'?"

"No." I nearly manage a smile, until he tugs me closer, and I flinch.

He lets go immediately. "Dammit. I'm sorry. I swore earlier I wouldn't do more than—"

"It's not that, it's . . ." There is not a part of me that does not ache, from my head to the smallest toe. "I can still smell the burns. Every time I breathe in. And we're both covered in blood or smoke, so I . . ."

My words taper off as Faolan watches me with the same calculation in his face I saw before he jumped into the waters at the Teeth. Eyes narrowed, lips curved up at one corner. And then he steps back into the swaying grass, sea oats flickering like scales at their tops. Reluctantly, I fall into step.

"Where are you going?"

"Think of the reward," he says as he turns.

Never the risk.

My hands are outstretched the moment the grasses close around me, tall enough to brush my shoulders with delicate white petals that smell as sweet as morning dew. I follow the sound of his boots, the dip and sway of his dark head, until after only a handful of seconds, we emerge at the mouth of a cave.

The colors are something out of a story. Amber, ruby, topaz, peridot—a thousand tiny gems painting a singular scene. Odhrán, patron god of this isle, rests at the center. Stags leap from each of his wide hands, as below, lovers tangle among wildflowers in a dozen different couplings.

"Guardian of passion, sensuality, fertility, and lovers." He winks. "Especially those star-crossed."

I touch my throat, where Odhrán's antler used to hang. "How do you know of this place?"

Faolan's smile is wry. "People tell me things. Even when they wish they hadn't." He reaches for his hem and then grunts as his injured arm protests. "Shite, I keep forgetting."

I don't believe him for a second. But I can't stop myself from drawing closer either. "Let me help."

Faolan searches my eyes as something sparks in his own. "Can you handle it? Lass, you blush if I so much as remove my boots in our cabin most days—"

He stops talking when I tug his shirt from the trousers, the damp fabric clinging to both our skins. I stretch onto my tiptoes and peel it free of his head.

Faolan is beautiful, his body made of rolling hills and sharp valleys, broad at the shoulders only to narrow the farther down it goes. I've rarely allowed myself to look beyond my lashes, even averting my gaze when I bathed him after the Teeth. I stare openly now. At the pale scars and thick muscles roped beneath his arms. The smattering of light hair across his chest, trailing down his stomach to disappear between the arrow of his hips.

Flames erupt beneath my skin, but Faolan's not laughing now. His eyes are focused. Intoxicating.

"Go on, then. If you want."

I hesitate, my bare fingers only an inch from his body. The magic could break open at our touch. It has before.

Faolan's lips drop to my temple, hands open at his sides. "It's your choice."

I flatten my palm against his stomach.

Both of us breathe in, tremulous and halting, as my fingertips slip along the top of his trousers. It's only to hold them steady—to tug the laces free.

A lie.

Not even a good one, as the material falls apart, and Faolan steps out as bare as the day he was born. I don't know where to rest my gaze—skin burning every time his hips brush the backs of my fingers or his hand trails down my arm. I'm shaking. He frowns.

"Saoirse—"

"I want to touch you." The words come from a place I'm not sure I even recognize—molten with longing, laced in fear. The drawings mock me from the cave walls. "I want to understand, Faolan. But I don't know how."

He is quiet for a long moment. I don't dare look at his face, heat scorching my own.

"Well, then."

Faolan turns his hand over, and I slip mine inside.

Together, we wade into the water's edge. It's warm—warmer than the open sea, and far more buoyant than I expected. Fabric swirls around my legs and clings to my hips in turn, chased by Faolan's fingers as he follows the line to my waist. Stops again when I lay a hand at his chest, shaking my head. His brows snap into a single arch.

"Tell me what you want and I'll do it, love. Trust me."

I do. That's the problem.

You should never put your trust in fairy tales.

"Show me how to touch you," I say instead, stepping forward as pebbles and seashells slide under my feet. Only a whisper of space remains between us. "Let me . . . let me thank you. Like you thanked me."

Something tugs at his expression—understanding? Regret?

But then he slides an arm around my waist, and I gasp as our bodies press flush in the water. My skirt tangles between us, a barrier as meaningless as an extra layer of skin. He takes a step, then another, until my back meets the cave wall and his eyes are all I can see in the flickering light.

"Kiss me first."

Another choice. And I'm half-drunk on the power of it as I slide a hand into his hair and drag my mouth over his. I kiss Faolan—the legend I heard stories of for years and the man I've lain beside every night for weeks—and in turn he wraps my thighs over his hips. Groans when I tighten their hold as he releases my legs.

For just a moment, worry bites through the warmth.

We're *so* close. It would take little effort for him to pull the skirt free. And even though part of me wants nothing more than to understand the fullness of it—of what it would be like to join another person's body with mine—the other part is terrified of the invasion. What sort of channel that would allow for the magic to escape. I've only just begun to understand the boundaries of who I am, or that I can even touch another person at all without hurting them. I'm not ready for what questions more would bring.

But Faolan doesn't press me. Instead, he drops his mouth to the curve of my neck and, on a rough string of swears, guides my hand between his hips.

"*Stars.*"

I'm not sure who breathes the word—Faolan or myself. His entire body curls around mine, taut and trembling, as I stroke a pattern taught by the sea. It's . . . intoxicating, watching the waves build beneath his skin. A hollow appears in his cheek as he clenches his jaw, swallowing another curse. When I turn my own mouth against his throat, parting my lips to taste salt, a hoarse groan rushes through my hair.

"Feck, you'll be the death of me—"

I know.

The fear is easy to ignore when he presses me harder to the

wall, hips rocking closer, hands wandering to my breasts. I blink
that first vision away and steal this moment—until Faolan is gasping my name, face buried in my shoulder as he releases control
and then catches himself with an arm on either side of me. Panting and shaking, something akin to wonder on his face.

I almost laugh. Almost.

Because for once, the Wolf of the Wild is utterly speechless.

And it was my power that commanded him so.

TWENTY-NINE

Darkness engulfs the cloudless blue skies in slow measures as our ship reaches the Scath-Díol three days later. Nessa tells me the Shadow Exchange was named for a particular kind of gem that allows someone to leave their earthly shape behind, bending shadows to disguise their form. It's forbidden to harvest among all six isles—but then so are most things sold at these black markets.

Far above the mast, a brilliant light starts to flicker around the sun's inky-black center, strange and cold. Tavin releases a long, slow whistle of warning, and we all duck our heads in unison to avoid the eclipse's full glare as the ship drops anchor below us. For once, I rock with the motion instead of falling, weight shifting from one leg to the other so I am one with the water instead of fighting against it.

When I glance up, Faolan's eyes are on me, a smile lighting up his face.

And damned if my heart doesn't try to fly directly into his palm.

"Nessa, you still have your contact from the Isle of Painted Claw?"

"Aye, Captain."

"Grand. Ask him about the ring—he was at that table. You and Lorcan find him and offload the crates from our last stop home. I'll handle the gills. The rest of you, be on the lookout for Captain Siobhan of Unbound Earth, and Rian of Reborn Stalk. He'll have Aoife with him wherever he goes, and he'll be missing his left ring finger—probably more by this point." Faolan loops a bag over his shoulder, and I force my gaze away.

Three days since the cove, and we've not spoken of it since. We pass each other like clouds—a touch gliding down my back or twirling a lock of hair, always gone the moment I turn my head to face him. He's asleep by the time I reach the bed, or doesn't come to it until after I've found a dream. Still, his words ring in my head.

My wife. My protection.

Ships hover in a wide-flung circle around us, their individual markings and flags obscured. I'm certain the crew will know where most come from, but it gives the illusion of privacy. Honor among thieves. Still, I pull at the fabric draped across my shoulders until it forms a proper hood, shielding my face from view. We don't know yet what story my father or the Stone King has spun.

"Here she comes."

Conversations die between one breath and the next as the ocean writhes beneath the eclipse's mark. Waters churn into a raging froth beneath the white ring of light and then split to reveal a land that was not there before. A secret island with golden sand that emerges only two or three times a year under a solar eclipse, according to Faolan. Time slows once the birthing is complete, and the earth remains still until the last drop of sunlight breaks free of the moon to send it all sinking back into the sea.

Between one blink and the next, the light shifts from white to red, and a ridged expanse of land as yellow as goldenrod emerges from the waters.

None of the boats hesitate to advance, our own currachs lowered to the water at once. There are stalls to set up, prices to haggle, cargo to unload, and time is already slipping away.

S ilence and stealth! Slip through the streets undetected with a painted claw. The birds are only sacred to keep you from having them."

"Fang of the diamond adder! One good poke will paralyze a man for twenty minutes straight."

Brona scoffs to my right. "Drop him dead, more like. You'd have to dilute the venom with meadowsweet an' honey to get only a paralysis." I strain to see the fang in question, but my boot catches for the hundredth time in an hour. Faolan wraps a steadying arm about my waist.

The market was half-formed by the time we made it to shore, but now rows of stalls and blankets piled high with wares cover every inch of the narrow land. Anything the Ring of Stars has banned or limited is laid out here, waiting for a buyer. There are flora and fauna like I've never seen, tinctures and instruments—and weapons.

So many weapons.

My gaze drifts aimlessly over blades forged from a volcano's heart, iron-studded shields, daggers crafted of ice, and colorful bows so finely wrought, I have to wonder if they're decorative. I'm running my fingers along the iridescent feathers of an arrow, watching how they turn the light, when I see it.

A sling.

It's been treated like an afterthought, looped over a sword's handle at the edge of a table. Five silver-threaded cords of leather are braided into two strands that taper at the ends into delicate loops, each woven piece roughly the length of my arm. At the place where they join, four bronze discs secure the straps to a central pocket large enough to fit a palm-sized stone.

I remember the ache it used to leave in my shoulder. The delicious rush in my chest whenever I found a perfectly round pebble to add to my brother's pouch. Secret lessons spent hitting targets on the beach.

And Aidan's grin when after months of nothing, my rock finally hit its mark.

Keep at it, Saoirse! Don't you dare give up.

My fingers flex in Faolan's as the memory passes through—bittersweet and far away. Yet as though he's felt the shift in my body, the break in my heart, Faolan tracks my gaze to the sling and raises a single dark brow.

"They call that a poor man's weapon. The humble shepherd's sling."

The words *I know* rest on the tip of my tongue; that was always my father's reason to dismiss it. He refused to allow Conal, his heir, to learn, but Aidan never much cared for Da's rules—and Da never cared enough about Aidan to stop him. And when my brother picked it up from a fisherman's son, he took his rebellion one step further and passed the knowledge on to me.

I tug on Faolan's hand. "Let's leave it, then."

He refuses to budge, eyes narrowed and mouth tugged to one side. "No, I don't think I will."

"Why? A sling is useless on a ship."

"Oh, you'd be surprised. Besides," Faolan says as he raises my hand to his lips, kissing each knuckle, "anything that makes your eyes shine like that is well worth the coin."

Before I can blink, Faolan's approached the merchant and has begun to haggle a price. I ought to protest—deny my interest or put up a proper fight. Instead, I linger near the table's edge and then force myself to move on. It's his fortune. He can spend it however he wishes.

Even if this one act sends my insides into an uproar.

My fingers trail over blankets spun of the finest wool I've ever touched as I find a new path through the market, but I jerk them back when a seller demonstrates what they're capable of on a fellow traveler. The moment her slight body is wrapped in it, she tips over and curls up in a deep sleep on the ground. Wool from the sheep of Painted Claw's highest hills, forbidden from use a decade ago.

Perhaps in another life with fewer enemies, I could use such a thing for a peaceful night's sleep. I haven't managed more than a few hours each night since the evening we were attacked.

I'm nearly past a new stall boasting honey that instantly seals any wound once applied—for a pretty price, naturally—when I notice the humming.

It stops me in my tracks.

My feet grind against loose stones, but for once, my body isn't taken over by panic. There is no pain or ice between my shoulder blades, no tug of the magic at my gut. I strain to listen—to seek and find. To my right, coin passes between two hands as a third swipes a bag of ice from the Dromlach Cliffs while the vendor is distracted. And to the left, so low to the ground my eyes nearly pass over her, is a woman sitting on a woven mat, her body bent with age.

It's not the humming of magic I hear. It's her.

She sings under her breath as her fingers work incredible knots through thread that gleams with every color I've ever seen, and quite a few I haven't. Together, they weave cloth charms in the shape of living creatures—a swan, bear, otter, and sheep.

"Would you like to know what they're for, lass?"

Kind brown eyes slanted as deep as Tavin's meet mine, though where his are framed by a curtain of dark hair, her hair is short and touched with silver. The woman smiles and pats the mat beside her, setting the half-formed animal down in her lap. I glance over my shoulder, but Faolan's still busy with the merchant. Careful not to sweep her creations into the dirt with my skirts, I lower myself to the mat's edge.

"These are my aisling de na sióga."

A laugh escapes me. Dream faeries. Clever little creatures that, once spun and sung into existence, can live for years like the animal they represent, curling up to your cheek at night to stave off bad dreams. I scoop the bear into my palm and smile as he comes to life, ambling across the network of lines to sniff around my fingers.

"Stars. I've only ever seen one in person, during the celebration of the autumn equinox." It was before the prayers and scoldings, before the proper magic began, when I was hardly big enough to matter. Rí Callen—only a child themself then—had a tiny cloth-woven dragon that would fly from their finger and circle our heads before returning on swift wings. When I'd asked Aidan for one later, he'd laughed and told me I'd have a better chance at taking flight myself than convincing Da to pay for one.

"I thought the only sióga-blooded lambs exist on the Isle of Painted Claw—and their numbers dwindle each year. How did you find enough to fashion these?"

A raspy laugh echoes from behind her scarf before she tugs the thing below her chin. I hesitate, then do the same, nudging my hood back as well so I can see her more clearly. "Look around you, girl. The world's a damned sight bigger than any of those crown-wearing fools want you to think." She winks, then goes still.

Staring at my eyes.

Gods. When did I stop hiding them?

Something turns in my stomach and I glance over my shoulder for Faolan or the others, but all I see are legs, cloaks, hoods. I tug mine back up, setting the bear down regretfully with the others.

"They are extraordinary, but I have to—"

"I know a song about speakers of the sea. Do you?"

I falter halfway to my feet, my knee catching in the folds of my skirts. "I'm sorry?"

"There were many names for them. People with the knowledge of the sea in their eyes. People like you."

My pulse quickens as sweat breaks out down my back. But as she tips her head deep to one side, I see the tattoo on her neck marking her as one of the sirens of the Isle of Painted Claw—a branch of the seanchaí. Women trained from the age of seven to master the songs of our lands, our histories, and our slaughtered gods.

Slowly, I settle to the ground once more. "People like me?"

She smirks, and all the while her fingers poke a bone needle through patches of shimmering thread. "You see anyone else round here with eyes that shift as yours do?"

Instantly, I jerk my hood lower until it shades my face again, my ears burning with the knowledge anyone could've heard her. Could guess what I hold inside me. "What does that have to do with speaking to the sea?"

"Everything." She laughs again, easier than before, but her eyes are curious. "All our lives come from the sea and the land she's birthed. Every life that's ever winked into existence bears her mark in the salt their flesh weeps beneath the sun, but *your* flesh—your people's—it knows better than most. You've got the ocean in your blood. I'd bet my whole collection on it."

My face is scarlet. I'm burning from the inside out, desperate to know more yet so aware she could be casting tricks. "That's a pretty sentiment." But a lie.

She levels me with a gaze and I wince. "We've the history of the world in our songs, lass. Stories of the gods, epic love, and raging storms—so why not of you?"

I clench my fingers so hard the nails dig into my palms.

Why not me?

Because I am wrong inside. Broken and unnatural, cursed with magic that killed one brother and might lead to the other's death someday if I can't get rid of it. Because my father terrified me and my mother looked away. Because Faolan's kisses made my whole body sing, and if she's right it means he only embraced me for the magic I possess and not the person I am beneath it.

Because I am the daughter of Dermot, once betrothed to the Stone King, wife of a legend, Wolf Tamer, Ocean Eyes, Trouble—*Saoirse.*

And I have no feckin' clue who that is anymore.

"If you'll just listen, lass, I think—"

"I can't." It's more bark than speech, and all I can manage as I push to my feet. "I'm sorry, but you're mistaken."

Her eyes narrow. "About the magic?"

My stomach twists so sharply, I have to hold my hand against it. "About me. I don't have any—"

"You don't see things as they ought to be? Feel what's to come—in living dreams or communion with the deep?"

Communion? I can't help an ugly laugh, one that fractures halfway through when there's another tug on my gut—not sickness, but a demand for attention. "I don't feel anything."

She is wrong. So horribly wrong. This magic is not patient or invited—it is a madness. A compulsion.

"It's there in your eyes, girl. They're churning even now."

"It's just a trick of the light." Where is Faolan? I turn on my heel twice, but he's nowhere in the crowd of shuffling figures. None of the crew is.

I wrap my arms hard over my stomach, trying to ignore the magic pulling like strings tied to my back.

"It's no trick; it's a mark of the sea's touch on your life. A gods' blessing—"

"The gods are dead!"

A dozen eyes land on us at my outburst and I crumple.

It's too many people. Too much attention.

I step closer, hunch my shoulders, and lower my voice to a scrape of a sound. "They're dead and gone, all right? And if—*if*—they ever gave someone sight like that, it would be a curse. Not a blessing."

She doesn't scowl or pull away in fright. Instead, she smiles until her face is as lined as crumpled linen.

"So long as a Soulgazer lives, the gods, once more, will rise."

THIRTY

Golden dust clings to my bootheels as I walk the shoreline, pushing myself as far from the clink of coins and overlapping voices as I can get. My fist clenches around the aisling de na sióga I didn't mean to take, squeezing the tiny wool bear until it wriggles against my fingers and goes still. Guilt wars with fury as I stuff it deep in my pocket. Patches of dry ground stretch between shallow pools, forcing my steps to slow as the dirt forms a viscous, shimmering sort of muck. It's only when my foot sticks deep in the earth and I stumble into a jagged pillar of rock sticking up that I realize these are not mere puddles.

The land is sinking again.

Gods.

I drop my forehead to the boulder and bite my lip until the turmoil eases inside my belly, unwinding from my heart. It doesn't stop pricking at my arms, though, raising gooseflesh across my skin.

You've got the ocean in your blood.

I give my arm a vicious swipe.

The old woman had no idea what she was saying. That or she's never witnessed the destructive power of the knowing sea. Without all his clever tricks, the goat hide and quartz for balance, Faolan's ship would crumple beneath the might of those waves during a storm. Aye, there is beauty in its savagery—and awe when the waters go as still as glass.

But there is danger in loving the sea.

Danger in loving *me*.

A *soulgazer*.

I release a harsh laugh as one by one, my fingers ease their white-knuckled grip on my skirts to flatten against the stone before me. An ache at the base of my skull creeps lower, humming as though a hive of bees has nested in my spine. My eyes are half-shut as the vibrations shift into words, then muted conversations, as shadowed figures flit behind my lids.

My hands curl into fists against the rock.

It's the bloody magic again.

I push back from the boulder and swear when pain lances between my shoulder blades. Unlike my wolf, the spiraled tattoo refuses to heal, burning my flesh anew every time the magic wants to surface. And that old woman called it a blessing?

The golden rock stretches like an arrow's tip turned to the sky, its surface shimmering in the light of the eclipse, scarred with deep ridges and spirals that almost seem purposeful. As though . . . a hand forged their path.

I stumble back—and then double over, gasping at the twin stabs of the magic's call and the tattoo's refusal to respond. Impulses war within my body, a battle of fire and ice, as I glare at the golden rock.

"You want me to touch it, don't you?"

It feels stupid to speak aloud. I've prayed most of my life, and not once has anyone answered.

But I am sick with the silence—sick of cowering belowdecks,

hiding beneath veils, and mourning this world when I've just barely begun to explore it. This magic is a hungry creature, yes, but *I* am the one who's spent my life half-starved.

Useless.

I raise my hand and press a fingertip over the carved lines.

"Saoirse!"

I startle, and my hand slips on a sharp point, the stone gouging my fingertip.

"Bollocks! Faolan, you—" I jerk my hand away, but blood already drips down the etchings, sprinkling the ground at my feet. My husband barely looks chagrined when he reaches my side, the silver-threaded sling tied onto his belt.

"Well, I didn't mean for you to cut yourself, did I?" Faolan asks as he bites down on the edge of his scarf and tears into the seam. One hard wrench, and a long strip comes free, which he wraps round my hand, pressing down to stop the bleeding. "I only wanted to bring you the sling. Honestly, who comes to the biggest black market in the Crescent and then runs off to talk with a bunch of rocks alone?"

"I wasn't talking to rocks, you absurd man, I was just—" My words tangle as a grin breaks his serious expression. I groan. "You can be such a—"

"Please, go on. I've been dying to hear you use one of those words you always bite back." Faolan's shoulders shake with repressed laughter as he ties off the cloth. "I'm such a . . . bastard?" He kisses my fingertip like that'll seal the cut. "Prick?"

"Pain in the arse."

I wrench my hand away and turn back to face what should be a mass of solid stone.

The boulder's surface ripples like freshly poured candle wax instead.

"What are you—feck!" Faolan catches my arm as I reach for it, fingertips a scant distance away from the swirls and lines sprinkled scarlet with my blood. Yet even as we watch, the patterns grow darker, drawing blood like ink into their lines as though starving for it.

As seven clear sigils burn dark red against the gold, Faolan swears and laughs in the same breath. "I've seen plenty round the Crescent, but this is . . ." He trails off as the marks disappear.

I lurch forward, a pang of longing and loss racking through my heart.

"Let me go."

"What?" Faolan's hand tightens at my elbow as I try to shake it free. "No. Trouble—"

"The magic's calling me. I need to see what's on the other side."

"Assuming there is one." He eyes the rock face warily, flexing his fingers as I reach for it again. "What if it eats you?"

A laugh catches me off guard, then stops when my hand meets the surface, warm and satin smooth. A touch of pressure, and my whole arm begins to melt through.

Faolan's hold drops to my waist, hauling me back so my hand falls free. "Right, that's enough of that. Let's go meet the crew and—"

"Faolan!" I squirm and press against his chest until finally he lets me go. There are sharp shadows beneath the line of his brow, lips no longer smiling but flat with concern. More bewildering still, he looks almost hurt that I've pushed him away.

I shake my head to clear it and back toward the stone. "I'm tired of waging war against myself. Tired of hiding, of being useless—Faolan, you took me from Maccus and my father for this magic, and for once I'm really trying to understand it."

"I know." Faolan tears a hand through his hair. "I know, it's just . . ."

"Do you want my magic or not?"

I've never seen a look of such agony cross his face—not when he was feverish and dying, not when my hand was a blackened, bloody mess. It's there and gone again in a second, leaving me to wonder if I ever saw it at all.

Faolan tips his head toward the sky, then offers his hand out for mine.

"We'll have to be quick about it, though. The island won't stay for long after the eclipse is done."

Hesitant, I knit my fingers slowly with his own. "We?"

"Aye." He smiles. "I'm not letting some dusty old rock swallow you without putting up a fight."

I nod and, together, we step forward into liquid gold.

We are creatures without weight or form, our beings swallowed alive by light. The only thing that is real is the grip of Faolan's hand around my own, and I focus what little of my consciousness is left on his calluses pressing into my palm.

We float, and then we fall in a tangle of limbs and low curses.

I gasp, drawing in deep lungfuls of stale air as Faolan rocks to his heels and casts a wild look about the chamber, cavernous and intimate all at once. Pillars surround us, joining walls that slope toward a near-perfect circle high above our heads, where an opening allows the sun to shine through.

Except it's not the sun. Inconstant where it should be steadfast, and blackened at the edges like a fallen star. It casts a strange silver light on the artwork that spills across the walls. Painted cranes, cracked mountains, toxic serpents.

"Just another adventure." Faolan's voice comes high and a touch tight as he stands, lifting me by the arm. My knees crack as I join him, a consequence of kneeling constantly in prayer.

"Right." I take a step, and my foot meets water with a delicate splash, the sound reverberating until an entire rain shower echoes around us. Beautiful but haunting. Like the figures stretched from floor to ceiling that grow clearer the more my eyes adjust, broken only by the pillars—

No. Not pillars.

Thrones.

My breath stops.

These are *thrones*. Impossibly huge, but unmistakable, and carved straight into stone beneath the portraits of the Slaughtered Ones.

"Faolan, do you see . . . ?"

I could swear a heart beats somewhere beneath the lingering damp. Humming through my blood, my bones. Gods, my teeth ache from clenching—the price of withholding the magic outside the rock.

I am so tired of fighting it.

My steps bring me to the nearest seat, and something catches hard in my throat when I recognize the patch of blueish-white veiled mushrooms at the goddess's feet. A cluster of stars painted above her dark curls I've always known to represent the formless babe nestled in its mother's belly.

Bandia Eabha, patron of the smallest island—*my* island—and protectress over childbirth, maidens, suffering, and forgetting. She holds life and death between her hands. To her left stands Clodagh, goddess of healing, justice, legacy, and the dawn. Her throne crawls with serpents, heather, and balancing scales.

I walk helplessly along the edge of the room and meet each

god's or goddess's eyes upon the wall—great beings I've spent my life begging to take away the very same magic that's led me to this place now. Róisín's eyes glint as I pass them, the goddess of artisans, shifters, storytellers, and twilight, who guards the Isle of Painted Claw. Patron of my old playmate Rí Callen.

I stop beside Faolan in front of Maira: goddess of Ashen Flame, guardian of the sunset and trade, warriors and horseflesh. His face is almost bitter as he studies her proud countenance and the vibrant swarm of equines that make up her skirts like a school of fish.

"Do you claim allegiance to any of them, Faolan?" I whisper, but the words still scatter across the ceiling above.

Discontent shifts to outright disgust on my husband's face as his gaze slides past Maira's throne to Clodagh. But then he blinks, and his smile emerges—startling. Flippant, even, as he shoves a hand through his hair. "No. They're more useful to us dead than they ever were alive. At least this way we have access to their magic on our own."

I wince at the irreverent words spoken so boldly beneath their watch, but he must be right. They are only stone and memory now.

Faolan cocks his head. "Funny, though. There should only be six."

"There are. Six gods for the six islands."

"Then why's there a seventh throne just behind you?"

My ankle nearly turns as I spin on my heel. He catches me with an arm about the waist. "No, that's not right. There are only six. Róisín, Eamon, Odhrán, Maira"—my eyes find each god in turn as I name them, reaching my patroness and passing her— "Clodagh, and Eabha."

But there between the portraits of the first god and the last lies another, just as Faolan said.

A seventh throne, as clear as day.

It's split nearly in half with the mark of a great hammer, cracking up the walls to distort her image above. Shards of labradorite drip from her empty eyes, clinging to the crumbled remains of her skirts. The only place untouched is her feet, licked by rolling coils of sea-foam.

I take a step, and the magic's call slides over my body like a second skin. Pain prickles in response, honing into a knife's point at my back with every subsequent step. By the time I reach the base, boots dragging through crystals and dust, I can barely catch a breath for its violent struggle within me.

"Tell me." I dig my hands into my sides to keep them from shaking. "Tell me what to do."

Kneel.

The impulse is so powerful, I drop to my knees and gasp when they bruise. Faolan reaches for my shoulder, but I push his hand away. "Not yet."

"All right. But if you're hurting, love—"

"I'm not." Not an intolerable amount, anyway. The pressure is building, but it will break with a vision. I *know* it.

I only hope that I don't break with it.

Glancing over my shoulder, I search for that kernel of pride in Faolan's face: the one I gleaned after climbing the Teeth. It's stifled by an unfamiliar emotion clouding his features so they're impossible to read. My grip on the ground slackens as I search his eyes for daring or mischief—belief.

"Tell me I can do this."

He blinks. Then his face softens as he cradles my neck, leaving me gasping as I *feel* his belief flood me at once.

"You *can* do this, Saoirse. I only wish . . ." Faolan growls and buries his mouth against my throat, hand stroking my jaw once.

"The gods are all bastards. You should never have had to hold this burden alone."

Yet that is all I've ever done.

"Let me go." My voice wavers as I lay my hands on my knees, palms up, and nudge his cheek once with mine. He fights me for a moment, then slowly releases his touch. The woad wolf at my wrist gleams in the silver light as I shift back, deep blue lines rippling as though she's preparing to howl. It's a comfort and a stroke of courage at once—a reminder that I belong to more than myself now.

A wolf is never really alone.

Tremors start at the back of my skull and glide down my spine, filling each groove of flesh until they nestle in my palms and tug them forward. Like I am a child again, and the magic is my nursemaid. I open my eyes enough to see my fingers outstretched to the ruined image's feet, and understanding settles in my gut.

I have never asked for the magic to come. Never wanted to know as much as it reveals.

I don't truly want it now.

But if this is the only way to understand—to commune with the sea, as the singer said—then I need to start here. Letting it in. Studying it, so that someday, I can wrench it free of my soul altogether.

Assuming the pain does not paralyze me first.

"If I—" My throat convulses around a swallow. "If I collapse . . ."

"I'll be here to catch you." Faolan drops to one knee beside me, gloved hand flat on the ground as he trains his gaze on my tense shoulders. "Whatever comes, I won't leave you here alone."

"Please don't."

I glance at the Wolf once more, then lower my hands to the goddess's feet.

THIRTY-ONE

I am endless. Savage and serene. There does not exist a single life untouched by my waters—my lifeblood fills their veins, leaving and joining in endless cycles of knowing.

Galaxies pass beneath my lids. My eyes witness all.

And then I am myself again—Saoirse. Only Saoirse.

Or at least I think I am.

I stand on legs that ought to be shaking, but when I glance down I can see right away they are not my own. Skirts sweep around their long, agile shapes in gauzy layers that mimic morning mist, roping up over breasts and arms and skin paler than mine's ever been—pale enough to have rarely touched the light.

"Is that all you have to say?"

Midnight hair whips across my shoulder as I turn to the speaker, my face dropping into a cold scowl. The sort Saoirse has never managed before. Eamon—god of earthquakes, mountains, and raging storms—stands before me while lightning crackles through his silver hair.

"It is all I have seen in the depths of the Knowing Sea." My lips move, but the voice that flows from them is resonant and unshakable. Nothing like mine.

"You'd better read the stars upon the waves again, little sister." Clodagh, goddess of judgment, steps forward with a face lined with concern. "This vision cannot be."

"I've seen it thrice. The Knowing Sea does not lie." An inexplicable wave of sorrow crashes through me, but I swallow it down and raise my chin higher. "Our time is coming to an end."

With a gesture, three maidens approach from the throne behind this body. Maidens with dark hair, mist-like gowns, and—

Ocean eyes. Every single one of them has eyes like Saoirse's.

No. Like mine.

My hand cups the tallest girl's cheek, and for just a moment recognition flares. There is something in the uncertain texture of her hair—the way her body curves in at the waist and sweeps wide above and below—that is achingly familiar.

She bites down on her lip as tears gather in her eyes, and then bows deep. When she walks away, it is to slice her thumb with a slender blade and press it to the amber wall behind my throne. A moment later, she is through, stepping through the very stone with the other two behind her.

A hand seizes my shoulder, whipping me around, but I am not angry. My fate is known—passed before my own eyes.

Wait.

Her eyes. Not mine.

I am Saoirse. I am a fanciful girl. I am—

"You star-gazing bitch. Do you not realize this prophecy damns us all? Including yourself?!" Eamon's eyes swarm with smoke, an eruption raging within. It is the same reason the people of his isle cry out against him and his constant storms that steal their young *and old, the heaving mountains that destroy livestock and shelter. He thrives on chaos, and it bleeds out onto his land—just as his body soon will.*

I nod, infuriating him further. He raises his arm, but my second sister, Eabha, catches hold before he can strike. "No! You know what happens if we spill our blood."

"Aye." He rips his arm free and steps back, hands in tight fists, waiting for me to flinch and take it all back.

"We cannot unwrite what fate has written. I am not her master, nor would I ever wish to be. I can only see. Only know."

"You can't tell me we're bound to its whims—not us. We are gods, damn you!"

"*Bound to our own power and laws, bound to our possibilities and desires.*" I allow my voice to drop until it pours like honeyed wine, as it has to a thousand petitioners across a thousand years.

No, I have only lived twenty-two years.

I am Saoirse. Wolf Tamer. Ocean Eyes.

Saoirse. Saoirse. Saoirse.

Eamon shoves me to the ground, and before I can blink, his fingers wrap around my throat. Their presence is a surprise, a horror—it forces my body to crumple until the cool earth bites at my back. Still, he does not let go, driving a knee into my stomach so that unearthly rattles fall from my lips.

"Take it back. Change it, damn you—do you want to die?!"

In his eyes, the rage recedes and fear takes its place when I do not fight for my life so preciously carved from the ocean itself. He does not want to harm me, truly. He wants to scare me, but I spread my fingers in the dirt instead as I feel his thumbs crush my windpipe, the fragile bones of my neck snapping one by one.

"No." It is the only word I can manage, and his fingers ease just long enough for me to take one final breath. "But I will be the first."

His eyes blacken to pitch. My lungs collapse beneath the point of his knee. I hear the screams of my sisters—their pleading—and the clash of a hammer to stone.

I choke on nothing—become nothing.

Am nothing.

THIRTY-TWO

My throat tears with screams that refuse to stop until a pair of arms crush me against a solid chest smelling of the sea. Pain explodes in my head, and I retch on air—gasping in futile heaves as my body vibrates with magic.

"Saoirse? Saoirse—feckin' stars, love, talk to me."

"Th-they—m-my throat—I c-couldn't—breathe." Faolan's arms tense, and I cling fiercely to his neck, my fingers stiff and pulse thrashing. "I couldn't get out."

"I couldn't *get* you out." His breath scatters hot across my forehead, then converges into one fine point that melts through my whole body where his lips brush my skin. "You were paler than a godsdamned corpse. I thought—and then you started seizing, and I was terrified to move you. Saoirse . . ."

Faolan's fingers slide into my hair, and for the briefest moment, I am someone treasured. Safe.

Then he pulls my hair to the side, allowing air to rush over my bare shoulders and the cruel tattoo between them.

"What the feck are these markings on your back?"

The world shudders to a stop. I scramble to get away, but Faolan's hold tightens—shifting from my hair to my shoulders, thumb finding the edge of one spiral. I can't hold back my scream. The ink from the caipín baís *burns*, as though Father's apothecary is digging his wicked needles beneath my skin even now.

Faolan snatches his hand away, staring at me openmouthed as I tremble and gasp. Still, he does not let me go. "I thought they were scars, the first time I saw them. You acted embarrassed and kept them covered up. But they lit up silver the second your vision started, and then—skies, it was like the more your eyes shifted, the brighter the tattoo burned. Is that . . ." His face contorts, concern morphing to suspicion. "Is that why you've avoided using it? Are they blocking the magic somehow?"

"Faolan—"

"Tell me what they are!"

I can't speak. Words spill into a sob as I grab on to his shirt, water pooling around our legs. "W-we have to go. The island is sinking, remember?"

He ignores me, accusation shifting to something else in his face. "Those markings cause you pain, don't they? You were writhing on the ground—crying."

I'm crying now. "It doesn't matter."

"Like hell it doesn't! Who gave them to you, Saoirse?" This time when Faolan touches me, it's like the lightest pass of a candle flame. He cups my jaw, and I cannot look away from the bottomless blue of his eyes. He is too beautiful, too clever. I was an idiot to think I could hide it for long.

My resolve crumbles, and he must see—why else would he lean closer? Whisper, like it isn't just us in this room.

"Tell me who hurt you, love."

As though the answer were simple. My father is the one who ordered the ink made, his apothecary wielded the tool, Mam held me down, but I—I'd wanted it too. Perhaps not quite in the way they'd planned, but enough not to rebel or push their hands away. Enough to stay as they tried it a second time. Faolan wants an enemy to fight, but I cannot give it.

There is no one else alive in this world who has hated me more than I hate myself.

"I'm sorry."

It's not an answer, and we both know it. Faolan starts to protest when water rushes in from the cracks in the walls, rising from the ground itself. He slides an arm beneath my trembling legs, jaw clicking as he bites down. "Do you know how to get out?"

Blinking past white spots that dance in the air, I point to the wall behind the demolished throne.

Faolan half carries, half drags me through ankle-deep water out the same gilded passage I opened earlier with my own blood. It absorbs us and spits us back out under the open sky. He doesn't slow as we pass the sellers packing the last of their wares, all anxious eyes locked on the horizon while waves lap farther onto the shore.

When we arrive at the currachs, Faolan stands a bit straighter—throwing out a hand before Tavin or Nessa can say a word as he scoops me into the nearest boat. "Leave it. We'll catch up to him."

I double over until my forehead touches my knees, my arms wrapped tight below my thighs. "Who?"

"You didn't tell her?" Nessa asks.

"We were a wee bit occupied. Just—get back to the ship, will you?" Faolan shoves the boat until it glides, then tucks himself into the opposite end. I stare at the gold-dusted soles of my boots and feel invisible hands crush my throat all over again.

Faolan knows. Or at least he's guessed some small piece of it—enough to suspect me of suppressing the magic his crew still knows nothing about. I trace the wolf tattooed at my wrist, pressing a finger over its heart.

Shame is my oldest companion, and it tastes vile on my tongue.

"Lass." A heavy warmth surrounds me and I know without looking it's Faolan's coat. He grabs the oars and pulls against the water until we're well away from the land and any keen ears, but I feel his gaze locked on me. It doesn't falter once. "Saoirse, look at me."

I do, stomach twisting all the while.

My husband is a preener. He cloaks himself in color and texture like a fine-feathered bird most days, priding himself on his storytelling and ferocity. He's generous with laughter, quick to act, and I've yet to understand how many shades of gray make up his morality. But however solemn a situation or furious he might be, Faolan has never once faced a problem without humor.

His smile is all wrong when it comes. Hesitant and weak as he folds the oars across his lap and loosens the cords of his leather glove.

"You have secrets. Stars know I do as well. As long as you can tell me what you saw down there, I . . . don't have to know the rest."

It's a barter, and not a very good one. I steal a hand to my throat and rub the skin near raw as salt trickles into the corner of my mouth on a tear. "The god of chaos and storms strangled me. I . . . died."

It's the truth. Bewildering and terrifying as it is. And though I know Faolan will believe me, I can't bring myself to look him in the eye. "Except I wasn't me, I was—*her*. The seventh goddess. They were all there in that chamber, the Slaughtered Ones, like it was their own Ring of Stars."

Faolan says nothing. He tugs at the ties of his glove until they lie flat once more, rings catching the light from his bare hand. "The Scath-Díol forms at the dead center of the Crescent. Brona can show you on the maps—and it's always been a strange strip of land, even for our world. If the gods were meeting anywhere . . . I suppose it makes sense it would be here."

I hug myself tighter. Hide my face so Faolan doesn't see me fall apart as the rest of the vision seeps into my memory past the growing pain in my head.

"I watched her foretell the fall of the gods. She warned them of the slaughter—said that people would rise against them all. She—" My voice fractures down the middle. I swallow to make it whole. "She didn't have to. The seventh goddess could have spared herself somehow, because she also knew that they would kill her. But she sent her handmaids away to safety, warned the other gods, and they *still*—"

I bite down on my palm as tears carve scalding paths down my face. Faolan doesn't reach for me this time, though, his face shifting through a dozen emotions at once. It hurts almost worse than the burning of my back.

"They killed her for it, Faolan. Crushed her throat. She was a goddess of fate and the sea—not its master, a mouthpiece. She only *knew* what would happen, just like—"

Me.

Just like me.

There were many names for them. People with the knowledge of the sea in their eyes.

I lift a trembling hand to my cheek, brushing it over the fragile crescent above the bone. "And their eyes . . . They had eyes like mine. The group of girls standing behind her."

"Handmaids, you called them?"

At my nod Faolan jerks back, but his lips split into a sudden grin. Unsettling and wild, like the one he gave just before I dove to find my grandmother's bones. I lean back in the boat, tucking my hands below my knees as he transforms from Faolan to the Wolf of the Wild before my eyes.

"Well, there's one answer at least. They must've been favored servants granted the sight—there are loads of songs about people blessed by the gods for their talents or devotion. You're probably descended from one."

I think of that familiar girl. The gentle hand on her cheek.

"No, that can't be right. The descendants of the gods were killed, too, during the uprising. The bastards and blessed as well—all the seanchaí agree on that. Anyone bearing magic—"

"You don't think at least one or two managed to escape?" Faolan barks a laugh, relief laced through the sound. My stomach clenches, and I wipe my face dry. "'Specially if they were only gods-blessed. It would be easier to hide than someone born with power—of course they'd keep quiet."

"I . . ." If that were the case, wouldn't there be more people like me? "I don't know."

The uprising was absolute, every lineage obliterated down to the last drop of divine blood. It started with the Daonnaí—my family's ancestor and the five others selected by their isles, armed with righteous anger, wit, and weapons forged by the gods themselves. If there were blessed handmaids among those hunted, I doubt they survived.

I shudder, too drained to do much more than fumble for the rope that hangs down as the currach bumps along the ship's side. But Faolan is buzzing with life.

"Feckin' hell, Saoirse, this *has* to be it." He claps his hands together, any concern left by the vision gone. "The other gods destroyed her image and throne, killed the poor creature, and sank the Isle of Lost Souls to cover up what they'd done! Why else would it've disappeared along with the gods if it weren't for that? It was one of the reasons the people rose up against them in the first place, wasn't it?"

My head throbs with the weight of it all. "I— What?"

Faolan catches my elbow and hauls me to my feet. "The lost goddess! The seventh. She's the patron of the Isle of Lost Souls, there's no way around it. And if you share blood with one of her blessed handmaids, it explains why you have visions—you can see past all the bullshite to the heart!" He takes my chin. "You're connected to the isle itself, Trouble. It really was you I was looking for, all this time."

I fist his coat in my hands, the rush of words a blur in my mind. "Faolan—"

He turns me around, nudging me forward to the rope ladder. "Come on. We've got to find that damned ring."

I have no more strength to fight him or ask questions. In less than a minute, I'm climbing the rope, no need to be tossed over his shoulder. I don't know when my legs and arms grew stronger, but even with fatigue settling in after the magic, they pull me over the railing without much effort.

But on the deck, it's all I can do to stand upright. Numb as I watch the crew gather for their captain. My eyes will barely stay open, swollen as they must be from crying.

That is, until Faolan throws himself over the railing, smiling wider than I've ever seen.

"Oi! Gather round, you lot. It's time I brought you out of the dark about why I married Saoirse in the first place. What this ocean-eyes business is really about."

Instantly, I am awake.

Painfully, furiously awake.

Dread coils low in my belly and shoots ice through my every vein as one by one, every pair of eyes flits from Faolan to me. And I shrink. Like a rabbit, my first instinct is to run—but we're on a ship surrounded by water, and there is not a damned place I could hide.

"Faolan. Don't."

The whisper is all I can manage with my voice wrung raw from screams, but I *know* he hears me.

I know it, like I know he'll ignore me, because he is a showman and I am the stupid fecking woman whose hopes of being accepted here—of finding friends and purpose—are being shattered with one bloody phrase.

"It's the tale of a girl who touched a soulstone. One blessed by a goddess with ocean eyes."

I hate him.

The thought boils up my throat seconds before the laughter begins, shaky and then overwhelming from the others. But Brona's reaction is worse. She regards me with the suspicion I'd thought we'd grown past.

"I'm serious, you lot. Listen!"

Faolan launches into an entire story that I know with a sickening lurch he must have been writing since the day we met—because that's his favorite thing, isn't it? The legend.

Never mind that he whispered words like *Wolf Tamer*, *wife*, and *love* to do it. Never mind that he's peeled back every damned layer I had to protect myself, touching me like he wanted me—listening like he actually fecking cared what I had to say.

Never mind that he's breaking my heart.

Blood rushes past my ears, flooding my face, neck, arms, until heat radiates off my skin. And still I cannot look away as Faolan describes his first time meeting me. How he'd planned to kidnap me if I didn't agree to his bargain—but then I locked him into marriage, something he sings the praises of now.

I die.

I die a little more when he talks about my grandmother and my lineage to a blessed one, and even more when he explains that our search for the Isle of Lost Souls depends solely on my ability to see a clear path. He swears once we find the ring, I can guide us straight there.

Because I've touched a soulstone and I have magic in my blood.

It wasn't meant to be like this. He told me the crew wouldn't have to know—not until I could control the magic. Not until it was *my* choice to tell, once I had some clearer answer to give than fractured visions and stifling pain. Faolan's kisses, the cove, that stupid song about ocean eyes.

One kiss from her lips.

Feck, it's all just another story to him.

"Imagine it. We'll find this island using *her*, and there'll be no more answering to Kiara in the future. No more runs around the Crescent or bowing to the Ring of Stars. *Freedom*. We can do exactly as we fecking please! And Saoirse will lead the way."

Freedom. What a sick, disgusting joke.

THIRTY-THREE

I run from the crew's stares and questions, their scoffs and Faolan's gaze. Run to his cabin, because nothing here is mine and I am not free and—gods above, my heart *hurts*. But the moment I fling myself through the doorway, I realize my mistake.

This room is full of memories now. Scented by sea salt and whiskey, our clothes from Aisling's Cove still rumpled on the floor. The dagger Brona lent me hangs from a bedpost just beside my pathetic, poorly knit scarf.

A furious sob climbs up my throat.

"Feck."

It's not real. It never was.

The room tilts as frantic footsteps pound down the hall, and I don't think. Don't breathe.

I slam the door shut between us, dropping the key with shaking fingers seconds before my body hits the ground. Distantly, I know he's knocking—know it will be so much worse once he finds a way inside—but it's not enough to keep me from crawling to the smallest corner of the room. Tucking my body as tight as it will go.

I should have cast you into the sea the moment you opened those eyes.

"Saoirse?" The door jerks on its hinges, wood groaning beneath his fists. "You knew I had to tell them at some point, lass."

I shut my eyes like that might make him disappear. Swallow the ugly scream that wants out.

You dare to ask for mercy?

"We could have waited, I suppose—I see that now. But think of the reward waiting at the end of this! You'll be a legend alongside me."

Metal scrapes against metal. Like the ends of an iron betrothal torc hitting my collarbone.

You're asking me to gamble the fate of our entire island on a fairy tale when she *has already cost me my heir.*

"They'll sing your praises when we find the isle, mark my words." A click as the bolt slides free. "It'll all be—"

Quiet.

Blessed quiet.

I know for a fact Faolan *hates* the quiet—will do anything to break it—yet somehow, this one lingers. Takes on weight. And a twisted bolt of pleasure shoots through me knowing I'm the cause. Whatever concern he painted in the gods' chamber, asking who hurt me as though he actually cared, it was only because he wants to be the hero of his own story. He is a masterful liar, and *that* is the truth that snaps across my lungs. It's unfamiliar but welcome, rooting in my heart, and for once in my life I don't want to fight it down.

I want Faolan to suffer. Want him to *hurt*.

"Saoir—"

"I thought it was *Ocean Eyes*." I lift my head, fingers twitching where they grip my legs like a vise. "Wasn't it? Or have you decided you like *Wolf Tamer* better?"

Faolan flinches when he meets my gaze. "Love."

"No, that's not it." A laugh pushes past my lips, bitter and hard. "The Wolf of the Wild doesn't have a love. Only legends. A crew member from every island, a lass at every port—a godsdamned ship spun of starlight." Another laugh, cold enough to prick at the skin running down my back. "And even *she* lacks a true name."

Faolan drops back against the doorframe, a mask sliding over his face. But there's sweat gathered along the curls at his temple. "If you're trying to insult me, you can do better than that."

Fine. I'll do better.

That wounded creature in my chest drags me to my feet, trembling as I brace against the opposite wall. "You're afraid. Terrified we'll look away from you for even a second—that you'll be just like the rest of us if you don't take up all the space there is."

Leather snaps as he adjusts the cords of his single glove. "And what's the alternative, then? Shrink myself so there's less of me to swallow?"

"Yes." The words taste sour as I spit them out. "It's impossible to *breathe* when you're in the same room. You steal all the air."

"And you allow me to." Faolan crosses his arms, raking his gaze over my rigid posture. My hands spread wide against the wall like that tether alone might keep me safe. "Saoirse, I've only ever taken what you offered first."

"Bullshite."

He scoffs, an edge to the sound. "Name a moment that I haven't."

"The cove."

Faolan's eyes snap to mine, dark as pitch. But I can't stop the words now they've broken through.

"Your cabin before the attack, that first storm, every night since—I gave you my magic, Faolan, but I never agreed to be your plaything. This marriage is *not* real."

He drops his head back. Kicks the heel of his boot once against the wooden door. "Is it my imagination, wife, or did you not kiss me back that first night?"

My body roots into place.

"And Aisling's Cove. You followed me there. Shade's breath, you all but commanded me to strip before you—did I force your hand?"

"No."

"Steal your heart?"

Shame burns a path up my throat. "That's not what I meant."

"Then what?"

I brace my fingertips against the curved wood behind me. Curl my toes against the ground. "I don't want to be just another one of your stories."

"Aye, you've made that pretty fecking clear." His voice drops near to a growl. "And yet for a woman who wore feathers the first time we met, I've never known another person to be so damned devoted to their own cage. So riddle me this."

Faolan's eyes lock onto my face with a hunter's focus, tracking the spread of color across my skin.

"What do you want from me, Saoirse?"

My mouth runs dry. "I want—I want to survive."

"No." His laugh is rough. "We're well past that now. What else?"

Only my nails brush the wall now. "I want to be free."

"Then prove it." Faolan sneers—a savage thing that calls to the beast cornered inside my own chest. Compels it until I'm crossing the room, feet striking the ground in a way they haven't since I was a child.

He doesn't move—doesn't have to. Between one shallow breath and the next, I'm standing before him. Hands raised, lip curled as

Faolan pushes a lock of hair back from my face. Searches my eyes like he wants to steal them. "Stop bloody caging yourself. Tell me what you want."

I react without thinking, my hand flying up toward his face.

It doesn't land. Not because Faolan caught it—his own hands are open at his sides—but because I cannot hurt him. As badly as I want to, as much as he deserves to feel every ounce of betrayal raging inside me, I can't do it. My body knows what happens when I fight back.

Tears gather sharp behind my eyes as I falter a step, until Faolan's hand wraps around my own.

"You're angry. And hurt."

My tongue is useless as he drags my hand to his chest.

"And you want to hurt me back." Faolan spreads my fingers with his own, pressing until they dig into his flesh. "So do it. I'll even admit I deserve it after that stunt on deck. But know this, Saoirse."

His eyes never once waver from their dark, liquid blue—a sight that will haunt me to my last days.

"Whatever story is spun about the two of us, I've meant every bloody word. Every moment. Every touch. Legends like ours don't die." Faolan's hands fall away, and I see the meaning in his face.

It's my choice. Just as it has been from the beginning.

I've lived in fear of power my entire life. Fear of myself, of those who raised me—of wanting anything too much, because desires can so easily be taken away or destroyed. I learned not to ask much of the world or my place in it. Learned that choice came with consequence, so it was better not to choose at all.

But Faolan's right. It's just another cage.

I twist my fingers into his shirt, and a flicker of a smile graces his lips.

Until I push him back against the door.

I *do* want. So fiercely. I wake up with my insides screaming for it every morning and fall into restless sleep every night. I strangle it into silence, pretend like nothing is amiss. And maybe it's selfish or wrong—I'm still furious, and my heart's an open wound.

But when Faolan's eyes drop to my lips, I drag him down and seal my mouth to his.

I kiss him like I'm scared someone might take him away. Full and ferocious—not the least bit tame. Faolan is still for only a heartbeat, and then his fingers knot in my hair, giving me no quarter to back down or regret it.

So I don't.

I part his lips like he taught me, catching the full bottom curve between my teeth. He jerks closer, body rolling into mine as his hands drop from my hair to hook beneath my thighs. One sharp tug and he lifts me, wrapping my legs around him so our chests flatten together as he turns to press my back into the wall.

"*Saoirse.*"

Pure heat bleeds into my soul when he whispers my name. Gathers lower as his mouth finds my throat, fingertips dragging beneath the hem of my shirt. I'd thought this was a game to him— coaxing me to play along. But I remember his face after the cove. The way he's avoided me since.

There is something here. Something I'm hungry to understand.

"You drive me mad," I groan.

His laugh is lost against my collarbone seconds before his tongue finds it. "And what is it you think you do to me, love? Having to lie beside you every night, not touching, knowing you disapprove of me. And—*feck*, your skin is soft here."

I can't control the noise that leaves my lips when his fingertips curl into my waist. Slide higher, bone by bone, until they reach that sweet, unsteady curve and—

"Wait!"

He goes still immediately, hand plastered against my chest. Our breaths tear the air apart between us, but I can't look at his face. I can only focus on the humming that fuses my jaw together, dancing up and down my spine only to lock in place at the spirals carved into my back.

Magic. Fighting my body to be free.

"I'm sorry." Faolan's head falls to my shoulder, breath skating across my collarbone. I feel it like lightning against my skin, his want bleeding into mine. "I shouldn't have—"

"It's not that. It's—"

Words fail as pain and pleasure form a wicked dance down my spine, drawing me to excruciating awareness. Of the ache between my legs—the restraint in his own. Calluses bite into my thigh where one of his hands rests, and leather scrapes my breast from the glove wrapped around his other.

A glove constantly laced and unlaced, but never taken off.

Even when we swim.

I drag Faolan's hand higher until it lies just over my thrashing heart. Dig my fingers into the laces. Swallow as he searches my eyes for permission, even as a weight drops in my stomach.

"Kiss me again."

Faolan's lips tug into a smile like sunlight before he drops his mouth to my throat again, and for a moment, I could believe the magic is lying. Whatever has drawn us together all this time is fate, nothing more. But I think of the vision in the gods' chambers, and the way wounded spirits call to me—how when the magic draws me in, the whole world falls away.

Like that first night at the Damhsa, when our eyes met across the fire.

Or the bone-deep yearning I feel whenever we touch.

His lips chase my pulse, kissing such a sweet path along my jaw that I want to die—something he's afraid of in spite of all his talk and teasing, the phrase he uses like a prayer: *Legends don't die.* Yet *death* is what calls to me, though I once believed it was the other way around.

I close my eyes and press my thumb into the knot of his laces, easing the cords apart.

"Please . . ."

Faolan goes still. But it's not until the laces unspool that my husband, the Wolf, realizes what I've done.

"No. Saoirse—wait!"

He's too late. I peel the leather back and expose a bare palm sliced by a gleaming abalone scar swirled at its center in a triskele, bright as moonlight.

The exact color of a soulstone.

THIRTY-FOUR

"Faolan, what is this?"

The words are barely audible, hoarse from his kisses and something else I'm fighting to keep down. Because I must be mistaken. It was *fate* that drew us together, not curses or death. Any moment he'll tell me the real story of how he got that scar—wrestling a silver-clawed bear or seducing a murúch who blessed his hand with her scales.

Except he wouldn't have bothered with the glove if it was only another adventure. He'd find excuses to show it off.

His jaw tightens as he slowly tries to close his hand, but I catch his fingers with my thumbs, flattening them until his palm tilts to the light. Silver streaked by violet, a touch of midnight and a splash of dawn. His hand holds the entirety of the world's colors, with a few wayward splotches along the joints where he must have squeezed it once.

Because in my heart, I know I'm not wrong. Faolan has held a soulstone in his palm.

Which means the Wolf is going to die.

"Put me down."

Faolan eases me to the planks, and I nearly crumple on legs as weak as a newborn foal's. His face is so familiar and so foreign. I don't recognize the way he chews his lip or the flush creeping up his throat. I can still taste him there, salt lingering on my tongue.

Gods, I need room to breathe—to think.

Except I can't think, because Faolan is marked and *I* am not, and—

I stare at my own bare hands. "This doesn't make sense."

"It does if your magic comes from your blood and not from a soulstone." Faolan's gaze lands heavy on me, his chest caving in with one hard breath. "You were never cursed, Saoirse."

A ringing strikes my ears. Settles deep in my bones until they want to fold. "I am."

"No"—he laughs, the sound raw—"you're not."

"Faolan, I touched a soulstone—"

"As a child, yes, I know." Faolan's smile drops. "But if you were purely mortal, or a soulstone had actually cursed you, your palm would bear the same colors as mine. Didn't you ever wonder why it didn't?"

I stare stupidly as light ripples across his ragged mark, silver bleeding into pink like the moon invading the morning sky. "I told you before, my father said the marks fade with time. He said most people—"

"Die before they can?" Faolan's laugh is empty as he raises his hand. "Aye, well, here's living proof that's a load of shite."

I shake my head. "But you're not mad. A-and you're not dead, so what did you—"

"I struck a soul bargain."

My mouth goes dry, my fingertips cold. "That's a myth."

"If I had a coin for every time—"

"*Faolan.*" His name comes out in a desperate lurch. "Be serious. Please."

"I am, love."

My bones turn to liquid as I search his brow for that quirk of humor, his swollen lips for any hint of a lie. The longer I look, the more the world tilts. Because if Faolan were teasing me, freckles would dance across the bridge of his nose and light would slant through the blue of his eyes.

Their color is flat, the depths of them still.

I shut my eyes. "A *soul bargain*."

It's an ancient, terrible magic I've always hoped was pure legend. Trickster gods once offered unthinkable gains in exchange for a person's soul: the strength of ten men, longevity of life, beauty to rival the mountains, immortality through stories and song.

But those ways ended with the gods, and while Faolan yearns to be a legend, he wouldn't claim it at the cost of his own life. There's nothing that could be so important he'd risk . . .

"Tell me you didn't." Any lingering heat flickers out. "Faolan, tell me you didn't do *this* for me."

He grips the back of his neck, glaring at the scar. "Technically it was for my life. The Isle of Lost Souls was just part of the deal. But I didn't realize what I was doing, and—"

My knees give out. I sink to the ground in a heap of tangled clothes and burning skin, my head held up only by the fingers clawing through my hair. I'm honestly not sure if it's a laugh that seizes my throat, or a sob.

"How the feck do you bargain away your *soul* without realizing? And who responded to you?! Faolan—the gods are dead!"

Questions fill my lungs like water until I'm drowning in them, my chest bound tight as air grows harder and harder to come by. I nearly jump out of my skin when I feel a hand—Faolan's hand—spread over my back, directly over my own damned secret.

"Breathe."

I can't help myself. I strike at his arm, his chest, flailing more than anything in an attempt to get away. Mercifully, he steps back and then collapses to the ground as well, legs folded together and shoulders slumped.

I can't read him—I don't want to read him—because another thought floats in to obliterate all the rest.

"You said you'd be honest with me. You *promised*."

His laugh is hollow. A ghost of its usual sound. "And you said you would use your magic to find the island while hiding the fact you've suppressed it. Guess that makes liars of the both of us."

I flinch. "I'm trying."

"Horseshite." Faolan crosses one booted ankle over the other, rubbing at the edge of the glowing mark. "If you want to talk honesty, Saoirse, why don't you start with telling me about the tattoos on your back?" His eyes flick between mine. "I think we both know by the color where they're from."

My stomach convulses as I reach for that spot, then falter. Close my hand into a fist. "You don't get to do this. You lied—"

"I'm a pirate. And I never *technically* lied."

This time, I don't contain the spite in my laugh. "No, you're careful of that, aren't you? You tell me—everyone—just enough truth to get us on your side and believe in your stories, and then you let the wolf split the lambskin clean off your back."

Faolan's lips curl into a snarl. "Call me a beast if you like, darling, but I've *never* pretended to be less than I am."

"Only more."

I wait for him to bite back. *Want* him to fight me.

He deflates instead, lips falling into a flat line as he shoves the dark curls from his face. "You hold actual power, Saoirse—magic the likes of which none of us could fathom, let alone hope to ever hold in our hands." His eyes catch mine. "I've always wanted to be more, but you *are* more. For all my stories, *you're* the one who will find the Isle of Lost Souls."

Just like that, every bit of fight abandons me.

"What if I don't?" My voice tilts alongside the world. "What if my magic isn't enough, o-or the right kind? What if I'm not fast enough, or clever enough, or—"

Free to use it because of the tattoo. The stupid fecking tattoo.

I thought it might protect us. Even half-formed, the caipín baís ink would keep the worst from coming out. But if there is no curse, only the magic within my blood . . .

Panic nearly chokes me. "Faolan, you've put your life into my hands, and I'm not even sure I can access the magic enough to see more than a few flashes of memory. Much less a path to the isle of the lost."

There is silence. Sick, slow silence.

"Then I figure I'll go out with a bang, and it'll make one hell of a final story."

His words are so flippant, I raise my head to curse him—and stop at the look on Faolan's face. So unlike anything I've seen from him before, so . . . mortal. He can't hold my eyes for long, tracing the abalone mark once across his palm before pushing to his feet. A moment later, he has a flask in hand.

The same one he carried the day I wed him.

A cord untethers inside me, allowing a part of my mind to drift from here—to hide—as I try to remember how long he said he searched for me. Eight months? Ten?

"Faolan?" My voice breaks, but he doesn't look at me. "How long do we have?"

He uncaps the flask, takes a long swallow, and then shoves the cork back in before tossing it to me.

"We have less than a month to find it."

Air escapes my lungs until I am empty. Numb. I pull the cork free and drink until a touch of heat returns to my belly. "A month."

"Twenty days, to be exact." Faolan's smile is weak as he clenches his fist to hide the mark. "Honestly, it's really a lot of time when you think about it in terms of hours. Minutes. Sec—"

"Tell me how you did it." He goes still as I drop the flask, hesitate, then take his hand in mine. "You said you didn't realize it was happening? I don't understand."

I study his face, taut lines blending into something softer the longer I look, until his head drops back and he sighs. "I was only thirteen."

Whatever I was expecting, this isn't it.

He takes a step back but doesn't release my hand, locking our fingers instead. His eyes drift to the window as a gull flits past. "I was thirteen. And I was dying."

"Faolan . . ."

He tightens his grip, pulling me to my feet. "You've heard the stories of how the Wolf of the Wild was started, aye? There once was a lad who survived three days on a patch of sea-worn rock by drinking the tears of merfolk."

I nod, and a smile flirts with his lips before fading away.

"Nice story, isn't it? Clean. Dramatic—even a wee bit heroic. Nobody talks about the parents broken to bits against the sharp rocks around him. The way he was blistered with burns, vomiting for days after, feverish and half-delirious. I've never heard even one version of it all that mentions the way he rambled about talking to a goddess for a whole week after they brought him back to shore."

Faolan turns to me, and I see it in his eyes now beneath the laughter and quick movements—the flurry of activity and lore that make up the man I've married.

Sorrow. He is stitched of the stuff, same as me.

"You said . . . you got the ring when you were thirteen. Did this happen before or—"

"The day after. On summer solstice." His temple dips as he swallows. "Told you I should've given the stupid thing back to your grandmother. But I didn't, and someone in our . . . village caught wind. They held to the old ways—didn't approve of stealing, and I'd got in trouble for it one too many times." Faolan cranes his neck back, eyes squeezing shut. "We were sent away, with barely enough to get back to Da's family on Ashen Flame. But it required a boat, and neither of them were sailors. They didn't know to look for signs of a storm."

Old panic ingrains itself into my skin where his fingers hold mine, but it's dull. A memory of a memory, pushed so deep inside himself it's nearly impossible to reach.

"The boat was too small, and we were unprepared. Within a few minutes, the wind blew us off course and into a patch of rocks. I'll never forget the look in my mother's eyes when the first one hit and water started gushing up from the bottom." Faolan traces a steady path along my knuckles with his fingertip. "The sea swept her away first. She was screaming my . . . my name. Then Da locked his arms around me when we were thrown from the boat, and it was his head that struck the rock, not mine."

I'm shaking my head, my heart threatening to split because it's too easy in this moment to picture Faolan small and scared and so painfully alone. "What did you do?"

Faolan leans against the wall. "Watched the waves sweep him off the rock too. Watched their bodies until—"

His voice catches and I squeeze his hand hard.

"Until the sharks came and there wasn't much left to see. Two days passed, and I kept hoping one of the . . . villagers would turn up. Change their mind and come find us. Or maybe the barkeep and his wife, who ran the pub I'd sneak off to? A fisherman, or—hell, my uncle, who was king at the time. Someone should've come, but nobody did. And when another storm hit the third night, a wave finally swept me off."

His smile is flat. Cold.

"I was too damned weak to swim for it, but I tried. Then when my legs got tangled up in weeds, I prayed for the first real time in my whole feckin' life—and wouldn't you know it, I was wearing that bloody ring when I felt myself start to drown."

Gráinne's bone ring. The one she gifted him in the pub.

My jaw goes slack.

"I didn't realize what the ring meant or I never would've let it get stolen, no matter how ugly the memory it sparked. But I held it so tight that night, begging for someone to hear, and when the soulstone began to form on my tongue, I clapped a hand over my mouth to keep it there. And that's when . . . she just . . ."

Faolan rubs at his eyes. Starts to turn his back on me.

Before I can think, I've wrapped my arms around his waist. He's stiff at first, enough that I wonder if this is welcome—if it's even something *I* want right now. But then he lays his arms across mine, and I drop my forehead to his back. Breathe in the scent of whiskey and wild as a vision flickers across my mind.

"It was her, wasn't it? The seventh goddess."

Faolan's stomach tenses beneath my hands. "Aye. I couldn't tell you now what she looked like—but her voice was like starlight. And I swear, Saoirse, there was no soulstone mark on my hand when I woke up. I thought it was only a dream."

I don't move as he recounts the goddess's offer: double his life. The chance to become a legend that wouldn't soon be forgotten—nothing like the starving boy clinging to a patch of stone. Thirteen years of learning the currents and tides, the quiet places where magic breeds strongest, the hearts most easily persuaded using knowledge gleaned from sailors' stories and the ocean's depths.

Thirteen years free of consequence, and then one to collect the girl with ocean eyes.

"I said yes, of course, and she put the soulstone back inside me. Put me to sleep. When I broke the water's surface a few minutes later, a fisherman was waiting to scoop me out. It was like I was a feckin' saint, the way the village gathered once we were back on land. I was bloody terrified—guessed I'd just gone mad at sea whenever the vision crossed my mind. Then, as time went on and the mark didn't come back, I tried to pretend it never happened. Focused on building a legend instead, serving Kiara's court while building my own world where I could."

Faolan's teeth flash in the window's reflection, expression as wry as mine is grim.

"I became the Wolf of the Wild. Forgot all about the vision, the ring—I let them all think it was murúch tears and gall that kept me alive. It wasn't until the bargainer's mark showed up eleven months ago that I started to believe it all again."

My fingers twist in his shirt. "That's when you approached Ríona Kiara about the Isle of Lost Souls?"

"Aye." His hands tighten over mine. "Spun her some shite into gold about a heroic hunt for the isle, and she backed me. With a heap of conditions, mind, and the promise I'd stop if after a year we'd found nothing. We were sailing the Crescent the very next day."

My voice is weak, muffled by his shirt. "And now we've only twenty days to find it?"

We both glance to the window and the pitch black of midnight.

"Nineteen, now."

"Faolan—"

A fist collides with the door in three sharp raps, jarring us apart. "We're nearing the vessel, Captain. He didn't have much of a head start."

It's Nessa's voice, colder than I've ever heard it. Of all the others, she is the one easiest to laugh. Faolan is still, gaping as his bargainer's mark catches the light, splashing colors across his face. My stomach coils to the point of pain.

"None of them know, do they?"

His eyes lock on mine as he gives the smallest shake of his head.

"Feck."

The fist comes again. "Captain?"

"Aye!" It's my voice that fills the room this time—too soft, cracked in the middle. But my movements are sure as I take Faolan's hand and pull the leather glove back into place. "We're coming on board. Prepare the approach!"

Part of me hates Faolan for looking so awed as I tie the cords across his wrist, drawing them tight until the leather conceals any hint of moonlight scored across his flesh. I'll be his secret keeper, for the sake of the crew. They may distrust me now, but they'll still follow the Wolf anywhere, so long as he can convince them of the story.

Faolan swallows as I tie off the cords. Tries to wrap his fingers over mine.

I draw back before he can.

THIRTY-FIVE

As we walk onto the deck, a throaty howl pierces the air.

I barely swallow my scream before another comes, and then a third, like a pack of wolves has found its way onto the sea. In the crow's nest, tiny Oona cups her palms around her mouth—but there's no way her voice alone could chill the air in my lungs.

I jerk back on my heel just as Faolan pulls a ring free of his smallest finger, made of wood braided with something thick and dark—fur? He cups his hand around it until the ring rests in the circle of his finger and thumb, then throws back his head and sets it to his lips.

The sound that escapes is bloodcurdling, dripping with restless hunger and an ageless hunt. Not Faolan's scream, but a wolf's unearthly howl. He catches my eye once his lungs are empty and shrugs, jerking his chin toward the prow, where a ship lies just beyond.

It's close enough that I could touch it if I tried. Red wood gleams in the firelight, a marigold-yellow flag tearing at the wind high above our heads—smaller than Faolan's, but only just. Below that flag is one of my own isle's colors. The crew stands straight-faced and cautious as they draw their sails until our ships run alongside each other, lanterns casting deep shadows across both of our decks.

"It was Rian who took the ring," Faolan says, lowering his hand to the dagger at his side. "We were questioning Siobhan at the Scath-Díol when the bastard sailed off. Brona spotted his ship on the horizon just before I left to find you."

"But we still don't know why he took it?"

"I've a fair idea about that, actually."

Annoyance tugs at my brow as I watch Faolan adjust a few ropes, smiling as though our fight never happened. "Would you care to explain?"

He laughs, a great gust of breath that shivers down my back as his arm slides around my waist. "What would be the fun in that? I'll show you instead. Hold on."

"What—"

Faolan steps up onto the ship's railing, dragging me with him, and it's all I can do to catch hold of his shoulders before we fly over the edge. It's only when we're plummeting toward the water, then coming up the other side, that I realize he wrapped a rope around his other arm. Our feet hit the opposite deck, and I nearly fall to my arse—then shove at his chest instead, coughing on the scream that never had a chance to leave my throat.

"I can't believe you—didn't warn me!"

"You never would've done it if I had." Faolan chucks me once under the chin, then turns to face Rian's crew.

Our own land in soft thumps around me, tying off their ropes one by one. It's an organized chaos I'd never gotten to witness, being trapped belowdecks during the attack by Maccus's men. Tavin wears a blade crossed over his back, Brona a wicked dagger strapped to her calf. They flank Faolan without direction, and I understand now the true power of being one of the Wolf's pack.

My face heats as I reach for a weapon—*any* weapon—to join the others, but they've never offered one beyond Brona's, and in truth I never asked. I catch the hilt of a knife on Faolan's belt just as he steps out of reach.

Nessa immediately claps a hand on my arm, dragging it down to my side with a grimace. "Hold it. Rian won't attack first. He owes Faolan too much."

"Attack *first*?"

"Well . . ." She trails off as a shirtless man steps around the mast with a sullen expression made more dramatic by the scar hooking from his absent left eye down to the corner of his mouth. At his side, a woman manages to scowl down her nose at Faolan despite the fact that she barely reaches his waist in height. Her body is small, as though at some point it simply stopped growing, but the weapons slung across her back and the sleek muscles of her arms prove she's a more formidable opponent than I could ever be.

It's she who marches straight up to Faolan and prods him in the stomach. "You said we'd have until spring to pay up. So why the feck were you asking questions and—"

"Aoife." The man—Captain Rian, I suppose—takes her by the shoulder and guides her back to his side before he turns a glower on Faolan. "I told you I'd have the shipment by the time the first ice melts, as we agreed. So why in shade's realm did you feel the need to hunt me down?"

Faolan grins, lifting one shoulder. "I wouldn't have bothered, if you hadn't run."

Rian's eyes narrow. "I ran because I don't need more bleedin' trouble—not the sort you're bringing in these days." His gaze lands squarely on me. "Courting king's fury for that, eh?"

My skin prickles, and I roll the wolf-hilt dagger slowly in my hand. But Faolan only laughs, warm and wild. It shouldn't be so unnerving. "Careful saying nasty things about my wife, lad, or I might have to return the compliment." He winks at the little woman, Aoife, who reaches for her weapon and finds Rian's hand instead. "But we're old friends, aren't we? You won't mind doing me a favor, considering the last three I've struck by you. Isn't that right?"

A muscle ticks in Rian's face as he looks from me to Faolan and takes a step back. "Depends on what the favor is."

Aoife's knuckles go white as she squeezes his hand. "Rian, no. We don't need more trouble."

"It doesn't have to be trouble. Not if you're willing to cooperate." A corner of Faolan's mouth twitches up. "Even if I don't often make a habit of tracking down thieves."

Rian's eyes tighten. "I've never stolen from you."

"No?" Faolan cocks his head. "Must've been a magpie, then, who swooped over our card table and made off with my ring."

A shadow flits over Rian's face, there and gone in a second. But it's enough. Faolan leans against a rope, fingers flexing over its waxen strands. "You see, I've never been much bothered by thieves. If you're careless enough to leave something unguarded, you can't be too mad when it's stolen away. How else do you think I got my lovely bride?"

My skin pricks as their eyes turn on me—until Faolan pulls his dagger free, blade seeming to cut straight through the lamplight. "But it just so happens the ring you stole is important to the Wolf Tamer, and so it's important to me as well. You remember it."

"I don't—"

"Bone-carved." Faolan flips his dagger, metal clinking against his own rings. "Blue stone at the center. Ugly thing, but you're the one who suggested I add it to the pot during our gamble, and if memory serves, *you* were the one who played the losing hand."

Rian is as still as stone, face unreadable, though his hand must ache from Aoife's grip. "Aye. I remember it well enough."

Faolan stops his play, dagger still in his hand. "Where is it?"

Rian snorts, but beneath the scowl, his skin rapidly pales. "It was a shite piece of jewelry. Didn't do anything special either. I only stole it out of spite—probably lost it shortly after. How d'you expect me to have kept track?"

Faolan's smile is chilling, a far cry from the one I know, as he taps a finger against the rope.

"Right."

With one hard jerk of his hand, he cuts through it. Wood groans—splinters—as the rope slackens and then spirals into the air. For a second, there is nothing. Then a sail comes tumbling from the dark, crashing onto the deck between our crew and the others.

"Nessa?" Faolan calls over his shoulder, never looking away from Rian. "How much would all these sails go for? The crew's weaponry, food stores, whatever they have in the hull?"

Nessa's grip eases off my arm as she smirks. It feels wrong as well—she's not herself. None of us are. "Might be enough to cover their debts, but I dunno, Captain. We went to a damned lot of trouble to get that last bit of cargo around the Ring o' Stars. Such a shame it went missing under Rian's watch, aye?"

Rian's teeth clench so tight, his words come out as a hiss. "We have until the next melting to pay it back. You gave your word."

"And you swore the cargo was lost in a storm, but here's an interesting bit of gossip we picked up last night. Three crates of that same silk you lost showed up at the Scath-Díol last season, while we just so happened to be busy with the winter council."

Rian glances to his wife, chest convulsing with every breath. "Just gossip. People are bored, making shite up."

"Aye, I'd wondered—but then I remembered something else curious." Faolan flips the dagger over his knuckles again, then holds its hilt to the light. "*You* added these knives to the betting pool. Carved with wolves' heads on the handles, perfect for a young lad making a name for himself. Your cards were quite good up to that point too—and I was a cocky son of a bitch at the time. Assumed I was more clever, or that it was fate. But now I find myself wondering if these were crafted special just for me. After all, where d'you see this kind of work outside the forges of the Isle of Unbound Earth?"

Aoife is gaping at her husband, while Rian looks as though he's turned half ghost. As still as death, sweat gathered over his lip.

"I told you that night, Faolan. I stole the daggers off—"

"The belt of a spoiled-to-shite son of a master blacksmith in a pub. Aye, I remember. But I also recollect *you* were struggling that year. The trade wasn't as lucrative; storms were ferocious. You could've sold them for a decent bit of coin. But instead you bet them on a game of cards."

"A gamble's worth it sometimes, isn't it? You say it yourself. Think of the reward—"

"Never the risk." Faolan stalks forward with the dagger, thumb tracing the wolf's sleek chest on its hilt. "And you were rewarded by someone, weren't you, Rian? Someone whose coin was worth more than those daggers or the betting pool combined."

Rian goes completely still, and it takes me a full breath to understand what's happened. We're standing on a game board years in the making.

And Faolan's just won.

"Where did you get the daggers, Rian? And why did they want the ring?"

Rian's free hand twitches once toward the sword strapped at his hip, but Faolan raises his own blade. "No more lies, or I swear—"

"All right!" Tension ripples across the deck, breaking into sweat along my brow as Rian shifts back and slowly raises both arms, nostrils flared. "He approached me at Scath-Díol, cloaked so heavy I wouldn't recognize him on the street. But the man walked like a skeleton, his eyes sunken and voice like a spider's crawl."

My body jerks at the image—the memory of a cold, slick hand spread across my back.

"He had coin. More than I'd made that year, and all I had to do was trade you a couple of daggers for a ring—look, I'm not proud of it." Rian swipes a hand across his face, shoving it back into his hair. "But you can't tell me you wouldn't have done the same in those days."

"Of course I would have. Anything to get ahead, aye?" Faolan reaches for another rope. "It's just that consequences are petty creatures that like to chase us to the grave. What else?"

"He used his left hand. Had a satchel that smelled of decaying earth and bottles of an elixir I've never seen before. And when he shook my hand . . ." Captain Rian's eyes flick to the side—to me. "His fingertips were colorless and flaking. Like ash."

Faolan's well-honed blade stops at the edge of a rope, fibers springing free. I nearly drop the dagger's twin, openmouthed and trembling.

The ring was stolen seven years ago.

Seven years.

Faolan lowers his blade. "I need a name, Rian. And you'd better be sure."

"I *don't* want to get involved in this."

"It's a little late for that."

The notch at his throat bobs as Rian takes Aoife's hand again, her expression twisted between concern and fury. "Your word that you'll leave my ship afterward, without harming it?"

Faolan shoves his dagger into its sheath, any pretense or play gone from his voice. "Aye. I'll even forgive one of the debts against you—just tell me who has it now."

Don't. Don't be right.

Rian looks directly at me, his gaze unfaltering. Words final.

"Dermot. The ring is with Rí Dermot of the Isle of Reborn Stalk."

THIRTY-SIX

No one is laughing now.

I sit alone beneath a murky sky, stars quenched by hungry clouds. The others tuck themselves into a half circle across the deck, and even Lorcan avoids my gaze. The fruit gathered at Aisling's Cove is gone, the fish from the Teeth as well. I crush a lump of crystalized honey against a wooden bowl with my spoon, dragging it through the boiled oats until they're edible once more. Still, the ache that began at the base of my skull last night radiates across my entire body, and for one ridiculous moment, I want to go home.

But that's exactly what we're doing.

"Right." Nessa taps her spoon once. She doesn't look at me. "We could cut our losses. Take on another adventure; quick enough, word will die out about the Isle of Lost Souls. Give them something else to talk about by the solstice—"

"That only works if the princess goes home." Brona's back is rigid as she speaks.

Faolan doesn't bother looking up from his place at a barrel, map laid out over its top. "Saoirse stays. You all agreed to it after I first met her."

Tavin shifts, Nessa exchanging a look with him before she rests the bowl against her knee. "That was before we knew about the soulstone business, Faolan. You never said her magic comes from those."

"And?"

"Can we really trust it?" I force a bite as Nessa's gaze burns against my skin. "There's a reason the Daonnaí rose up against the gods."

"Saoirse's *not* a god."

"Aye, but you claim she's descended from one of their handmaids. Touched with their magic, even if it's only a drop in her blood. Once upon a time, lad, a drop was enough to behead someone." Nessa nudges Tavin's boot, and he scowls at the nautilus shell in his hands. As the seanchaí of the ship, he should be the first demanding honesty and quoting the ancient laws. It would only be just, after all, if they voted to expel me.

I would do the same, wouldn't I?

Tavin sighs when Nessa kicks him again. "Stealing a bride on the eve of her wedding is one thing, Faolan, but what we're talking about here . . . She's not an ordinary girl. And clearly her father knew that, or he wouldn't have been so keen to steal the ring back, let alone hide her away."

"*Or,*" Faolan says, finally looking up. "Rí Dermot's a greedy bastard through and through, and he doesn't want Kiara to be the one to find the Isle of Lost Souls."

"So he was going to use Saoirse to find the isle himself?" Tavin frowns. "If that's so, why marry her off to Rí Maccus?"

The spiraled tattoo scorches beneath my skin. I grimace and press my back to the railing until it bruises more than burns. I'm so tired of their questions. Tired of my useless tongue.

"Her father doesn't believe in the Isle of Lost Souls. He only wants the power Maccus has to offer."

"So let him have it," Brona snaps, tossing her bowl to the ground. "You swore when I signed on to the crew that we'd have nothing to do with Rí Dermot, yet here we are charting a course for his island while his *daughter* sits there, sulking—"

I jerk to my feet, but Faolan raises his hand. "Saoirse is my wife. Whatever ties bound her before, they were cut the moment she pledged herself to me."

"So that's why you really married her?" Brona laughs, and that heat inside me shifts. Grows teeth. "Please. All it would take when we enter her father's waters is for Saoirse to say we kidnapped her, forced her into a handfasting, and then she'd be free to—"

"To what?" My voice strikes the air like a blade I don't have the strength to soften anymore. "Flee into the loving embrace of my father? It's clear you know what he's like. So perhaps you meant my mother, a woman whose only advice was to keep quiet, please, and obey my husband on my wedding night."

Faolan starts toward me, but it's my turn to stop him. "Or is that who you mean I should run back to? The Stone King."

Some tiny part of me whispers caution as I meet Brona's steady dark brown eyes. Feel the wide gazes of the others on my spine. The things I say cannot be swallowed back down—but for once, I have no will to.

I am hungry to be heard.

"You're right, all of you. I could go back and be his queen. What was it he told my father—first payment when the marriage is consummated, second when my belly swells, third after I've borne him a child that survives? Assuming *I* survive long enough to create one."

Faolan tries to come between us. "Love, you don't have to—"

My hand doesn't falter as I hold it firm against his chest. "*I made the choice to come.* I struck the deal with Faolan, I concealed my magic from everyone, and whatever that makes me, I am *not* my father's daughter. I—" My voice breaks as I catch sight of the woad wolf at my wrist, howling the sweetest silent song. It would break me to never hear it again, to forget that one night I belonged.

The wind shifts, and my grip on the fury falters. Dissolves it enough for pain to slip through.

Stars above.

I turn so I don't have to see their faces, forcing myself to breathe past the stinging in my eyes. I want to burn those words to ash and run. Not to my old home, not to the life that once awaited me, but back to who I was becoming mere days ago. It's unbearable to think I'm losing her already.

"I never wanted this magic. And I'm sorry I didn't tell you about it from the start." Tears slip past my defenses. I blot them away with my hand. "It's—terrifying to see things happen inside your mind. You think you're going mad, or maybe that you cause them to come true by bearing witness."

Conal's face flashes across my mind. I shake my head to clear it.

"But I can *use* this magic. I had a vision while holding my grandmother's soulstone at the Teeth, which led me to this ring, and if I can actually find the Isle of Lost Souls with it, then . . ."

My voice falters, and Faolan steps closer, until my palm lies flat over his beating heart. "Then we all have something to gain."

The crew shifts their focus, and I might collapse were it not for the steady pulse beneath my fingertips, held down by his own. Faolan is unwavering now, indigo eyes locked on the others.

"I told you at the start of this journey that *this* would be the quest. The one we'll be remembered for—and not just in clever pub songs, but real history. The sort of tale grandmothers pass on to the weans in the dark of night." His thumb traces the tattoo at my wrist. "The wolves who salvaged a dying world."

I want to laugh. I want to weep.

Whatever magic I possess, it's nothing compared to Faolan's silver tongue.

"We'll buy our freedom with the Isle of Lost Souls. No more errands for Kiara, or backward political deals, no more lost spirits wandering the lands or debts tying us down—just *freedom*. Can't you taste it?"

Their faces are torn in half. Brona's on the fringe of their cluster, arms folded tight across her chest. Nessa abandoned her own bowl to hug her knees to her chest as Lorcan rubs at his brow.

Tavin rolls the nautilus shell against his palm, glancing from my husband to me. "We're risking death if we fail. Kiara won't take a bad gamble—you know that, Faolan. If we're caught on Dermot's isle, I'm not sure even her word would be enough to protect you."

Faolan opens his mouth to speak, but I press my hand down until he stops. "Then I'll go alone."

"*What?*"

"I said I can go alone." I straighten until my spine hurts, aware of every drop of caipín baís ink below my skin. My hands are numb beneath Faolan's grasp. "After a Damhsa is done, Father spends weeks courting favor among the other five rulers, and he almost never returns until summer solstice strikes. I could take a horse by land—no one would recognize me. I was kept far from the public eye."

Tavin stops fiddling with the shell. "And what of the ship? We can't lay anchor without his guard taking notice."

"You can off the southern tip. I watched the waters every day, and it was rare a ship ever passed by. The land is remote there, hardly populated. The waters themselves are so shallow between ours and the Isle of Frozen Hearth that most don't bother coasting there."

Faolan is staring at me. I turn my face away, pulling until he releases his grip.

"I'm sorry for breaking all your trust. I have no right to expect you'll give it to me again—but I want to try." My gaze finds Brona's, and I startle to see that beneath the rage is a raw sort of pain. One I know all too well.

Muscles draw tight across my neck as I swallow.

"Give me three days to find the ring. You'll be safe as long as you stay on the southern tip, and if for any reason I'm caught or you're spotted, you can leave me behind. I'll tell my father I paid you in jewels to take me, or stowed away on your ship. And you"—my throat closes in—"you can tell everyone I was just some fanciful girl who fell in love with a pirate. No one has to think he was stupid enough to have ever loved me back."

"Saoirse—"

I turn my wrist over, so that we can all see the woad wolf. "Angry or not, I *am* one of you now. Let me try to prove it. Please."

Their silence is deafening. For a long, agonizing moment I stand alone again in the murky dark, wind lashing my face as it blows in from the east.

And then Lorcan stands with a sad sort of smile, tugging his collar to the side so that I see his own tattoo. "Once a wolf, always a wolf."

My vision blurs as I step forward, pressing a hand over my mouth.

Nessa is next, groaning as she pushes onto her feet and catches me by the back of the head, pressing our foreheads together. "I'm fine with having an oracle on board, as long as you don't scold me for all the dirty thoughts."

"I can't see into your mind."

"Sure you can't." She grins and jerks her chin at the others. "To freedom, then?"

Tavin still frowns as he taps his scrying shell, then tucks it into his pocket. "Freedom."

"Freedom!" Lorcan shouts to the open sky, relief in every part of the word. He reaches for Brona, but she ducks under his arm and heads directly for the map. And Faolan—

Faolan watches me like a wounded creature.

I retreat toward our cabin as Tavin gives orders, the sails and ropes shifting above the deck. It's become a haven these last few weeks, being surrounded by Faolan's treasures, falling asleep to the steady beat of his heart. I'm almost to the door when Faolan appears, blocking it with his arm.

"You can't go alone."

"I can."

"Love—" He winces under my cold stare. "*Lass*, we've been over this before. You're too rare to risk."

"Do *you* know the secret passages around my father's castle?" I fold my arms over my ribs. "Did *you* spend your childhood sneaking in and out of them, or avoiding other people because they might set off your magic? I can do this, Faolan—let me do this."

His full lips tug into a frown, and it's all I can do not to linger on them. His pull has an unfair advantage on me, drawing me closer like a silver spider's web.

I force my focus onto his gloved hand, remembering just why his soul seems to call out to me stronger than most. "You should tell the crew."

He balks. "Why?"

"Because you love your pack of wolves." Faolan's arm drops to his side, lips parting and then locking shut. He doesn't deny it. I reach for the door handle and take in one slow breath of his scent. Whiskey and salt. "And they love you."

I push inside, but I'm not a step past when his words bite at my heels.

"Aren't you a wolf now, too, Saoirse?"

The door swings shut before I can respond.

THIRTY-SEVEN

The first time I laid eyes on my cottage seven years ago, I didn't see the thatched roof fraying at the edges from frequent storms, nor the crumbling stones at its base with holes for mice to slip through. Instead, I fixed my sight on the garden and learned how to breathe again.

Dirt packs beneath my nails as I pause on the worn path and tear another weed free. The garden's been neglected since I left for the Damhsa, thyme and yarrow flowering as the rest of the herbs go to seed. I break a stem off, arrow-point leaves scattered with purple blooms, and relish its scent.

It's good to feel steady earth again. And strange.

My body rocks on instinct as I reach the cottage door and lift the stubborn latch free.

Inside is nothing special, yet once it was everything to me. A window looking out over the ocean, wooden rafters half covered by cobwebs, a bed tucked into one corner and a trunk at its feet. I took two of the quilts with me, stowed on my father's ship, but one pink treasure remains. The fireplace is blackened and cold, a table and chair lonely beside it without my candlesticks and cloth. But the other table, nearest the door, is as beautiful as ever.

Neat rows of jars and cloth-wrapped bundles of herbs remain undisturbed on the scarred wood, tucked just below a second window. I brush a finger down the line: a clay pot of dried dandelion root to ease the pain of a monthly cycle, a jar of chamomile and valerian to brew for a restless mind, yarrow in case of injury. I hesitate to touch the sachet full of lavender and dried honeycomb—a vanity of mine once, meant to soften the skin and make it fragrant and sweet.

Perfect for a new bride.

"You're really going through with it, then?"

I lower my hand and shut my eyes in a useless attempt to hide from Brona. We haven't spoken in the days since our fight, too busy summoning the wind by burning falcon's feathers from Frozen Hearth, or rowing when the breeze refused to be caught.

"Aye. I haven't much of a choice." Not with only two weeks left.

I pack a few of the jars and bundles into a small leather rucksack, right alongside the poisonous little vial of caipín baís ink. "At least it's only my own life I'll be risking."

I shut the door with a heavy shudder and lean against it. "And like you said, I'm worthless to my father dead. Whatever consequence comes, it won't be that."

She quiets. Kicks once at the ground.

"I shouldn't have said any of it." Brona's dark hair falls into her face, lacking the usual braid, and she shoves it back with a scowl. "I just—I didn't know."

My shoulders tense as I study her face, but the anger isn't directed at me. With her arms crossed and head down, she looks less certain than I've ever seen her. "I never told you."

Her jaw sets. "You never had to. Everyone knows Maccus has a bloody heart of stone—and Dermot?" Brona shakes her head, laugh bitter. "He's a feckin' monster."

The word drops heavily between us, but even standing on the same island I learned to walk on, I can find nothing in me to defend my father. He's doubled the number of caverns on our isle and the size of our coffers with it, aye, but there are so many rumors. Collapses and brutal injuries. Villagers who imbibe the mushrooms, drink tinctures developed by his apothecary, or inhale spores directly and forget half their lives in one day.

And then there's the version of Da no one else has witnessed.

I should have cast you into the sea the moment you opened those eyes.

"How . . . how are you able to see it?" I swallow past the shame, the lingering fear. The way his words fit like an old skin I'm long past ready to shed. "No one else does."

"My sister." I don't think Brona meant to say it. Her fingers dig into her arms as she glares at the ground for several long seconds, twin slashes of red appearing on her cheeks. Just when I think she's about to run, she releases a sigh that could break the world. "She was a navigator too."

Was.

Dread creeps down my back as I search Brona's eyes. "What happened?"

"Dermot destroyed her." Brona balls her fists against her sides. "Ma taught us both the ways of the stars, how to track storms and currents—taught a whole school since she lost her leg and couldn't find work on ships any longer. But when your da showed up one day, it wasn't any of the others from the Dromlach Cliffs he went for. It was my older sister. Orla."

Her name is wrapped in pain, still tender at the edges.

But it's Brona's stubborn jerk of the chin that keeps me still.

"She was seventeen when she took the job—all bright smiles and dimples. She used to laugh, you know, and knew the story of *every* constellation no matter how wee. Even made up her own sometimes."

Brona no longer meets my eyes. "They brought her body and stone back two years after she left. Said she died in a storm— but there were scars. Deliberate ones. And . . . and her belly was swollen."

My own stomach plummets. "How long ago?"

"Three years next season." Brona swallows. Wipes away a tear that I pretend not to notice. "I hoped it was a mistake. Or water bloat, or a thousand other things besides. But I was wrong. She walks my dreams at night, since we brought the soulstone home, even after we buried the body. And she shows me—"

Her voice falters. I recognize the horror in her eyes.

"She shows me her memories of the ship. How Dermot started with gifts—combs carved of shell so fine, it was a wonder they didn't break, necklaces of violet-blue pearls, and sweets the likes of which we'd never seen. At first it felt like a blessing. Until the night he came to her room."

Brona glares at the ceiling, tears spilling over her eyes.

"She didn't feel she could refuse him. He made *sure* she couldn't refuse him. The level of power he held over that ship, over *her*. The rest of the crew was well paid not to care, and the money was too good for her to pass up. She had to take care of me—of Mam. So she allowed it until . . ."

She swipes at her eyes. Inhales a knife-sharp breath. "My sister wanted to get rid of it, but the surgeon's herbs didn't work once she'd missed her second month's courses. She wanted to be free, be *done*, and she was so close to leaving that ship until the day Dermot saw her stomach. He blamed her for being careless, a-and when she said she'd tried to end it and couldn't, he—" A strangled sound catches in her throat. "He threw her from the hatch down into the hull in his fury."

"Brona—"

She crumples, but this time I don't hesitate.

I wrap her tight in my arms, like I always wished someone would do for me. Brona flinches, but doesn't stiffen or push me off. Instead, she turns her face into my shoulder and breathes deep, already fighting to contain her own storm.

But I understand it now. It's not disgust or contempt for feelings that drives her walls up so high.

It's an effort to protect her own.

"I'm sorry."

Brona sniffs. Rubs at her eyes with the back of one hand. "Don't. I've been cruel to you."

"My father is cruel. You've only been unkind."

She laughs, the sound muffled and wet, until she steps back to meet my eyes again. "Aye. It's just . . . when Faolan first talked about that feckin' island, I got so—so angry. Because it's supposed to be a myth."

"I thought the same." *I'm scared I still might.*

Brona searches my eyes like they're the lines on her map. "But if it's not—I mean, if you can really find it, then that means freedom for Orla. Rest for me. I can't bring Dermot to justice, nobody would give a shite, but at least we could have *peace.* And that's just my story—one soulstone. Imagine what finding the isle would mean for the Crescent."

I don't. I can't.

Brona laughs weakly. Wipes her face on her sleeve. "I want to believe in you, Saoirse. I know you're not Dermot's daughter—not in the way I accused. I just . . . I need you to look me in the eye and swear you're not lying. That it's not some grand story from Faolan? I need you to tell me you really think you can find the Isle of Lost Souls."

Her words paralyze me. She wants me to swear by faith in myself—the one thing I've never been able to manage, though loathing comes as easy as breathing. Only days ago, I thought this magic was a curse—a harbinger of death and destruction. And even after I saw the seventh goddess speak about how prophecy is not a punishment, and those of us who see are not responsible for what comes to pass, it's still hard to believe.

"I—"

My gaze drifts across the garden and locks on Faolan standing at the end of the path, his curious gaze on the cottage I called home for seven years. I swear I feel the sun dip a little lower in the sky to mock me with its passage of time.

Faolan is going to die, and I have to pretend he's not. The only path forward is to find the Isle of Lost Souls. I *have* to believe in it—to chase it with everything I have—because without it, I'll end up with nothing and no one.

"I swear it, Brona."

No matter how much I wish I didn't have to.

Brona studies my face for another long moment, then releases a tight smile and squeezes my hand before letting it go. "Okay. Then I'm behind you."

Gods.

"It makes a sort of sense, actually." Brona rubs her nose on a sleeve, then parts her hair into three sections with her fingers. "That we'll be finding the Isle of Lost Souls now when the last time Muireal cradled the moon between her palms, the isle sank into the sea."

My arms go limp. "What are you talking about?"

"Muireal." Brona nods to the clouded sky, then shrugs, halfway through her plait. "Some called her a siren, others a whisperer of fate or collector of stars—caught in her own pattern forever when the sea eventually tired of her song. The constellation's on its way to peak right at the next full moon. Hasn't happened in five generations, if you listen to my mother."

The next breath I take puts me back in the water, faced with my grandmother's bones.

"They say when she holds the moon in her hands, even the staunchest skeptics believe faeries walk the earth again and anything is possible." Brona rolls her eyes as she ties off the braid. "A bit trite, all that, but the timing makes sense. Don't you think?"

Aye.

Far too much.

Before I can ask anything else, Faolan whistles my tune as he strolls up the garden path—a wistful three-note trill—and then smiles as though we haven't spent the last few days avoiding each other. "Ready, Saoirse?"

"A-aye." I'm still gaping at Brona, but between one blink and the next, she's off to join Nessa by the path's end. "I've just got to—why do you have a pack?"

My voice falls sharply enough to stop him mid-step, but then he shrugs and adjusts the traveling cloak slung over his shoulders.

"I'm coming with you, of course."

The leather bag creaks beneath my grip. "No. No, we decided it would only be me. I know the land around the castle, know the ways in and out—you agreed, Faolan."

"That you'd risk only *your* life, aye." His smile belongs to a sea demon. "But then I got to thinking on what Kiara said at the hand-fasting. Something about our paths being struck together, and how we're not to abandon each other. Isn't that right?" He scoops the rucksack out of my hands and loops it over one shoulder. "Your life counts as mine now. So I'm coming along. Need anything else from the cottage before we set out?"

He glances over my shoulder, and for a heartbeat I think of letting him inside to see the space that's *mine*. Would he tease me for the dozens of socks stored in the trunk? Find the stars I carved into the walls at seventeen, when I dreamed one day the Wolf would appear and take me away?

I glance over my shoulder at my cottage—my sanctuary.

My prison.

I know the precise curve of the walls and the places it's bent with age, doorways sliding to one side and plaster sagging to reveal patches of stone. I know how cold it gets in the winter no matter how much wood is piled on the fire, and what corners the spiders like to claim as their own. It's the only place left in the world that truly knows me, and it's terrifying to think of letting Faolan inside.

I don't move from the entrance. But I don't close the door either. "Damn you and your tricks."

His eyes soften, hand brushing mine. "Is that a yes?"

I draw my own cloak tight, digging my fingers into the wool. "We'll have to get extra gills. I was going to swim up the old ferrier's entrance to get to the family crypt. You can't make it by boat any longer, so no one keeps watch."

"Perfect. And if we can't make it in there?"

"I have a few other ideas." His face falls when I don't elaborate, but I pretend not to see it. "It's two hours to the nearest village. We'd best get going."

THIRTY-EIGHT

The pain starts in the first village, if you could call it that. The houses are low and cramped, close together, the people dressed in cloth worn as thin as their faces. Every hand we pass is stained a chalky, porous white from harvesting the caipín baís. Even the children's.

My stomach turns violently when a girl of three catches my fingers in her pale, mottled ones to lead me to the pitiful stable where we buy the only horse fit enough to travel. As I press an extra coin into the girl's hand, I slip my little dream bear from the siren into her pocket as well. I hadn't meant to take it with me from the Scath-Díol in the first place, but if I can't fill the girl's belly beyond tonight, at least her dreams will be kind.

The second village is worse. Muddy streets filled by gaunt figures with vacant eyes, so lost in the magic of the stalks, they've forgotten their families and homes. Their own names.

The third is so full of wandering spirits, I no longer try to put distance between my back and Faolan's chest, but let him hold me until their hurt stops eating at my mind, pulsing beneath the marks on my back. But it doesn't keep my soul from aching as we pass the final altar glimmering with aged soulstones until the dark forest swallows us again.

"Right. That's enough." Faolan eases the reins from my limp fingers once we've left the others far enough behind, tightening his arm around my waist as he pulls the horse to a stop. "Best stop here for the night."

I don't argue. I don't say anything—barely have all day. Not since the little girl told me that each night at the eleventh hour, the ghosts shriek through the woods, their stones buried beneath rock and sea from a cavern collapse just before she was born.

"Saoirse?"

I blink and curl my leg over the horse's shoulder to slide to the ground. Try to ignore the sharp pangs in my thighs, the ache rooted in my skull that crawls to every limb. "Sorry."

"Don't be."

Faolan lands beside me, and for a moment we are apart. Then he catches my wrist, easing me to face him for the first time in hours. It takes everything I have left to look him in the eye. When I do, all I can think about is the way he watched me only a week ago with his fingers tangled in my hair, lips swollen from hard kisses.

Lips of a liar, same as mine.

Whatever he has to say, I'm not ready to listen.

I step back until my arm breaks free from his fingers and I can shake my head. "I-I'll gather wood for the fire."

"Hang on—" But I'm already walking away, unwilling to feel his pain alongside mine. The magic's left me far too sensitive, my body vulnerable, spirit small.

When I return, he has the roll unfurled on the ground and the horse tied up, a circle of stones and packed dirt waiting for kindling. From one of the packs, he pulls out a loaf of bread crusted with nuts, and a bundle of dried meat, as I stack the wood. One crack of a Bruidin leaf from the tin in Faolan's pack, and warmth bleeds through the air into our skin.

I'd forgotten how cold it gets on my isle by night, even in the dead of summer as we are. It's all the pocks in the land, I think, letting in the sea and chill with it. Half of it's gone to bog, strewn with peat moss and *always* the scent of decay. I'm halfway through rubbing life back into my fingers when I feel his gaze on me.

My heart launches a weak protest when I meet it.

Faolan sits with his knees drawn to his chest, dark hair pulled back neatly into a knot for once as he tears the bread in half and offers me a portion. His shirt lacks embellishment; the rings he loves so much are gone. The cloak is the only thing that gives him away, and only because it's hanging half off one shoulder instead of pulled low over his head as it's been all day.

"You're really going to ignore me, then? Along with everyone else?"

I almost laugh as I take the bread. It's like sand in my mouth. Of course it's not actually me Faolan misses. It's the attention.

I feel nothing. I want nothing. I am nothing.

I repeat the phrases in my mind until the pain dulls into something manageable, then force myself to meet his gaze. We couldn't have the Wolf of the Wild spotted in case anyone talked, so I was the one to secure the horse and purchase lunch, facing my own people for the first time in my life. They wouldn't recognize me. Not only because my parents kept us separate in the castle and the keep, but because I know well how to hide myself from the world. What's more, I don't even mind it when it serves me.

For Faolan, though, it's little more than a small series of tortures.

"I'm not ignoring you."

His scoff sets my teeth on edge. "Right. It's just the ground is wildly intriguing at the moment, aye?"

"Stop feeling sorry for yourself." Faolan's eyes latch on to mine, wide and affronted, and I can't help the smallest smile. But it's brittle, as I remember the look on his face when his glove fell away. His story about a promise, a voice in the sea, and a girl with ocean eyes. "I'm thinking."

"You could think aloud with me." The hope on his face is boyish. Impossible to reconcile with everything else. Quiet descends for a beat too long, and his smile drops along with his face into his hands. "What'll it take, lass? I'm going mad, guessing what's running through your mind all on my own."

I fix my eyes staunchly on the fire, insides twisting again. "Is there a god that could turn back time? Or make you tell me the whole truth before I—" I can't finish the sentence, not aloud.

Before I boarded the ship? Married him? Or back to the moment before he told me I was worthy of so much more than I'd been dealt?

I feel nothing. I want nothing. I am nothing.

He must sense some small part of what I'm holding back, because his shoulders drop as he pushes a log too hard in the fire, and the whole little pyre collapses in a shower of sparks. "No. But there's a goddess of fate who set this all up nice and tidy, and she's a real bitch."

My laugh catches me off guard, breaking the heavy quiet before I can clap a hand over it. I glance toward the stars, where they peek out from behind leaves, half afraid she'll manifest from my visions and lash out at Faolan. But it's only us and the quiet. Finally, I drop my forehead to my knees and release all the breath that's been trapped in my chest since the moment his glove fell away.

"Aye, she is. But you still played your part."

"So did you."

"At least I've owned mine."

I almost regret the stillness that follows. But I can no longer swallow blame that is not my own, just for the sake of keeping the peace. Even if it means this fragile warmth between us is snuffed out.

"I'm sorry."

My head jerks up. I hunt his face, his eyes, for the lie. The manipulation that must be there.

But it's only Faolan—the boy who survived a shipwreck to carve an entire legend out of this vicious, hungry world. And still I wonder if it's my ears that have got it wrong. "What?"

"I said I'm sorry." Faolan's lips flick up at the corners, but his eyes are sober when they meet my own. "I should have told you from the start, or at least after we were handfasted, but I'm . . ." His smile falters, then drops away. "I'm a selfish bastard at heart, and a proud one. I've worked bloody hard to get the ship, the name, and if I could never remember what it was like to be on those feckin' rocks, nameless and completely alone—"

"You forget I was alone too."

Wind rustles the leaves above our heads, as though the trees are listening as well. Smoke gathers between us, then trickles into the air. His calluses scrape my wrist, drawing me back to my body—to him. But I can't meet his eyes. Not for this.

"Do you know that silence has a sound?" I curl my toes into the dirt. "It's memory. Ghosts. You can think a million different thoughts and hear each one as though someone's shouted it across the room. *Murderer. Cursed. Worthless.*"

My breath shudders when I take it in. "I used to press up against a wall to pretend someone was holding me. By the time I was sixteen, my left side almost always had a bruise. I didn't talk to anyone for months—my father sent someone with supplies every full moon, but they were instructed to leave them at the path, as though I were contagious."

"Saoirse . . ."

"And I would tell myself I feel nothing. I want nothing. I am nothing."

Faolan has never gone so rigid as he does now. His knuckles are white where his fingers hold mine, breath trembling as it pours free from his lungs. "Is that what you tell yourself now? In the times when you go quiet, lost so far inside yourself that I cannot reach you?"

I squeeze my eyes shut until stars appear behind them, then nod as his thumb presses over mine. "It makes it easier."

"Easier to what?"

"To forget the pain. The things I've done—or what's been done to me. My . . . my father isn't a good person."

Faolan blinks, clearly taken aback. I almost want to laugh again, but I shake my head instead. "You asked me to share my thoughts. And that's it. Even without seeing all we did today, or hearing Brona's story, he's never apologized after he did wrong. Not once, not ever." I wonder if it would be better or worse if he had. "I never thanked you for taking me away from him."

Faolan's fingers pull on mine until I look up. He's frowning at me, lips slightly parted until he leans in and tucks a dark lock of my hair back from my face. I'd hardly noticed it fall. "You're the one who chose to leave him, lass. Hell, you swam across the bloody ocean to get away—don't think I've forgotten that moment." His thumb brushes my bottom lip. "All I've done is provide a ship and name to protect you, and a hell of a lot of trouble."

I can't help the smile, as out of place as it feels on my mouth. "I did, didn't I?"

"Aye." His gaze drops from my eyes to my lips, and it's only then I realize his hand's still holding my cheek. My stomach tightens in a way that's familiar now, holding fast to the moth wings inside so they don't escape when he touches his lips to mine. But as he leans forward with firelight flickering across his face and my head tips back, something unfurls inside my mind.

A glove removed. A secret shared.

The death sentence weighing heavier on my shoulders with each day that's wasted.

I turn my head so his lips meet my cheek instead, wincing at the tender brush of it. "I can't. Not after . . . I just . . . I can't yet."

His fingers stiffen on my jaw, but it's surprise I see when I pull back, not anger. "Why?" He searches my face, fingertip stroking my jaw. "I could make it all up to you. Banish those nasty thoughts of nothing from your head. Bring you so much pleasure, if you'd let me—"

"No." The word is so foreign on my tongue, it takes effort to push it free. But its power is immediate, sending Faolan back on his heels, his touch sliding from my face. I grab his hand before it can drop fully away. "I want this, Faolan. Want *you*. But I can't—not until I can trust you again."

He flinches, and it nearly breaks my resolve.

"I'm sorr—"

"Don't say it." His laugh is as sudden and quick as a bird taking flight, fingers raking over the reddish-brown scruff at his jaw before he clears his throat. "You're absolutely feckin' right. Just . . . stars above, I wish—" He bites the words off and leans his elbows on his knees. "I'll earn it back. I swear it to you now, all right?"

The final knot of anger in my heart unfurls, and with it an idea.

I glance toward the fire, then slowly reach into the small leather satchel, glass clinking as I extract the vial of grayish-white ink.

"You could start with this."

THIRTY-NINE

The bottle of ink looks innocent enough. Barely the length of my thumb, it swirls with shades of white not unlike the ones I've glimpsed in the sky right before a world-ending storm. But where even clouds contain specks of light, the ink absorbs any to be found.

Understanding flashes across his face as he looks from the bottle to me, his brows knitting together. "The inverted triskele on your back."

"Aye." I set the vial between us, then wrap an arm around my legs. "You were right when you guessed about the color. It's made with caipín baís ink."

"Feck." Faolan goes to touch my shoulder, then thinks better of it. His fist falls hard to the ground between us. "The bastard poisoned you."

I drop my face against my knees. "Mam said it was to help me." But even then, in the midst of their plans, I remember how wrong those words had felt. "But I think—I think Da was afraid of me. And maybe he should've been, Faolan. I thought I killed my brother with this magic."

A part of me still worries that I did.

The ground shifts, pebbles scraping one another as he moves beside me. I keep my eyes shut.

"I heard stories about Dermot's daughter being sent away. But I never . . ." His sigh catches in my hair. "How did it happen?"

Every part of my body rebels against this story. The one I've concealed inside for seven long years.

But trust comes in parts, and how can I expect him to earn mine if I'm always terrified of losing his?

"We were playing on the beach. I was fifteen—isolated from most people by that point, because the amulets weren't as effective since I started bleeding, and it was awful trying to be around them. But Aidan snuck Conal out of his lessons one day, and the both of them dragged me along."

I remember it, the way their affection blazed across my loneliness like a comet.

"I always wore an amulet before—you remember the one? In the same pattern as the tattoo."

"Aye, carved in white ink, just like this."

I nod. "Da said it was blessed in our patron goddess Eabha's well. And I believed it until he told me otherwise the night Rí Maccus claimed my hand." My nose scrunches as I rock my head left, then right. "I never took it off, because he told me it would stop the magic—and in a way, it did. Like standing outside in the middle of winter, until everything goes a bit numb. It was better than feeling mad."

Faolan shifts again, and I sense his hand before I feel it. But this time when it wraps over my knuckles, I don't push him away.

"We were going to swim. Conal and Aidan were wrestling each other, tearing their clothes off, and I was a few steps behind. Dresses are harder to sort out."

"I'm well aware."

I laugh, the sound a touch wet. "The amulet caught on my laces when I was tugging it overhead, and broke on the stones below. I knew I wasn't supposed to be without it, but Aidan and Conal were already swimming and I'd never felt the full consequences of the magic—only vague feelings, never visions. So I left it on the shore and went to take their hands. And the moment our skin touched . . ."

It still exists there, in my body. That gut-wrenching sensation, like an invisible hand had reached for my spine and tugged it straight out.

"I saw what would happen. I *knew* that if three of us went into the water, only two would come out again. When the vision ended, I tried to tell them. Fought them to get out of the water, and then stayed by myself onshore, because I thought if I stayed on the beach, then the vision couldn't come true. But they took it as a game."

Conal's mirth swirls between my temples. Escapes as a trickle down my cheek.

"They tugged me back into the waves between them, even though I was screaming at them to stop. I tried to get back to shore—I thought if I didn't stay, it wouldn't count. But a cavern had just collapsed, and there was no way to tell until the current caught Aidan under the water. Conal got him free, but . . . he didn't make it out himself."

The fire cracks beneath a gentle breeze, wrapping us in smoke. Faolan eases a strand of my hair back. Catches the trail of tears with his thumb.

"I'm sorry for that. Sorry you had to live through it. But, lass, how the hell could you think that it's your fault?"

"Because I knew what would happen." I sit up, wiping at my face. "I knew, and I did nothing. I was still onshore when the two of them started to drown."

"Could you have managed to help them?"

I blink. "No. But—"

"You were a child. Could you have tossed one of them over your back and swam them both to shore? Or—let's say all three of you *were* in the water. If the current caught you instead, would they have just let you drown without a fight?"

Every joint in my body locks into place, chest caving in around each breath. "N-no. But I could have run once I knew what would happen, so they could never get me into the water in the first place."

Faolan huffs—almost a laugh, but even he's not that flippant. "I doubt they'd have been swayed, if they were young lads playing a game. Besides, what if on the other side of some rocks, another person was swimming, too, to make it three? Or what if you hadn't had the vision—don't you think it would've still come true? It's not like seeing it is what made that cavern collapse."

I'm speechless. Searching for words, even as the ones the goddess spoke ripple through my soul.

We cannot unwrite what fate has written. I am not her master, nor would I ever wish to be. I can only see. Only know.

I think of the other gods' reactions to her prophecy. Of my father's to what he could never understand—the lies he's told to gain whatever serves his purpose best. Making me dangerous. A monster. A curse.

Until I feared myself enough to want to lock her away.

Faolan watches me as I curl over, spreading my fingers against the moss-laden ground. It's excruciating to unwind this knot inside me—the knot that *was* me for years of my life. Almost unbearable.

Because I am not a monster. Or a murderer.

I am not cursed.

"Saoirse?" Faolan cups my cheek, and I lean desperately into that touch—gasping at its gentleness, its warmth. "It's time to name yourself, instead of listening to all your father's shite. You're not a killer, and you're certainly not *nothing*. So tell me what you are."

The answer flies to my lips, taken from my grandmother's vision, the siren's story at the Scath-Díol. Yet even as it emerges, I know in my bones that it is true.

"A Soulgazer."

Faolan's thumb skates along my lashes, resting at the corner of my eye as he grins. "There you are. I see you."

But *I* can't see our path ahead if I'm willing to wear a blindfold.

My fingers are stiff, damp with soil and specks of green. Still, I manage to undo the laces of my shirt enough to spread the collar open, shrugging it down my shoulders. Cool air rushes across the sensitive skin along my back when I pull my hair to one side, and the hitch of his breath confirms he's seen it.

The tattoo.

He touches the silvery-white marks with the tip of a finger, tracing one, two, then the start of the third. "They didn't finish?"

I wince. "No. My body seized after the second was complete, and Da told his apothecary to finish the third the night I left for your ship."

Faolan grunts. "No wonder you were desperate enough to swim for it."

Once, I might have glared at him for the irreverence, but I understand him better now. How humor cuts through the darkness like a well-timed swipe of a dagger in a fight. "I couldn't go through with it. They said they'd tried it before, and some of the people they tested it on lost use of their limbs. Their ability to think. I didn't . . . I didn't want to be nothing after all."

"You couldn't if you tried." Faolan sweeps a touch over one of the swirls before he reaches across my lap to the bottle. "You nicked the ink?"

My laugh is shaky. "I'd just agreed to marry a pirate. I figured I'd better start learning to thieve somewhere."

His lips touch my back next, and heat pools in my thighs. "Clever girl."

I swallow. "I wanted it in case we failed. I wanted a way to lock the curse away myself. But . . . if it's not a curse, or a danger . . ." I reach back and tap the top of the tattoo. "Then this is all that's standing between us and the Isle of Lost Souls."

Faolan's breath hitches once. Escapes in a slow, uneasy stream. "Death-cap ink ingrained into your skin. Right. Dermot's made it easy for us, hasn't he?"

I twist until I can see his face. Bite my lip until it almost bleeds.

"You could burn it off with your knife."

Faolan jerks back, brows snapping low. "You want me to brand you?"

"Aye." I wait to regret the words, or for an uneasy lurch in my stomach. But for once, it's as steady as a rock. I reach into the satchel beside us and remove two other glass jars, a length of cloth folded around herbs. "The caipín báis have few natural antidotes, but I brought them in case. Something to quell the pain, a salve for healing—I wasn't sure what we'd face. That's why I went into my cottage before we came."

Faolan's touch slides down my jaw, turning my face back to his own. "This is a damn lot of trust to be putting in my hands. You're sure you're ready for it, Saoirse?"

I meet his gaze, bright even in the darkness. Rather than sinking, it makes my body feel like floating on the warmest summer sea. The thought of losing that feeling—of losing *him* because of a lock on myself I never asked for in the first place—is intolerable.

"Aye. Caipín báis are temperamental—they only grow in the deepest caverns, which is why our island is sinking as it is. I don't think the ink will withstand heat. And a brand would disrupt the pattern locking it in place. At least . . ." I reach for the vial of ink and hesitate only a second before uncorking it to pour the contents into the fire. Instantly, the flames flare white, then silvery black and finally gray—spitting and consuming it until after only another second, they've returned to orange. "I hope so."

My hands shake as I cork the bottle and drop it to the ground. "A salve should do the rest."

Faolan only stares. For a long moment I think he'll refuse. That I'll somehow have to do it myself, shoving a blade in the fire and hoping I hit the right spot on my back. But then his hand curls back into my hair, and he drags my face forward until his lips settle on my forehead.

"You're the bravest fecking woman I've ever met. You know that, right?"

I don't, but I'm powerless to do anything except linger in his arms until he slowly sits back, wiping the sweat from his brow. "All right. Ah—here." He tugs the leather sheath free of his belt and passes it to me. "Bite down on this, and don't dare let up until I say it's through."

My hand only jerks a little as I reach first for the enchanted willow bark, chewing until a delicious sort of ice has coated my insides. Faolan fishes the box of Bruidin flame from his pouch and cracks three more leaves into the fire. Then he slides his dagger into the flames, resting it just over the embers until it glows cherry red. His gaze flicks to mine as he takes it out, turning it this way and that to inspect the metal—make sure it's clean.

"Ready?"

I slip my hand into his, leather and skin warm against my palm. "Ready."

I bite down on the leather and lock eyes with him until he moves behind me, searing the tattoo away with a press of his blade.

The fire pops, disguising my muffled cry as a white-hot chill strikes my body with the violence of lightning. It's like nothing I've ever felt—*pain* is familiar. This is something else entirely.

Another wave hits, brighter and hotter than before. My back arches as the leather sheath absorbs my groan and Faolan grasps my hand tighter, his thumb easing the fingers apart.

Faolan.

I see flashes of him as a wee lad in a seaside pub, soaking up stories like they alone sustain him. In a village as a youth, wearing plain wool, restless and desperate to know the sea himself—scrawny surrounded by royals at court, then caught and chained shortly after. He'd told me Kiara spared his life, but I couldn't fathom what it was like when they were both younger. Hungrier. She offered a leash in exchange for the noose, and Faolan has felt like her lapdog ever since.

He wants to be free to make his name. More than jewels, more than life, more than anything.

"Why—" I stare at our hands, panting as the leather drops to my lap. "Why did you marry me?"

Faolan nearly drops the dagger, swearing as his pinky meets the still-hot blade. He tosses it into the dirt. "You know why."

"No, I don't." The pain is more bearable now, though my skin crawls with sensation. I take up the pot of salve and hold it out to him with shaking hands. "You said you'd planned to kidnap me if I refused to seek the isle. So why did you agree to the marriage?"

Faolan runs a fingertip along my earlobe, then dips it into the pot. "Maybe I like a bit of trouble."

My skin warms as he eases the salve along my wound, cooling

the branded flesh until my shoulders unwind. Yet still I hold my tongue. In all these weeks traveling together, I've learned it's the silence he can never stand.

Only a moment or two pass before his sigh ruffles my hair.

"You were dressed as a magpie."

The answer catches me off guard. I twist to look at him, but his hand rests at my shoulder, keeping me straight. He reaches past me for the other pot and roll of bandages.

"They were my mother's favorite bird—something she used to tease me with given my habit of collecting bits and bobs. She'd tell me if I were ever to build a proper nest, I'd need another magpie along. And then there you came, when I least expected you." Faolan lays the poultice of moss and herbs I crafted this morning over my damaged skin, then gently unwinds the bandage. I hardly dare breathe. "I could tell you were a collector, just from the way you exist in the world—flinching when it draws too near, but wide-eyed the rest of the time. You line your feathers with stories, and hoard the things people say to you like treasures, even when they're pure bullshite. You can't let anything go."

He guides my arm up, wrapping the bandage across my ribs and between my breasts. Again, twice more.

"And your offer was so damn clever, I was tempted to see it through."

My husband tucks the end of the bandage just over my heart, and I pray he can't feel how hard it's beating.

Until he speaks, and breaks it all over again.

"It's a good story, anyway, isn't it? The Magpie and the Wolf."

Faolan helps me back into my shirt, and I turn my face away so he can't see my frown.

Legends may not die, but stories always end.

FORTY

Seven years and three months have passed since my brother died, yet still I expect his ghost to thrash among the waves. The night before my banishment, I saw him from my window in the castle above, but as we climb the narrow path down the cliffside, there is no glint of silvery blue against a sea turned black by the pebbles below. I search for the figure, throat straining with the need to call out.

But Conal is gone.

A rock slides beneath my foot, and I start to slip until Faolan catches me below the arm. He doesn't let go, and it's only then I realize I'm shaking.

"All right?"

My nod is a weak thing. Still, I can't seem to walk on until I've found Faolan's hand with mine. Not for the first time, I glance at the top of the cliffs, where my father's home splits the evening fog. Black stone that glints green in daylight, torn from the land along with so much else. He's always been so proud of replacing the rotting walls his ancestors built of wood, thinking himself clever.

But how many backs broke to haul it up that cliffside and secure it in place? How much weaker is the ground we stand on, matching the wide bogs in the center of the isle and spreading round its edges?

How many years until the entire island sinks?

I force my gaze to the ground ahead, taking one step after another in the night until our feet meet the narrow beach that holds nearly every good memory I have of my childhood, as well as the very worst. It takes effort to block them without the tattoo's forceful shield. Yet as Faolan squeezes my hand, guiding me until my back is to the waves and we're both facing the cliffs, it grows easier. Our damaged souls seem aligned.

"That's it, then?" he asks.

"The oldest entrance, aye." It gapes open halfway to the cliff's bottom, formations clinging to the top like fangs. With every low tide, it breathes out the rot of the isle. "It looks open from here, but when you make it inside you'll see. The interior collapsed the day my brother . . ."

His fingers tighten on mine and I'm grateful I don't have to finish that thought. I clear my throat instead. "You're sure you can get your message to the ship if something goes wrong?"

If *I* am wrong. If my father is here and not away like he'd planned. If the gills don't work though we've tested them twice.

"Aye. It's a sand dollar from off the coast of the Isle of Ashen Flame. Dried out; all you have to do is crack it open and tell the wee doves where to fly. Nessa said they could have the ship here in a matter of hours, hang the consequences if we're spotted."

"All right." Glancing at the old entrance one more time, I tug Faolan past the mouth and its crumbled interior toward the outer lip, where deep water meets the cliffs. "The ferrier's tunnel should be just round this way. If the rocks haven't collapsed, we'll see the top of the entrance as the tide drops."

"And if they have collapsed?" Faolan is smiling as he asks, wait-

ing for my list of worries he only half paid attention to this morning. Something in me shifts as I study the constellation of freckles
on his cheek, tugging my lips up to match.

"Think of the reward, never the risk?"

His eyes widen, then dance with light, and it's all I can do to
turn away and force my feet along until we're both balanced on
the barest edge of rock, slick with sea spray. It's a good distraction,
forcing my heart to race for other reasons, though I have my own
goat-hide bands knotted round my ankles now, ensuring it'll take
a damned strong wind or wave to get me off this rock.

My mind grasps the truth of it well enough, but my body is still
shaking like a leaf by the time we reach the ferrier's path, marked
only with a deeply etched pattern we find by sweeping our fingertips along the cliffside. A triskele, the same as those three-spiraled
marks on a soulstone.

Faolan cracks his neck and shakes his hands off before crouching to shuffle through his bag. He hands over the gills and I grimace as I fix them to my throat, the mist awakening the magic so
they fuse to my skin. But any discomfort passes quickly as Faolan
tugs his shirt over his head. "Well?"

Right. This part.

I watch a touch helplessly as Faolan works his boots free one
after the other, then ties his hair back with a leather cord. Mercifully, he keeps his trousers on—except it's not a mercy because
every pale, freckled, beautiful muscle shifts into the next as he
moves, and when he stretches his arms overhead, the sleek bones
of his hips glide beneath the skin in an arrowhead that—

He clears his throat and I whirl around to loosen the ties on my
own shirt, then do the same for my boots. Those I drop into the
bag alongside his, but I hesitate just a second before pulling my
shirt free as well.

It's different than the cabin or the cove, when my dress was still laced, body hidden below. My skin immediately breaks into goose-flesh when it meets the air, speckled with water by the next breaking of waves. The place he's branded stings, but the salve has already repaired the worst of its damage. Still, awareness creeps across my skin, and *gods*. It hurts to breathe.

"Saoirse?"

Right. The magic—the gills. The crypt.

I run a finger over the long, wide strip of cloth that's looped over each shoulder and wrapped across and beneath my breasts to secure them. It hasn't moved, and at least that's one thing to be grateful for, though there's a hand's width of soft flesh exposed above my trousers.

My face is burning hot when I turn to hand over the shirt, one arm wrapped tight over my middle. His eyes dart down as if I've caught him doing something wrong, and I can't tell if I'm relieved or disappointed when they don't return to me.

"Done." Faolan straightens with the bag over his shoulder, and I swallow as I face the black waves. Ghostly blue flashes at the very edge of my vision, and I start to turn my head when Faolan's hand drops to my lower back. His fingers spread wide against the bare skin. "Are you ready?"

No. I truly can't breathe now, and I've no idea where to place the blame. Instead, I force my chin down in a nod, brace the balls of my feet against the rock's edge, and jump into the sea with Faolan.

The ferrier's tunnel is almost completely engulfed by the ocean. As we swim closer, I see most of the entrance is covered in a thick layer of barnacles, some of which have grown as big as my own head. It's terrifying to think we're about to go through there. Paralyzing not to know what we'll find on the other side, if we make it at all.

Faolan's fingers brush over my neck this time, catching on my braid before he flashes a smile and tugs the large moon crystal from his pocket, casting a purplish light between us. He ties the cord round his neck, takes my hand, and swims straight for the entrance.

Silence has never existed so completely as it does in this narrow passage of stone.

It devours us like a thing half-starved. If not for Faolan's constant touch reminding me I am not alone here, I'm certain my body would rebel against my mind and claw its way out of the dark. Instead, we carry forward as the tunnel gets tighter around us, jagged rock growing straight out of the sculpted sides and top. One of my ancestors—or perhaps the goddess herself—carved this space from the cliff to allow our soulstones a sacred passage back to the mother sea.

Nature is simply reclaiming her stolen land.

My skull brushes against rock and I try to swim lower, but my belly meets the bottom, and the water—

Gods, the water pushes faster against my feet. It tugs Faolan ahead in a sharp move, and as the light in his hand passes through, I see with horror that three of those angry growths of stone cross over one another so the opening in the middle is barely wide enough for a person to fit. Faolan tries to catch hold, but it's all he can do to adjust his shoulders and avoid smashing his head.

And then he's through, the rapid stream forcing my body into the space left behind. Something goes wrong—something doesn't *fit*. And the world goes black, my chest collapsing with a scream that bounces off the rock all around me, in front of me— against me.

I'm trapped.

Holy stars—I'm *trapped*.

Ropes of water burn my skin now, tearing at my clothes and threatening to rip the hair from my head as my hips wedge even tighter against the rock until it digs into my skin.

Pain and fear explode in my mind and I become a wild thing without reason or thought. I lash out, twisting and crying out in streams of bubbles when the rock does break my skin, slicing the fleshy part of my hip so that the next pass of water through my mouth tastes of blood.

I'm going to die here. It was all for nothing.

Something slides against my neck, and I jerk away, only for a pair of steady hands to catch the back of my head before it can break against stone.

Faolan.

I'd weep if I could, but instead I force my body to go still as his hands travel down my throat, my torso, all the way to my hips, which he takes in hand and pushes back. One gentle twist and my body flies through the narrow opening into his, both of us spinning and grasping for something to hold on to, until the tunnel abruptly ends, spitting us into a pool of water too deep for my feet to touch the bottom. I barely have time to orient myself when Faolan catches my waist, dragging us both to the surface.

The first breath stings, sending vibrations to the deepest places within me. The second releases in a near shout of relief.

I'm alive. We are alive.

"Are you—all right?"

"Aye." I twist to catch sight of Faolan as he hauls me to the pool's edge. "What about . . ."

His face is bathed in a gentle blue-tinged light emanating from the walls. They're covered in long strands of living algae cultivated for whole lifetimes to grow up and cross over along the ceiling.

Gods. I forgot how large this cavern was—said to be the home of Goddess Eabha herself, when it first appeared centuries ago.

Before my ancestors took it as their tomb.

"What about yourself?"

Faolan doesn't answer. I glance at him and find his eyes have stopped hunting my body for injury. They linger now, where his fingers perch at the space between my ribs. Soaked fabric clings to the fullness of my thighs and draws tight across my breasts, leaving little doubt as to my shape. On instinct, I start to curl in on myself—arm about my waist, legs crossed. Anything to appear smaller.

But his eyes glint with something like hunger and my mouth goes dry.

Slowly, I straighten my shoulders. Lift my chin. Welcoming his gaze despite the fierce heat blooming across my skin.

Faolan rocks a small step back, brows shooting up, before he grins and meets my eyes again. With a slight shake of his head, he swipes a hand over his face and turns away. "Going to be the death of me, aren't you?"

A drop of ice cuts through the heat as I remember that first touch. First vision.

"Something like that."

He sets his pack down and, as we dress, I force my eyes from his body to the walls. The one behind him is littered with carefully hewn alcoves like honeycomb in a hive, each one bearing the body and soulstone of an ancestor. A network of algae runs along the strips of wall between hollows, illuminating bones and long-ruined cloth, tarnished jewelry and the untouched stones that shimmer like abalone.

Like Faolan's scar.

I nearly reach for his hand as I glance at the collapsed old entrance—then look again. My jaw slackens at the sight of near a hundred caipín baís littering the mound of earth, their stalks as slender as a pointed finger, the domes ashen gray and speckled black. By these traits alone, they'd be easily missed, were it not for the pallid mourner's veil caging each of them in an intricate web of lace.

"Those are meant to be rare," I say, voice tilting as I take a step closer. "It's why Father demands more caverns each year, in hopes more will grow. Why wouldn't he just—"

"Don't be so sure he isn't. Look."

Faolan jabs a finger at the nearest cluster growing in one of my ancestors' graves. Half of them have been clipped, their stumps weeping pearly tears that turn my stomach. Twist it into knots.

I rub firmly at the spot. "This is where he got it, then. The death-cap ink? That one bottle must have taken dozens to produce. But why—"

"Why would he make his own people suffer trying to find the wee veiled ladies when all this time he's had a hoard of his own?" Faolan snorts, turning his back on the sight. "How do you think gods become gods? Or the Daonnaí who slaughtered them, the rí and ríona now—they're all the same feckless creatures, Trouble. Your da just took better advantage of the magical resources he had at his disposal. After all, it's hard to be angry enough for revolution when you can't remember your own name."

Faolan's words stick like a knife between my ribs so that my next breath comes painful and slow.

Or maybe it's the caipín baís forcing ice into my lungs.

Maybe the restless dead?

I swallow my tears before they can rise, and walk the row of empty slots carved for my father and mother at the center of the cavern, the spaces for my siblings, the empty grave meant for me. Only the smallest is filled, a mound of bones covered in a tattered silk shroud for a child not even formed enough to produce a soul-stone.

Conal's remains in shadow.

I frown as rocks clatter behind me, Faolan swearing from where he must have stumbled near the stairs carved into the wall. But it's late. Half of my father's men will be at his side on the tour of the other isles, and the rest like to drink and play games late into the night, lulled by the summer breeze.

I take a step, then another, fingertips skating the edge of the hollow where Conal's body should be.

"Come help me with the door, would you?" Faolan grunts.

My hand meets empty air.

That sick feeling in my gut explodes into dread as metal clicks against wood behind me, and the caipín baís leak poison below. *Freshly clipped.*

I whirl around, already running as the latch starts to give beneath the slide of Faolan's blade.

"Wait, Faolan—don't!"

The door swings open.

And my father, his apothecary, and a half dozen guards stand on the other side.

FORTY-ONE

Y ou stupid, selfish whore!"
I barely have time to shield my face before Da shoves me through the doors of the great hall, sending me sprawling onto uneven flagstone. My knee splits wide open when I fall. "Do you have any idea what your reckless frolic with that lad has cost me?!"

I scramble to my feet, keeping my eyes on his polished boots as blood spreads across my trousers. Behind me, bodies collide and Faolan curses, but I don't dare look back to see if he's all right. History in my father's house demands that I keep my eyes down.

I squeeze my hands into fists to hide their shaking. The woad wolf dances as my tendons shift below.

"Because of the delay, Rí Maccus has refused to send his stone-masons to reinforce the central caverns. Two collapsed in the last storm, taking a row of cottages with them."

My gaze drags up to his waist and the gleaming bronze of his belt. Higher to each flash of gold, silver, and glittering gems wrapped along his knuckles as he gestures through the air. They are nothing like the chalk-tipped fingers of that little girl.

Heat creeps up the back of my neck as cold takes over the rest.

"Fifteen dead. Elders, mothers—an infant only days old."

Bodies swim before my eyes—too thin by half, hands ashen practically from birth, their eyes dulled not by death but by exhaustion and hunger or the mushrooms they're sent to harvest. Meanwhile my father's own stomach has rounded in the last five years, stretching silk he never used to wear, and my jaw threatens to break from clenching.

"All of them gone, thanks to your selfishness."

I look up, teeth bared like the wolf that I've become.

"*My* selfishness, Father?"

His pupils draw to pinpricks as ice fractures the air between us. But when his hand meets the back of my neck, I shove his arm away before he can force my head down.

My rage leaves no space for a collar I've long since outgrown.

"You've carved holes into an island that's already sinking. Ten new caverns in the past year along the center and south, the fields left to seed as you demand higher taxes and longer nights. And the temples?" My laughter is a knife's edge, cutting through the sound of a scuffle behind me. "When the people go hungry, when accidents plague the new caverns or half a harvest is destroyed by pests and storms—you blame *their* lack of piety to gods you don't even believe in!"

His hand strikes through the air like a snake's bite, and I flinch against a slap that never lands.

When I look up, Faolan stands between us, his lip bloody and chest heaving as he grips my father's wrist, white-knuckled with fury, wrapping his other hand around Da's throat. The guards are at his back in an instant, weapons drawn, but Faolan does not yield.

"Lay another hand on my wife, Dermot, and you'll lose it."

My wife.

My entire body curls around the word as its effect ripples through the court. Strikes my father. For a second, his eyes widen and he looks as if he might believe Faolan. But then a nasty smile splits his face and he steps back, waving off the guards with his free hand.

"You sound a touch possessive for a boy who holds no real claim over my daughter." His gaze levels on us as Faolan steps back to my side, his arm locking around my waist. "Whatever she's told you, it's a lie. Her mind's muddled—just like my mother's—and as such, any vows you might have exchanged are null and void by the word of her king."

"If her mind's no good, why do you keep pushing Maccus on her, then?"

Da's eyes narrow, and I wrap my hand over Faolan's at my waist, threading our fingers tight.

Da lifts one brow. "Rí Maccus does not need a mind. He needs a body. And I need—"

"To pull that great stick out your arse. Saoirse is as clear-minded as a sage, and my cousin Ríona Kiara can speak to that fact herself. *She's* the one who conducted the handfasting."

All expression drops from my father's face, and my mouth goes dry because I know what comes next. But Faolan doesn't stop—he doesn't know what it means when Dermot goes silent.

"And if you think my cousin, the *queen* of Ashen Flame, will take kindly to how you've treated us today—"

"Can Kiara attest to the consummation as well?"

My fingers fall from Faolan's as he releases a tight breath meant to sound like a scoff. But Da is not watching Faolan; he's reading *me*. And I've rarely succeeded at hiding anything from his eyes.

"Kiara has the proof of it, right enough," Faolan says. "What, you think I'd sign on to a marriage and *not* take my rights? What sort of man wouldn't?"

"Whatever cords she carries or trick of bloodstained sheets means nothing to me. The truth is bare in front of us."

Heat stains my face, rushes down my throat to my chest, burns in every limb, as I watch satisfaction settle onto my father's face. I don't see it when a hand clamps over my upper arm, nor when Faolan swears and his touch is ripped away. I only look when he shouts my name, driving his elbow into one guard's throat, wrenching against the grip of a second.

"Get your fecking hands off her," Faolan snarls. "You want money? I can buy you stonemasons—Kiara can as well. You have no idea what I'm capable of finding and the coin I can make you. Dermot—"

"This goes far beyond coin, lad. There's no need for dramatics." Da's voice carries across the vaulted stone ceiling. "Your cousin will be summoned to account for your actions, and I'd suggest you change your story by the time that day comes if you want to taste freedom again. The rest of you?" He raises his voice, gaze sweeping the hall. "Out."

Faolan's face is wild as two guards bind his arms; he bares his teeth as they drag him bodily through a doorway behind the rest of the court. "Dermot, I swear on the stars, the Slaughtered Ones, and every feckin' stone on this island, *if you hurt her*—"

The door slams shut, cloaking the room in a sickening silence. The quiet of a wood when hunters are near.

I don't dare speak, or beg, or breathe.

Not until Da releases a soft laugh, his attention fixed on an object nestled between his fingers.

"The audacity of children." He rolls the thing slowly across his palm. "Tell me, Saoirse, did you truly think I wouldn't know the moment that fool pup of yours crossed into my waters? Let alone my home?"

My chest aches as I try to force a smile. Fail. "It was my home, too, once, Father. Or have you forgotten?"

The dismissive flick of his eyes is a dagger meeting its mark. "I forget nothing." He tilts his head. "The ink you stole. Do you have any idea how long it took to create? The cost of it?"

I bite down until my teeth nearly crack.

He glowers and then catches my shirt collar before I can react. Exposes the bandages beneath, the scent of herbs drifting free from the salve. His lip curls when he sees the wolf tattoo on my wrist as well. "You've mutilated yourself. And it'll take months to complete another vial. Useless girl."

I scramble back, but it's then the object he's toyed with catches the light.

The sight drains my face of blood.

"My mother never took this off, as long as she was alive." Da slides the bone ring onto his smallest finger, where it balances so poorly above the knuckle, I hold my breath as though that could keep it from falling. "Told me it was made of a god's bone and the ocean's tears. Just like she swore it wasn't madness in her eyes, but dreams." His smirk becomes a grimace as he spins it once, then closes his hand into a fist, hiding the ring from view. "Swore it up to the day she held your head under the waves, because she said the damned sea told her to."

I flinch. Shut my eyes so I don't have to see the rigid line of his shoulders or set to his jaw, the marks of a man in pain. Da regrets saving me that night. He regrets my very birth—told me so in words I bear on my flesh, clear as any other scar. He cannot hurt over a memory he's longed to be true.

Can he?

"Mam said . . . you cried the day I was born." I regret the words as soon as they're out, wrapping my arms across my chest like that might shield me. "Was that a lie?"

"No." The word startles me enough to look again, but Da's not watching me.

He's studying the tapestries behind his throne now, filled with our ancestors. For a moment in the quiet, my heart turns traitor, twisting violently with its need to be held by my father's hands.

I start to reach for them, a child again. "Da—"

"I wept because I knew the cost of sparing your life, and still I was too weak to end it."

I am a fool.

My hands clutch at my stomach as I fight for breath that does not come, and when he faces me again there is contempt laced in the brutal mask he's worn all my life. "I paid the price with my son." He turns his hand over, and we both watch the ring slip through the air. "A mistake I'll not make again."

I drop to my knees a second too late. His boot shatters the bone ring into pieces, cleaving its gleaming blue stone neatly in two.

A dam breaks inside me with it, the walls split by an unholy scream that tears my throat raw as I lurch forward and meet an arm as unbending as iron, lifting me to my feet. Da tightens his hold so severely, I start to choke—and it's only then that he takes my face in hand, jerking my head against his shoulder so I have no choice but to meet his eyes.

His cold, dismissive, hateful eyes.

"You'll thank me for it one day, lass. Maybe not until my death-bed. But you'll thank me." His lips curl just before he presses them to my tear-slicked cheek. The same one he meant to strike.

Da releases me after. Lets me sink back to the ground, where I gather the jagged, useless fragments into my hand. Before I can store them in a pocket, however, he steals those pieces as well.

"Brigid, put the cuffs on her when you get to the room. And you'll want to bandage her knee first so she might spend her nights praying Rí Maccus is a more forgiving master than I."

"My king." Soft hands replace my father's, and I lose any will to fight as the old nursemaid leads me from the chamber.

"Please don't do this," I whisper, my steps faltering as we reach the door. "Please. Faolan will die if—"

"Now do you understand why we sent her away?" My father turns his back to me as a tall man peels himself out of the shadows. Dark, curly hair, soft blue eyes, and a tunic stitched with the caipín baís in silver thread. "She's gone feral. A danger to herself as well as those around her."

"She seemed afraid."

Aidan.

He doesn't look at me as he approaches our father, and shame binds me in place.

"Pity is a weakness, son. You'll do well to remember that." Da tips the ring's fragments from one palm to the other with a look of disgust. "I'll dispose of these. Send word to Maccus. He needs to claim his bride."

Brigid nudges me from the room, and I fall to my bloody knees in the hall. A sob wrenches out of my throat as two guards haul me to my feet and up a flight of stairs. I stop fighting. Stop caring. Before week's end, I'll exchange the sea for a bed of stone. And it won't matter whether I have a handfasting or a husband's life to save, or even gods-blessed sight.

The ring is broken now.

And so am I.

FORTY-TWO

Brigid strips me bare as though I am the same child to whom this room once belonged.

Perhaps I've become her again. Because I don't fight as she scours the sweat, salt, and sea from my flesh, replacing it with the cloyingly sweet lilac oils favored by my mother. I don't struggle when Brigid slides metal cuffs that are harsher, unsightly versions of the amulet I wore most of my life into place. For once I welcome the fog they bring—until Brigid lifts the shears.

"Don't."

I glare as a dozen wrinkles form around her lips, the shears dangling limply from her hand. "It's an order, miss. To hide your . . . well, your eyes. Rí Dermot—"

"Can cut them himself if he wishes to hide my eyes again." I'm less surprised by the harshness in my voice than by the way she flinches from it. She ducks her head in a low curtsy, stepping back, and my face screws up even as I pull the towel close around my shoulders. "I'm sorry. Don't tell him, just—leave it, aye? I'll answer for it."

I always do.

Brigid falters, her cheeks paling as she glances once to the door and then back to me before shaking her head. "You . . . You'll need something to wear. I'll check your mother's wardrobe."

"Wait—" She's already gone, a bolt sliding shut behind her.

Right. It never did lock from the inside.

My heart beats slower with every second the cuffs bind my wrists. I want to sink into the floor until I become nothing but stone. Let the fog overtake my mind, drown my wits in tears, and forget . . . everything.

Faolan's lips carving a path along my throat. Wind whipping past my face as I fell off the Teeth, Brona just beside me. Nessa's laughter, or Lorcan's tight embrace, and the way Faolan's eyes burn through the dark when we're lying alongside each other trying not to touch.

You're becoming a wolf, you know.

I don't want to forget.

My throat works as I push onto my feet and snatch up the damp shirt and clammy trousers that smell of the tide. I turn my face into the fabric and breathe, slow and deep, until my head feels right. It's only then I lock eyes on the wardrobe. Carved of oak into a forest scene, the inside is fixed with a false wood backing, leading to a small passage on the other side.

I fling open the door and freeze as rows of dark gowns in simple cuts stop me where I stand. They seem impossibly small, meant for a fifteen-year-old girl who always knew for certain that her father's love was meant for his sons. He could never make room for a daughter.

My touch lands on a fine gray dress with a torn hem, and I shudder.

There isn't time.

I shove the entire row to the side, kicking shoes and scarves out of the way until there is space to run my hand along the smooth wood of the back. But there will be a seam, a knot, and when I press just so, a door will open and reveal—

Nothing.

"Feck!" I pitch myself against the wall of mortar and stone that was once a small tunnel meant to save my life in case of an attack, but it doesn't give. My heart climbs in my throat as I try again. Racing to the fireplace for the poker, I wield it like the crew wield their swords and thrust it against the mortar again and again until sparks fly and all I've accomplished is a few shavings on the wardrobe floor.

My breaths are ugly, desperate things now, full of dust and decay.

Rot.

The air is rotting here—so full of the dead and dying. Of *memories* I no longer wish to have. But the window is latched like the door, and I cannot breathe.

I cannot breathe.

I—

Sprays of glass cascade over the room and down the castle wall as I lower the iron poker and cling to the window frame, allowing the wind to consume me. It's only when my head stops spinning that I catch sight of a woman reflected in a stubborn shard of glass clinging to the side. Raw anger burns in the line of her broad shoulders and tilt of her chin—strength in the set of her strange eyes, the muscles that weave in harmony with her curves.

A sound catches in the back of my throat as I fight the urge to reach for her, because she is intimate and foreign, yes, but she is also *mine*.

"Saoirse?"

The voice lands like a slap. An impossibility. But glass crunches beneath a heavy step as my bedroom door creaks shut, and then I see *his* face. Pale and sharply angled, warped in the glass beside mine. Not Conal, the brother I spent seven years believing I'd killed, but the other—my favorite.

The wind blows our hair wild as I face Aidan at last.

Seven years have stretched and hardened my gentle brother into a warrior. A weapon. I remember how Da used to push him to keep up with Conal. How Mam would sneak Aidan away from the sword to play the harp for her instead, claiming his elegant fingers were better suited to the strings. When Mam and Da argued over it, Aidan would take my hand and we would run to hide among the faerie pools. Da had little patience or consideration for a second son.

Not until the first one was lost.

I search for the laughter that used to play a constant dance in Aidan's eyes, the lips that were always seconds away from a smile. I find nothing but a fraught sort of curiosity, and a tiny wrinkle to his brow.

"Aidan?"

He startles, raising his hands defensively before he curls them into fists and drops them by his sides. I'd laugh if it didn't hurt so much. Of course he's afraid of me. The last time we saw each other outside the hall below, I was half-mad on the beach, screaming with shifting eyes, and he was dragging Conal's corpse from the waves.

Now he's spent seven years under the weight of our father's sole focus, determined to make him fill the space his heir left behind.

"What has Da done to you?" The words are out before I can swallow them down. For just a moment, something like regret crosses his face. But then Aidan wipes his expression clean in a way he could never manage when we were children.

"I'd think with your curse, you'd know better than I could ever tell you." His voice is a shock to my system—familiar enough to have crossed my dreams a hundred times, lofty enough to be a stranger's.

I shake my head, rolling the fire poker against my palm. "My magic doesn't work like that."

The word cracks through his mask. "Magic?"

I release a heavy breath edged in mirthless laughter. Glance at the shimmering blanket of glass on the ground. "Aye. Gods-given, like the mushrooms and the painted crane feathers and all the rest. It was never a soulstone curse."

Aidan's brows knit a furious line. "Da says you're like a bean sídhe. That it was a mistake to ever let you walk among us." He casts a look over his shoulder, then takes a step inside. "Are you a death bringer? Is that why Conal—"

"No." Biting my lip, I carefully lay the fire poker down. "I thought so, too, because of my first vision—it happened that day on the beach. I thought . . . I thought I caused it. That something in me killed Conal, or that I brought it about."

"You didn't?"

I have to fight myself to hold his gaze. It's been such a long time, and Aidan looks so much like Conal now. "I only saw that it would happen in my mind. Just as I see things now—in glimpses or flashes, or a feeling of what's coming to pass. But if I could bring about death with my sight . . ." Something sour climbs my throat, remembering Da's lips against my forehead, and all his gentle lies. I swallow it down. "Do you truly think it would have been Conal's that I sought?"

Aidan takes a step back, and I catch the sides of my gown to keep from reaching for him, cuffs weighing my wrists down.

"I tried to change Conal's fate," I say, "running out of the water and begging you to join. And I swear if I thought for a second that I could go back and trade my life for his—"

"Stop." Aidan's hands land on my shoulders, grip too tight. His jaw locked, fingers shaking. "Saoirse, you—"

He swallows. Lips wobbling from their harsh set. "You shouldn't have . . ."

I wait for him to push me back then. To disappear behind Da's training.

Instead, Aidan's fingers dig into my collarbone and then he pulls me forward into his chest. Both arms wrap around me as he buries his face in my hair. When his body shudders, I tighten my hold, thinking of Faolan's arms the night of that first storm. Every nudge from Brona, ruffle to my hair from Lorcan, and rough embrace from Nessa—they've all found a home in me.

"I'm sorry," I whisper.

Sorry I didn't fight you both harder to stay onshore with me.

Sorry it wouldn't have done any good even if I had, because fate is cruel, as Faolan said.

Sorry that I've been so lost in my own wounds, I've never stopped to wonder what it's like to be the one who's alive only because our brother died saving his life.

Aidan's breath shudders through my hair, something hot and wet dripping down the back of my neck. When I pull away, he wipes a sleeve across his face. "I begged them to let you stay, Saoirse. And when that didn't work, I tried to go after you, but I never made it far. I should have tried harder—should've fought them both."

I search his face, my chest tight. "We were only children. We had to survive."

He quiets, brow furrowed and lips apart. I see the passage of time in his jaw, shadowed and rough-cut along the edge. His beautiful hands shake before he folds them behind his back, calluses marking the wrong spots on his skin. They used to grow at his fingertips where he'd pluck the lyre strings, or halfway down his knuckles where the sling dug in. Now they form a mountain's ridge where a sword's hilt must rest.

"Aidan?"

He shakes his head. "How did you survive?"

I fall back against the wardrobe, gripping its wooden side. "I told myself stories. The ones we used to make up, or ones you brought back from court."

Aidan's face clears of confusion, a playful glint slipping into his eye. "The Wolf of the Wild?"

My face floods with heat.

"Right. Would you care to tell me, little sister, how the *hell* you managed to marry him?"

FORTY-THREE

The fire becomes a handful of embers, its reddish glow marred by the gray of predawn filtering in through the open window. I watch numbly as one of them flickers out, my mind spiraling over my own stories. Meeting Faolan at the Damhsa, trying to swim to his ship, the Teeth and Maccus's attack, Scath-Díol and boarding Rian's vessel. The only parts I omit are those to do with the numbing ink made of caipín baís and the tattoo it created. Both would paint Da in a light I'm not certain Aidan's ready to see.

Still, at first I wasn't sure whether Aidan truly believed me. His smile was too amused in parts, his eyes flicking up like they wanted to roll when I told him what it was like to meet Faolan for the first time. But by the end, all Aidan can do is utter a single soft curse.

"It sounds mad, I know." Another ember goes dark. "But it's true."

"I . . . believe you. I think." Aidan rubs at his jaw. "Even if it's strange. But I guess I'd be more annoyed at the fact the magic only chooses lasses if the things it showed you weren't so fecking awful."

I laugh and drop my head back against a chair, though I'm curled on the rug below. "I don't know whether to pray for better visions or none at all."

"Do you still pray?"

I touch the bare space on my throat where the gods' charms and tokens used to hang, and feel the drag of Faolan's wolf ring along my collarbone instead. "Not really. The gods are truly gone."

I felt one of them die.

"So why do you still have this magic?"

My laugh is empty as I adjust the shackles on my wrists. "Da told at least one truth among the lies. Our grandmother *did* awaken the magic with a soulstone." And perhaps tried to drown me as well. "But even Faolan agrees she'd gone mad with it by the end of her days."

Ash lifts on a plume of smoke between us, and Aidan catches it in his fist. Crumbles it between his fingers. The ease between us draws a bit tight. "Are you worried about that happening to you?"

I turn the wolf's-head ring over once. Twice. "Yes. But for all I know, the magic could leave me once we find the Isle of Lost Souls."

Aidan goes still, dark curls falling into his eyes. "Would you miss it?"

His question lodges in my stomach and stays there.

I prayed for so long that I'd never feel the magic's touch again. On Faolan's ship, diving for Gráinne's bones, at the Scath-Díol and every moment after, whenever it arose in me, I'd fight it down the best I could. Yet for a brief handful of hours, from last night to this morning, I was *free*. Alive in a way I've deprived myself of for twenty-two years.

And now, chained and numb once more, I finally understand why Faolan craves freedom so.

Better to feel anything than *nothing*.

"Aye." I lower my head to study my ragged nails, heart

constricting until I fear it will stop. "I would. But it doesn't matter now. Da crushed the bone ring, and there's no getting it back. He's going to destroy the pieces, which means we can't find the Isle of Lost Souls, and Faolan—"

My voice breaks as his abalone scar flashes across my mind.

"Faolan is going to die."

Aidan startles to his feet, gripping the back of his neck. "No. Saoirse—obviously Da wouldn't have him killed. Do you know the uproar he'd receive?"

"That's not what I meant. It's . . ."

The words die on my tongue. I've already asked Aidan to believe so much, it feels like a step too far trying to explain the soul-bargain mark as well. There's a reason Faolan hasn't confided in his crew, isn't there?

I bite the edge of my thumb instead. "What is Da's plan for us?"

Aidan lowers his gaze, shifting from one foot to the other. "He's already contacted Ríona Kiara to collect Faolan after the wed— after a few days pass. He thinks it will do the Wolf some good to stay dungeon-bound."

Faolan will hate that. My body drains of warmth as Aidan watches the ground, one arm stretched over his head. Layers of muscle strain at the seams of his shirt, scars spanning skin wherever it's exposed—so many more now than when he was seventeen. He used to prize his smooth skin, claiming it a future canvas for the colorful tattoos of Painted Claw.

I nudge his foot with mine. "You're close to Da now?"

"Close enough to track his movements." Aidan grimaces, kicking the fire poker aside. "Right down to the bowels."

I don't laugh, though some distant part of me wishes to.

After a moment, Aidan's rueful smile falls and he stalks to the shattered window, looking outside. "I have Father's ear now, as much as he allows it. But he still keeps his secrets, even from me."

"Including the apothecary's work?"

Aidan keeps his back to me. "Aye."

He's lying. I see it in the redness of his ears, a habit from childhood, yet I cannot fathom why. Da already let slip that they haven't had time to brew fresh ink for my skin—unless Aidan knows about the bottles in the apothecary's cabin. Concoctions brewed of caipín baís, then sold at the Scath-Díol to avoid scrutiny.

I think of the girl with the pallid fingers, her mother's vacant stare, and the smell of rotting things. None of them are visible here, yet their fingerprints are obvious in the fine clothing Da wore and the beautiful weave of Aidan's belt. My own dresses are cut from cloth purchased by the villagers' labor and the apothecary's designs.

I open my mouth to press Aidan, then stop. Study the taut, unfamiliar line of his neck.

Aidan may dislike our father, or disagree with his tactics, but loyalty in our home has never been a choice. We filled our roles as commanded, ignored the ugly parts, and lived behind walls that meant we never saw what it took to build them.

Seven years is a long time apart.

"You were going to say Kiara will come after the wedding, weren't you? Do you know about the marriage treaty to Maccus?"

Aidan's boots drag against stone, but I turn my eyes to the last dying embers before he can face me again. "Maccus has had his eye on a secure alliance for years, Saoirse. You're just the easiest route to take."

I laugh, though there's no humor in the sound. "It's never been about me, then. I was merely the wax sealing the contract."

Aidan nods, and I drop my head against my knees. Something unnamed passes through me, relief mixed with what, I do not know. Revulsion? Disturbance?

I shiver as the fire dies beside us, remembering Maccus's cold smile. "You have to help us get away, Aidan. Please."

"Of course I will!" The indignation in his voice jerks me back upright as Aidan crosses the room in two easy strides. He reaches for me, hand unfurling like a sail over my head, then hesitates. It's only when I lean forward until my hair brushes his palm that he settles it fully over my crown, thumb brushing the divot between my brows. "I wanted to fight for you last time, but I was too young. Couldn't see a way out. But I know better now."

Aidan brushes a kiss to my forehead, and I squeeze my eyes tight, willing myself to believe that he can do it. That there's *any* path off my father's island that won't require a toll of blood to be paid.

"Please" is all I can manage as the cuffs leach poison into my skin, numbing my fear and hope. My thoughts as well. I shake my head to clear it and dislodge his hand by accident. He pinches me lightly on the cheek instead.

It reminds me of someone—equal parts irritating and endearing, a stroke of sunlight breaking through the caipín baís cloud. "Could you get a message to Faolan?"

Aidan sits back on his heels, and I raise my head in time to see his lips twitch to one side. "You're not worried I'll steal your husband from you?"

"Have him. You'll send him packing within a day, I promise."

Aidan bursts into laughter, and I can't help but join him. After weeks among Faolan's family, hearing their banter crack across the ship, I understand its power better now. Humor makes sense of the shadows and light.

Aidan rubs at his chest and glances to the door again. "You know they're calling you Wolf Tamer now, right?"

"Who?" My smile slips. "The crew? We've been confined to a ship."

"I heard it in the pub just yesterday, from a group of sailors who'd passed through Aisling's Cove." Aidan's nose wrinkles when he grins, just like when we were small. "Odd thing to hear a song about my sister's thighs, though, I'll tell you. Something like 'She was quite wee, yet broad in the—'"

"Feckin' stars, I'll kill that man." I groan as Aidan doubles over on another laugh. "He must have sung it for the crew at some point, the bastard."

"Bandia Eabha, you really *are* a pirate, aren't you, with that tongue?" Aidan's smile is pure devilry now. "Be fair to the poor lad, he composed a whole bloody song about you. Anyone that besotted must be worth a second look."

"Faolan is not besotted, he's just—"

Irritating. Beautiful. Awe-inspiring.

"Full of himself."

"A wee bit." Aidan winks. "What's the message?"

The humor bleeds from me as fast as it came. "Tell him . . ." I hesitate, glancing from Aidan's full smile to the softness in his eyes. "Tell him not to be stupid. He doesn't need to try for an escape. And tell him you're coming up with a plan—but for star's sake, don't ask his advice. Nessa and Tavin are usually the strategists."

Aidan tilts his head slowly to the side. "You really have become one of them, haven't you?"

I touch the wolf tattoo at my wrist, a lump growing in my throat. "I always wanted to."

The last log breaks apart, sparks flaring in the semidarkness as

Aidan drops to the rug beside me, nudging my hand with his. "It'll take some time to sort out. Da's men have to track Maccus's ship down and make the voyage back. Then there's the servants preparing the house for a royal wedding."

"I know." I lace our fingers tight, and for a second he stiffens. Neither of us is used to touching much anymore. But I'm not so afraid, and as the sparks die in the fire, he runs his thumb over the back of my hand.

Aidan sighs. "I'll have to arrange a boat."

"Faolan's crew is docked near my cottage at the southern tip."

He jerks back. "What?!"

"We planned for the wolves to leave if we didn't return by tonight, but I don't trust them to keep that promise. They love Faolan too much to be wise."

Aidan gapes at me, and I release his hand to curl my legs tighter, chin resting on my folded arms. "If you have someone you trust, or could chance it yourself, the ship is fast. We could tell them to stay as they are while Faolan and I slip out in a currach—or take a horse by land as we did before."

He shakes his head. "Our guards would have you before you made it halfway through the bog." Aidan pinches the bridge of his nose. "Let me think on it. I'll—try to get a message to the wolves to stay put, but our focus needs to be on *you*, Saoirse. Faolan will be all right."

That damned soulstone mark fills my vision when I blink, until ice from the cuffs at my wrists chases it away. I shake them until some feeling returns. "How long do you think it will take?"

"A week. Maybe less? I'll have to find the key to *those*," he says, nodding to my wrists. "And manage all the communications without Da taking notice. It'll be a few days at least."

My eyes flick back to the last ember, flaring bright for one last breath.

Is that what it will be like when Faolan meets death?

We have so little time left.

"All right. One week."

I blink, and the ember goes dark.

FORTY-FOUR

Hanging across my room, there is a tapestry of Carys the Clever and her fork-tongued riddles. She is said to have been born unsightly but bewitched the hearts of kings with a wicked trick, painting herself with oils each night from the last serpent created purely by a god's hand.

Faolan told me the real story weeks ago, whispered into my ear as he held me upright during a vicious storm.

Carys was chosen by her village to stand sacrifice on the spring equinox, when the mighty serpent would shed its skin and deliver blessings for the year to come. As Carys walked into the water, she shouted not, begged not, wept not. Instead, she sang in the serpent's own tongue, luring him to her side until he coiled like a kitten at her feet. She stroked his mighty head, crooning all the while, and then ripped out one of his fangs, driving the venomous edge directly between his eyes.

I have no fang. No siren's song.

Only a faded tapestry, an absent brother, and a new betrothal torc worn so close to my skin, it bruises with every breath.

All it lacks is a chain.

"Keep still, child."

A laugh pushes between my trembling lips as Brigid stains them red. Another servant tightens the laces of my gown until I'm forced to sit straighter, my breasts put on display along with those godsdamned childbearing hips Maccus was so concerned with.

"Am I a child? Or perhaps only a plaything?"

His plaything.

Holy stars.

Brigid ignores my outburst just as she's done for the past five and a half days, and sets a wreath of freshly woven forget-me-nots like a crown upon my head. "There. I think you'll please the Stone King well, Princess."

His title hollows out my belly. Heedless of the lip paint, I thrust the back of my hand against my mouth and bite down to trap the scream. Force myself to breathe through my nose and out past my fingers as heat stings behind my eyes.

This can't be how it ends. Me in Maccus's bed, Da's pockets laced in jewels.

My one saving grace is the ink I ruined, the tattoo they have no time to replicate. But Faolan—*feck*, how many days does he have? Will he die alone in that cell, cut off from the wind and sea he so loves?

A rug does little to warm the ground as I walk away from Brigid and the serving girl, delicate blue silk frothing over my feet. Hours of fittings and it's still quite impossible to believe this wedding gown is *mine*. A month ago, I'd have admired the daring cut of the bodice or traced the ribbons tied over each shoulder, never once understanding whose touch they were meant to entice.

A shudder wracks my body, and I start for the window, desperate for air—only to remember, no, I'm not even allowed that anymore. Da had it boarded up for fear I'd jump.

"Please, just—get out." The words are strangled by my panic, but the two women don't falter. They've done their part, haven't they? Created a soft, submissive version of me.

I'm going to be sick.

But no sooner has the door shut behind them than it opens again. I spin on my heel, already snarling. "I said get—"

Aidan stands frozen in the doorway, face pale against the deep blue hue of his courtly trappings. The colors represent our island, mushrooms embroidered for our claim to godly magic. It's the sort that doesn't draw shame or speculation but is bottled up and sold to anyone with the coin.

My shoulders drop. "Maccus is here. Isn't he? You . . ."

But I can't finish the words. Aidan looks ready for a court visit, and I—I was always alone, wasn't I? Loyalty is everything in our father's household, and we're not children anymore. Aidan looks every part the royal heir.

"They sent you to escort me?"

Aidan jolts like a man woken from sleep, raising a hand smudged gray. "No! No, a summer storm's delayed Rí Maccus. We have another couple of hours. I just—gods, Saoirse, I never thought to see you like this." But as quickly as he takes in my own finery, he must read the hurt in my face. The fury.

I battle to hold it in. "You didn't come back. I waited for you *every* night—I thought you'd changed your mind."

"Stars, no! Saoirse, just—come here." Aidan beckons me, and I dig my feet harder into the ground, not able to trust that this is real. Not until he slips a hand into his pocket and retrieves the fragments of the bone ring.

Everything in me melts away. "How? Father took them, and I— *Aidan*."

"It was a right son of a bitch to collect it without Da noticing." Aidan catches my hand and drops every piece into it, coating my skin with ash, same as his. When he looks up, he smiles and I feel its incredulous echo stretching my own face. "Why do you think it took me so long? I couldn't have anyone watching while I looked for them. It was only this morning I spotted them in his fireplace, while he ran preparations for the ceremony."

The bones dig into my skin as I search his eyes, then take a tentative step closer. "And the rest of the plan?"

"Starts with this."

Aidan nudges my elbow higher until the cuff catches the light, and then he slips a key from his other pocket. One hard twist and the ugly metal pieces fall to the ground.

Sensation steals my breath. I double over, gasping and clawing for something to hold on to as the initial flood passes through me. Aidan unlocks the second cuff, and I fall to my knees, gripping the ground until my nails threaten to break at the ends. Flickers of confusion, pain, and love pass from his fingers to my skin until they withdraw. But it's all only a wave. After a few seconds, it sinks back into the sea of myself.

Aidan stands warily across the rug, mouth agape as I shift back onto my heels. Smile.

"Thank you."

"I— Of course." His laugh skates through my hair as he catches my elbows and hauls me to my feet. I lean into his chest and feel an old melody slip through me. Sad and sweet. The song of my brother.

A clatter down the hall splits the music in half, footsteps pounding the flagstone.

Aidan breaks his hold at once. "I arranged Faolan's release this morning. They've probably just realized. Take the servants' pass to the right of the hall, cut through the old playroom, and he'll be waiting at the bottom of the stairs on the other side. Then—"

Voices echo down the hall. Sweat gathers at Aidan's temple.

"You'll take the old kitchen passage—remember when we used to sneak sweets? I've left clothes for you both. People have come for the wedding, so with luck you'll be able to blend in and make your way to the docks. Faolan knows where to go from there, all right?"

I nod, my heart in my throat. "This is goodbye, then?"

"Aye." Aidan crushes me into his arms again. "Wait two minutes. I'll distract the guards, and you run as fast as you can."

"I love you."

He touches my chin, then disappears. Two minutes pass in a blink and a century. The quiet is stifling, but when I finally press my ear to the crack at the door, I don't hear a sound.

Take the servants' pass.

My steps falter as I push the wooden door open and pad down the corridor. It's larger than I remember, the walls sculpted up into points over my head. Tapestries line near every wall, telling stories of the gods or of our people, Bandia Eabha and her blessing of caipín baís.

I remember the clusters of them in our crypt.

Conal's empty grave.

Blood pushes fast through my veins, and I gasp. Force myself to walk down the hall.

I have to reach the servants' pass.

Except a touch skates up my spine like the coldest of hands, and I barely contain a scream, bruising my lip in the process. Whispers hum in the back of my head and stretch out like a complicated web as I curl my fists so tight, the wolf ring bites through my skin until blood wells up, spills down my wrist.

Sweat beads cold against my palm.

"*Saoirse . . . SAOIRSE!*"

I cannot have a vision now. Not when I'm so close to reaching Faolan. Breaking *free*.

My steps quicken, heels driving into stone as my breath crashes against itself like a torrent of waves. Conal's voice echoes in my mind—*"Saoirse, stay onshore! Help me spot him. Aidan!"*—and I want to be numb again, because his pain is my pain and I cannot *bear* the weight of them together.

This magic is ferocious. It's eating me alive—pulling viciously as the current dragged Aidan down so Conal was forced to follow. It tugs me to a chamber at the wrong end of the hall, marked by a beam and long strips of graying silk that flutter without provocation.

I don't want to go inside. I fight with everything I possess, but it drags me through like the tide. As the last kiss of silk fades, my eyes adjust to the dim light of a single window and fall upon an altar in the center of the room.

Conal's body rests on top.

Gods.

The magic fades like a candle snuffed, until only a whisper of its smoke lingers. His voice is just a memory in my mind. I hesitate and then trace the edge of his burial shroud, mapping the way it sculpts what must be petrified flesh now, if any remains at all. It doesn't make sense why it's here—why they haven't put him in the crypt with the others to seek rest until the Isle of Lost Souls can be found.

My touch lingers on the embroidery at the silk's edge. I wonder vaguely if Mam stitched the embroidery alone, since I wasn't allowed to help. Da banished me before the druid could complete the first funeral rites, after all.

His face crosses my lids, and I flinch away.

I shouldn't be here. I turn to go, but a flicker catches my eye. Rippling like moonlight.

Conal's soulstone.

Not cracked or porous or blackened at the edges; no sign it's been corrupted. But it's faded somehow. The three swirls of a triskele on its top worn so smooth, they're almost invisible—like the waves tumbled it over pebbles until someone could fetch it back from the sea.

I step closer, and my lips part as magic flutters through my belly and draws my touch back, hand hovering over the soulstone until the very air hums with longing. Because it *is* calling me—No. Conal is calling me. Just like Gráinne did, deep in the water. His soul yearns to be seen, held, protected.

Released.

I could release his spirit to the wild. I could—

"Saoirse!"

My father fills the doorway, the whites of his eyes on full display. He tears his gaze from my outstretched hand to Conal's body and back again, going white with shock and then purple with fury. "You . . . you worthless, traitorous—"

"I wasn't going to do anything. I swear!"

"It wasn't enough that you took his life. You want to steal his soul now as well?!"

"No, Da, please—"

He crosses the room in two strides and seizes my throat, startling me so violently that I curl my bare, bloodied fingers fast around the soulstone.

FORTY-FIVE

I am five, shaken and bruised from a fall off my very first horse. But Da scoops me up, his laugh as warm as the quilt Mam patches every time I rip a new hole in its edges. "You'll make a fine king—look at you! Not a bone broken. Clever boy, rolling as you did." Da's smiles are my favorite sight in the world.

They vanish one night, after Mam screams for an entire day and a baby is left to show for it—a girl this time. The smiles don't return for years.

I'm thirteen, and girls take up too much of my mind, Da says. He tells me to either kiss the laundress's daughter and be done with it, or he'll dismiss her. I do, and kissing is far less interesting than I thought it might be. It's easy to stick to training after that, until I'm sixteen and bed the lass. She smells so sweet, with a body as soft as spun wool, but the act is unsettling. Too animal. I leave the rutting and romance to Aidan and his favored stable lad after that.

I am eighteen, a week away from my first Damhsa. But Aidan and I are restless, knowing the grown world is minutes away from swallowing us alive. We want to live before it happens. He wrestles me in the pebbled cove while wee Saoirse searches for flat stones to skip. She never meets my eyes anymore, and I miss the strange colors.

But when we go to swim, she clasps our hands—then bursts into tears and begs us to stop. White as bone, her eyes churning like a wave.

The hairs rise along my nape.

She asks if we can go inside, but every inch of me rebels. The walls hold our parents and rules, stuffy tailors keen to dress me like a damned cock for the lasses to pluck during the ritual. I shove Aidan toward the water instead, dragging her between us. Saoirse pleads, but we're already up to our knees. I'm chilled to the bone by the end of the first dive, tilting my face back to the sun, laughing because we are young and perfectly free.

And then there's no laughter. No air.

Tentacles of water wrap around my body, pulling me down like a monster of the deep. A current. But I know how to break free of these—Da taught me as soon as I could swim through our isle's vicious waters. I twist my body, hold my breath, kick out instead of against until a glimpse of pale flesh banishes every feckin' instinct.

Aidan.

My life becomes forfeit to his. I grab him around the middle and push him high, kicking with everything I have until his head breaks the surface and he can breathe, while my chest is wrapped in burning irons that tighten more with every passing moment.

If I can just hold on. If I can just kick harder.

We break free, but water finds home in my lungs. Aidan is alive, kicking for the surface, his fingers clawing mine because mine have gone limp and I am hollowed out.

Drowning. Dying.

It's not peaceful as the poets sing, but violent. My lungs battle with the sea, my body twitching and thrashing in nonsense patterns, black spots dancing across my vision as I scream my rage against the absence of life—

Until the last fleeting glimpse of it winks out.

FORTY-SIX

I taste salt.

Bitter and raw, tears streak down my cheeks as a keening moan escapes my lungs. They were burning with water only seconds ago, trapped inside my brother's mind. The room forms around me in fragments—the altar and shroud, the soulstone in my palm.

The stains glow like freshly spilled starlight reaching up my arms, just like Faolan's scar.

My stomach wrenches and my lips part in horror as I stare at the abalone scars and the soulstone, waiting for its light to fade and my own life to crack in two. Neither comes to pass. I feel no pain as the marks glow stronger once, then sink slowly into my skin until nothing, not even a streak, is left behind.

"Holy gods."

I nearly drop the stone when a strangled scream emanates from the ground.

My father writhes against the edge of the altar, clawing at his throat in the same place his hands trapped mine. The scorching silver marks beneath them do not fade. His skin rips beneath his nails, and I choke on a cry of my own as I shove the soulstone into my pocket, falling to my knees.

"Father? Da?!" His eyes aren't here, and he makes a sound—gurgling and rasping, as though he's drowning.

Drowning . . . just as Conal had. As *I* had in the vision.

When Da grasped my neck, did I somehow drag him through with me?

I catch his wrists and try to drag his hands away from his throat, but he's too strong. He rolls, throwing me into the altar with an unearthly scream. When he turns on his side and buries his hands in his hair, I swear I see streams of water escape his lips.

"Da, stop—please *stop*!"

"Stop it. Make it stop—I'll make it stop!" Da says, and in spite of everything I told Aidan, I start to pray. Earnestly and hungrily, I pray I haven't filled his soul with the ghost of his son—haven't sliced through the tethers of his mind. It's too clever for me to disrupt or break. It always has been.

But the gods give no answer, and my father gives in to madness.

Da shifts onto his knees and I reach for his arm to help him up, though my legs tremble like a colt's—then stop when I see my bloodied fingertips, remembering how they opened the entrance to the gods' chamber. It's a mistake. He throws himself to the ground as I hesitate, bashing his own forehead against the stone.

My scream echoes all around us as I jolt forward and try to pin him to the ground. But he is a warrior in spite of his indulgences, and I am no match for his strength.

"HELP! Gods, please, someone!" I wrap my arms over Da again and again, heedless of the scrapes and bruises he delivers every time he throws me off. I've just tilted my head back to shout for help a third time when a figure at the door catches my eye.

Aidan, his face a map of horror.

"Please, it wasn't me—I swear I didn't mean to! It was the soulstone—Da grabbed me just as I touched it. I didn't realize my hand was b-bloody until the vision took us both. I think—I think the magic's breaking his mind!" The words sound like fanciful lies, because I am a fanciful fecking girl with uncontrollable magic, and a family I've all but ruined, and whatever ground I gained with Aidan five days ago is wiped free from his face.

One blink, and it hardens into the face of the heir our father trained him to be.

"Don't touch him." Aidan shoves me off, grabbing Da's shoulders to pin him to the ground.

I'm sobbing, powerless to stop it. "Aidan, please—I *swear.* I swear I didn't do it. Not on purpose."

"Stop—just stop it!" Aidan's shouting now as he fights our father, who's intent on ending the torment in his mind, face coated in blood from a nose broken by the ground.

"I didn't do it," I plead, but Aidan's eyes are cold with fury when he finally looks at me again.

"You said if you could control your magic, that it wouldn't be Conal you killed. Didn't you?"

"I . . ." I cannot speak. My stomach rolls into sickening knots. "I didn't do it."

"I don't believe you, Saoirse. Not this time."

"Aidan—"

Da howls and tries to drive his head back into Aidan's nose just as guards flood in from the doorway. All eyes are fixed on the struggling bodies before us, Aidan's focus on keeping Da from harming himself further under what he believes is my curse.

And perhaps I am a curse after all. Wreaking death and pain everywhere I step, a thing to be hated and feared.

Conal's soulstone weighs heavy in my pocket as I bite down on my wrist to keep another sob from escaping, and run out the door.

Late-afternoon light flares through uneven windows as I race down the servants' pass, landing like a slap across my face every time. The playroom becomes a blur as I run through it next, and down the stairs beyond.

I don't believe you.

My ankle rolls on the bottom step and I cry out as I fall forward, colliding with a surface that's soft and hard at once and smells of—

"Saoirse?! Stars o' fire." Faolan crushes me to his chest. "Your brother said you'd be here twenty minutes ago. Kiara's waiting—took her a feckin' age to arrive, thanks to the storm. Tavin's scrying shell requires moonlight to send a message, and . . . What's wrong?"

I try to say something, or maybe I don't, because I feel so far from myself as Faolan pulls me along. My lips are useless, teeth chattering. I can't speak—until he opens the door at the end. The *wrong* door, which leads to the entry hall, where half a dozen guards wait to greet the Stone King.

"Bastard!" Faolan tries to slam the door, but one of the guards holds it open with her shoulder as two others rush inside. Faolan drops his grip on me in favor of raising his fists, but finally life rushes back into my limbs enough that I take his arm and pull him behind me.

"Stop." He edges around me and I plant my feet. "Faolan, stop!"

"We have to *go*, Saoirse."

"You're not going anywhere until you put his mind back together." Aidan breaks through the guards, his shirt blood-smeared and eyes dark and distant—as cold as our father's.

Faolan tears his gaze from the guards to face my brother, then slowly glances back at me.

Magic still courses through my body in rapid, tumbling channels. He must see it swirl within my eyes.

"I-I didn't mean to."

"Shite," Faolan murmurs, confusion melting into concern as he palms my cheek. "I know, love, just—tell me what happened?"

"She's driven our father mad, that's what." Aidan speaks through his teeth, face pale with outrage. "Her bloody curse scrambled his brains, and—Saoirse, stop shaking your *fecking* head!"

I try to force stillness, gripping my hands hard enough that more blood seeps through the wounds on my palm. "I'm sorry. I'm so sorry—I swear I didn't mean to."

"Obviously you didn't." Faolan sets his shoulders and steps half in front of me to face Aidan head-on. "But even if she had, could you blame her? Have you *seen* the state of her back?"

Aidan's fury slips, and for a second he's only my brother again. "What are you talking about?"

"She didn't tell you what that bastard did to her? The tattoo?"

"I . . ."

A servant approaches with owl-wide eyes, saving me from speech. "Ríona Kiara is at the main doors, my prince. She demands an audience with the king."

It stops Aidan in his tracks, face going to ash as he looks toward the stairs behind us, then slowly down to his hands and shirt. Blood speckles the fabric, staining his skin. "Feck." He swipes a hand over his brow, then stares at the two of us.

I cannot imagine what he sees.

"Keep her at the entrance. Serve her and her people wine, food, whatever they want. I need time to—"

The central doors fling wide as Kiara strides in, her body outlined by the sun. It catches in the short strands of coppery-red hair spilling over to one side, highlighting the crest stamped in gold hanging round her neck. She takes in the sight of us with one hard sweep of her pale green eyes and cocks a brow.

"I came to speak with the king, not a princeling."

Aidan straightens in an attempt to match her height, bloody hands in fists at his sides. "Rí Dermot has fallen ill. As his heir apparent—"

Kiara snorts. "Is that what you call yourself?" She sizes him up, then dismisses him with a flick of her gaze. "I've come to collect my cousin and his bride. I have the cords of their handfasting if you need proof, but the fact that your king thought it appropriate to seize a member of my court will not go unmarked." From her pocket, she pulls the flimsy braid of fabric that once reordered our lives.

Aidan locks his jaw. "Faolan may be yours, but Saoirse is a daughter of Dermot's house."

"Not by the tradition of a handfasting. I conducted the ceremony myself." Kiara casts the braided cord at his feet like a bone. "They are bound in the eyes of our law."

"Unless it was only a farce."

Faolan's indignation shudders through me, drawn by the magic into my body to perfectly match my own. He wraps an arm slowly around my waist as Aidan shifts under Kiara's heavy gaze.

She cocks her head to one side. "What are you on about, lad?"

"Saoirse told me the truth." Aidan glances at me, then firmly away. "She confessed it was all a lie—that the only reason you wed them was to protect her if they were caught. But they don't live as husband and wife."

Kiara laughs outright, and Faolan's grip on me tightens. "You're saying there's been no consummation?"

Aidan's neck flushes red, but he nods.

Kiara snorts. "Stars, lad, if you need a witness, I can give you plenty. The ship's not so big and noise carries far too well, and you can hardly expect your sister to confide about *that*. But if you need further proof, Ríona Etain's niece, Aisling, can attest to a tryst in her very own cove two weeks past."

"That's not—" Aidan breathes out once, then jerks his chin. "Whatever the state of things, Saoirse must face the consequences of what she's done. She attacked Rí Dermot."

"Can you prove it?"

Aidan startles back a step. "What?"

"Did you witness the attack?" Kiara sounds almost bored as she collects the cord from the ground. "Can you prove it was her hand on the blade that stabbed him, or her fingers around his throat?"

"It's not a—physical harm. His mind is . . ."

Kiara smirks, and Aidan turns red. Suddenly, he is *not* the brother I know, shadows gouged into his face so that it looks like Da's. Terrible and wrong. When he speaks again, it's with the quiet, sharp force of a rock released from a sling. Kiara's response is a thousand arrows lit aflame.

"Wait," I say, my voice barely a croak.

But the word means nothing to them.

Aidan starts forward until Kiara steps in his path, and their shouts are too much for my mind, which feels as fragile as Da's in the rooms above. I reach for Faolan's hand again, but he releases me to stalk Aidan's steps, heedless of the guards who dog his path. My husband is not one to miss a fight.

"Wait—*please*."

Aidan is seconds from drawing his sword because that's what they've forced him to learn, his knuckles white on the hilt. Kiara's own hand drifts to the back of her belt, where a dagger sits. Blood will splash the tiles of my childhood home and it will be *my* fault.

All my fault.

I fling myself between them, hands raised to either side. "Stop!"

My shout echoes off the high ceiling, drawing every eye—except they're not looking at my face. They're staring at the brilliant gossamer streaks painted again down my hands and arms, all leading to Conal's soulstone resting in my bare palm.

But I have no memory of withdrawing it. My mind has become my enemy once more, and I feel so far away.

Still, I have to explain. I have to *try*.

"Conal was calling to me in the rooms above. I didn't understand it until I saw his soulstone. H-he's been afraid for so long—*dying* over and over, and I-I just wanted to help him. I need to give him rest. But I didn't realize I was bleeding, and I didn't *mean* to touch the soulstone!"

Faolan lowers his hand from the bronze wolf strapped to his side, coming closer. His eyes are afraid. "Saoirse?"

I step back before Faolan can reach me, terrified of losing the very last person to regard me with anything close to affection. And beneath my skin, the bright colors spread faster, clinging to my very veins.

"Da was furious when he found me. He attacked me, and it scared me so much that I—I grabbed the stone. But I didn't mean to bring him into the vision. I think that's where he still is. *Drowning.*" My voice wavers. Breaks. "I don't know how to bring him back."

Kiara's face turns thoughtful even as she takes a wary step back, but Aidan . . .

Any hint of gentleness or love is gone from his face now, replaced with pure disgust. "You tampered with Conal's soulstone."

"*No.*" I hold it higher, and all of them stumble back. "It's not broken—I would never hurt him! He *called* to me, Aidan. I have to help him. Don't you understand?"

"Guard. Fetch a chest."

I clutch the last piece of my eldest brother as the guard disappears through a door and returns with a small chest, her hands protected by thick leather gloves. "Wait. No—please don't take him back there. He's so cold—so *alone*. Aidan, I'm going to find the Isle of Lost Souls like I said. I-I'm going to bring him there, give him peace. Please!"

It takes little effort for the guard to pry it from my fingers, weak as I am. Not even Faolan dares come closer. The scream that leaves my lips is one of pure agony, a sound I do not recognize as my own—until she shuts the chest, severing a tether I hadn't realized was there.

I drop my forehead to the ground in a wash of relief and guilt, and so many other things, watching as the marks fade back into my skin. "I'm sorry."

I don't know if Aidan hears my whisper. Faolan catches one of my arms as Kiara takes the other, pulling me to stand on legs that threaten to give out at any moment. Aidan stands apart, shaken and pale, his eyes gone flat.

"We're leaving." Kiara's voice is a wall of stone, her grip just as hard. "If you wish to accuse Saoirse, you can take it before the Ring of Stars, but until then she lies under my protection."

Aidan squares his shoulders, wipes his expression clean. "Get out, then."

My legs threaten to give way. "Aidan—"

"Go."

FORTY-SEVEN

The coastline disappears into pure horizon behind us as night falls, yet still I cannot stop trembling. I'd thought Da was wrong. That my magic wasn't dangerous or misspent, but a blessing of true sight. I'd earnestly believed that I could be free of fear—of *shame*—no matter what visions came or emotions wound their way in currents between myself and whoever was around me.

I'd stopped craving nothingness.

But then I lost myself in my brother's soul, and my grandmother's in the sea before that. And I realize now, it's not the knowing that scares me.

It's the power of a damaged soul and how easily I respond to its call.

"Easy, love." Faolan smooths a hand over my hair, fingers catching in the wreath of forget-me-nots, and I drop my head to his shoulder. "It's all behind us now."

Brona appears at his shoulder, a blanket tossed over her arm. Nessa isn't far behind, fussing with ropes though her eyes land on me between one knot and the next. None of them spoke much after helping us onto the ship, too focused on getting out before Maccus or the other royals arrived.

"You should eat something." Brona holds out the blanket, and Faolan wraps it over my bare shoulders. I hadn't even realized I was cold. "It'll help with the shock."

"I can't." The words fumble across my tongue.

"Bollocks on that. Lorcan?" Brona calls over her shoulder, and the bosun appears less than a breath later. His smile reaches into my chest like a hand, squeezing my heart until it hurts.

"Can you at least manage some bread? We sneaked into the village the second day after you left. It's a bit stale but better than the usual fare. Or I have some broth below."

Lorcan holds out a hunk of nutty-brown bread wrapped in wax cloth, lines scored across the top to mimic mushrooms. My throat burns when I try to swallow down tears.

"Thank you." I manage to take it in hand but turn my face into Faolan's neck before he can force me to try a bite. "I'm sorry."

"Stop apologizing," he murmurs, drawing me closer as he looks over my head. "What's done is done."

"But I—"

"*Stop.*" His lips find my forehead, and I choke down a sob as Brona crosses her arms and sinks to the ground nearby. I can't look at her face. Can't bear the disappointment. Lorcan leans against the railing just beside her, and Nessa leaves the ropes to sit on his other side.

Faolan sighs. "Well that's it, then. We give up on the Isle of Lost Souls."

"What?" I push against Faolan's chest, searching for his eyes. They meet mine without hesitation, mouth pulled into a grim smile. His fingers curl tighter at my hip.

"We didn't get the ring. That was the whole bloody point, wasn't it?"

I drop the bread. "No."

"It's fine. We had a good run of it."

"No, you're not going to—"

Die.

I glance around the deck, and his wolves peer back. Nessa with a hand buried in her hair, smile uncertain now. Brona surreptitiously holding on to Lorcan's hand, half-hidden behind her folded legs. Tavin stands at the wheel beside Kiara farther down, grip bone white on the spokes.

"You can't leave them." The words are soft, meant only for him.

"Enough, Saoirse." Faolan tucks my hair back, then reaches over to salvage the bread. But I twist away, fingers working between us until they slip into the pocket tangled in my skirts. The pieces of the ring tumble together in my palm. For a moment, I wish I still believed in prayer. That if I could simply will it to heal, it would.

A whimper catches in my throat as I pull the ash-coated shards free.

There is silence as the others take it in, and then Faolan's chest jumps with a soft laugh.

"Feckin' stars. Did you really just—"

"My father broke it." I curl my trembling fingers around the mess. "I couldn't stop him."

"That doesn't matter."

"Yes, it does."

"Saoirse, you found the *ring.*" Faolan takes my jaw between his hands, capturing my eyes with his. "Hang the rest, I thought—" He shakes his head. Strokes my cheek with his thumb. "We'll figure out how to heal it, just like you sorted out my arm. Your magic's free now—"

"I can't trust it, Faolan. I thought I could, but I was wrong."

"*No.*" He catches my hand, lips painting a sweet path over my knuckles. "You're not. Whatever happened with your father, he had it coming to him. You're brilliant, love."

I don't believe you, Saoirse. Not this time.

I pull my hand back, pressing a fist over my heart. "What if you're wrong?"

"Me?" Faolan's eyes wrinkle at the corners as he smiles. "Haven't you learned by now? I'm never wrong."

My chest lurches with what might be a laugh as his eyes flit over my face. Drop to my lips.

Kiara storms down the deck. "What the feck are you two playing at?"

Faolan stiffens. "Kiara—"

"You need to consummate this union."

Faolan lets go of my face, shoving to his feet. "Why is everyone so bloody concerned all of a sudden?"

"Because she told her *brother*, eejit, and I'm sure her father suspected. If Dermot gains sense again or Maccus catches up to you, you'd damn well better be able to convince them it's done. It's far easier for them to gain an annulment than to break the handfasting of a couple unwilling to end it."

Faolan's fist meets the railing. "You wouldn't stand against them? Isn't that the whole point of our godsdamned arrangement, *my queen*?"

She glares at the mocking twist he gives her title, eyes the color of liquid green flame. "I've fulfilled my end of this bargain, Wolf, though I wonder if even that's enough to save your sorry arse by this point. It's time you cleaned up your own mess."

I can't help myself. My laugh breaks free.

It's brittle and ugly, coming so hard that I roll onto my hands and knees, and then the wild laughter morphs into a mess of tears and gasping breaths. *I* am the mess. It was absurd to think I could live a single moment of my life outside the dictates of those men. Our *entire world* belongs to them. My body, dreams, desires—the *magic* I possess—what do they matter against the power Maccus and my father hold?

"Dammit, Kiara." Warmth surrounds me as Faolan scoops me up, tucking my face back into his neck. "You can't take it easy on her?"

Kiara doesn't flinch. "You need to grow up. Both of you. There is more at stake here than a story."

Faolan bristles beneath me. "You don't think I know that?"

"I think it's easy for you to forget."

Faolan's hand tightens beneath my thighs, the fingers of his other hand splayed across my ribs. "I'm taking her to bed. We'll talk later."

"Good. You're learning to obey."

I feel her eyes like another brand as Faolan turns his back on her, carrying me to our cabin. He kicks the door shut behind him, cursing under his breath, and I want to laugh all over again at the way my bridal gown catches in the door, tearing at the hem.

Faolan sets me on my still-bare feet and I hold numbly on to his shoulder as he hesitates, eyes racing over my damp dress, the crown of flowers in my hair. When his fingers meet my skin, a piece of him bleeds into me without either of us asking for it—envy mixed with longing.

Good. This, at least, is something we can both do.

My fingers shake as I reach for his arms, but he takes my betrothal torc instead, jerking it free of my throat. "Never again." He tosses it below the bed to be forgotten as I wipe at my damp face with the waifish skirts, then reach behind to pull the laces free one after another.

It stops Faolan where he stands, hands still hovering in the air between us. He hesitates, then starts to turn away.

"Don't."

The fabric eases its hold on my chest as the first knot comes free. Faolan's gaze darts down once. His throat works as he clears it. "Someone's not quite so shy anymore, then, is she?"

I want to smile at the joke, weak as it is. Want to blush and turn away. Want to do anything but this—the only thing I *know* I can do right, because people have been doing it since we were first born of the sea.

The careful bows on the dress knot together. I swear and reach for the ribbons at my shoulders instead.

"Saoirse?" Faolan's voice is softer, the tease gone. I can't look at him as I pull one of the bows free, the clever bodice falling away like a petal. The shift beneath is hardly a whisper of fabric.

My throat feels raw when I swallow.

Maccus was meant to see me like this, his face impassive, hands efficient and cold. Was Mam the one who directed the seamstress? Did she run her fingers along the fabrics, choosing the one that might entice his interest the most?

Something skates down my cheek.

"Saoirse, what are you—? Slow down, lass."

"Why? You heard your cousin. We need to con-consum—" My teeth lock together and I can't push the word out and take this off at the same time. "I've seen enough of nature to know it can be done quickly, and this is *one* thing we can do right, s-so—"

I glance up and freeze as another layer of soft blue silk slips free. His gaze is wary and dark at once, hands half raised like he's about to hold me still and yet terrified to touch.

My throat runs dry. "You said you wanted me. The night of the market—you said you wanted this."

His breath is shaky when it comes. "Aye."

"Then take it."

He doesn't move, and my heart lashes my chest, so I reach for the dagger at his belt and take a fistful of the dress in hand. One flick and it tears straight down to my navel—cuts through the shift as well. I drop the knife just as Faolan curses and steps forward. But instead of shoving the material off like I expect—like maybe I'd want if I weren't so bloody lost inside myself—he catches my hands and traps them against his chest.

"No." His grip tightens when I try to pull back. "*No.* When we lie together—and we will do that, Saoirse—it's not going to be on my cousin's orders. And it sure as feck isn't going to be when you're in a state like this."

Fury claws up my throat and I thrash against him. "I'm fine!"

"Are you?" He releases one wrist only to sweep a finger below my eye. It comes away wet, and when I blink I feel tiny drops sliding down. When did I begin to cry?

Or have I never stopped?

My head lolls as I try to shake it, spreading forget-me-nots like rain, but instead of letting me go or pushing me back on the bed, Faolan just wraps me tight against his chest and shakes his head. "You're hurting, love. But you're not fecking alone anymore."

The words break my resolve.

I release everything I have in an ugly, broken wail and collapse against his chest.

FORTY-EIGHT

A full night's sleep wrapped in Faolan's arms is like a rebirth, soothing all those jagged edges of my soul. I wake to his fingers trickling down my back in a gentler version of the rains that beat the window all night. His skin is rough, warming me to my bones, where it lingers. Hair a mess of curls I've rarely had the privilege to see considering the fact that he's too restless by half to stay in bed for long when daylight comes.

"Morning," he whispers.

I blink when his lips meet my forehead. Fingertips turning to a hand that presses flat at the small of my back.

"You stayed."

"I told you I wouldn't leave. Not when you were like tha'." Faolan's voice is rough with the morning, a growl caught in his chest. Something aches inside at knowing I've missed out on it for a week. His fingers trace my jaw, coaxing me to meet his gaze.

He doesn't ask me if I'm all right—the answer must be obvious—but I'm a little more whole than I was when I went to sleep. That has to be enough.

I push onto my elbows, then still and roll slowly onto my side, tugging the torn halves of my dress back together as heat burns into my face. "Last night—"

Faolan drags the quilt up to my collarbone and touches my jaw once. "Never mind it. Just tell me what happened, aye?"

My stomach flips, but I clutch the blanket to my chest. Fold my free arm beneath my head and tell him everything. What it was like growing up with my father at Aidan's and Conal's sides. How it felt to lose them both at once. How I'd thought the Damhsa might be a fresh start, until the magic took me over though I'd fought long to be free.

And for a time, Faolan doesn't say a word. He plucks spare forget-me-nots from my tangled hair as he listens and arranges them in a constellation across the pillow. My words falter as I stare at the design, thinking of Brona's story about the moon held between Muireal's palms in the sky.

"I splintered my father's mind without even meaning to." Finally, Faolan meets my gaze, and the tightness in my chest eases just a bit. "Maybe he was right, and I shouldn't have removed the tattoo. Maybe I am dangerous."

"Well, I could've told you that."

I hit his chest. "Be serious."

He catches my hand. "I am. Trouble, never in my life have I met something *or* someone who was well and truly harmless. Even kittens are born with claws. And might I remind you that within a day of meeting, you—the mighty, wee Saoirse—wrangled me into a handfasting."

I push onto my elbow, spreading my fingers against his bare chest until they find the steady pulse. "You needed me. It's not like you could've said no."

"I beg your pardon." Faolan sits up, and for a moment we are back to the beginning. His teasing smile and my frozen wonder, separated by a torn dress and a bedsheet. But then he tweaks one of my curls gently around his finger and sits back against the frame. "Remember, I had a damned good plan to kidnap you without all the vowing and forced celibacy. Just ask Tavin. Our resident seanchaí should have woven it into a proper song by now."

A true laugh bubbles out of me, and though guilt bites it off at the end, it helps. "Fine. I'm dangerous. But I think if I can only— if I can understand the magic . . ." I shake my head. "Maybe I can stop being so controlled by its whims."

Maybe, if I could find a way to harness it, I could protect those I love from its power.

"Worth exploring." Faolan spreads his fingers over my hip. Before I can register the touch, he's pulled the bone shards from my pocket, rolling the cracked pieces across his palm. He casts me a look, one brow gently raised.

I bite my lip and slowly extend a hand.

It's nearly dusk by the time I take a break, dropping my aching head against the ship railing. Hours I've been at it and gotten nowhere. Faolan and Kiara are arguing again, their voices carrying down from the helm, the usual threads of resigned affection gone from their voices. I curl tighter against the pile of ropes that's more or less become my nest.

"Have a bit of faith . . ."

". . . waste of time."

Useless.

I curl my fingers tighter to keep from hurling the shards into the sea.

"Chew this for a spell." Brona's voice draws me sharply up just before she shoves a small bundle of herbs into my hand. "You look ready to lose your lunch."

"What is it?"

"Dried butterbur we used to grow on the cliffs by the lighthouse. It'll cure your head all right. I get a mean ache before every storm myself."

She drops to a crouch before me and frowns at the broken ring that's caused us all such trouble. "You still can't get it to do whatever it's meant for?"

I shake my head, wince, and then bite down on the herbs, pressing the bundle against my cheek with my tongue after. "No. It's not . . . alive anymore." I don't know how else to explain the draw a soul has on me. But try though I might, there is nothing within the pieces I'm able to coax out.

"Right." Brona glances over her shoulder as the tension between Kiara and Faolan breaks into full-on shouts. I push to my feet and lean over the nearest rail to spit the bundle of herbs into the water, the ache dulled to barely a nudge at the base of my skull. "And we can't just stick it together with sap?"

Her words are so dry, I can't help but laugh. "Even if we tried, the blue stone at its center is split. See?" I press a fingertip along one half, the brilliant color dulled to a pitiful imitation now, and gasp when the ragged edge nearly breaks my skin.

It's sharp, aye, but the memories it recalls are razor-edged.

Blood smeared across a door made of gold, giving entry to the hall of gods. And again on my brother's soulstone before Da touched my skin. Every god requires a sacrifice . . . and every great vision has required a piece of *me* in return.

I stare at the angry red mark on my skin and slowly press it back against that same edge. My flesh protests, bending without breaking around the point, until I force it through and a crimson pearl emerges in its place.

"What are you doing?"

I hesitate for only a second before smearing my fingertip along the outer curve, painting the cloudy stone red.

"Saoirse . . ." Brona's words trail off into a gasp, then a curse, as we watch the blood trickle between the two halves until the stone snaps together, whole once more.

I drop to the deck, shoving all the pieces of the ring together—marking each with my blood—until they fuse together one after another. Pores in the bone draw close together, the surface gone from aged yellow to a gleaming white. Cracks dissolve into seams, then nothing, as the ring knits itself into being. With one final drop, the opalesque stone throws brilliant colors across my palm and the deck between us.

"Holy feckin' stars," Brona says on a mad sort of laugh. "Faolan, get over here!"

I shake my head and bring my split finger to my lips as footsteps pound the deck, others responding to Brona's call. One of them kneels before me—Faolan—and he starts to reach for the ring, but I drop it to my lap and catch his hands, shaking my head instead. Da's madness is fresh on my mind.

"Don't touch it. I don't know what it can do."

"It better do *something*," Kiara said, but even her hard voice holds a sliver of awe, respect. Something I never could've hoped to command from such a figure before. "Will it show you the island?"

I don't know. I'm afraid to know. But when I look to Faolan again, I think of the days we've wasted, how few we have left, and any lingering doubts turn to vapor easily banished with a flick of the wrist.

"I hope so." I cast one final look at my husband, then close my eyes and slip the ring onto my finger.

"This way, little Soulgazer. Come along."

A weathered face peers down at me as I walk across shifting pebbles and watch the ocean roar. That's what it does when it storms—Aidan says so. Her skin runs deep with wrinkles, her silver hair escaping its braid in five places, and her eyes—

Her eyes are a weakened version of my own, their colors shifting in fractured rhythms with no reason or rest.

Maybe it should scare me, but her smile is so warm that I feel a matching one stretch across my lips. I know this woman who sneaks into my room in the dark and sings to me every now and then. Even here in the grayish dawn, as she glances furtively over her shoulder before lifting me into bony arms, I don't fight as she walks directly into the foaming waves.

My feet strike a delighted rhythm against her hips as salty wind rushes over us, tearing at my nightgown and dark curls— as fine as duck's down, Mam said with a tut on my third birthday.

"Are we going to swim?" My voice is high, more air than anything, as she sets me into the water with a tight hold on my wrists. I shriek when the next wave merely laps at her knees and soaks me to my shoulders.

"Not quite. Do you remember the song, Saoirse?"

I nod as I twist away from the open sea and try to bury myself against her legs, hide from the cold in her skirts. "The island one?"

"That's it. Sing it for me, will you? I forget."

"Gran, it's so cold—"

"Sing it." Her fingers bite and I flinch. Swallow.

"D-daughter of the knowing sea . . ." The rest of the words disappear from my mind as though washed by the rain that pelts my face, and her frown is so severe, I want to cry. But she sighs and smooths my hair, kissing the top of my head before turning me by the shoulders to face the waters again.

> "Daughter of the knowing sea
> Gaze sworn long ago to me
> Captive soul, your blood shall free
> The Isle of the Lost
>
> Painted lips and bronze-capped tail
> Past stones of deepest shadow sail
> Recall to breath, the waters pale
> End their ageless frost
>
> Silver streams our great moon wept
> While mistress fate for cent'ries slept
> Rot across the lands has crept
> To claim their wicked cost
>
> Heir of sight, vision reviled
> Death awaits, my star-touched child
> Flee to the waters and the wild
> A home time unlost."

Her arms shake as she grips my shoulders tighter. "Death awaits, my star-touched child."

She pushes my body down.

No. I don't want to go.

"Gran!" I writhe as she forces me to my knees on the scratchy stones, cough when ocean spray slaps my face. And then I wail. "I don't want to!"

"Hush. Weren't you listening, little Soulgazer?"

The word resonates through the vision, settles deep in my bones, until a fresh wave brings me back to this present, and the pressure on my shoulders, the clouds raging above our heads.

Gran pushes harder, and finally I pitch forward, arms flailing against water I don't know how to navigate. My wail becomes a scream as she kisses my cheek and wraps a hand over my eyes.

"Star-touched child. Don't you see? I lost the pure sight when you were born, but this way—this way I can gain it back. Find the island—appease the knowing sea. Release your grandfather from his torment."

Her voice runs feather soft as I scream one last time and then breathe lungfuls of icy water.

But the pain lasts only seconds. One moment, my vision goes black, and the next, the world blurs past as my father cradles me to his chest.

"You fecking madwoman. You'll never touch my family again! As king of this island, I banish you to the southernmost tip—how dare you laugh?"

The sound is unhinged and vibrant, crawling across my skin. "Band of fools, all of you. Trying your damnedest to tame that which will never be yours. You'll learn soon enough." Gran straightens, her eyes unfettered and terrifying in the way they see everything.

Like she's spent a lifetime looking and has forgotten how to stop.

"Get out!" Da cradles the back of my head as two guards step forward and catch either of her frail arms, but still she laughs as they drag her from the water.

"She'll be the last of us, then. Gods know I tried. Mark my words."

"She's nothing like you. She won't be—"

"Look into her eyes. You know the truth of it!" Her words turn shrill, body wrenching against the guards' hold until they are forced to turn with her, and her smile is the most frightening thing I've seen in my life.

"Fate does not bend the knee to the will of kings, my son, no more than it obeyed the will of gods."

FORTY-NINE

"Right, toss out the pretty phrasing—all that shite we already know about daughter of sight and the gloomy bits. The important stuff's in the second part. Painted lips, bronze-capped tail, past some dark stones and pale waters."

Nessa steps over Faolan, balancing a steaming bowl as she does. "And the frost."

Faolan claps his hands and throws an arm about her neck. "Aye, the frost! So where does tha' leave us?"

The ring glows in my hand as though it was forged of winter ice, beautiful and threatening in turn. It's a lifeline I cling to, while the rest of the ship devolves into shouting, theories dropping through the air like falling stars.

My own thoughts drown them out.

Heir of sight. *Soulgazer.* The words weigh heavier each time I remember them, but not so heavy as the knowledge that once, at least for a little while, my father loved me. I *knew* I hadn't imagined it. Even though his love was not strong—even though it never lasted—Mam remembered too. Is that why she allowed him to hurt me over and over again?

Laughter cuts through the shouting as Nessa suggests we try

the Isle of Bridled Stag, where there are an abundance of painted lips and plenty of holy wells, and I can't take it anymore.

I've done my part. They can damn well figure out the rest now.

My own bowl is left empty as I walk toward the bow. I'm halfway there when footsteps fall in a counter-rhythm to mine—irritating and precise. I whirl around, expecting Faolan or Brona. But it's Kiara who stands tall behind me, the wind mussing her cropped red hair.

Gritting my teeth, I bow once and slip the ring into my pocket. "Forgive me for leaving so suddenly."

"Gods, don't apologize for that. It's a welcome change from when I first met you, little Wolf Tamer."

"Your cousin certainly seems to think so." I regret the words as soon as they're out of my mouth, glancing over my shoulder at Faolan as he sweeps his arms wide, then grabs Brona and shoves one of her star charts into her hand. He speaks with his entire body, and it tugs hard at the strings of my heart.

"Does he?" Kiara's tone crawls with amusement, and heat creeps up my throat. "The lad loves to create drama, aye. I've no doubt he's managed to prod your temper plenty, even with all those pretty chains you wrapped around yourself at the handfasting."

I clutch my throat as though the torc might still be there. "I did what?"

She snorts. "'I vow to follow the path you lay, honor your name, kiss your boots'—tell me, has your marriage followed through on all those promises?"

I can't help but laugh, remembering keenly now what I said and how they'd all reacted. Stars above, I'd meant every word then. "No. Not a bit."

Kiara tips her head back on a laugh, the family resemblance striking. "Good. Faolan has a big enough head as it is." Her smile is an invitation, a shade sharper than Faolan's own. I do my best to return it, knowing it falls flat.

She doesn't falter, though, shrugging off her coat so the ever-present wind tugs at her shirt.

"What is it you want, Saoirse?"

The question startles me, prickling beneath my skin. "What?"

"Faolan is obsessed with his freedom, making a mark on the world, but I have to ask . . . what about his bride?"

Faolan's wolf's-head ring catches on my skirt as I face her, lips parted and stomach clenched. No words come. Kiara studies me a moment, then takes a half step closer. "After you've found the Isle of Lost Souls for me, and I've released Faolan from his leash, what do *you* want?"

My heart races. I can barely breathe. Images of this morning trickle across my mind, from Faolan's tender smile to the pile of forget-me-nots he plucked from my hair. Because in spite of what I told Aidan about a temporary marriage, I still managed to forget that this was never meant to be mine.

"I . . . I want . . ."

I close my eyes, picturing the question again, and try to force my old answers to fit.

I wanted to survive, until Faolan taught me that it was not enough. I wanted to understand myself, and I hold the answers now. I wanted to belong, and the crew made me a wolf. I want—

Love.

No. More than that, I want to *be* loved.

By touches like raindrops that slide down my bare skin, kisses that drift across the sweet bow of my lip, and labored breaths that whisper my name. I want to be loved by a pair of sleepy sapphire eyes and gentle smiles, a laugh too loud and energy unbound. By murmurs and shouts and belly-deep groans.

I want the impossible.

My body curls into itself and I lean my elbows on the railing, wrapping both hands across my mouth as I stare into the churning water.

This pain is unreal. It buries itself like a fist in my stomach, robbing me of air, because Faolan is a man of his word and the only promise he's ever made is a few months of his life in exchange for this island.

It's a good story, anyway, isn't it? The Magpie and the Wolf.

The clever bastard.

I squeeze my eyes against the threat of tears.

"Faolan means well." Kiara's voice comes from far away. "But the moment our deal's fulfilled, he'll be off like a hare fleeing the fox. And you can go with him, to be sure, keep your place on his crew, enjoy his affections. While they last, anyway. But what comes after?"

I can see it without the need for magic or visions. And if I was ever lonely before, it will be nothing compared to what I'll be after all this is over. I might be one of the wolves, aye, but could I stomach living among them once Faolan had lost interest in me? Watch him pursue others as I stood quietly by?

"You don't have to say another word. I already know." I wipe my cheeks and then drop my head to my hands. "What's your point with all this?"

Kiara taps the railing beside my arm, her voice softer. "You're vulnerable. What happened with your father might've been an accident, but it won't be seen that way. If you were hoping to cut ties after the Isle of Lost Souls and disappear, you certainly won't be able to now. Not to mention you've picked a fight with Rí Maccus as well. Twice."

I groan into my hands, unable to help myself. It's not bloody fair—I didn't ask for *any* of this. Not Faolan's attention, not a broken betrothal, not this *damned* magic.

"You need protection, lass, and I'm telling you now Faolan cannot be counted on to provide it."

Kiara takes my arm and pulls none too gently until I'm standing straight and meeting her gaze full-on, the kindly confidant replaced by a warrior queen. "But I can. And it will be built on concrete ideals and a fair trade, not flights of fancy or desperation." She strokes my hair from my face, then crosses her arms. "Protection from whoever wants to harm you. Money. A home on the island of your true ancestors if it's inhabitable."

I stare at her through wet lashes, searching for the trap. "In exchange for what?"

Kiara smiles. "The magic, of course. You have the power to see or know what others are trying to hide, what tragedies may come. I'll call upon you no more than four times a year to provide your sight, and the rest of that life is yours to lead how you wish."

A life like Faolan has led for years, free on the surface but always tethered to Kiara's will. He could not bear the burden of her reach, no matter how long or flexible it may have been.

And yet.

Kiara lifts one shoulder. "You're welcome to refuse. I won't force you. You can test his affection, see if you can prove me wrong. Honestly, I'm damned curious if he has it in him to commit to one woman or venture past a few moons. But think about my offer, would you?" She pushes off the railing with a shake of her head. "You've survived plenty so far, Saoirse. Don't stop now."

The clouds swirl like wayward ribbons above her head as she walks away, and suddenly I wish I could control my magic better. Wish I knew how to search for a specific path and, what's more, how to make it a reality. Because if there was even the smallest chance Faolan could want me too . . .

My chest jerks with a laugh. Wasn't it only last night he claimed he did? But in a carnal sense, the sort stirred by months of lying beside temptation only to vanish as soon as it's satisfied. Nothing like the sort of soul-deep yearning that catches my being whenever I look at him.

Gods, when did this happen? How could I be such a fool?

I've seen the way his moods shift. Faolan uses charm like a second skin, trading touches and kisses to get whatever he wants. The first time we met, he whispered I was special, and a part of him had to mean it for the manipulation to work.

And that's the root of it.

Because no matter the looks we've shared, the healing of my hand, the stories of his childhood, or the ways he's held me close, I'll never be able to tell if it's me he truly wants, or the magic I possess.

"Saoirse! Come see this!"

Faolan's eyes light up with a wild look, and it's like the sun lodges in my chest.

Stars above.

I push off the railing, but have barely reached the helm when I stop, gaping at the wood shavings and haphazard carved lines littered across the deck. "Why—"

"We needed a visual. Look!" Faolan grabs my shoulders and turns me to face the strange circlet of six misshapen blobs, some bigger, some smaller, all of them coming to two points on the right like . . .

"A crescent moon?"

He points to the bottom right. "Isle of Painted Claw, and there?

Isle of Reborn Stalk. That's the sixth and the first in the lines of thrones, aye?"

"Aye, so—wait. *Painted* Claw. You're not saying—"

He nods, grinning madly as he taps the bottom island with his knuckle. "Lips, and tail." He knocks the isle above it in the sequence, then scratches an X in between. "There's the line about the moon, and really, it only makes sense, aye? It's reborn and so it's a great snake. And there's a whole bloody lost goddess, so why wouldn't her seventh island finish off the circle with the others?"

"Right." I'm laughing—I can't help myself from feeling the relief because, broken heart or not, the number of days left in Faolan's life is dwindling. He must feel the same because he wraps his arms around me, one over my middle and the other across my chest, burying his face in my neck, and *gods*, it hurts to exist.

"Brona remembered a patch of nubby black rocks right in between that we always avoid, because there've been a fair few shipwrecks tha' way—figure it's as good a chance as any they're the 'stones of shadow.' And with the full moon affecting the tide, we should be able to avoid the worst of the dangers."

"What about the pale waters? The frost?"

He falters, then squeezes me so tight I truly lose my breath. "We'll figure that out when we get there. Think of the—"

"Reward, never the risk." I'm smiling like a fool when I say it, but Brona, Tavin, Nessa, Lorcan—all of them are watching me expectantly. "What?"

"So you agree?" Faolan lets me go to slip around my side, keeping an arm around my shoulders until he can meet my eyes. "That's our heading?"

My smile drops as the full realization hits me. My voice has gained respect here. They want *me* to decide.

I swallow as I think over the song, the meeting place of the gods in the center of it all, and . . . it all fits. I can't speak, my throat too tight, but I nod and Faolan claps his hands like thunder and bolts off to the wheel, already shouting orders. Nessa grins at me as she passes, Brona touches my arm, and for the first time in my life I truly feel I belong somewhere.

Until my eyes catch on Kiara as she studies the map, and I remember I do not truly belong anywhere.

Not yet.

FIFTY

Lamplight glints off the silver wolf on my finger as Faolan's shadow dances across the wall. His arms bend like tree branches, dark lines crossing one another when he removes his shirt. They pass over the silver-threaded sling hanging on the wall, the green coat I often steal. Arms bound across my chest, I lie as still as I can and try to keep my heart from escaping, because I know exactly what I want now.

No matter how much it will hurt tomorrow.

Faolan's weight sinks into the bed behind me, heat radiating off his skin like it always does, and I squeeze my eyes shut.

Someday, I will be nothing more than a story to him. The girl who tamed the Wolf of the Wild for a summer. Every moment we've shared will be spun into a fantasy, beautiful and stagnant, and I'll never know which parts were dreams or manipulations and which parts were true.

Except for one.

"Faolan?"

He shifts, and the mattress moves with him. "Aye, lass?"

I roll onto my side until our bodies nestle at the center. Reach a hand slowly toward his cheek. Faolan doesn't flinch, eyes curious even in the half dark, but he doesn't move forward either. Hands caught lightly in the sheets, waiting on me.

He doesn't have to wait for long.

I kiss him and hope to the gods he can't feel the turmoil in my lips like I feel the relief in his own. It starts off delicate—and ends too soon, my fingers vibrating with the need to touch him again.

Faolan strokes my hair back to study my face. "Lass?"

"You told me . . ." My voice shakes, and I force myself to swallow. Look into his eyes. "You told me when you fixed my hand to ask you again at a better time. So I'm asking."

Silence stretches my nerves to a single thread before his fingers fall to the quilt covering my arm. Eyes hunting my face, too perceptive by half. "Asking what?"

My heart matches the force of the drums on the night we first met. I remember what it was like, to be touched for the first time by this man made of wild.

Before the legends.

Before the magic and danger and death.

"I'm asking you to show me . . . what it means for a man to worship a woman."

Faolan stiffens, and I turn my face into the pillow.

Dammit.

He didn't mean it. I misread everything—he doesn't want me, he only wanted—

Faolan curls a hand over my shoulder, tugging until I'm on my back, our faces inches apart. "Saoirse, we talked about this. The consummation—"

"Has nothing to do with it, I swear. I want . . ." His mouth softens beneath the fingertip I've placed there, and I can't help but trace the curve of his bottom lip. Swallow when he takes it into his mouth. "I want you, Faolan. I've never felt drawn to another person as I am to you. And I want—I *need*—to know what will happen if I give in."

The lines of his face ease as he searches for a lie that isn't there, because it's one of the truest things I've said. I want to know what it is to drown in another person and come out newly alive on the other side—with *him*. The Wolf of the Wild. I want the legend who haunted my dreams as a girl, and the man who haunts my days as a woman. It's unfair, the way he's tattooed himself on my heart so it sings just one name, over and over again.

Faolan. Faolan. Faolan.

Faolan murmurs a soft curse against my fingers and then drops his head to nuzzle my palm right after.

"Damn me to the shade's realm if I have the power to resist that." Smiling once, he sweeps my hair back and then draws his touch over my throat. Along the dip of my collarbone, down to the ties of my shift. He wavers at the laces for only a moment, then hooks the first and pulls it slowly free.

"I'll show you this part, then. But if you don't want the rest—"

"I want it." I'm startled by the power in my voice, and it shocks a grin out of him as well.

"Aye, but if you suddenly *don't*, just tell me. I can't peep into people's minds like someone I know."

I push onto my elbows, heedless of the way it draws the loosened fabric abruptly apart so it slips down my shoulders. "I can't peep into minds! Only memories sometimes—"

His lips burn a path down my throat, and the words die on my tongue. A calloused finger sweeps one firm line down to my navel, dragging the rest of the laces free, and then his hand flattens between my breasts directly over the strike of my heart.

"D'you want to guess how long I've thought of you like this?"

I shiver when the brush of lips turns to a gentle bite just over the bone, fisting the sheets in my fight to keep still. He shifts, hand sweeping over my bare ribs to drag my shift low over my arms as his kisses move lower.

Lower.

"Saoirse?"

I gasp, because his mouth's found a new curve, drawing toward the peak, and I barely understand the movements of my own body—restless, with embers burning deep in my belly. But it doesn't scare me as it did before the cabin, before the cove.

A gentle tug on either wrist and my shift falls entirely free of my upper body. It's never been so difficult to breathe before. "Since the fever? And that stupid song about—about my thighs?"

He pauses and then laughs. "Obsessed with those thighs, aren't you?"

"*You're* the one who wrote a song about—*feck*."

The scrape of his beard against my breast draws my back off the bed. Faolan slides an arm along the arch it makes, coaxing it higher as his mouth drifts to the tiny dip of my belly button, tongue finding the barest curve of bone to the side of my hip where the shift is newly trapped.

I grit my teeth against the urge to cry out, or beg and plead for more.

I want *more*.

"I should've written another verse. One for either breast, weapons of torture against an innocent man trying to get some rest with them pressed to his back most nights."

Heat flushes beneath my skin until my face surely burns scarlet. Faolan releases my back only to catch my hands instead, weaving our fingers together.

"For your belly, soft and rounded—gods, so sweet." He nips the curve, then catches fabric between his teeth and tugs it down. Past my hips, peeling it over my thighs. His eyes meet mine over the slopes of my stomach and breasts, and some small part of me tries to reach for the old shame. But I can't find it. Not when he looks at me like this.

Not with the ghost of his mouth on my skin.

"I've thought about you for far longer than that song."

His voice is rough as he guides my hands to his shoulders and then nudges my legs apart to kneel between them. Presses a kiss beside my knee as he lifts my hips in his hands, pulling the shift all the way free.

"Since the night of the storm?"

"Longer than that."

I close my eyes. Stars above. I've never felt so bare as the moment I hear the shift drop to the ground, until Faolan releases a shaking breath just after.

"Much." He moves, tugging my body closer as his hand drags higher up my thigh. "Much." His lips drop a kiss to the innermost curve, and I forget how to breathe entirely. "Longer."

He hooks my leg over his shoulder, and my eyes fly open because his kisses—

I bite down hard on the fleshy part of my palm to contain the raw cry that tries to escape. Suddenly, I understand *exactly* what they all meant about worship. In all those years of prayer, I've never felt so pure—so holy—as I do now.

But then he stops. Smiles against the crease of my thigh. "Guess again, Trouble."

A moan tears free of my chest. "You're not being—fair!"

"Pirate."

He nuzzles once. Licks. A shudder wracks my body that has *nothing* to do with the gods and everything to do with the ordinary magic of another person's touch.

"Saoirse?"

Another stroke, this time with his finger, and I burrow back against the bed. "The bloody—Damhsa!"

His groan is my reward. "Good girl."

Faolan stops his teasing, and it's almost too much to bear. My hand falls from my mouth to the sheets, his shoulders—threading in his ruddy hair. He growls when I tighten them into fists, his kisses more fervent, drawing my body as taut as a bowstring.

When I find release, it's nothing like what comes from the furtive passes of my own fingertips in the dark nor even what he gave me after that fevered day by the Teeth. This feeling sweeps through every part of me, down to the deepest, darkest corners I hide from the world—quiet and powerful, caught in a belly-deep moan I do everything I can to contain.

Until Faolan bites gently down on my hip, forcing a bit of the cry to break free. And then his body slides up, his elbows driving into the mattress by my ribs as his bare chest presses to mine. "Don't hide, Saoirse. Not from me."

I can barely think when he kisses me after, but it doesn't keep my limbs from twining around his own.

Parts of my being weave into a new pattern that matches this moment, the colors he's painting across my world. His touch to my face is exceedingly gentle, thumb carving the slope of my cheek. It makes me want to be soft, as warm as melted wax—until his hips press to mine. Something animal takes me over then.

"Take them off."

My demand takes him by surprise. I feel it in the small jerk of his stomach, or perhaps that's just a response to me slipping my hands over the ties of his trousers between us. "Are you sure—"

"*Yes.*"

Whatever control he possessed before snaps, and from there it's a rush to push the clothing free, to spend as little time apart as he kicks his trousers off the bed until our bodies press without barriers—an array of flesh both soft and smooth, bone pale and sun browned. Even the ever-present glove comes off, leather falling to the floor.

Faolan's lips find my ear as he draws my leg high around his hips, teaching me the ways bodies can find each other. And I don't fear the physical pain that will come. Only the emptiness, after. But it *has* to be enough.

"Say it again, Saoirse. Tell me what you want." His forehead drops to mine, eyes midnight dark, and my heart falls completely out of my chest.

"You." It's a breath, a promise, a plea. "I want *you*."

The noise he makes is harsh and sweet as he drops his lips to my throat one last time, then rolls his hips, joining his body with mine.

I gasp his name as pain splits through the heat—but it's short-lived. Gentle words soothing the ache spoken against my jaw, fingers sweeping distracting circles until it starts to ebb away. From there it's a dance my body knows on instinct, drawing me deeper with every stroke of his thumb to my pulse, pass of his lips over mine, curl of his fingers in my hair. Soon I'm twisting up to meet him, holding on to him, and he's losing himself with me until there is nothing of the legend here.

Only the man.

One night. One memory.

One perfectly honest thing between us.

I bury my face against Faolan's throat when pleasure finds him—and he parts our bodies just seconds before it does. It's all the sweeter for his protection, his promise kept after all this time. Our ragged breaths and pounding hearts are the only sounds for a long, still moment until he rolls onto his side, pressing a kiss to my sweaty curls.

"You're so fecking beautiful."

I blink as a wave of *longing* seeps from his mouth into my mind—as all-consuming as our pleasure was moments ago. His lips drift to my temple, hand flexing over my chest, and a rush of sweetness and sorrow tangles in my blood.

"Of all the treasures I've stolen . . . All the years I've searched . . ."

Tears prick as I arch closer, afraid to untangle our limbs. Heat radiates off his palm like sunlight, burying golden arrows in my heart. It's not affection. Not amusement or arousal, either. It's something—unnameable, yet I must try to name it.

Names mean everything to him.

"Saoirse, *nothing* compares to . . ."

Faolan stops.

Stares at me with confusion that turns swiftly to alarm.

I don't understand until he peels his palm free of my chest, leaving a glowing, iridescent handprint behind. I flinch as the connection severs between us, our soulstone marks flaring with light before his dulls and mine fades to nothing, taking all my warmth with it.

"I'm fine," I say, even as Faolan rolls off the bed. If I'd felt empty when our bodies parted, it's nothing compared to this. "It's already gone. Come back and we can—"

"I need to check the sails." He tugs the leather glove on, fingers shaking as he does up the knots. "Mind the crew. Kiara wanted to talk as well."

"Can't that wait?"

I hate how pathetic my voice sounds. Hate the way Faolan avoids me as he does up his trousers, then reaches for a shirt. I snatch it away before he can, hugging it to my chest so he has no choice but to look.

Immediately, I wish I hadn't.

"Saoirse—"

I hand him the shirt, then roll over so I don't have to see the regret lining his face. For a moment, we're both still, his shadow a rueful ghost on the wall. One of its arms reaches out, hovering over the lump that must be me. It stops a hairsbreadth above my shoulder.

Then fabric rustles as Faolan dons his shirt and walks toward the door.

"You've done your part, Trouble. Sleep now. I'll handle the rest."

My heart cracks as the door falls shut, but I press the heel of my hand against it. Roll until I'm sure it's beating in a solid rhythm again. It doesn't matter what we both felt, that unnamed thing floating between us. Kiara was right. Faolan was never going to stay. He's never made me any promises beyond the legend we'd create—and that's all this journey is. A story that will eventually end.

But no matter how many years come to pass, or how Faolan runs from the truth of it, I'll know *this* was real.

And no one can take that from me.

FIFTY-ONE

I wake alone, and it's alone that I step through the memories of last night scattered across the floor. By the time I've scrubbed my face clean and found clothing that doesn't smell like him, it's only the unfamiliar twinge between my legs that reminds me last night wasn't a dream.

It was real. And now it's over.

I give my head a ruthless shake and head for the deck—pulling up sharply at its threshold. Tension knots the air as though a storm is brewing, centered around Brona and Kiara at the wheel.

"If you're so keen to direct us, then *here*. Please, be my guest." Brona shoves one of her dotted star charts at Kiara, who rolls her eyes.

"Is it such a lofty request, asking for the coordinates, navigator? I need Tavin to send a message to Aisling—Maccus won't give up so easy, the bastard. You'll want them to be accurate."

"They *are* accurate," Brona snaps. "As close as I can get, following a damned song for guidance! You're better off spending your time praying for fair winds if we're to make it by the solstice."

"We'll make it."

Faolan's voice shivers down my spine though it's spoken to the air and not my skin. It takes everything in me not to turn like a flower to the sun as I step across the deck.

"We don't have much choice, do we?" Kiara asks. "You swore this ship could outpace anyone, so please tell me why his sails are on the horizon?"

"He's not as stupid as he looks. If I had to guess, one of his spies bought some Stiff Wind at the Scath-Díol, same as us. And then there's Aidan, eager to point the way."

Kiara groans, pushing her hair back as the currents shift once again, like the sea itself wants to slow us down. "His entire bloody court was set to arrive only a few hours after we left. Did you really think he'd take the insult of stealing his bride *twice* from her wedding day without retribution?"

"Obviously not," Faolan says, his expression hard as he studies the clouds that roll over themselves like sausages. "We'll lose him in the fog tonight, buy ourselves some time. Have a bit of trust, Kiara."

"It's dwindling by the second."

Faolan stalks past her to take the wheel as Brona curses them both and gathers up her maps to take shelter in the hall. "Tell Aisling to meet us there. At least then you'll have a guarantee of escape if everything turns wrong."

"Oh, I plan on it."

Kiara glares at Faolan, then kicks a boot against the railing. Releases a hard breath into the air. "You've done well over the years, Faolan. We were both dealt a shite hand in life, but we've built something worthwhile out of it. Together. All I'm asking is that you don't muck it up now."

His nostrils flare as he grips the wheel tight. "Yes, my queen."

Kiara is quiet for a time, watching her cousin. Then her gaze pins on me. "And you, Wolf Tamer?"

I lurch from my spot tucked by the doorway, heart beating loud enough to drown out the sea. Faolan doesn't look at me, and I'm not sure whether to be grateful or hurt. "Aye?"

"Sort out your magic." Kiara folds her arms over her chest. "If that song is right, you're the one who will free the Isle of Lost Souls from whatever spell the gods laid upon it, and we don't have an age to get it done."

I bite down my protest, knowing how little good it would do. None of us knows what we're getting into—a risk with no guarantee of reward. Even the location is a gamble.

Death awaits, my star-touched child.

"Saoirse?" Faolan's eyes find mine over the wheel, leather glove wrapped neatly over the bargainer's mark. His face is rueful, lips turned down.

We are out of other choices. There are only a few days left.

I swallow and turn away.

"I'll sort it out."

F or four days, we sail without breaking. A storm comes to sweep us off course after the first day passes. By the third, we're back to chasing the line where the sky meets the sea, and Muireal's constellation edges closer to the center. She seems so lonely without her moon.

Gods. I thought I understood loneliness before.

But Faolan is a man possessed. He avoids stillness, most especially if it's shared with me. His smiles are fast but his feet faster as he jokes and slips free of conversation or my touch like it's a noose, seeing to tasks along the ship. I sleep alone and wake alone, and it's only after the second dawn I learn that Faolan strung a hammock between the mast and ship's railing, keen to keep an eye out at all hours and dive into whatever needs to be done. I remind myself it doesn't matter; the Wolf was never going to be mine.

And all the while, Maccus's fleet haunts our horizon.

The old rhythms of song and laughter on the deck are gone, replaced with fraught conversation and skirmishes over stupid asides. Glances are cast with wariness at first, then fear the more my magic grows—and it *is* growing. Our one reassurance that this path to the island is true. For the closer we get, the more that *pull* of it threatens to undo me at the seams.

My skin ripens until it's ready to split with the humming in my veins. The crew's desires brush against my mind even without touching—their frustrations, annoyances, and wounds. I can't read their thoughts exactly, but it's invasive all the same, leaving me just as tangled inside as the hours drag on.

So I avoid them too. I take to following my old rules, not daring to touch another person, or the bone ring either.

Perhaps the day is coming when even that much control will be lost to me.

Perhaps I will long for the days when I could hide.

But there is no stopping this.

Soon, the isle of the lost will rise.

FIFTY-TWO

"S top." The words are out of my mouth before I'm fully awake, tumbling from the pile of sails I'd slept on as lightning heat licks down my spine. I manage a single deep breath from the ground, and then I shout as loud as I can manage. "Stop the ship!"

Brona runs up, and two other pairs of feet follow. "We're not to the mainland yet, Saoirse. It should be dead center, shouldn't it?"

"I don't know, but—" I double over as the humming grows too intense, clenching every muscle until a whimper tears free of my throat. "No. It's here. We have to stop *here*."

There is quiet for only a second, and then Faolan kneels before me. It's the first time he's met my eyes in days; I hate that it's when I'm weak and vulnerable. "Maccus is barely a league behind us. We can't afford a mistake here."

"I—" Another wave, strong enough to force tears into my eyes. "I'm not mistaken."

"What's this?" Kiara walks up, half-dressed, with crinkles stretched across her cheek as though she's just rolled out of bed.

"The island—Saoirse says it's near."

"How the feck can she tell? It's already dusk." Kiara glances to a sky that's gone hazy purple, but Faolan looks at me again and finally offers his gloved hand.

"A bit of trust, Kiara?" The words are meant to sound clever, but for the first time I see he's as worn through as the rest of us. Possibly more. I've never seen such shadows beneath his eyes, his skin stretched tight over bone—and his hand trembles where he extends it.

Shite. How many days, exactly, have passed since he told me? I try to count backward, but he must read the question on my face because his smile is small and strained as he takes my elbow and lifts me to my feet.

"Saoirse . . ."

"It's today. Isn't it?"

He nods, scratching the back of his neck. "Aye. I reckon I have until midnight, since that's about when it all happened."

"Faolan—"

"We've plenty of time to sort it out, but I . . . brought this along." He dips a hand in his pocket, flashing me the half-filled vial of water that healed my hand. "Figured it couldn't hurt."

I reach for his face, until I remember the way he avoided my touch. I can't be angry, though. The magic is too strong. I start to draw my hand back, but he steps closer. Hesitates, and then pulls my palm up to his cheek, allowing me to see him for what he is beneath the legend. Beneath even the man.

Faolan is just a boy crafted by want, terrified of being forgotten.

I try to speak. To say anything that might bolster him, even as the magic spikes across my skin. But my mind's too crowded by the island's call for visions, so in the end, I can only step forward and press a single kiss to his brow.

Faolan sucks in a breath, then reaches for me. "Feck. Saoirse, I'm sorr—"

"This can't be right."

Brona's voice jerks us apart, and I force myself to step away from whatever he was about to do or say, turning to the railing where she stands facing the water.

And the ghost of an island just beyond.

Rock of pitch black stretches into a steep peak at the center, like a volcano once erupted to create this space before vanishing deep into the earth. It drags out into a circle of sorts, a cluster of stones standing sentry near their outstretched tips. Between them, a channel connects to a calm, round bay with enough room for a ship—if we can make it past the massive waves crashing between the pillars first.

"We've stopped here before, Saoirse. There's not so much as a fly left alive on the place." Brona sweeps a hand through her hair, grimacing when it finds a knot. "Even fish won't tolerate the waters. I must have got the calculations wrong."

"No." I cannot tear my gaze away from the desolate land—not when its call still sings in my bones. "This is it. Those are the rocks of deepest shadow. I'm certain."

They look at one another, at their captain—not at me.

Not this time.

Faolan pales but drags a smile onto his lips, trying to be the dashing leader they've followed all this way. "Saoirse, if you're sure—"

"*If?*" I round on him, any lingering softness evaporating in the face of his favorite mask. "For feck's sake, you wanted my magic—you married me for it—and I'm telling you *this* place is the Isle of Lost Souls. Stay here on the ship if you like, but I'm going."

Faolan's jaw works twice as he looks from my eyes to the ship. It's too dark to note where Maccus's fleet rests on the ocean beyond, and we both know the risk of leaving our advantage behind. I draw Faolan's gaze back with a touch to his jaw.

"Either you trust me or you don't."

Nodding once, Faolan rolls his shoulders back and starts for the railing. "Get the currachs ready."

Our first steps on the island's shore are like a drunkard's, the rocks uneven and almost angry. Above our heads, the black mountain peak stretches up like it wants to break into the sky open, lines carved into the sides where streams must once have flowed. A smattering of bare-limbed trees cages its side.

Not a single drop of water marks the land.

"Well, Faolan? Is this the weight of your promises to me?" Kiara kicks away a rock that splits in two beneath her boot, as brittle as the rest of this place. My palms are coated in sweat. I flatten them against my thighs.

"Give her a minute," Faolan mutters, but I can see sweat dotting his own brow despite the chill in the air.

> *"Recall to breath, the waters pale*
> *End their ageless frost"*

I glance at the peak again, those empty lines where rivulets once ran. "I think we need to climb."

"Climb, she says." Kiara laughs outright, turning away from the peak to look over the waters beyond. "This was a mistake."

The last of my patience breaks.

"Then go back!" I turn on the others as well, sure I must look half-mad. "Leave. Take the ship, and sail wherever the feck you want. I didn't ask for any of this, I never wanted it—I *hate* that I can feel this place in my head. But whatever's calling me is here, and I'm going to bloody well find it."

I turn before any of them can respond, and stare down the island that's caused nothing but pain in my past.

"Whoever you are—" I start to pray out of habit, then bite my tongue and reach deep into the pocket of Faolan's coat. He's not the only thief on the ship, and I believe I've earned the right to claim it. "You called me here."

The bone ring is ridged, carving a smooth, supple line beneath my finger. I trace the circle's edge.

"Show yourself."

I slide it on, and the world melts with color and light.

This vision does not swallow me like the others have, but instead paints *this* world anew. The island is made of life like I've never witnessed it, every inch covered in rich carpets of moss and nutty-brown earth—a living tapestry speckled with amethyst-colored flowers and fat, golden butterflies. I crane my neck to see the mountain above, silvery white at the very top and streaked blue-purple all the way down to its base, where a pool of pale water lies, threaded in silver as well.

"Stars o' fire," I breathe, not sure whether I'm seeing a vision of the past or what could be again. Whatever it is, it's achingly lovely.

"Saoirse?"

I turn on my heel to see Faolan—not as he is now, but as vibrant as the stories he spins. His skin and hair glow with light, lips twisted up into a mischievous smile, hands unstained by abalone scars.

Please let it be real.

I reach for him and gasp when our fingers connect. Just as at our first encounter, visions unspool behind my eyes at his touch— not ruin or death, but *everything* we could be. Bickering in the most beautiful waters, a cove of our own at my back. My belly swollen, eyes alive, laughter.

So much laughter.

The ring has restored the world to possibility. Perfect, untouched possibility.

He tugs at my hand. "What do you see, love?"

"The Isle of Lost Souls. I can see what it should be."

What *I* could make it again? The thought is dangerous and far-reaching.

Seductive.

As I take in the sights, greedy for more, I see something I hadn't noticed before. A path bent around two fat trees with amber bark, one of them carved with the same swirling triskele that marks a soulstone.

"*There.* I need to go there."

"Wait—"

I want to laugh that it's Faolan who's saying the word to me for once instead of the other way around. It's the easiest thing in the world to pull free of his hold and step onto the path, watching as tiny white flowers bloom around my feet.

"She's lost it," Kiara mutters.

"No, Saoirse is just— The magic's strange, all right?"

"She's acting mad. Or drunk."

"What's the other option than to follow her? It's a bit late to cut our losses."

The whispers hardly matter, because the song is drifting through the leaves above and I'm humming alongside it.

> *"Daughter of the knowing sea*
> *Gaze sworn long ago to me*
> *Captive soul, your blood shall free*
> *The Isle of the Lost."*

I climb for minutes or hours; it hardly matters now.

> *"Flee to the waters and the wild*
> *A home time unlost."*

Home.

I'm coming *home*.

The sky is split between the moon and her starry companions as she rises slowly into the night. Muireal's constellation is almost perfectly aligned. I walk until my legs burn, and the earth plateaus beneath my feet. Without looking, I know we've reached the very center of the isle.

It's strange, though. I'm not winded or sore or even scared, because for once in my life, I know exactly where to direct my steps. I *know* that the path winds through narrow, sweeping cliffs to hide away the heart of the isle from the world outside. One by one I navigate them, fingers tracing the patterns and symbols carved into rock, until I step through a wall of mist into a scene of pure paradise.

A series of pools lines the rock going all the way up to the snowcapped top that soaks up moonlight all but one night a month and pours it into the waters that flow down, down, down to collect just before our feet. I've never heard such lovely music as the sound the water makes, passed from one pool to the next, paler than bone or sand or snow, their shallows gleaming like mother-of-pearl with all the discarded soulstones.

"It's here! I told you." I'm laughing as I turn to see Faolan and the others, but none of them are smiling. Faolan steps forward, his beautiful jaw set tight as he reaches for my hands to pull the ring free.

"No!" I jerk back, but this time he doesn't yield.

He removes the ring, and the earth turns as black as shadow. We are standing on brittle bones and forgotten memories, with barren scoops of earth holding only foul, stagnant muck.

The Isle of Lost Souls.

"This . . . this isn't right." I crane my neck to search for Muireal's constellation in the sky, but clouds streak over the moon, blurring its position. "We're here. We tracked the moon, I-I found the stupid ring—it's not supposed to be this way."

I swipe the ring from Faolan, and he drops his head, searching the ground fruitlessly for a clever way out like he's managed to take all his life. I see the cracks form until the mask crumbles. Falls away entirely. "No. It's not."

Kiara steps forward, face gone to stone. "Faolan, you'd best figure this out *now*. I'll not face Maccus empty-handed when he appears. For all we know, he's already laid anchor."

"What do you care?" he asks, voice chained at the edges like he's barely restrained a scream. "You'll have Aisling to back you and—"

"*She* means war." Kiara flings a hand my way, and nausea takes me over. "Your choice to take Saoirse means war, and I was willing to fight it with you, but without this damned island—*awake* and alive—to negotiate with, we're all fecked."

The words should cut like a knife, but I'm as empty as the land beneath my feet, its veins dry of the magic that once dwelt in the goddess.

Magic . . . that now lives in me.

My fingers waver as I roll the ring between them and stare at the perfect blue gem that throws a thousand different colors every time it catches the light. It's almost like a living thing, this relic worn by my ancestors.

Restored by my blood.

A chill sweeps my neck, but I tilt my head and slowly slide the ring onto my finger.

Captive soul, your blood shall free . . .

Is that truly all it would take? It seems so simple. A prick of the finger, a couple of drops, just what it took to fix the ring and walk through that doorway. Yes, the gods were slaughtered like animals—bled like them, too, until the earth drank everything they had—but they were *gods*. My line is only blessed. And this island already held magic before they hid it away. Surely all I need to do is recall it to life?

I ignore the arguments around me, the sound of my name being called, as I tug a dagger free from my belt and nick my smallest finger. One, two, three drops fall to the ground, and I hold my breath, waiting for something to happen.

Nothing does.

"Saoirse, we need to go."

I want to scream. To rage. I'm about to slam my hand into the earth and *make* it work when someone seizes my arms and lifts me as though I were a child—lifts until my feet clear the ground, until I forget what it is to breathe, as I come face-to-face with the man I have now fled twice. Rí Maccus.

Stars save me from the Stone King.

FIFTY-THREE

We are going to break each other.

     I am shattering in a thousand different places as I watch Rí Maccus sink his fists into Faolan. Still, the cries he releases are nothing to the soul-wrenching sound he made when he first saw the kiss of fire upon the sky as they dragged us away from the pools and down closer to shore—like an animal mourning.

Because his ship's sails are afire, lit up like a phoenix's wing. A great and terrible beauty that I swear I feel rip straight through his heart and into my own.

"Stop it!" My throat is raw with the shout, but like all the others it's pointless. I writhe against a guard's hold on my wrists, whimpering when one nearly gives way—the same one Maccus twisted after I tried to stab him with my knife. "Please—whatever you want, I'll pay it. We'll both pay!"

"You're as foolish as your old man if you think money will atone for what you've done." Maccus's laugh is a soft, cruel thing he casts over his shoulder like it costs him nothing. "But you're welcome to beg."

Faolan spits. I go boneless as the glob lands square on Maccus's cheek, sliding slowly down his jaw.

"Bastard," Faolan coughs out—or maybe he laughs.

Gods, don't let it be a laugh.

Maccus moves faster than I thought possible, grabbing hold of Faolan's hair in one hand as he drives his fist so hard into Faolan's gut, we all hear the crack of his rib. The men drop Faolan to the ground, where he curls onto his side, clenching his teeth against a groan.

My own echoes across the clearing, until Maccus grasps my jaw in one gloved hand and snaps my head back to meet his eyes. I don't look down—not this time. And something shifts in his expression, almost like . . . amusement.

"Go on, then. Make your offer, girl."

I blink, my lips parting and then pressing feverishly tight at the glint in his eyes. The only thing I have to offer will cost him nothing, and me *everything*. I dart a glance to Faolan, who's just barely recovered enough to raise his head. Even hollow-eyed with fury, dirt-streaked and panting on the ground, he is beautiful. My proud, fanciful Wolf.

Legends don't die.

It's a promise I make myself as I look back at Maccus, forcing my lips to form the word as my heart tears to pieces.

"Marriage."

"No!"

Two guards dive onto Faolan as he protests with a vicious snarl, but Maccus only laughs—the sound scornful and deep, vibrating from his center straight to the hold on my jaw. "You're worthless for that now, though. Aren't you?"

My hand meets his cheek in a vicious slap before I'm even aware I'd torn it free from the guard.

A whisper of memory chases in my mind from the touch—*loss*. So all-consuming, it ate his heart whole.

We stare at each other, the Stone King and I, until his jaw quirks as he drops his hold to wrap his fingers round my throat instead. I claw at his hand, nails dragging uselessly over the leather as Faolan and the others rage around me, fighting their restraints, but it's an impossible feat. Maccus seems truly made of stone.

"Even if the Wolf hadn't already made you his *bitch*, you'd be worthless as a wife." Maccus strokes a thumb over my pulse, and bile rises in my throat. "Your blood is tainted, and I won't be driven mad like your father. What else is there to give me?"

"The—island." The words waver as they leave my mouth, every syllable dripping with lies. I failed to awaken the Isle of Lost Souls, just as I'll fail to save my husband and our crew.

Maccus's lips draw into an outright sneer as he looks over the arid rock washed in silver light, seeing none of its magic and *all* its blight. "Worthless."

"You're wrong! I—" His fingers tighten, and I choke on the next words. "It's the—Isle of Lost Souls, I swear to you now. You just have to . . ."

I trail off as my vision blackens, my head lolling back as moonlight slips past the columns of smoke, revealing a cluster of stars in the dark silk sky. The moon is a gleaming pearl hanging just above the constellation of three stars mirroring one another below, cupped like gentle hands.

Some called her a siren, others a whisperer of fate or collector of stars—caught in her own pattern forever when the sea eventually tired of her song.

I blink furiously, twitching under Maccus's grip. But I don't stop staring at the constellation even as somewhere nearby, a wolf roars my name.

The last time Muireal cradled the moon between her palms, the isle sank into the sea.

Muireal . . . my lips shape the name—and then wrench apart in a gasp as understanding dawns with a violent streak of sensation down my spine, forcing my body to buck against Maccus while he fights to contain me. But I don't cower away this time. I writhe, claw, and *bite* until his fingers loosen enough for me to breathe—to shout.

Because the seventh goddess is coming. Tonight, she will rise.

"Let me go! Muireal is returning—don't you see her in the sky? I have to awaken the isle before she releases the moon from her stars, or else Faolan—"

"*Quiet*, you raving madwoman!" Maccus's hand digs tighter, until my breath trickles to a feeble stream. "You think you can play tricks on me? That I'm someone to be fooled by the stars?!"

"She proved you were," Faolan rasps, bent over on the ground with his bloody lips drawn into a snarl. "*Twice*. Now let go of my wife, you sick son of a—"

Maccus is going to kill him. I don't need magic to see it.

White spots dance across my vision like snow, mocking me as I reach out toward the Stone King, seeking any part of him uncovered by cloth. His focus lies on Faolan, so fiercely he doesn't notice my hand until it scrapes against his cheek.

For a moment, we lock eyes and I see *nothing* in the depths of his own. The king is a living ghost—no, not quite alive. But not dead either. Something . . . other.

Maccus releases my throat and shoves me to the ground, breaking the spell. "You seek to drive out my mind, same as your father's."

"N-no! I'm only trying to—"

"I've heard enough."

I cry out as he reaches for his sword just as the moonlight brightens, then seems to grab at the air around me. It urges the magic's hum into a roar—soft and then so loud it seems to want to split my mind.

Maccus stops. Stares openmouthed. The others are watching, too—I feel their eyes like fingers as I collapse to the ground, grateful and horrified at once to see the moon is nearly aligned with the stars, which means I was *right* and Faolan won't die.

But maybe I will.

Because power demands sacrifice, especially when wielded by the gods, and when Muireal planted *this* power in my bloodline, it was never meant to lie dormant. Yet five generations of my family have ignored it, allowing its roots to grow bitter and *hungry* in our souls. I was a fool to think only a few drops would suffice as payment.

This magic wants to devour me to the bone.

Daughter of the knowing sea . . . Captive soul, your blood shall free . . .

I should have cast you into the sea the moment you opened those eyes.

I feel nothing. I want nothing. I am nothing.

It's you.

Memories and magic crowd my mind until I scream, nails breaking where my fingers curl into the earth. I'm bleeding again from three different places, but still nothing happens. My whole body shakes as I turn my shrieks toward the sky, where the moon hangs a hairsbreadth from Muireal's palms. "Release him! Release his bargain and take my soul instead—I'm here, damn you. I'm *here!*"

"*Shut up!*" Maccus fists my hair in his hand, ripping me around to face him again. This time, with a sword pressed to my throat. "Shut up, you insignificant little wretch. You speak of bargains and souls as though you've ever had to reap them—as though you've held life in your hands as it slipped through your fingers like water. You know nothing—you are *nothing.*"

"I am everything!" A sob breaks from my throat as the blade

bites into my skin. But I do not flinch. Not this time. "I am Faolan, our wolves, the soldiers—*you*. I am all your damage and all your desire—every morsel of pain or scrap of joy; all of it dwells in *me*. You cannot hide from me, Rí Maccus, even with your heart of stone. I *see* you."

Maccus's fingers go slack and I tear myself free, backing off before he can reach for me again. Blood runs down my neck, and I welcome its hot kiss. My rage is boundless, even as the boundaries of who I am blur. Yet as the moonlight grows rich and all of them regard me with a mixture of pity, horror, and awe, there is only one person who tethers me to this world.

One person who will be lost for good if I don't see this through.

"Faolan—"

"*Enough.*"

The world stops with the swing of Maccus's sword.

I fall back with a cry—but it's not me he strikes. It's the ropes binding Faolan's wrists behind his back.

"Arm yourself." Maccus tosses a blade at Faolan's feet and I watch as my husband assembles himself upright like a wooden doll, wincing with every movement. Too godsdamned stubborn not to take the bait.

Gods. This is it, isn't it? The ruin I saw for us both at the start—the scars Faolan will never heal from, tearing through the world like arrows, blood shed across the beach.

Maccus's sword sings as it slices through the air. "I won't kick a dog while he's down."

"Didn't seem to be a problem before," Faolan says, darting me a desperate glance, and I understand at once what he's doing, distracting the Stone King's ire from me. I want to strike his smart mouth—kiss it until we're both bloody.

Except I already am.

I stare at my red fingers, the places where they tore against the earth or collected drops from my throat like jewels. When I tilt my hand so one hits the ground, it glimmers faintly silver and then sinks into the blackened earth. But no ruptures form, the moon still minutes away from Muireal's control. Still, I shudder as I recall the way those soulstone marks glowed and then sank beneath my skin. How when my magic activates the world around me, opening gates to the past or an entrance to the divine realm . . . it always starts with a cut.

Like the magic springing forth from our islands after the gods bled upon the land.

"No."

My whole body curls in on itself as an impossible thought creeps into my mind, past the relentless tug of the island or the collective pain and panic wracking our crew. I can accept that I am gods-blessed—or even that I was made to be a *sacrifice* for the good of the Crescent and all its lost souls.

But I cannot be . . .

"Daughter of the knowing sea, gaze sworn long ago to me. Ca-captive soul, your blood shall free—"

I cannot breathe. My heart convulses and I reach for my pocket, where the goddess's ring is stored. I draw it out over my chest to try to contain the agony there, but when my finger slips through the circle and bone meets my bare flesh, the truth sears across my mind.

Hundreds of supplicants litter the isle, hundreds of soulstones brought forth by sacred ferriers, until mortals learned to use the power of a broken soul. Until the precious stones became currency like all other things, and mistress fate demanded her toll for all those lost souls.

There was a prophecy. A warning.

A goddess with ocean eyes.

Muireal, they called her—me.

I was immortal, but I died—yet unlike the others, no blood was shed when they killed me. No.

My blood was threaded first with that of a mortal fisherman, and the daughter we loved—the daughter I refused to claim, because I could see what was coming for the gods and their named children. I left a single child nameless and hidden, bearing a ring carved from my own finger to gift her with choice and legacy, then walked to my own death with open eyes.

Five generations of mourning passed. Five generations of sight, each weaker than the last as one after another rejected my gifts and embraced madness until freedom was born to a king with a drop of gods' blood in her veins.

Saoirse.

The name rolls through me like a wave, until the vision breaks and I remember it is *mine*.

I drop the ring and then press my hands into the ashen earth—feeling the magic I once feared and loathed that was always meant to lead me here to the Isle of Lost Souls.

My birthright, if I choose to claim it.

And that is the answer.

Choice.

The sharp slap of metal drags me back, and by the time my vision fully clears, they are already at blows: my Wolf of the Wild and the Stone King.

"Stop!" I fumble for the silver-threaded sling at my side, knowing it must be as good as useless in my hand after seven years without practice, and then twist to search for Kiara. The queen who gained amnesty the moment Maccus arrived. She denied helping us, handed over the handfasting cords herself for him to burn, and whispered to Faolan as they were dragging us here that their bargain was done. He'd found her the island as promised. He was free.

It only cost him his whole world.

She stands at the line of the petrified trees half-hidden by shadow, eyes glinting catlike in a way that churns my stomach.

Hands seize me by the arms and I whirl around with a cry as a soldier catches my wrists and jerks them behind me until I'm forced to my knees—forced to watch as the others put up a fight but not nearly good enough for the number of Maccus's crew. Nessa with a line cut down her cheek. Tavin holding off two women at once, more worn down with each second. Brona handling herself against one fighter without ever seeing another walking behind her, his sword raised, until Lorcan smashes his head in with a rock.

The fighting shifts, and there is Faolan.

Faolan, bleeding from five different wounds.

Faolan, howling as Maccus slips past his guard and swipes a blade down the same ribs he broke.

Faolan, seconds from death.

"Kiara!" I wrench so hard against the man's hold, my shoulder threatens to slide out of place. But there she is, watching me instead of the bloodshed, her expression unfathomable.

Tears leap into my eyes, and for a split second, I hate her. Hate all of them for their games and lies, their schemes. Hate her for offering a trickster's bargain, determined to harness my magic before anyone else can.

I hate her, because I cannot survive outside her cage.

"I accept your offer. I'll do it. My magic for Faolan's life—just stop this. Save him. Please!"

Kiara narrows her eyes, and for just a moment, all I see is death. Then she flings her hand out and releases a blade over my head into the soldier's eye. There is no time to balk or second-guess. I have all of three seconds to snatch up a rock and fit my fingers through the loops of my sling, swinging it over my head again and again just like Aidan taught me.

You don't have to be clever. You don't have to be strong. Just know when it's time to let go.

As Maccus raises his arm for the killing blow, I release the stone from my sling.

It strikes Maccus's hand with a sickening crack, knocking the sword from his hand as blood pours from his knuckles to the ground. His enraged gaze snaps to mine.

"Rí Maccus!" Kiara's shout surpasses all the groans and clashes of metal, drawing the king's focus at once. I fumble for another rock, then see she's armed herself with a bow that is trained on his chest. The Stone King's lips twist into a scowl just before he releases a high, piercing whistle, and his men fall away.

I search for Faolan at once—kneeling on black pebbles, his shirt hanging in bloody tatters, hair matted to his face. He's *alive*.

But my relief lasts only a second.

Because the light shifts from pale to a pure silver frost, and all eyes turn to the heavens as Muireal finally cradles the moon between her palms.

FIFTY-FOUR

I collapse into the shallow, dried-up pit behind me where a stream once flowed from the top of the mountain to the sea. Scored into the earth as though by claws, the pathways are cracked and spent, a mirror to the dying woods from which they come. Beneath the cracks, though, a touch of silver frost peeks through. I turn my hand until the bone ring's brilliant opalesque stone catches the light once more, unable to decide if the gleam is cruel or kind.

There's no more time to reconsider. To wait.

Five generations of my ancestors bound their magic so tightly within themselves their minds frayed at the edges. They never knew the legend they could claim—the power of a goddess planted deep in their souls. Were they taught to fear it? Did they believe themselves monsters in need of cages, harbingers of curses and death?

Did they hate themselves too?

My teeth sink into my bottom lip as I touch the ring to my forehead and wait for fear to return. For loathing to settle deep. But there is only me and the magic now.

Tears stream down my cheeks, hot and human, as I raise the

dagger to my right wrist and let the words pour from my lips even as they tremble.

"I call upon the knowing sea. The whispering stars. The great mother's depths."

The blade is cold against my skin, laid over a net of deep blue veins. Somewhere behind me, I hear my name. It's a question, then a shout, feet pounding earth until they slide through rocks and stop at the barren stream's edge.

"Saoirse!"

Faolan's voice breaks through the sweet mist of my mind. He's draped in shadow, huddled beneath the weight of his injuries as the others draw near. Whatever he sees makes his face pale, as though his soul's already abandoned its vessel. "What the feck are you doing?"

I look to the knife again, and for a moment caution flickers through my certainty. Maybe there was a reason my ancestors rejected this path. Perhaps it required too much. But if I can save Faolan—save *everyone*—from a fate of wandering the earth, trapped in eternal torment . . . is that not worth my life?

"Only the goddess Muireal can awaken the island. And her magic is in my blood."

Realization dawns, and Faolan darts forward to try to grab my arm—but he can't. Something keeps him from me, even as it causes his bargainer's mark to glow beneath the glove. I press the blade's edge down until my skin bends but does not break.

"*No!* Wait, love—please. Whatever those voices are telling you, they're asking too much. Opening a stone door, fixing the ring, those feats only took a few drops. But the whole feckin' island?!"

Death awaits, my star-touched child.

"It's the only way."

Kiara steps beside him, her face unreadable, arrow still trained on Maccus, who paces like a bear. "Faolan, back down. Think of the reward, never the—"

Faolan whirls on Kiara, anger vibrating through him. "*She is not a risk I'm willing to take!*" I watch as the legend crumbles into dust, the man falling to his knees and throwing himself at a barrier he cannot possibly break. "Saoirse, *please!*" His voice cracks, and with it, my heart. "I'm begging you, put down the dagger."

Doubt rips through my concentration for just a second, halting the slip of the blade. "You'll die if I do."

"I don't feckin' *care!*" Rage explodes across his face once more as he rips the laces of his glove apart, then slams his bare hand against the silver barrier of moonlight. He turns his face to the sky as the bargainer's mark ripples, screaming at a god he barely believes in. "Do you hear me, damn you?! Let her go! I've had my thirteen years—she's barely begun to live. *Let her g—*"

"Faolan! This is my choice. *Mine.*"

"Then don't make it," Faolan snarls in response, body coiled against an enemy neither of us can fight. But his eyes . . . his eyes are wounded and wild. Two glistening halves of the same treacherous sea I've always yearned to drown in.

I'm drowning now as that sea spills over.

"Don't make this choice, Saoirse. Don't—*don't leave me.*"

I take a step closer, and his iron jaw quivers. Another step, and all my husband's fury implodes on a keening wail. It brings me to my knees until we mirror each other—the fallen magpie and her wretched wolf.

"We were just a story, remember?" My lips tremble from the weight of a smile. "One of your epic tales. When I was grieving and homesick, completely alone, walking those cliffs by the cottage and praying I could just fall . . . *you* were what called me back from the edge. The Wolf of the Wild saved me long before I was the Stone King's bride."

Tears blur my vision as I reach for his hand, flattening mine to the barrier just over his soulstone mark. The colors ripple in response.

"You were always my favorite legend, Faolan."

His eyes drop to the dagger.

"And legends don't *die*."

I slit myself open from elbow to wrist as Faolan screams my name in the same savage howl he released when they burned his ship.

The dagger drops into the dirt at my feet as blood laces down my arm, beautiful and macabre. It breaks across my skin in a dozen tiny rivulets, then showers to the ground.

Silver-tinged waters erupt wherever my blood falls.

This is magic.

Raw and unbound, it pours from the earth in rivulets that flow not toward the sea, but above—to the mountain, and the heart of the Isle of Lost Souls. They swallow the moonlight from above and replicate it in silver streams that climb over my feet. Blood drips from my fingertips and the waters reach up to meet it, until some of the light slips into my veins, pulsing beneath my skin to the very heart of me.

I scream at the first touch of the goddess's might. Scream like a woman bringing life into the world and a babe drawing its first breath, the beauty and pain wound tight into one vibrant being. Then I collapse onto my hands and knees as the water laps at my thighs, circles my waist, and finally covers my head.

And there she is. Hovering just above me.

The lost goddess.

Her hair is the night sky, swirling with stars and draped over skin that glows with the moon's caress. If the ocean is reflected in my eyes, it was born first within hers. Her hand grazes my jaw, as lined as the riverbanks after a drought, and gently she tips my head back.

"Heir of sight. Daughter mine."

Tears stream down my face. "I'm here."

I'm *home*.

She smiles, and it's as if I've waited a lifetime to feel its warmth on my face. Nothing about my body feels strange now. The magic's hum is no more than a butterfly's wing at the back of my mind. I am as lush as the island recalled fully to life, part of the earth and stardust that formed it, breathing in sunlight and shadow both. I am not useless, or worthless, or *nothing*.

I am. And that is enough.

Her lips meet my forehead, and I swear it makes my blood sing.

"We've waited a long time for you."

"What do you . . ."

She casts her hair back with the sweep of an arm, and five figures emerge from the dark. My mothers. Grandmothers. Women who neglected their magic and forgot who they were.

It's clear they remember themselves now.

Gráinne stands at the front, no longer a specter but flushed with promise, her eyes alight. Beside her is another version of us, with my nose and Gráinne's high cheeks. The others are unrecognizable, born in the age of the Daonnaí, but all our eyes are carved from the sea.

"Little Soulgazer."

I turn to the goddess again, my heart filling the quiet of this place. "I never knew."

"It was not for you to know."

What else is this world made of that we cannot see? I glance to the walls of swirling water around us, shadows shifting behind their might. "Why now? Why *me*?"

The lost goddess lifts her hands, and between them appears an orb. It pulls on my insides like the ocean's tide, drawing me close. And yet it's familiar as well.

I tilt my head, considering the freckles at her wrists. A mark at her shoulder.

"Muireal?"

Her smile is a comet's blaze, lighting the night sky. "You found my relic." She gestures to the bone ring. "As well as my name."

I shake my head. "No, my friend Brona—she told me of the constellation. It's an old story, passed down for . . ." My eyes skate over the women as the pieces fall into place. "Five generations."

Muireal brings her palms together until the moon sinks into her flesh. "Fate preserved my name in the stars, though the others stole the rest. You witnessed their destruction?" I nod. "It is the lot of a Soulgazer to see too much. You will draw love. You will draw hatred."

"I . . . *will*?" I glance down at my hands, bloody and pale. "But I thought . . ."

"You have a choice to make: rest or awaken. Should you choose to sleep, your spirit will part to the next realm and your body will decay. Should you choose to awaken, your body will heal as your spirit expands within its boundaries." Muireal lifts my chin with a finger, until I meet her fathomless eyes. "But be warned. If you go back, there is no escaping the magic. You will be bound to the dead, releasing their souls and tied forever to this land."

For a moment, I doubt my choice as my life hangs in the space between us.

I could draw back now. Turn my head, reject my birthright,

bleed all my magic into the land and live on as nothing more than a legend. The story of a fanciful girl who carried the blood of a goddess, wed the Wolf of the Wild, and sacrificed herself to resurrect an island lost to myth.

I could be loved that way, shaped into whatever the seanchaí desired.

Let me make a legend of you.

The voice wraps around my flesh—salt and silk.

Faolan's voice.

"Awaken."

I blink and wait to regret my impulse. The choice that promises all risk and very little reward. But Muireal only smiles like she knew I'd choose it all along.

"Then take my breath, and return."

I take one more look at Muireal's midnight hair and starlight skin, memorizing it for when I'm only mortal again. Then I tilt my face forward and seal my lips to hers.

FIFTY-FIVE

The magic does not rush or ruin me like I might have expected, but trickles back in like the gentlest of rains. It comes in awareness of the living souls on land, their hurts and fears and disbelief. The knowing settles in my bones and remains, not a thing to fear, but to guide me along in quiet ebbs and flows I must learn to read. And the stars—I tip my head back to see through the water, even as they whisper in the darkness.

I must learn their language. Learn the sea.

Learn myself.

I am one with the magic now, neither master of fate nor bound to its whims. I will listen and watch, speak her truth, and guard the souls.

There are so many souls to call home.

The water breaks around me, and just like that, the world is all noise and rough edges and fury again.

"She's *alive*—let me go! Damn you, Nessa—"

"Look at her, mate. You want to go as mad as her old man?"

I glance down and swallow a cry at the sight of my skin glowing like the goddess's—or perhaps it's just a reflection off the streams that disappear into the forest and climb the mountain like winged creatures of mist above. My right arm no longer bleeds, the wound closed and marked by a silver scar. A beautiful, macabre match for the woad wolf on my left. The ring—a relic I now know was carved from the goddess herself—wavers with light and shadow on my finger. Slowly, I stand and step free of the stream.

My legs buckle like a newborn foal's, light leaving my body until I am a creature of earth again.

Faolan wastes no time breaking free of the others to haul me into his arms. His lips make quick passes across my brow, temple, cheeks. Then he curses and pushes me back, trembling fingers delving into my hair as he locks my gaze with his. "Saoirse, what happened?!"

My lips are numb, my tongue heavy and head thick. But there is one last thing I need to do before Muireal releases the moon. I lean into his chest, gently taking his hand. I feel his broken soul cry out.

"Love?"

I shake my head and twist in his arms, fumbling for the edge of the stream. I don't know if there is some ritual I am meant to follow, a sacred song or gesture to complete. All I can manage is one whispered, desperate "Please" as I spread my hand across Faolan's palm and lower them both into the water.

The humming returns, gentle at first, and then powerful enough to shake my bones. If I'd found it painful to bear the regrowth of flesh on my hand, it is nothing to the weight of knitting a broken soul back together. Agony laces down my spine and tears from my throat in a wretched sound that Faolan buries against his chest. His hold on me tightens in spite of the danger—in spite of whatever pain he must be feeling himself as the pieces of his bargain are stripped away, returned to their source.

It is endless, and it is a breath. And then it is over.

When I open my eyes, panting and barely able to hold on to him, I see it. The mark still wraps over his palm, gleaming with light, but the edges are black now. The colors fixed.

And its twin lies in a perfect reflection across my own palm.

"It's done." I bring his hand to my lips and kiss the very center. "You're free."

But his frown is fierce as he pulls me farther into the shield of his body, staring not at me, but at all those who just witnessed the awakening of the goddess once again.

"You released him." Maccus's voice splinters the calm, his face contorted by wariness and curiosity. "*You* released a soul from a bargain." He shakes his head, disbelief thick in his laugh. "No. No, it's not possible—Kiara, stand down."

Her grip tightens on the bowstring. "I don't think I will. Not when you're threatening the life of a king."

Maccus rears back, then laughs well and truly, the sound full-bodied and razor-edged. "What are you playing at? Faolan's no king—"

"He's wed to a queen. Or have you forgotten the laws of the Daonnaí—the very ones that granted you a throne? We are all bound to follow them, are we not?"

Maccus's entire demeanor shifts like a quaking of the earth, and I hold on to Faolan's arm as it locks over my waist. Kiara smirks, then lowers her bow just a touch and turns her face to the side. She never removes her eyes from the Stone King. "Tavin. You are the seanchaí I assigned to Faolan's ship, though my cousin does like to play the role of storyteller often enough. Tell us, how did the Daonnaí determine who was fit to rule? How does a rí or ríona claim their crown?"

The quartermaster emerges from the pack, his long hair loose around his shoulders, a cut bleeding on his brow. He staunchly avoids Faolan's gaze, which shifts from shocked to hostile in seconds. But I can't understand why.

"Under the first light of rebellion, at the end of the godly age—"

"Tavin!" Faolan snaps. "Not one more word."

Tavin stares at him, brow knotted and hands trembling. But it's Kiara who responds.

"It's the law, Faolan. He's sworn to speak what's true."

"Hang the law—Tavin, we made you a *wolf.*"

"I . . ." The quartermaster rubs at the spot where his tattoo lies. "I know. I'm sorry." He turns his head. "Under the first light of rebellion, at the end of the godly age, the Daonnaí agreed that mortal rulers would take over the gods' seats on their respective islands, guarding the lands and people within. Whoever best presented the traits of the isle, and the gifts bestowed by the god's original form—the strength of a mountain, the brilliance of dawn—would prove worthy of their crown."

"*Turncoat!*" Faolan swears. "Bloody turncoat. After ten years, you—"

"You knew all along he was mine," Kiara says, glaring as she dismisses Tavin with a wave of her hand. "And would we not all agree this is a gods-touched isle?" She turns toward the mountain peak behind us, the blanket of newly grown trees, and then back to me. "And that this is a gods-touched girl."

Their eyes rake over my flesh—I can feel them. I know they're there, but my own gaze is steady on Faolan, watching a thousand stories play across his face.

"Not just touched," Kiara says, and Faolan jerks to his feet, leaving me behind.

"Kiara, don't—"

"Saoirse is a true descendant of the divine patron of this island. Goddess of fate and keeper of lost souls. That makes her a queen."

The words are a ring of iron wrapped around my throat. Faolan's eyes lock on mine, and in a blink, I see it all disappear. The story he promised we'd write. Freedom from the endless webs we were born into. A life on the sea, answering to no one but ourselves.

Gone in the space of a single breath.

I stumble forward onto my feet—not toward Kiara, but to Faolan's side, until my fingers meet his. "I'm sorry," I whisper, then bite my cheek. I want to live in the lie. I want it so badly the magic shows me what could be by the mere press of his fingertips to mine.

A version of Faolan appears in my mind, older and sharper, with a little boy on his shoulders whose mischief matches his da's. I see a wee lass peering out from my arms with eyes I'll never teach her to hate. A ship with a name, because it is home to us.

I blink, and the scene disappears as Faolan pulls away with stiff fingers, unraveling the final thread of that impossible future. I swallow the bitterness of my hurt.

It was only ever pretend, anyway.

"Saoirse is the only person alive who can lay true claim to this land or its magic. We all saw it. Without her touch, all our dead will remain trapped and even more will corrupt than have already done so."

"She is a child!" Maccus's voice breaks into a snarl, the most emotion he's shown. "Addled in the mind, claiming magic. Kiara, if you think I'll let you play this hand—"

"Is this a game to you?" A new voice comes from the trees, as smooth as honey and just as warm, before Ríona Etain's granddaughter, Aisling, steps out.

Heir to the Isle of Bridled Stag, she is small and soft in all the places Kiara is sharp and tall, her eyes two shades darker brown than her skin. I've never seen the princess of the pleasure island dressed so casually, her hair braided in a single black rope down her shoulder, though the end is wrapped in a red scarf I recognize as Kiara's own from the Damhsa all those weeks ago.

Aisling takes her place by Kiara's side and Maccus goes scarlet.

"You nasty, conniving, bitc—"

"I've already sent word of the island's discovery to the others of the Ring of Stars." Aisling flicks her braid back and smooths the mustard-yellow skirts she wears, adjusting the gold-braided belt at her waist. "How lucky Kiara was able to inform me before you torched her cousin's ship. A council will convene here in two weeks' time with their island's stones. Or at least the ones they care for most."

Kiara lifts her chin, leveling Maccus with a look. "If she can truly restore them to the waters and allow the spirits to pass on, I challenge you to find a single ruler of the Crescent who'd dare refuse her a place on the Ring of Stars."

"I-I don't want it." The words fall from my lips like drops of poison, souring her expression. I don't regret it—the truth pulls from the deepest corners of my person, the ones I've only just learned to accept. "I don't want any of it. I don't want that sort of power, I just wanted—I thought I'd have—"

Freedom.

My eyes wander helplessly to Faolan, but he's staring hard at the ground, blood dripping down his chin from a raw gash above his brow. Even trapped by my father, facing off Maccus, he was never this quiet or contained.

An animal saved from slaughter and dropped into a cage. That's what I've made him with my bargain to Kiara.

Her hand falls on my shoulder—I never heard her move—and her face is hard as she speaks again. "Want it or not, it's yours to bear. Turn away the Ring of Stars and their swaths of dead when you're the first chance they've had at peace in five centuries, and you won't live past the next morning. Not freely, anyway."

I laugh, because it's all I can do. "This isn't freedom."

"It's as good as you'll get, Wolf Tamer." Her eyes flit from me to Faolan, and I see now what he's been running from all this time in the slightest touch of smugness to her smile. "Imagine the story, if that makes it easier. The Girl with Ocean Eyes and the Wolf of the Wild turned king and queen of all the lost souls."

"You feckin' knew," Faolan whispers, the words barely contained. "Aisling could have stopped it. My ship—"

"I've done you a favor, cousin. You're king consort now." Kiara touches his cheek and he recoils, only faltering when the wound on his leg forces him to give way. Kiara smiles wider, then walks back to rejoin her lover. "Embrace it."

I stare at her back for a long moment, then look to see what's left of Faolan's rigging and sails hanging in burning strips that fall to the deck just as the skies above erupt into angry groans, dropping rain like a blanket over the earth. I turn back to tell him I'm sorry again, to swear I'll find some way to repair his ship and fix this, but he's already disappearing into the trees.

FIFTY-SIX

"Faolan?"

The shadows bend around me, branches caressing my shoulders and leaves stroking my face. He's close—I can feel him in the anger pulsing just below his surface, the pain raking his heart raw. It takes me a moment to understand that his *soul* calls to me.

I round a small copse of boulders and there he is, bent over a stream as he tries to pull what's left of his shirt free and tend to his wounds. He gets his arms only halfway over his head before he flinches and releases a garbled cry, jerking the fabric forward rather than letting go.

His hurt goes so much deeper than skin.

"Faolan, stop. Please—"

"Why? Can I not even remove my own damned shirt without your permission now, my *queen*?"

The words are a slap I'm not prepared for. I fall back heavily against roughened bark and watch as he grits his teeth and finally pulls a dagger free from the back of his boot. The shirt falls away in seconds, revealing the tears in his flesh from Maccus's blade.

"I didn't know Kiara meant to do that," I say.

His laugh is vicious and mocking, and my own anger surfaces as I push off the tree. "Faolan, I never wanted any of this! I never wanted either of us trapped."

"Well it's a bloody perfect time for you to figure that out, aye? Except that wasn't the first time you talked to her about a bargain. Was it?"

"It's not—" I bury my face in my hands, desperate to pray, knowing there is no one left to listen. "What choice did I have? I was just trying to make sure I survived all this, and she gave me a choice: use my sight in exchange for protection. You never promised me anything—"

"To feck with tha'!" Faolan rounds on me and stalks forward, never mind the blood and wounds. "I bound myself to your body, my spirit to your own. Does that mean *nothing* to you?"

"It means everything!" Tears spring to my eyes, and I swipe them firmly away. "But what happens when that time is up? Or we move to another island and you meet a girl who's more interesting, more beautiful—what happens when I'm not enough anymore?"

He stares at me, his mouth agape, before his fingers curl into fists that he presses against his temples. "Saoirse, I've told you things I've never told another living soul. About my parents, what it felt like holding on to that rock, dying. Hell, I *married* you—"

I whirl on him, rage releasing my tongue. "So you could use me to find the island! To save *yourself*—you can't tell me those weren't your motivations, because you made that perfectly clear from the start."

Faolan lurches forward and then snarls in pain, grabbing his ribs. "And after? You think I was playing a game when I healed your hand, kissed you after the market—*lay* with you?"

"I don't know." I can't meet his eyes now. I stare at the sky instead, what dark pieces I can see behind rain-soaked leaves. "You're so damned hard to read, and even the things you say twist around on themselves. I've seen you tell stories and charm your way through your crew, the markets, all of it. You use affection like it's coin, and never promised anything outside our first vows—and I couldn't wait for you to. How was I to know it all meant *anything* to you?"

Faolan's laugh is bitter, his eyes near black. "How the feck could you have shared that night with me and believed it was nothing?"

Flames erupt in my belly, scorching my cheeks as I turn on him. "*You left.*"

He stops moving. I don't.

"You left our bed, and then *ignored* me for five days after. And I—" My voice breaks, pain and fury spilling into tears that I don't bother trying to hide. "I knew better, but I waited for you, and y-you wouldn't look at me or *touch* me—"

"Because I didn't want you sensing my bloody feelings! Lass, you—" Faolan rocks forward and then stops, every tendon strained, every muscle taut. "Your eyes were changing color. Then my scar left a mark, and—stars above, the way you can know a person, know *me*, by a touch scares the shite out of me, Saoirse."

His chest heaves as he looks at me. *Really* looks.

"I thought you'd be able to tell . . . that you knew . . ."

Faolan bites off the words, and I nearly swallow my tongue.

It's another trick. A lie. I have to believe that.

Because if it were the truth, it would damn us both to a life neither of us wants, corrupting and twisting us over time like the souls who've remained here for generations.

I stagger back. Shake my head. "It's not too late for you, Faolan."
I ball my fingers into the ends of my shirt to keep them still. "I'm
tied to the island now, sworn to help your cousin. But you . . . you
could still be free."

His eyes stay on the ground, and my breath shakes when it
comes out.

"I can sever the handfasting."

"No."

I shut my eyes tight against a growing nausea and spread my
hands over my stomach to keep steady. "Faolan, son of Barden—"

"Stop it." Faolan grabs my hips, shaking me. "I won't listen—
dammit, Trouble, I can't leave you to Kiara and the rest of the
sharks."

"You *can*, and you will." My voice steadies as more tears slide
down my face and neck. "Faolan, son of Barden and Iona, I re-
nounce our bond and release you from your—"

My words cut off as Faolan yanks me forward and seals his lips
to mine.

Longing bursts from the contact, chased by anguish, desire,
determination, and resignation. As our kiss deepens, a future unspools beneath my lids—not the one I saw with the bone ring's
help, but *his* imaginings.

Faolan's fantasies of *me*.

A rose-tinted sunrise over mountain peaks I've never seen.
Nights bundled in the crow's nest, teaching the stars to sing. My
wrists tangled in ropes—hands open in sweet surrender, body
arching off our bed. The scrap of red silk, blue ribbon, and leather
cord that tangled our lives together, hanging always above our bed.

I gasp as Faolan spreads his fingers along my jaw, ensuring the
soulstone mark meets my cheek. The touch opens such a clear

path between us that I cannot doubt his meaning. Cannot doubt what we both feel. His hold on my waist tightens as I break the kiss on a sob. "No. I'm supposed to let you go."

His thumb scrapes my lips like the first time we met, and my eyes fly open to meet his—as blue as sea glass forged in fire.

"It's too late, Saoirse. I'm already in love with you."

EPILOGUE

Faolan

The day my luck runs out, swallowed by the knowing sea or torn from my lungs on the tip of a blade, it'll be her name tangled in my last, dying breath.

Saoirse.

The stones by the pool's edge gleam with freshly wrought moss and moody violets as kings and queens step into the heart of the island, taking its measure. Silver water flows into a basin of rock—the same water Saoirse's blood commanded to flow. They didn't see it swallow her up. They don't know what it cost to awaken this place.

They only see the trussed-up version of my wife Kiara crafted last night.

Nessa jostles my arm when Maccus walks in, and I return a tight smile. Scratch at a spot on my back just above the knife hidden there—wince when it tugs at the threads keeping my shoulder together. An ugly red scar left by his own damned sword.

"Bastard." Nessa spits out my own thought, and I snort. My

smile only brightens when Kiara shoots a glare my way. I'd bow just to piss her off if Saoirse hadn't looked up right then, stealing the very air I breathe.

She's coiled her hair into dark waves that toss like the winter sea over her bare shoulders, skin as pale as bone. The dress Kiara stuck her in is unearthly, flirting with every hint of breeze. She's pleated the flimsy fabric in a dozen places, holding the fabric tight enough to show her toes beneath the hem.

I bite down the urge to throw myself at her feet. Worship her the way she asked me to weeks ago, voice trembling so much I would have denied her if not for the unflinching truth in her gaze. Stars help me, I was lost from the first moment I held it. And what a powerful damnation that was for a man built on lies.

Yearning rests in the softness of her eyes now—a terrible kind of tenderness, wounded and wanting.

My breath comes out half snarl.

Kiara touches Saoirse's arm, and it's like time starts again when she looks away. This time when Nessa nudges me, I can't laugh. Can't even smile.

Saoirse is the dawn and dusk wrapped into one gorgeous creature, and I'm a man doomed.

"Descendants of the Daonnaí, rí and ríona of the Crescent." Kiara's voice cleaves every conversation, and it's only then I notice the other head of dark curls tucked into the crowd. Aidan, standing pale and thin, a smooth box tucked under one arm.

Alone.

"Welcome to the Isle of Lost Souls."

I feel Saoirse's gaze like the brush of her fingers that night in the woods as she tried to cut me free. Daft bloody woman. How the hell was I supposed to stop loving the sea?

"For generations, we've sought these waters as our dead consumed the land. Riotous, wayward spirits corrupted without flesh or solid stone to contain them. We've sacrificed hundreds to this pursuit, chasing rumors only to find storms or madness."

"Should she be smiling like that?" Nessa mutters. This time, I don't have to fake my grin.

"What, and give people the idea she has a heart?"

Nessa chuckles as Kiara goes on, spinning the story she snatched from my own blood-streaked hands. I don't laugh. Don't look away from Saoirse, who's gone so damn rigid I'd think she'd turned statue were it not for the restless churning of her eyes. They haven't stopped shifting since she emerged from the waters imbued with far more than a couple of drops of divine blood.

"We thought we'd lost our salvation with the age of the gods, a pathway to the next realm, yet here we stand on sacred ground."

Saoirse bites down on her bottom lip, a habit I chided with my tongue last night between promises to stay. To remain landlocked and fight until we're both free of Kiara's web. She didn't believe them—doesn't. My word's still not much in her eyes, and I can't blame her.

But for the first time in my life, I meant it.

Kiara strikes a fist into her palm, eyes gleaming as she takes us all in. "Our search is over. The isle has awakened."

A map of bruises and welts shrieks across my body as I slip forward until I'm standing to the left of Maccus, just out of his line of sight. The dagger presses steadily into my palm, hilt tucked against calluses once wrapped by a leather glove. I'd rather stand naked than openly bear the bargainer's mark, but Kiara's orders were clear: no more hiding.

One of many offenses my cousin has to answer for.

"Let us embark on a new age." Kiara touches Saoirse's shoulder and steps back with sharp eyes. Smiles when Saoirse turns away from the collection of kings and queens to lower her feet into the pool. "A new tithe."

I force my blood to quell its raging as the water burns bright, glowing as though her skin is the source of its light. For all I know, it is. Some gasp; others curse—Maccus stiffens and my dagger slides half-free of its sheath, ready to be buried between his ribs should he so much as twitch in the direction of my wife. But he already knows what she is.

Rí Tadhg of Frozen Hearth walks forward in his fur-lined gray cloak to place a basket of warped, cracked soulstones on the rock where she's perched. He cuts a shallow bow, eyes hard, but the doubt in them shifts to awe the moment Saoirse takes one into her bare hand. Because as rigid as she'd gone at the sight of a king bending the knee, Saoirse's movements run fluid once she holds the stones.

Of course Kiara's words about a first tithe were all bullshite. She's had Saoirse practicing for two weeks straight.

> *"Daughter of the knowing sea*
> *Gaze sworn long ago to me . . ."*

Saoirse pricks her finger on the needle-point end of her brooch until a bead of blood threatens to stain her gown. She smears it over the soulstones instead, tracing it into the swirling grooves across their tops.

> *"Captive soul, your blood shall free . . ."*

She lowers the entire basket into the water and stills as the stones light up.

> *"The Isle of the Lost."*

There's no grimace on her face, no stiffness to her body. These must not be broken, only forgotten. We've learned the patterns over the past few days—the toll they demand.

It keeps on, and as the seconds trickle past, my grip on the knife eases. The lines of Maccus's shoulders don't drop—but then the Stone King's not exactly known for breaking form. One by one, the souls unfurl from the soulstones to join the ether at the top of the mountain looming above us. The next basket is brought forth, and the next, until Saoirse's voice runs raw, humming instead of singing the tune that's begun to haunt my dreams.

And the water rises. Froths by the third basket, light flickering in strange patterns as though following the music's rhythm.

Maccus is king of the second island, but it's not until the fourth bout of souls have been released that he finally walks forward. I spot a woven bowl in his hand with only one stone, small compared to the ornate hammer resting at his hip. His face remains blank as Saoirse takes them, fighting the tremors lacing up her legs. When she draws blood upon the pieces, a weathered old man even larger than the other souls ascends, gaze lingering on his son.

I don't relax until Maccus rejoins the others, flick my fingers to warn Tavin, tucked near a cluster of ivy, to stand down with his bow, the disloyal bastard. I catch Saoirse's eye—smile reassuringly, knowing I can do feck all else right now. Her gaze softens when it meets mine, some of the tension leaving her shoulders.

But when Aidan approaches, Saoirse falters at last. He doesn't meet her eyes as he shoves a small chest toward her, crafted of leather and wood burned with the sigil of their house. I expect to see the same weathered soulstone they forced her to give up—the one holding her eldest brother's soul. But there are two within: one cracked and blackened, the other glimmering like starlight.

Fresh. New.

Feck.

"I-I don't understand," Saoirse says, voice cracking down the middle.

Aidan lifts his head, and even from behind I know there's steel in his eyes. "You will."

I try to move to Saoirse's side, but Nessa clamps a hand down on my good shoulder as Kiara's gaze burns a hole in my side.

Stick to the ceremony. Follow my exact orders. Leave Saoirse to her task. Then, and only then, will I leave you both for a time to adjust. But I expect your presence at the first council of autumn.

Freedom wrapped in choking vines covered in poison thorns.

Exactly what I always dreamed of.

By the time I've shaken Nessa off, glaring at my cousin, it's done. Saoirse's brother's spirit rises from his stone and she gasps, tears flooding her eyes. But just as I suspected, her father follows shortly after.

"Da?" The word dips out of Saoirse's lips as Dermot's silver spirit hovers, watching her . . . nothing hostile in his expression. Nothing at all. In life, his lips were always twisted, his eyes cold and cruel, yet there is an emptiness there as he watches his daughter until he spies the eldest brother's shade. Warmth blooms at last, painted across his features in a broad smile before they both rise to the mountain and out of sight.

My eyes dart from Aidan to my wife, both wounded and clearly trying to pretend they're not.

Still, I wait for any hint she'll collapse, any sign of tears—a reason to shove these miserable stars out of their carefully woven sky to get her in my arms.

But she only stares into the distance as her heart flutters at her throat. No music, no accusations or jokes. Not until Kiara clears her throat, and Saoirse blinks, turning to climb free of the water.

No one dares touch her—not until the glow leaves her skin along with whatever energy she has left. Saoirse nearly crumples, and I finally break free of the crowd, catching her with an arm around her waist. I coax her to lean heavily into my chest, ignoring the way my heartbeat wants to choke me.

"It's all right. I've got you," I murmur into her ear, but I don't dare try to tease this away. Not with what I know comes next.

"So let it be finished." Kiara smiles at us, then faces the gathering. "The first reaping of souls in five generations. Let any who would oppose the laws the Daonnaí laid down say so now."

No one moves. Not even Maccus.

There's not one among them who'd dare oppose her now. Not yet, anyway, damn them.

But they're thinking on it. Saoirse feels it, too, the way she's tensed up beneath my arm. Their faces shift like beasts, every one spinning something new—calculating, fearful, desirous, infuriated. Kiara may hold our strings, but every single one of them has a blade in their back pocket.

"Very well." Kiara's voice was trained to conquer. Once, it spurred me on to steal the best pastries at family dinners so we could share them beneath a table: a victor's feast. Now it bends even the most ironclad will into place.

I stroke the back of Saoirse's cold fingers. Lift them to my lips just as she tilts her head back onto my shoulder, her eyes finding mine. I drop my forehead to hers before she can read the defeat there. There's no going back from this gilded fecking cage.

I'm already in love with you.

"All hail Ríona Saoirse and her husband, Rí Faolan. Queen and king of the Isle of Souls."

ACKNOWLEDGMENTS

When I wrote this book at the start of the pandemic, I had a sexy pirate, the saddest girl who ever lived, BIG FEELINGS, and very little plot. Half a decade later, only the first three remain true, and it's largely due to the list of people below. Thank you all!

To my quick-witted, multitalented mastermind of an agent, Sheyla Knigge: you are made of pure magic. I cannot fathom trying to navigate this journey without you at my side and feel endlessly lucky that we found each other. Thank you.

To Sareer Khader, my brilliant editor, who's displayed endless kindness and imagination (and who may be even more in love with Faolan than I am): thank you. In your hands, my book *finally* lined up exactly with the vision in my head. I cannot wait to repeat the process for book two.

Thank you to the entire team at Penguin Random House! Stephanie Felty, Kalie Barnes-Young, Christine Legon, Alaina Christensen, Kristin del Rosario, and Adam Auerbach. I couldn't ask for better champions. And thank you Charlie Bowater.

Thank you, Katie, my first and oldest writing friend, for reminding me over the years just how joyfully unserious storytelling can be. Thank you to K.B. Hoyle and Beth Mitchell for being some of my earliest champions and critics.

Thank you to Kaitlin H., Megan S., and Cassie Malmo, for reading early versions of this book and holding my hand through critique. Thank you to Jordan Gray for offering your brilliant mind and friendship: you saved this book from at least a dozen plot holes. Thank you, Diya, for listening to me blab about the book for two hours at YALLfest. And thank you to Sonja, my first beta reader, who made it all feel real.

Thank you, Jazzi, Carolyn, and Bri, for our pandemic video chats, and the push to revise this story from YA to adult. Thank you, Megan P., for hosting me in Germany as I made a mad dash through said revisions, and Megan B., for all those evenings talking story and pulling cards on your couch.

Thank you to Adrienne Young: if you hadn't used my submission as an example of voice on a random Instagram story in December 2019, my life would look very different. Thank you for Writing with the Soul, the adventure in Scotland in 2022, and all the tiny check-ins since.

Thank you, Meghan, Audrey, Emma, and Jonathan, for bringing me into your family, and encouraging me as I squeezed the earliest drafts of this book into naptimes and early-morning shifts. And thank you, Amy, for creating a home out of an empty shell. I already miss our commune.

To Kathryn and Richard (my parents, who I swear are nothing like Saoirse's!) and my little sister, Vera, thank you for always supporting me—even when I was writing fanfiction nonstop daily for fourteen years, and you were starting to get concerned. Look at me now!

To Kaitlin and Alan . . . thank you for everything. Loving me as I ugly cried on the filthy living room floor over this book, hyping me up before networking events, asking what I truly wanted, then challenging me to grow as an artist and human until I could reach it. You gave me courage, and now you've given me three of the brightest gifts in Harrison, Corinne, and Merryn. I am eternally grateful, and owe you a trip to France.

To Kyle, thank you for returning to my life at the most dramatic moment possible, fulfilling my lifelong fantasy of living a second-chance romance. You make me feel giddy, wild, and wise, like standing on the shores of a misty lake beneath a mountain. I love you dearly.

To Jaime Johnson . . . thank you. What more could I possibly say? I spent my whole life longing for a friend like you. You are my bosom sister, platonic soulmate, and singlehandedly responsible for the fact this book ever reached "The End." I love you a million.

Finally, thank you, Libba Bray. You don't know me, we might never meet, but your stories are the reason this book exists. Why I still exist. Thank you.

SOULGAZER

MAGGIE RAPIER

READERS GUIDE

BEHIND THE BOOK

I was raised to submit—to my parents, God, or the husband I was promised as long as I remained good. Wanting was for Jezebels, pleasure was a sin, curves were distasteful, and my voice was not welcome.

In every way possible, I was born too much for that world. So I tried to be less.

And less.

And less.

Until one day, the cage they'd convinced me to build around myself burst wide open and I was free. For the first time in my life, I had choice. Power. But I didn't trust it. In fact, I was terrified—feeling raw and exposed as I gathered the shattered bars that contained me and tried one last time to *make* myself fit. But they disintegrated in my hands, and in the end, all that was left was . . . me.

That is how Saoirse came to exist.

Her story is one that belongs to thousands of other young women who grew up deprived of themselves—who were taught by institutions or patriarchal culture that the best thing you can do with your life is to submit. To be less, because that is the only way you will ever be loved.

That is where Faolan comes in.

In writing their romance, I was able to expose that lie. When Saoirse bites her tongue, Faolan refuses to speak until she releases it. When she's determined to stay small, he pokes at her until she unfolds. He plays the antagonist as much as the love interest, helping her navigate her trauma and harmful beliefs with a playful sort of wisdom that's equal parts irritating and adoring as he challenges her to know herself and claim her space in the world.

Yet even at the end of this story, Saoirse is not a badass. She's not a natural fighter, and she doesn't want to burn the world down—at least not yet. She was written for the soft girls: the ones who were told they were damaged goods. Anger does not drive her narrative, but loss. Grief.

It's exquisitely painful to face your past and realize how much of it was illusion. To mourn what you could have been all those years, had you not spent all your energy trying to fit an impossible mold. Saoirse's grief is seen in her guilt for her brothers, her struggle with magic and power, and in the lingering spirits that color their world. But the point isn't her sadness.

The point is that she heals.

Saoirse and Faolan are my love letter to the deepest, most complicated parts of myself—parts I once believed I needed to suppress in order to be happy. To be loved. Faolan is my wild and levity, with his ferocious appetite for life and refusal to let it be anything ordinary. Saoirse is all of my longing and heartbreak, with all her wounds and wonder on full display.

I love them, because writing them healed something in me. Their story is a much more fantastical mirror to my life—and while I can't say I've ever fended off a furious ex at sword point or made out in a steamy island cove, I know what it is to lose everything you ever thought you were, and to sculpt something new from the ashes. I also know what it is to laugh over the glorious mess you've become along the way.

Thank you, Saoirse and Faolan, for teaching me that.

And thank *you* for reading.

DISCUSSION QUESTIONS

1. Saoirse's main conflict in this book centers around her relationship to her magic—or in essence, her power. She fears it and wants to strip it away until, ultimately, she accepts it as her own. Would you have made the same choice in her place? Why?

2. Faolan clearly loves his crew, yet he never discloses his secrets about Saoirse or his scar to any of them. If you could have told any of the Wolves the truth, who would it be and why? Do you think it would have made a difference to the story?

3. Think about Saoirse's trek through her father's island and the realities she encountered throughout the Crescent, as well as through her relationship to Brona. What parallels could you draw between the conflicts in *Soulgazer*'s world and our own?

4. In *Soulgazer*, the magic comes from the land after an uprising against the gods. Knowing how the story went, do you agree with the peoples' decision to slaughter the gods and claim the magic for themselves? Do you think it played out how they wanted?

5. If you could have a magical item from the world of *Soulgazer*, or explore one of the islands in particular, which would it be and why?

6. Faolan tends to charm his way through life, laughing at conflict and shrugging off the consequences. Do you think he's as careless as he seems, or do you think it's all a facade?

7. There is an adage in this world: "we are a people who cannot mourn, for the dead cannot pass on." What do you think it means to live constantly alongside your ghosts in a dying world? Does it excuse the antagonists' actions, or shift your view of them?

8. Saoirse and Faolan are in a marriage of convenience, but clearly that changes along the way. When would you argue that she fell in love with Faolan? When did he fall for her?

MAGGIE'S "BOOKS THAT MADE ME"

The Song of Achilles, Madeline Miller

Spinning Silver, Naomi Novik

A Great and Terrible Beauty, Libba Bray

Serpent & Dove, Shelby Mahurin

Raybearer, Jordan Ifueko

A Far Wilder Magic, Allison Saft

Juniper & Thorn, Ava Reid

Women Who Run with the Wolves, Clarissa Pinkola Estés

Suddenly You, Lisa Kleypas

Author photo by Mary Fehr

Born in the South with a healthy streak of wanderlust, **Maggie Rapier** is an incurable romantic who loves nothing more than wordplay and witchcraft—except, perhaps, her sourdough starter. When she's not marketing French antiques or writing about moody girls and sexy pirates, you can find her wandering in the woods with her partner, and a basket in hand.

VISIT MAGGIE RAPIER ONLINE

TheDailyMagpie.com
TheDailyMagpie

Ready to find
your next great read?

Let us help.

Visit prh.com/nextread

Penguin
Random
House